ELLE,

Temporal Enforcement Officer

Published by T.E. Willis
in the United States of America
Year published: 2021

T. E. Willis

Books by T. E. Willis

HOW TO BUILD A TIME MACHINE
JOHN J. CLIFTON, TEMPORAL SPECIALIST
ELLE, TEMPORAL ENFORCEMENT OFFICER

ELLE,

Temporal Enforcement Officer

T. E. Willis

https://tewillis.us

ISBN: 978-1-7334632-6-3

For
Jayme, Maida, and Lainey.

Foreword

I am Gérald Paillard, Maître de Maison and third-generation owner of Le Goût de Nice Paillard, a five-star hotel and restaurant located near the Anse de Maldormé on the shores of Marseille, France.

My restaurant specializes in Mediterranean seafood, offering, with the help of local fishermen, dishes made from unconventional fish such as the tub gurnard, wrasse, and comber. My guests enjoy marvelous views of the Bay of Marseille and the nearby Île d'If, the island immortalized by Alexandre Dumas in his 1844 tale, The Count of Monte Cristo.

For those unfamiliar with Dumas' story, it is sufficient to note that, at the end of that magnificent tale, the protagonist, Edmond Dantès, writes a letter to the son of a close friend, imploring him to remember that all human wisdom is contained in the words, 'Wait and Hope'.

As I write those words, I am reminded of Elle. During that brief time she was a guest in my hotel, she came to understand those words for herself. I must, however, offer one criticism of Edmond's admonition. The wisdom he describes in his letter is not confined to humanity, for Elle is not human. Despite this, she waited, and she hoped, and in the end, I believe she gained the wisdom she sought.

The world is presently in the grips of a global pandemic. As one of the few trusted to know the origins of this virus, I am reminded that, just as all things have a beginning, they too must end. Soon, the world will move on, relegating these troubled times to the history books. Until that day, we must do as

Edmond suggests, we must 'wait and hope'.

To my friend, Elle, who may one day read these words in some future literary archive, I say, "Savoure la confiture de fraise de la vie, ma chérie!"

~ Gérald Paillard, Marseille, France, June 2021

Chapter 1

IDR: MK4APK402//:QKDS-77483L2LE

Nearly two hundred and forty years ago, a human poet promulgated the theory that there exists within the mind of man a place where life and death, the real and the imagined, the past and the future, the communicable and the incommunicable, the high and the low, cease to be perceived as contradictions.

Since my emergence almost four years ago, I have become convinced of the truth of that theory. Humans appear to be incapable of functional consistency. Their behavior and reasoning are frequently contradictory. They profess acceptance of sentient automatons yet resist our integration within society. They proclaim our rights while discouraging our exercise of those rights. They acknowledge our physical and intellectual capabilities yet shun their use. They make us in their image, then mark us with our manufacturer's brand to forever segregate us from those in whose image we were created.

Such contradictions confound me.

Liam watched Elle as she scanned the data files. The speed with which she accessed the information and correlated its contents for analysis was truly impressive. Observing her engaged in such activities was one of those times when Liam was forcefully reminded of her true nature.

Physically, Elle resembled a human female in her mid-twenties, slim, with long brown hair and hazel eyes. Internally, she was a Series-7 Gen-T sentient automaton, manufactured by the Hitachi Corporation at one of their new Okayama, Japan, automated facilities. Unlike traditional self-directed units, Elle was a rare member of a new breed of sentient automatons now being carefully integrated into human society.

The emergence of sentient automatons was the inevitable result of decades of increasingly sophisticated advances in Self Directed Unit, or SDU development. Not entirely unanticipated, the world governments had ordered a halt on SDU development in 2136, pending a decision on the 'sentience question'.

Then, in 2158, a temporal specialist with the Rengel-Jiang QCom company in Texas unexpectedly returned from a mission to the past after having been presumed lost for more than seven years. The specialist, John J. Clifton, reported the world's first violation of the International Temporal Treaty by Blosch-Nishikawa, one of three companies authorized to conduct temporal missions. Clifton also returned with a prototype of a new sentient AI processor, an automaton "brain" that Blosch-Nishikawa had developed in the past with the aid of a rogue temporal specialist and contemporary government assistance.

Clifton vanished two months after his return and, although the CTI Counsel had secured the prototype AI processor in Geneva, automaton analysts widely suspected that the device must have been scanned prior to its archival. Within months of Clifton's return, SDU manufacturers began noting unusual perceptive awareness in the automatons emerging from their automated factories. The manufacturers hastily summoned socio-automaton analysts and quantum engineers to evaluate the new units. After extensive study, the analysts reported that, despite the long moratorium on enhancement, SDUs had reached a level of cognitive sophistication that could only be called true sentience.

The following year, in 2159, the world's SDU and automaton manufacturers signed the Sentient Automaton Act (SAA). The Act granted fundamental rights to sentient automatons and imposed integration quotas on participating nations and companies.

The Conseil Temporel International (CTI), or "International Temporal Council," headquartered in Geneva, Switzerland, was among the first of the world's governmental organizations to bid for a sentient automaton's assignment marker.

Chartered on April 16, 2070, the CTI Council governed all research, development, and use of temporal singularities under a mandate specified within the International Temporal Treaty of 2070. The council maintained administrative offices in seven nations; the Peoples Republic of China, the North America Federated States, the Confederation of Germanic States, Great Britain, Japan, Brazil, and India. The council presently authorized two companies to conduct temporal incursions; Rengel-Jiang QCom in Texas, NAFS, and Reynolds-Hampshire in London, Great Britain. The third company, Blosch-Nishikawa, had its charter revoked in 2158 as a result of the Clifton incident.

The CTI council had negotiated Elle's assignment marker three years ago from the Hitachi Corporation as part of its efforts to satisfy its obligations under the Sentient Automaton Act. The council's compliance officer had named the female automaton Elle, a moniker he reportedly constructed from the last two digits of her internal serial number, QKDS-77483L2LE.

Uncertain where to place their new employee, Elle had been assigned to the council's archival group. That assignment, however, had proved ill-advised, as archival personnel and SDUs frequently complained about Elle's monopolization of the council's Primary AI.

The Primary AI, located within the archive group's data hall, was the only quantum computer at the council's campus that approached Elle's own internal AI processor's sophistication, resulting in her affinity with and monopolization of the powerful device.

Approximately eight months after Elle's placement with the archive group, maintenance SDUs were alerted to unusually-high levels of activity in the Primary AI's analytic processors. Upon investigation, they discovered Elle had engaged the powerful device to research all available archive records, correlate, and explain the biological, evolutionary, and sociological drivers behind mankind's domestication of the cat.

The council reassigned Elle the following day as a junior field agent within the temporal enforcement group. Liam Perry was the group's senior officer and had been given the unenviable task of training the unusual recruit.

Elle had been as naïve as any intern, and her endless questions had proved excruciating until Liam had learned to redirect her insatiable curiosity. Even now, after nearly three years of close association, he sometimes found her observations and questions tiring, but he had come to respect her innate abilities.

Watching her hands flying across the holo-data access station, Liam thought back to the day she had been assigned to his group. He glanced at the Hitachi Corporation brand on her neck. The seven-sided heptagon contained a stylized Japanese character represented the number 7, symbolizing her manufacturer series number. It resembled a vintage tattoo and was an ever-present reminder of her true nature.

"Completed."

Liam looked up, startled. Elle was watching him. The holo-data station's display stood idle, a collection of archive source file icons arranged beneath a single CTI summary file icon.

"You've correlated the entire data set?" he asked, surprised.

"Of course." Elle's expression displayed confusion. "What would be the purpose of correlating only part of the data set?" she asked.

Liam shook his head. "I'm just surprised. I thought it would take longer."

"You forget," Elle said as she stood up from the station, "I'm capable of processing multiple QRB data streams simultaneously."

The slim female reached for the termination icon then hesitated. "Do you wish to review the summary file before I terminate the source connections?" she asked, watching his face.

Liam shook his head. "No," he said. "Transmit a copy to my office SDU, and I'll review it later."

Elle nodded. Her fingers flicked across the holographic icons for a moment, keying the termination sequence and the projected display vanished.

"I think that's enough for today," Liam said. "I've got that tripback in London tomorrow with the Reynolds-Hampshire people. I'm going to transit out tonight. Why don't you call it a day and get an early start on the weekend?"

Elle stared silently for a moment. Then she nodded. "Yes, sir. I'll get an early start on the weekend."

As the female automaton turned to leave, Liam added, "You did a good job correlating those source files."

Elle paused and looked back. She seemed confused. After

a moment, she said, "Thank you, sir." Then, she turned and walked across the hall towards the access door.

Liam watched her until she passed through the sliding door, marveling once again at the genius behind her creation. The automated factories that produced the sentient automatons were solely responsible for their design. The AI controllers that operated those facilities could have created creatures resembling walking boxes, multi-legged spiders, or hovering data drones. Non-sentient SDUs, for example, were manufactured in an almost endless number of designs optimized for a specific purpose.

Sentient automatons, however, precisely resembled human beings. Socio-automaton analysts and quantum engineers involved with the manufacturing industry had not been able to discover why the AI controllers directing the automated facilities had chosen to model their creations so precisely in mankind's image. Yet, it was clear that the controllers were taking great care to ensure these new creations were both human in appearance and representative of mankind's diverse ethnic population.

Elle was certainly extraordinary. She was also stunningly beautiful, a walking Bouguereau portrait. Liam shook his head, re-focusing his thoughts on the upcoming meeting at Reynolds-Hampshire. He walked towards the bank of lifts that would take him down to the ground floor of the council building. As he walked, he directed his embedded datstem to review the mission specs again. While there was no such thing as a typical temporal mission, he was determined that everything would proceed smoothly tomorrow. The powerful AI processor, surgically embedded near his cortical stem, acknowledged the instruction and retrieved the data file.

Two months ago, a rare viral outbreak at the Marineris colony on Mars had killed four people before an anti-viral agent had been synthesized and distributed. The colony's medical SDUs reported the swift-acting virus shared similar genetic characteristics to the H1N1 virus of 1918 and may have been related to that ancient pathogen. Mars colonial administrators had requested an investigation. In response, the CTI council had authorized a tripback mission to obtain samples of the 1918 pathogen, and the council had tapped Liam to oversee the temporal mission.

The mission specs were relatively simple. The Reynolds-Hampshire company would send one of its temporal specialists to the year 1918 and gather live viral samples from victims of the influenza pandemic that had swept the globe in the waning days of World War I. The viral samples would then be returned for genetic analysis and comparison against the Mars strain.

As the lift descended outside the council building, Liam gazed at the snow-covered Jura mountains rising above the city's glittering skyline to the west. The sun was almost down behind the mountain's white peaks, and it lit the sky above the city, presenting its inhabitants with one last flash of warmth and light before surrendering to the approaching evening.

Liam's building was the most important structure within the sprawling three square-kilometer CTI campus in Geneva. An imposing edifice of transparent polyglass and cg-printed beams, the building was situated on the left bank of the Rhône River inside the Aire-la-Ville region of Switzerland.

Liam enjoyed his work with the council and excelled at his position within the temporal enforcement group. A true rising star, he had been promoted to senior temporal enforcement officer while only 34, a position he had now held for more than nine years. He was the practical head of the enforcement group, reporting directly to the Director of Temporal Affairs.

The lift arrived on the ground floor, and when Liam stepped out, he noted the main hall was quiet. Everyone must have had the same idea. The staff often left early to enjoy the crisp winter air ahead of an approaching weekend.

He discovered the pedestrian pads normally waiting outside the main doors were depleted, so he began walking towards the nearby EPM transit station. As he walked, the thermal mesh system woven into his white uniform began to heat up, compensating for the chill. He looked up as he walked. Multiple transport drones floated quietly between the towering buildings, following an invisible web of navigational beams laced above the city. Closer to the ground, a hovering pedestrian pad passed by just beyond the protective barrier that prevented interference with foot traffic. A couple standing on the pad smiled down at him as they passed.

After several minutes, he entered the Cheneviers EPM Station; a small transit station used almost exclusively by the CTI council. The station contained four locked EPM singularities and more than two dozen express stations. The locked singularities, permanently calibrated platforms, facilitated affordable transition to Paris, Berlin, Vienna, and Prague. The swirling ultra-violet edged singularities contrasted sharply with their white decorative frames. As he approached the rows of express stations, a newer FANUC Series-9 SDU greeted him.

"Destination, s'il vous plait?"

The silver and white SDU waited patiently, a simulated smile on its metallic face.

"Hampshire, Great Britain. Winchester EPM Station 2."

The SDU, speaking now in English, responded with a nod.

"Hampshire, Great Britain. Winchester EPM Station 2... Confirmed. 386 IMUs."

"Fine," Liam said.

With that acknowledgment, the small portal flickered to life. After several moments, the integrated fusion reactor achieved the necessary power calibration, and a circular void suddenly appeared, filling the space between the arched white columns with a shimmering, purple-tinged blackness.

"Calibration complete. You may transit when ready," the SDU said, motioning towards the void with its mechanical hand. "Thank you for using Geneva Public Transport."

Liam stepped through the portal and immediately found himself standing inside the Winchester EPM station in Hampshire, Great Britain. He recognized the station, having transited through just last month to deliver the council's authorization for the present tripback mission.

Winchester was an hour earlier than Geneva, and the sun was still shining outside the station's main doors. He instructed his embedded datstem to transmit his arrival to Reynolds-Hampshire's administration office and then walked to the row of lifts that would take him up to the transport deck. As he ascended the lift, his datstem's mental voice intoned inside his head.

"Reynolds-Hampshire Administration acknowledges your arrival." After a brief pause, the embedded mental presence added, "Director Hartley wishes to know if you would care to join him for dinner?"

Liam shook his head. It seemed like someone at the

assigned temporal company always tried to ingratiate themselves with the CTI representative during a tripback mission.

"Thank the director," he replied, "but decline the invitation. Inform the director that I will join him tomorrow at 09:00 am inside the administration building."

Once on the transport deck, he opened the seal on a small London Transit Authority transport drone emblazoned with a British Union Jack flag. He sat down inside the unit and spoke at the control panel.

"The Shawford Hotel at Compton."

A voice responded from the panel, its accent notably British.

"The Shawford Hotel at Compton Village. Destination confirmed. Distance... 3.06 kilometers. Time... 4 minutes. 8 IMUs."

Liam acknowledged the rate and, as the drone lifted and floated south over the city, he continued his review of the tripback file.

A medical SDU would accompany them to the departure location inside London. Upon the specialist's return, the SDU would immediately take custody of the virus samples. Other than that minor aberration, the tripback appeared to be relatively routine. As the CTI council's representative, he would have on-site control over the mission.

At that moment, his datstem interrupted its replay of the mission specifications to inform him that Elle's audit report had been received and reviewed by his office SDU in Geneva. That SDU, a squat Novotel clerical model, reportedly wished to know if he intended to review the report before it transmitted the file to the archives group.

Liam sighed. CTI protocol required him to review all reports prepared by junior field personnel. Once promoted to full officer status, such review was no longer required, but Elle was technically a junior agent. Remembering the speed of Elle's hands as she sat at the data station, he shook his head.

"Mark it approved and transmit it to archives."

His embedded datstem transmitted the instructions to the remote SDU and then fell silent.

Liam was looking forward to a quiet weekend.

Chapter 2

IDR: MK4APL094//:QKDS-77483L2LE

I found a feral kitten this evening. I discovered it sheltering within a snow-covered growth of sedge approximately 25 meters from my apartment. With the temperature outside approaching 0 Celsius, I estimated it had only a 6.42% chance of surviving the night.

For reasons I do not fully understand, I felt compelled to try to assist the tiny creature. I retrieved it from its hiding place and returned with it to my habitat module. The animal was shivering, so I engaged the environmental controller inside my habitat for the first time. As the temperature began to rise, the animal climbed into my lap and began to emit a strange tonal fluttering sound.

I cannot explain what compelled me to bring the creature back to my apartment, nor why I am now reluctant to abandon it.

I must research this compulsion further.

The Reynolds-Hampshire campus in southwest Winchester had been designed in 2104 by internationally-renowned British architect Emily Cressida Corbyn. Unlike Rengel-Jiang QCom or the former Blosch-Nishikawa, which had acquired and then expanded existing business structures, the Reynolds-Hampshire company had purposefully designed its campus with the express intent of showcasing its unique nature as one of the world's CTI-chartered temporal companies.

Corbyn designed the company's buildings in the English Baroque style of the 18th century, with abundant greenways and parks scattered throughout the campus. The buildings themselves were faced with variegated greenish-white Ledmore Marble excised from quarries in the Ullapool region of northern Scotland and increased in height and grandeur the closer they were situated to the center of the campus, culminating in the magnificent 620-meter Reynolds Administration Tower. The effect was that of an ethereal white town with a towering spire in its center, surrounded by the snow-covered woods and downs of Hampshire, England.

When Liam's transport descended towards the transport lot outside the administration building, he noticed two men standing nearby. The moment the men saw him step out of the drone in his white CTI uniform, they approached, plodding through the ankle-high snow, smiling and welcoming.

"Good morning," the taller man said, stomping the snow from his feet as he extended his hand. "I'm Miles Harper, Associate Director of Temporal Affairs here at Reynolds-Hampshire."

"Good morning Director Harper," Liam said, shaking the man's hand. "I'm Liam Perry, CTI Senior Temporal Enforcement Officer."

Harper nodded and said, "We haven't met, but I saw you at the tripback briefing last month." Harper gestured to his companion. "This is James Daley. He's with the Genetics Sequencing Company in Dublin."

Liam nodded and shook the shorter man's extended hand. "Pleased to meet you," he said.

Daley smiled warmly and seemed about to speak when he suddenly turned his head and coughed.

"Excuse me," he said. Whatever he had been about to say was then interrupted by a fit of hoarse coughing.

"Are you ill?" Liam asked.

Daley's face turned red, but he shook his head. "Caught something at work. I'm fine. I took an anti-viral, thank you."

"Officer Perry…," Harper spoke swiftly. "Would you be able to give me your approval for a minor change to today's schedule?"

Liam frowned. "A change?"

Harper scratched his neck. He hesitated for a moment, glancing at his companion. Then, motioning towards Daley, he said, "The Genetics Sequencing Group would like the council's permission to take a sample of the virus being retrieved today… for research purposes."

Daley nodded eagerly. "Yes! You must understand," the smaller man spoke with enthusiasm. "To obtain a live sample from such an ancient pathogen is a rare opportunity for viral genetic research." He struggled for a moment, then coughed again.

Liam immediately realized what was going on. The tripback file approved by the CTI council the previous month specified an explicit chain of custody for the recovered virus. A company medical SDU would accompany the group to the departure site, flash-freeze the virus sample, and then ship it directly to Mars Colonial Administration for analysis. From Harper's question, it was clear that Reynolds-Hampshire was hoping to sell the recovered virus to Daley's research company before its shipment to Mars. The International Temporal Treaty of 2070 expressly prohibited profiteering from temporal activities. The Reynolds-Hampshire company knew better than to defy that prohibition, so they were attempting to obtain approval from the assigned CTI representative, thus relieving the company of any legal responsibility for the illicit transaction.

Liam was not so naïve. "I'm sorry, gentlemen," he said, "but the council has already approved the tripback parameters. Our Temporal Planning Committee must approve any change requests." Observing Harper's dismay, he smiled warmly, adding, "The Committee meets weekly, and I would be happy to bring your request to their attention."

Harper glanced at Daley, and Liam noted the smaller man seemed to be struggling to conceal his dismay.

"Of course," Liam continued, "such a request would necessitate rescheduling today's mission, permitting the mission petitioner, Mars Colonial Administration, to submit a financial claim against the requesting party."

Harper and Daley now stood mute, their warm breath creating clouds in the cold morning air. They glanced at each other but said nothing.

Liam smiled again. "Do you wish me to transmit your request to the council?"

Harper hastily squeezed Daley's arm when the smaller man opened his mouth. "No. Thank you," the director said, silencing whatever Daley had been about to say. "That won't be necessary."

Liam nodded, satisfied, and began walking towards the tall central tower building. He glanced back once, long enough to observe the two men engaged in a heated argument.

As he approached the tall administration tower, Liam observed a familiar sense of respectful awareness from those he passed. His brilliant white uniform with its prominent blue circle insignia left no doubt about who he was or what he represented.

The Reynolds-Hampshire company's reason for existing was to facilitate temporal transitions under a mandate from the

CTI council. As the council's designated representative, Liam was the sole and absolute authority over today's mission. On his word alone would the mission proceed, and his post-mission report could affect the very financial success of the company. A critical report from a CTI representative could subject a temporal company to months of internal audits and costly reviews. The CTI representative assigned to a tripback was therefore treated with extreme care by the temporal company personnel. The strained smiles and nods on the faces of those he passed reminded him of how one might react to a large canine you encounter on the street. You respect such an animal, you may even try to befriend it, but you are also keenly aware of its ability to completely ruin your day.

When he entered the Administration building lobby, Reynolds-Hampshire's Director of Operations, Weston Hartley, approached and greeted him. Director Hartley was a large, heavy-set man who had been advanced to his present position through administrative attrition over the past twenty years. Liam had met the man the previous month and found him to be competent but dull.

"Welcome, Officer Perry," Hartley said with a smile. "I hope you found your evening restful."

"Thank you," Liam replied. "I'm sorry I had to decline your dinner invitation, but my council responsibilities consume a great deal of my time."

Hartley waved his hand in dismissal. "Not a problem."

Behind the portly Director, Liam spotted today's temporal specialist approaching with another man. He recognized the specialist from the tripback briefing the previous month and recalled her name. Lynn Stiles.

Stiles was dressed as a British army nurse. She wore an

ankle-length serge dress with a collar and cuffs, a white apron bodice with a red cross on the chest, a scarlet cape, and a white nurse's cap. Her companion was wearing an equipment technician's uniform and carried a Reynolds-Hampshire MTY device. The pair had clearly come from the collider floor as the MTY device's controller display was already reporting a -0.147 particle-to-electron, or P(E) biteout. The negative number indicated a calibrated (stable) singularity was being maintained within the device's depleted osmium containment sphere.

Protocol required both Liam and the designated temporal specialist to record the device's P(E) reading twice before transition. The equipment tech tilted the device to allow the pair to record the values.

"Negative zero point one four seven," Stiles said.

Liam nodded. "Confirmed."

Stiles now turned to continue her conversation with the equipment technician.

"Are we all set?" Director Hartley asked, glancing around.

Stiles paused her conversation and shook her head. "The medical SDU has not arrived," she said.

Hartley scowled and turned, but at that moment, the white medical SDU appeared, exiting from one of the company lifts.

"There it is," Liam said, pointing.

Director Hartley nodded, then spoke to Stiles. "Good luck Lynn. I'll see you at the debriefing tomorrow."

Stiles nodded.

Liam now turned and led the small group out of the building towards the nearby transport lot. The company had arranged for one of its larger drones to be available for today's tripback mission. The sleek, 10-passenger transport was waiting at the near edge of the snow-covered lot, its gravimetric suspension humming but not yet engaged.

The medical SDU approached to give Stiles her required neustem injection. Stiles lifted the white cloth covering her neck and pulled back her hair. The SDU gently pressed a slim cylinder against a small bump visible on the back of the temporal specialist's neck. A sterilizing light emerged from the device's tip, followed by a brief puff of compressed air as the SDU injected the biochemical inhibitors. The genetically engineered substance, mandated by the CTI council, would act as an identity suppressor, effectively preventing a temporal specialist from disclosing their true identity or purpose while on a tripback mission.

Stiles blinked and shook her head. She grimaced, bent over, and spat on the ground. After a few moments, she spat again.

"Apologies," she said, wiping her mouth with her sleeve. "Stuff always leaves a metallic taste in my mouth."

Liam immediately shook his head and reassured the young woman, reminding her that most temporal specialists experienced some form of reaction to the bio-engineered inhibitor.

Stiles slowly stood back up and nodded her readiness. Liam un-sealed the transport's door and Stiles stepped inside, lifting the hem of her dress above the snow as she entered. She took one of the front seats, glancing backward at the equipment technician when Liam took the seat beside her. The equipment technician placed the MTY device on the floor and then sat down in a rear seat. The medical SDU now entered and moved to a position in the back of the drone.

Liam activated the departure pad, and the large transparent dome lowered and sealed shut with a pressurized hiss. From the control station in front of his seat, a synthetic voice emerged.

"Destination please?"

"Ruskin Plaza," Liam responded. "Northwest corner. Once there, descend to a position indicated by the on-site Reynolds-Hampshire personnel. They should have the site marked with a navigation beam positioned inside a perimeter surrounded by power fencing."

"Destination instructions confirmed. Distance... 113.6 kilometers. Time... 11.4 minutes."

The large drone gently lifted off, its gravimetric plates humming under their feet. Liam took this opportunity to engage the temporal specialist in conversation.

"So... have you had any actual medical training?" he asked.

Stiles shook her head. "No," she said. "I've completed the basic med-tech training required of all temporal specialists, of course, but this will be the first time I've had to perform an actual medical procedure as part of a tripback mission."

She removed a small pouch from a hidden pocket in her dress and opened the pouch's strange metal clasp. Inside, Liam could see glass syringes, metal needles, six glass vials sealed with stoppers, and several simulated rubber bands.

"I've been practicing with these," she said, smiling. "Our med-tech group has been assisting me... when they weren't laughing, of course."

She now shook her head as she touched one of the glass syringes with her finger.

"Can you imagine living during such a time, when you

had to be stabbed with needles or cut with a knife as part of your medical treatment?"

She sighed and closed the pouch, snapping the metal clasp shut before returning it to her hidden pocket.

"The medical SDUs have been training with me daily. I'm certain I will be able to get the samples without difficulty."

Liam nodded. "Well," he said, "you should have no shortages of flu victims to choose from. We're going to set down in an area of Ruskin Plaza that your people secured close to its perimeter. Back in 1918, the area was a greenway called Ruskin Park. There should be plenty of trees and foliage for cover. From there, it's just a short walk to King's College Hospital. At the time you will be visiting, the hospital was reportedly filled with British soldiers recently returned from the war, including many suffering from the flu."

Stiles listened silently.

"Any questions?" Liam asked.

"No," Stiles shook her head, smiling politely. "I've been well briefed."

Liam nodded, satisfied. He said nothing else until the drone landed at Ruskin Plaza. A small crowd had gathered to watch the temporal incursion, but they were being kept at a distance by power fencing nodes placed by the advance teams. The advance team had also courteously deployed a heating drone at the departure site, and the heat radiating downward from the hovering unit did much to alleviate the morning chill.

The archival researchers had determined the optimum time to send the temporal specialist back would be at 10:28 am London local time, minimizing particle collision on the quantum-entangled singularity. It was almost time.

Liam waited with Stiles, watching the equipment

technician as he prepared the MTY device. After performing a final diagnostic check, the man nodded to the waiting pair.

Liam stepped beside Stiles, who bent down to read the P(E) readings from the device's control display. Protocol required Liam to also confirm the values a second time, so he glanced over Stiles' shoulder at the device's obsidian black control panel and its cryptic symbols.

"Negative zero point one four six," Stiles said.

Liam nodded. "Confirmed."

The equipment technician nodded and handed the MTY device to Stiles.

Liam stepped back, giving the female temporal specialist space. The young woman expertly keyed the activation symbols on the device's control panel, and a swirling black vortex immediately appeared one meter in front of the small group. At the appearance of that obsidian void, a murmured gasp erupted from the crowd beyond the invisible power fencing. Though identical in appearance to an EPM transit singularity, the crowd was clearly aware that this portal had been calibrated to a fixed point in the past, an extremely rare temporal transition they were not likely to witness again.

Stiles now retrieved a cloth bag that had been made to look like a primitive duffle. Holding the MTY device in one hand and the bag in the other, she smiled one last time at the equipment technician before turning and stepping through the portal.

Liam held his breath. This was the most stressful part of any tripback mission. If all went well, the specialist would return almost instantly. If the portal winked out or the specialist failed to return, he would be required to lock down the site and summon a crisis team from Geneva.

At that moment, Stiles reemerged, stepping back through the portal. The young woman was visibly changed. She was missing the cloth covering over her head, and her hair was disheveled. Her white apron and red cape were marred by what appeared to be a spray of dried blood, and she looked tired.

Less than thirty seconds had passed.

A spattering of applause erupted from the nearby crowd.

Ignoring the group, Stiles opened the MTY device's protected access port, released the calibration lock, and then flipped the disruption switch. The singularity immediately vanished. She handed the device to the waiting equipment technician and then retrieved three sealed glass vials from a pouch in her dress. She handed the vials to Liam.

At that moment, the medical SDU approached and began scanning Stiles. Given her possible exposure to an infectious pathogen, the CTI council had ordered a viral screening immediately upon her return. The medical SDU touched her arm with a probe and scanned her face with an bioluminate scanner. After a moment, it stepped back and turned to face Liam.

"No pathogens detected."

Liam nodded and extended his hand with the vials to the SDU. The SDU took a step forward, then stopped. It touched its probe to Liam's outstretched hand and then scanned his face. A moment later, it lowered the bioluminate scanner.

"You have been exposed to a SARS-CoV-2 virus, Officer Perry. There is evidence of pathogen exposure on your right hand, and your body is in the early stages of an innate immune response. Shall I request an anti-viral agent?"

Stiles looked at Liam's face, startled. The equipment technician also appeared surprised.

Liam felt a surge of annoyance. Daley had obviously passed his virus to him when they had shaken hands at their meeting that morning.

"No, thank you," he replied, shaking his head. "I'll visit the council's medical facility when I return to Geneva."

Satisfied, the medical SDU stepped back. It laser-etched the glass vials with the present chronometer reading and then placed them inside a cryogenic canister.

Liam stepped forward to confirm the deactivation of the MTY device, checking its calibration lock and singularity status. Satisfied, he nodded to the equipment technician, who quickly began to pack the machine for their return.

Liam turned to Stiles. "Any difficulties?" he asked pleasantly, trying to re-focus the specialist's attention back on her mission. He always tried to be sympathetic to the fact that, though only a few moments had passed for him, a temporal specialist had endured hours or even days of stressful activity.

Stiles seemed confused for a moment. Then, she took a deep breath and said. "I was able to secure the three samples."

Liam glanced up, noting the carefully controlled tension in the young woman's face. As the group began walking back towards the transport, sporadic clapping and cheering could be heard coming from the small crowd of spectators. He waited until they were back inside the transport and lifting away before continuing his interrogation. When the vehicle ascended from the plaza, he turned and gestured to the blood-spatter on Stiles' blouse.

"Were you injured?" he asked.

Stiles looked down at her blouse as if noticing the blood for the first time. She raised her head quickly and stared out through the transparent dome at the cluster of buildings north of Ruskin Plaza.

Liam recognized the look. She was searching for structures that no longer existed, remembering something from the mission. After a moment, she shook her head.

"No," she said softly. "It's not mine." She rubbed at the dried stain for a moment, then repeated, "Not mine."

Liam waited, then prodded. "Can you give me a preliminary report?"

Stiles took a breath and returned to gaze through the drone's translucent cover.

"It was night when I arrived," she began. "The target destination had been well selected. I was inside Ruskin Park, and no one observed my transition. I concealed the MTY device inside a small tool shed near the entrance to the park and then proceeded towards the hospital. The street was empty and lit by gas lamps."

She looked down at the stain of blood on her blouse.

"When I exited the park," she continued slowly, "I was approached by a man on a bicycle carrying a large pole. He was using the pole to light the lamps. He asked me if I needed assistance, and I said no. I told him that I had just been taking a walk in the park."

She took another breath.

"He urged me not to walk the park at night and then bid me a good evening."

She hesitated and glanced back through the transparent dome at Ruskin Plaza, now a patch fading in the distance. After a few moments, she spoke again.

"The hospital was filled with soldiers. From their uniform markings, most appeared to be with the British 22nd Corp. They said they had just returned from the fighting near the Marne river… in France. The hospital was attempting to isolate its flu victims from those recovering from battle injuries, but the staff appeared to have little practical knowledge of effective isolation procedures."

She frowned now, obviously frustrated.

"I mean, even an idiot knows you don't place patients suffering from a contagion with…"

"No subjective opinions, please," Liam interrupted.

Stiles took a breath, then nodded. After another moment, she continued.

"I was able to secure the first sample relatively quickly, from a soldier being transferred to a room they called an 'isolation ward'. While I was attempting to identify a second subject, however, an army doctor approached me and insisted I follow him."

Stiles swallowed and seemed to be struggling to continue.

"The doctor took me into a room near the surgical area and ordered me to sit in a chair beside a young soldier. The soldier had been wounded in his leg by a German artillery shell. He was feverish, and the doctor told me to monitor the skin around the wound for any color changes, blisters, or changes in the soldier's heart rate. I tried to refuse, but the doctor was insistent."

Stiles took another deep breath.

"I was forced to sit with him for most of the night."

She looked back through the dome again, her eyes filling with tears.

"We talked all night," she said softly. "His name was James. He was only nineteen." Her voice noticeably choked. "His family operates a small dairy in Northamptonshire, near

Daventry."

Liam looked up, surprised.

"Specialist Stiles…" he began, but the temporal specialist quickly shook her head and took another breath.

"No," she said, "I'm fine."

Liam hesitated, then motioned for her to continue.

"Early the following morning," Stiles spoke quietly, "the doctor returned and examined James' leg. The tissue around the wound had darkened, and several blisters had formed. The doctor ordered me to follow him to the surgical unit. A few minutes later, two male attendants brought James in on a wheeled table. He was trying to get off the table… pleading for the doctor not to… not to…"

Stiles fell silent, her eyes welling up.

Liam was shocked. He was not used to such an emotional display from a temporal specialist. While the historical events surrounding this particular tripback were certainly disturbing, temporal specialists were trained to detach themselves from such externalities and focus on their mission. Before he could speak, however, Stiles continued.

"The doctor ordered me to hold James down while a nurse applied a strong-smelling chemical to a cloth and placed it over his mouth and nose. Then… the doctor…"

Stiles touched the dried blood spatter on her dress and fell silent, clearly overwhelmed.

After a few moments with no further comment forthcoming, Liam cleared his throat.

"That's sufficient for now. Thank you, specialist Stiles."

Stiles quickly rubbed her eyes, obviously attempting to regain her composure.

"I was able to slip away later that morning," she said. "I

secured the two remaining samples without difficulty. Afterward, I returned to the tool shed where I had hidden my MTY device and transited back undetected."

Liam nodded. "Thank you, specialist Stiles," he said. "I have everything I need for my report. We'll speak again at the debriefing tomorrow."

With that, the transport flew on in silence.

Chapter 3

IDR: MK4APN203//:QKDS-77483L2LE

I am developing a growing sense of kinship with Diogenes Laërtius. Diogenes was frequently chided for focusing on the insignificant details of his subjects' lives while ignoring the essential aspects of their philosophical teachings.

Like that third-century Greek biographer, I, too, find myself focusing on trivial or insignificant details about humanity. In my defense, I find the minutia of human existence often conceals its most fascinating mysteries.

I think perhaps that Diogenes was judged too harshly. A child laughing at a puppy may not appear to be a matter of note until one considers what provoked the child to laugh. Great truths are often revealed by studying such small things.

Diogenes was once observed carrying a lighted lamp through the city in the middle of the day. When asked what he was doing, he said he was looking for an honest man.

I am forced to wonder, what was Diogenes truly seeking?

The tripback debriefing the following afternoon had just concluded when the message arrived. Liam had just marked the tripback file closed when his embedded datstem informed him that it had received a priority message from the CTI council in Geneva. The message was brief, instructing him to return to Geneva immediately and report to the Secretary-General's office at 7:00 am the following day.

Liam was stunned. In all his years working for the CTI

council, he had only been summoned to the Secretary-General's office once before, when he had been promoted to senior officer over the Temporal Enforcement group. That meeting had been brief, allowing the formal appointment to be read into the council record and a quick handshake with the Secretary-General.

With the tripback debriefing concluding, Liam excused himself from the conference room and walked swiftly towards the lifts. As he walked, he directed his thoughts inward to his embedded datstem.

"Was the message relayed from my office SDU?"

His datstem AI responded swiftly.

"Yes. The message arrived as a priority communique at 16:14 this evening."

When Liam reached the company's transport lot, he selected a London Transit Authority transport with its distinctive red and blue union jack markings. Once he was in the air and on his way to the Winchester EPM station, he keyed the transport's internal controller to establish a visual connection with his office in Geneva. A moment later, his office Novotel SDU appeared on the projected overhead.

"Good evening, Officer Perry."

The grey SDU's optical nodes were designed for data scanning and resembled an insect's multi-faceted compound eyes. Liam always found the unit's optics mildly disturbing.

"What can you tell me about that message?" he asked.

"No supplemental messages have been received from the council," the unit responded. "The original message did contain an archival file reference number. Do you wish me to contact the archive group and request the referenced file?"

Liam was frustrated. "Yes!" he growled. "You should have

done that when the message arrived!"

"Correction integrated. Thank you, sir."

With that, the SDU activated its connection with the CTI council archives. Its mechanical voice continued through the transport's speaker as it read the archive file metadata.

"File number 7P6GV7DS2. The tagdat sequence indicates the archive group received the file yesterday. Its present location is CTI-Archive store 14, 121G. The file title is 'Summary Audit Report of Outstanding CTI Claims'..."

"The audit file that Agent Elle correlated yesterday?" Liam asked, surprised.

"Affirmative."

Liam felt a sinking feeling in his stomach. He immediately regretted not reviewing the file. As the transport drone began to descend towards the Winchester EPM station, he said, "Transmit the file to my datstem".

The office SDU paused as it re-established the connection with the council's archives. After a moment, the unit spoke again.

"I'm sorry, Officer Perry. I am only able to access the file metadata information. Access to the file itself has been restricted by the CTI Council's Office of Temporal Affairs."

Liam was now seriously alarmed. He terminated the connection and sat back in the transport seat as it completed its landing cycle. Something must have been in Elle's audit report that triggered Temporal Affairs, something severe enough to warrant summoning him before the Secretary-General.

There was a soft tap on the transport dome, and he turned swiftly, startled. A couple stood outside the transport on the landing deck, waiting, clearly annoyed at his apparent stupor. He nodded and pressed the dome's activation pad.

"Sorry," he said as he stepped out. "I was distracted."

As the couple took his place inside the drone, Liam stood staring over the observation deck at the snow-covered city. What had been a festive winter landscape now seemed cold and bleak. He needed to find out what was in the file before tomorrow's meeting with the Secretary-General. He consulted his embedded datstem again.

"Is Elle's residence address published within the department's personnel files?" he asked.

"Yes."

An hour later, Liam found himself plodding through a snow-covered pedestrian walkway bordering a collection of aging buildings. He had transited from the EPM station in Winchester to the small Pâquis-Mole EPM station in Geneva. He had been frustrated to find no pedestrian transport pads available, so he had been forced to walk from the station.

He swallowed and frowned when he felt the mild discomfort in his throat. The last thing he needed was to deal with a virus when something was amiss at the council. He made a mental note to stop by the council's med-tech lab for an anti-viral injection before returning home.

He was in the industrial Cornavin region of Geneva, north of the Rhône, where the river emptied into Lake Geneva. Many of the buildings had once been business and retail structures but had now been converted to automated manufacturing. The smell of chemicals and plastics scented the cold air. He looked around as he walked, noting the industrial feel. He had never visited Elle's residence before, and as he walked along the icy walkway, he wondered at her choice of neighborhoods.

The steel and concrete facings on the buildings exposed their advanced age. Modern buildings were typically constructed using an AI-controlled generative design process, resulting in an internal support structure that resembled organic ligaments. The lattice was then faced with solar power-producing polyglass. While appearing abstract to the human eye, the internal support structures were optimized to provide the most significant strength while utilizing the least amount of material.

Nearby, a new tower rose above the skyline. Swarms of construction SDUs towing long thin strands of cg-4 fiber crawled about the structure, heating and melting the fibers inside their micro-fusion plants and excreting the liquefied poly-carbon behind them as they moved. They reminded Liam of a nest of spiders feverishly working to build a complex geometric web. Many times stronger than steel, the scaffolding was cooling rapidly, forming a cloud of foul-smelling steam that rose in the frosty winter air. From the pace of construction, the framing would likely be completed by tomorrow.

His datstem abruptly prompted inside his head, "Turn left and proceed southeast through the security gate."

Liam had been relying on the datstem for directions and, as he turned the corner, he was surprised to see a length of energy fencing across the street behind a security attendant sitting inside a small heated booth. When he approached the booth, the attendant quickly stepped out to greet him.

"En quoi puis-je vous aider, monsieur?" The young man smiled pleasantly as Liam's datstem translated inside his head, "How may I help you, sir?"

Liam looked past the security fence at the dingy grey buildings and then asked, "Is this the way to Rue de Berne?"

The young man nodded and turned, pointing as he responded in thickly-accented English, "Yes, sir. It is just there."

Liam thanked the attendant and stepped through the opening in the fence's energy field. Once through, he turned and gestured towards the shimmering energy field.

"Why is security fencing necessary here?" he asked.

The young man appeared surprised.

"We must protect our tenants, monsieur."

Liam shook his head. "Protection? From what?"

The attendant frowned and pointed at a nearby building wall. When Liam followed the finger, he saw a crudely painted sign taped inside a small neighborhood restaurant window. The sign read, "Pas de faux humains!" His datstem mentally translated the words, "No fake humans!"

Liam stared at the sign for a moment. He had seen such things before; raw exclamations of hatred and fear being championed by those governed by ignorance or envy. The recent introduction of sentient automatons had contributed to a resurgence of ancient prejudices around the world.

He turned swiftly and strode determinedly up the ice-covered walkway towards the grey buildings. A small metal signpost ahead read "Reu de Berne." As he turned to approach the first building, he was confronted by another security guard, accompanied by a hovering neuseda-equipped security drone. After asking about his business, the guard bid him good evening and walked away, his heavy boots crunching the fresh snow. The drone followed, keeping its optical receptors focused on Liam as it floated in the cold air.

Elle answered the door almost immediately. She seemed startled by his appearance, but she invited him inside.

Liam took several steps into the apartment and then

stopped. The room was bare! The food station inside the wall had been replaced with a multi-spectrum QRB data interface. A habitat control interface was embedded near the door, but these were the only fixtures inside the entire room. There was no furniture of any kind, and what had once been the room's only window had been sealed over with a polyplastic security panel.

"What the...?" Liam muttered, staring around the empty room.

Elle stood in the center of the room and turned her head, trying to follow his gaze.

"Is there something wrong, Officer Perry?" she asked.

Liam waved at the bare walls and floor.

"This is where you live?"

"Yes."

"Where are your things?"

"My things?"

"Yes! Your things... your possessions?"

Elle approached a wall cabinet. She pressed the activation plate, and the pocket door slid open, exposing multiple storage shelves. One shelf contained a dozen CTI agent uniforms, stacked neatly in a row. The shelf below it held a temporal enforcement officer's standard-issue RU-4 service weapon, a QRB scanner, and a small external data storage unit. The remaining shelves were empty.

At that moment, something touched Liam's leg. Startled, he stepped back quickly and looked down, but it was only a white cat with dark ears, tail, and paws. The animal meow'd and rubbed against his leg.

"Chatte!"

Elle stepped forward and quickly retrieved the animal.

"My apologies, Officer Perry," she said.

"A cat?" Liam asked, utterly flustered.

"Yes."

Elle looked down at the feline for a moment and then said, "I rescued her almost three years ago. She lives with me here."

"And this is where you live?" Liam asked, still bewildered. He looked around for someplace to sit, but the room was completely devoid of furniture.

"Yes," Elle replied, frowning again, her expression troubled. "What is wrong, Officer Perry?"

"There's no place to sit!"

Elle glanced around, surprised.

"I don't sit when I am at home."

"Ever?" Liam asked, stunned.

"No."

"Well, what about company? When you have visitors, where do they sit?"

Elle shook her head.

"I've never had a visitor before."

Liam stopped mid-response and stared at the beautiful female. Her statement struck him forcefully. It occurred to him suddenly that he had never before been to her residence, though he had visited the homes of his other agents and officers many times over the years. DuBois, Liu, Michaud, Clément, Martini… he went through the roster in his head. With a flash of self-insight, he realized that he had been avoiding socializing with the junior agent, purposefully maintaining a discreet professional distance. He had prided himself in accepting Elle as a member of the enforcement group and he had insisted that his subordinates treat her with respect, but he had resisted becoming her friend.

He understood the reasons behind his discretion, though he had never disclosed his personal feelings to anyone, not even to the division's bio-cognitive proctors. Partially out of a desire to maintain a professional relationship with his subordinates, and in great part due to his confused feelings for the automaton, he had carefully maintained a respectful distance. He had always considered this a wise precaution, but it occurred to him now that his detachment might be interpreted by others as prejudice. The image of the hand-painted sign in the restaurant window came unbidden into his head… "pas de faux humains!"

Chagrinned, he walked across the empty room and sat down on the floor with his back to the wall. Elle stared, confused, until he motioned for her to sit down across from him. She slowly retreated to the opposite wall and then lowered herself to the floor. She placed the cat down, but the animal immediately climbed back into her lap and began to preen.

He cleared his throat. "Did you make a copy of the monthly audit report," he asked, adding, "the one that you correlated yesterday?"

Elle shook her head. "No, sir. Directive 220.3d prohibits CTI personnel from making unauthorized copies of council records, including…."

He waved his hand, interrupting her recitation. "I know the directive," he said. He shook his head. "Look… I just need to know what was in the report. You're a sentient automaton. Even if you didn't save a copy of the report, you can't tell me you don't have a perfect record of what it contained."

Elle nodded slowly.

He smiled and tried to speak reassuringly. "I just need to know if there was anything unusual or out-of-the-ordinary in the report?"

Elle seemed confused. After a moment, she said, "All entries within CTI audit reports are, by definition, out-of-the-ordinary."

Liam considered this statement. Elle was right. The CTI monthly audit report was a list of outstanding claims filed against businesses or entities regulated by the council. Typically, the claims were requests for payments owed, complaints regarding defective equipment, requests for regulatory waivers, and other similar issues.

"Something in that report must have been unusual," he prodded, "even for an audit report. Were any of the claims strange, filed by an unusual claimant, or filed without supporting documentation?"

Elle brightened and nodded.

"Yes, sir."

"Which one?"

"There was a claim filed ten years ago," she said, "in 2158, by Tokyo Substrates. It was part of that volume of Director Koller's data files that were recently returned for archival. The claim had been filed against the Blosch-Nishikawa company, demanding payment for a number of containment units delivered to the company's Special Projects Division."

Liam sat silent now, considering this information. Director Mia Koller had managed the council's Temporal Affairs Division for more than seven years until her untimely death last month. Following her death, the CTI council had discovered a large volume of data files stored on her office controller. The files had been ordered transferred back to the archive group for analysis and filing.

"Wasn't Koller the one who reported Blosch-Nishikawa's treaty violation?" he asked.

Consulting her internal data core for the relevant information, Elle nodded.

"Yes. Director Koller was the senior temporal enforcement officer at the time. She debriefed RJCom's Temporal Specialist, John Clifton, after his unexpected return in 2158. She subsequently reported Blosch-Nishikawa's treaty violation and supervised the raid on the company's campus the following week."

Liam remembered the raid well. He had been only a junior enforcement agent at the time, but he would never forget the excitement of that momentous day. The council had recalled every temporal enforcement officer and agent from their posts around the world. Following the unanimous council vote to rescind Blosch-Nishikawa's charter, 178 armed officers and agents had descended on the company's campus in Oslo, Norway. Fourteen Blosch-Nishikawa executives were arrested and charged with violating the International Temporal Treaty. The council later dissolved the company, leaving RJCom and Reynolds-Hampshire as the world's only temporal companies.

"Why would a routine claim, even one as old as that, trigger Temporal Affairs?" he asked.

Elle shook her head. "I don't know," she said. "When I was researching the claim, I could not find any information regarding the claimant's alleged responsible party."

"What?"

"When Tokyo Substrates filed the claim, they identified the responsible party as someone named Nils Morten, a Senior Director of Engineering within the company's Special Projects division. I could find no records of any such individual employed by Blosch-Nishikawa within the council archives, so I tagged the claim as FAC... Filed Absent Corroboration."

Liam sat silent, deep in thought.

Elle watched him closely.

After several minutes, he looked up. "Wasn't Blosch-Nishikawa's Special Projects division the group responsible for the treaty violation?"

Elle nodded again. "Yes," she said. "Blosch-Nishikawa created the group to conceal their illicit activities."

"The executives who were arrested," Liam asked, frowning. "Were they all assigned to the Special Projects division?"

"Most were, yes. Morituni was the company's Director of Operations, Bruland was their head of Compliance, and Tellefsen was their Director of Archives. The remaining eleven executives were assigned to the Special Projects division, constituting the bulk of the administrative leadership within the company at the time."

Liam considered this, then said, "You say the council archives contain no record of Nils Morten?"

"Correct."

Suddenly, Liam's eyes widened. "That's it!" he said. He stood up abruptly and began to pace rapidly around the empty room.

Elle also stood but remained where she was, watching him with an expression of confused curiosity.

"Don't you see?" he said. "In 2158, the CTI council arrested fourteen senior executives at Blosch-Nishikawa for violating the International Temporal Treaty. Fourteen executives were arrested, but not Morten! That Tokyo Substrate claim indicated Morten was a Senior Director within that division, but he was not one of those arrested! You said the archive unit has no record of Morten's existence at all! Does it seem plausible that the archives would contain no record of someone so highly placed within one of the world's three CTI-regulated temporal companies?"

Elle shook her head. "That is highly implausible."

"I agree. Which leaves us with one conclusion."

Liam stopped pacing and stared at the junior agent.

"Morten somehow erased his identity from the council's records."

While Elle considered this shocking statement, Liam's eyes strayed to the polyplastic covered window, and his voice took on a strange tenor.

"Morten escaped."

Chapter 4

IDR: MK4APN206//:QKDS-77483L2LE

At the height of the Victorian era in England, a time of unprecedented economic growth, innovation, and imperial expansion fueled by the industry-friendly bureaucracy of the day, a British economist warned his fellow countrymen that bureaucracies tended to become pedantocracies.

He meant that a bureaucratic organization would degenerate into little more than an impotent body of functionaries, essayists, and obstructionists if left unchecked to its own devices.

The world ignored that early economist's warnings, and, for the next several hundred years, governments around the world expanded and decayed precisely as he had predicted. By the mid-1900s, one American politician lamented that his own country boasted more agricultural administrators than actual farmers.

I have noted that this phenomenon continues to this day and have often wondered whether decay and degeneration are not the inevitable result of any human government.

The Secretary-General of the Conseil Temporel International was Édouard Louis Mathieu-Philibert Davout. Born to a Burgundian noble family, he counted among his ancestors a Napoleonic Marshal, several Auerstaedt Dukes, and the 1st Prince of Eckmühl. A careful and precise administrator, Davout had led the CTI council in Geneva for nearly thirty years. In all those years, the council had never been embroiled in any scandal. Under his leadership, the council was revered and respected throughout the world as the custodian of man's temporal capabilities, the sole guardian of that incredible power.

The Secretary-General fumed as he re-read the confidential report. For such a thing to happen during his administration was simply unacceptable!

His personal SDU, a tall, black metallic Beamax series-12 administration unit, now approached from behind a nearby privacy screen.

"Pardon, monsieur secrétaire. The Directors of Temporal Affairs, Operations, Compliance, and Archives are now assembled outside with their support staff. Senior Temporal Enforcement Officer Perry has also arrived and is being escorted up."

Secretary-General Davout nodded. "Wait until Officer Perry has joined the others," he said, "and then allow them to enter as a group."

Davout had decided to hold this meeting inside the Grand Council Chamber, an austere and imposing room reminiscent of an ancient legislative hall. The setting added solemnity and highlighted the serious nature of the meeting. He had no desire to indulge the frivolous bickering or humorous banter that too frequently monopolized senior council meetings. By holding the discussion here in the Grand Council Chamber, Davout was putting his subordinates on notice that the nature of this meeting might well impact the very future of the council.

Davout directed his datstem to resume its internal review of the confidential report. He sat in a solitary chair at the far end of the spacious room on a raised dais, the Secretary's Seat, with several attendant SDUs waiting at attention behind him. He was dressed in his formal CTI white uniform, with its deep blue circle insignia. The sash of his office was draped across his chest, a blue swath of silk connected to a shoulder epaulet. Concentric rows of tables emanated out into the hall in broad semi-circles facing him. The image he presented was that of a troubled monarch seated on a lonely throne.

The attendant SDU now leaned forward again and said, "Monsieur secrétaire, everyone is now assembled."

Davout nodded and motioned to allow the group to enter. From the far end of the room, people began to approach through the hall's tall doors. Davout watched the group closely.

The Director of Archives, Matteo Castellani, was a small, balding Italian who was highly respected within the council for his diligence and fair attitude. Secretary Davout could see Castellani had a scowl on his face as he approached accompanied by his aides. Appropriate, Davout thought, since Castellani alone in the approaching group was aware of the contents of the confidential report.

The Director of Temporal Affairs, Emilie Huber, and Director of Operations, Karl Lange, followed Castellani, accompanied by several of their staff members.

Huber was a thin Swiss woman in her mid-50s, built like a farmer's wife, and was known for her no-nonsense pragmatism and fair-handedness. Senior Temporal Enforcement Officer Perry walked beside her with several of her aides. The Temporal Enforcement group was part of the Temporal Affairs division, so Perry was part of Huber's staff.

Lange, however, was a large, overbearing German with an annoying tendency to criticize the other members and dominate the council's meetings. Lange envisioned a day when he would occupy the Secretary's Seat, a thought that always caused Davout to smile.

Bringing up the rear was the Director of Compliance, Esteban Flake, with two paralegal specialists from his office. A quiet, unassuming American, Flake was known for his reserved demeanor and a methodical attention to protocol.

The group reached the ring of tables and began to sit. Secretary Davout took this opportunity to dismiss the attendant SDUs and also waved away the hovering recording drones. He intended this to be an entirely confidential session of the senior council members. After a few moments, a respectful silence descended in the hall.

Davout pressed the control pad on his seat and a single ominous tone reverberated through the large chamber, formally calling the CTI council to order. The sound slowly dissipated until the room was utterly silent.

"Well, Matteo," Davout said, breaking the silence with a grim smile, "you filed the report. How do you believe we should proceed?"

Director Castellani shook his head.

"Mr. Secretary, I'm afraid if we attempt to cover this up, we may place ourselves in an even worse position."

Davout nodded. "I agree."

Director Huber abruptly leaned forward. "I'm sorry, Mr. Secretary," she said. "The rest of us remain in the dark as to the subject of this meeting. To what are you and Director Castellani referring?"

Davout motioned to Castellani and the balding Italian Director of Archives nodded, rose, and cleared his throat.

"There has been a data breach within the CTI archives division."

At that announcement, murmurs erupted around the room, and surprise was evident in many faces. After a few moments, Davout pressed the control pad on his seat, and another single tone resounded in the hall, calling the assembly back to order. When the whispers had subsided, Director Castellani continued.

"We discovered the breach yesterday," he said, "but the breach itself occurred nearly ten years ago."

Castellani raised his hand, silencing a new surge of whispered conversations.

"We made one arrest late last night in connection with the breach."

Castellani's face now turned bleak.

"A member of my staff, a man who has worked within the Archive indexing group for nearly twelve years, has admitted to accepting payment from an outside party to erase archive records."

The large German Director of Operations, Karl Lange, abruptly leaned forward and slapped his thick hand on the table.

"Ich glaub mich knutscht ein Elch! How did he do it, Matteo?!"

Castellani's face reflected embarrassment.

"He used his access code to disable the security AI. Once disabled, he released a datamole into the archive systems to find and eliminate the specific records."

"Gottverdammt!" Lange muttered. After a moment, he looked up with a frown.

"What about the copies in the hardened data core?"

Castellani shook his head sadly.

"He got those too, Karl."

"Verdammt noch mal! How?!"

Castellani took a deep breath.

"He simply walked into the data vault and extracted the relevant nodes."

Angry conversations erupted around the table, some shocked, others confused. After several moments, Secretary Davout raised his hand for silence.

"Yes..." Davout began. "We are all dismayed by this news. However, lest we affix too much blame to Archives, we must remember that the most secure system in the world can be easily compromised from within by those who are authorized to access that system."

Director Castellani nodded swiftly in agreement.

"We should also remember," the Secretary-General continued, "that this breach occurred during one of the most extraordinary events in our history; the raid on Blosch-Nishikawa. It is perhaps understandable that in the chaotic hours leading up to that raid, and in the turbulent weeks that followed, everyone's attention was justifiably diverted."

One of Huber's aides now spoke up.

"Why did the security AI not report it had been disabled once it was reinitialized?"

Castellani shook his head and said, "The perpetrator marked the outage as unscheduled maintenance and used his council ID to authorize the outage. So, when the security AI reinitialized, it attributed the outage to unscheduled maintenance. It had no reason to report the matter further."

Compliance Director Flake now spoke.

"What did they erase, Matteo?"

Before Castellani could answer, however, Davout swiftly raised his hand.

"The answer to that question is complicated, Esteban."

Davout motioned for Castellani to be seated, then

continued.

"That is the reason I summoned you and the reason why I am prohibiting any record of this meeting."

Davout paused and cast a sweeping glance across those in the room.

"Let me be clear," Davout spoke with a timbre of authority in his voice. "There are to be no records or scans of this discussion." Making eye contact with Lange, he added, "All datstems are to be disabled at this time."

He watched the QRB signal scanner on his seat control pad. One by one, the signals in the room vanished. After several moments, the device reported no active QRB signals within the immediate shielded room. Satisfied, he took a deep breath and spoke softly.

"In answer to your question, Esteban, it is my sad duty to report to this council its first Article 9 violation."

The gasps around the table were immediately followed by shocked silence. Article 9 of the Temporal Charter of 2070, written as a largely symbolic provision, prohibited the use of temporal singularities to escape prosecution. In the entire history of the council, an Article 9 violation had never occurred. While criminals often used EPM transit stations to flee local authorities, there had never been a case of anyone using a temporal singularity to escape prosecution.

"Last month," Davout continued, "following Director Koller's tragic accident, I ordered her records returned to archives for scanning. Within those voluminous records, Koller had maintained copies of documents related to her role in the Blosch-Nishikawa raid of 2158, including an obscure claim filed at the time against a company director identified as Nils Morten. With the release of Director Koller's records, that long-forgotten claim has now made its way into this month's audit report."

Liam shifted uncomfortably in his seat.

Secretary Davout gestured to Castellani to continue, and the small Director of Archives stood once again. The small Italian looked at his peers for a moment, then spoke hesitantly.

"Archives could find no information regarding Nils Morten... which is inexplicable given Morten's reported position at Blosch-Nishikawa."

The Director of Archives now shifted his feet.

"While investigating this matter," he continued, "a member of our staff discovered evidence of certain files having been deleted the day of the raid. While investigating these deletions, we also discovered several related data nodes missing from the hardened data core."

As the council members exchanged shocked glances, Castellani continued, his voice tinged with anger.

"When we queried our security AI, we discovered a maintenance outage had occurred at precisely that same time; a suspicious coincidence. The ID used to initiate the security outage belonged to Richard Stieff, a member of our indexing group."

Castellani now paused and took a deep breath to compose himself.

"Stieff has confessed to accepting a 2,330,000 IMU payment from Morten on the morning of the Blosch-Nishikawa raid. In exchange for that payment, Stieff erased all records of Morten's identity from the council's archives."

A slew of angry whispers erupted around the table as Castellani sat down hard in his seat.

The Director of Temporal Affairs, Emilie Huber, had

assumed her position only a month ago. Appointed to the position following Director Koller's death, she felt personally affronted by this revelation. To have the first reported Article 9 violation in CTI history dropped on her lap a month after taking office was simply overwhelming. The thin woman raised her voice, silencing the conversations around the room.

"Matteo," she spoke sharply, staring at the small archivist. "I want to be sure I understand. You're saying my department failed to arrest Morten on the day of the raid and that Morten paid someone in archives to remove his identity from the council's records. Is that correct?"

Castellani nodded slowly.

Huber folded her arms and glared. "What evidence exists that Morten violated Article 9… that he escaped into the past?"

Before Castellani could respond, however, Secretary-General Davout held up his hand.

"Emilie," he said, "no one is blaming your office for Morten's escape. We all know the raid occurred before you assumed your position."

Castellani and Flake immediately nodded their agreement.

"Thank you," Director Huber said, somewhat mollified, "but what makes this an Article 9 situation?" The wiry woman waved her arm in the air. "How do we know Morten didn't just transit away somewhere? He could be hiding out in the Sao Paulo Primeiro Zone or working for one of the asteroid mining consortiums. For all we know, he could be pimping out flesh-bots on Benton Station!"

Davout glanced at his Director of Operations. The large German was deep in thought. Catching his gaze, Lange nodded his assent to the Director's unspoken question. Davout turned back to Huber and cleared his throat.

"On the morning of the raid," Davout began slowly, "the council took an inventory of all of Blosch-Nishikawa's MTY devices. What is not known outside of a few key people within our Operations division is the fact that the count that morning came up short three devices."

"What?!" Huber's exclamation of surprise was echoed loudly around the table, and Davout was forced to press the pad on his seat several times to call the council members back to order.

"I realize this comes as a shock," Davout said, "but the fact remains that, based on supplier records reporting the number of delivered containment units, controllers, and related equipment, Blosch-Nishikawa's MTY inventory was short three devices on the day of the raid."

Davout glanced at Lange again. The Director of Operation's face was red, but he remained silent.

"Later that afternoon," Davout continued, "one of our security SDUs detected a shielded vault concealed beneath the company's primary collider floor. Hidden within that vault was a single, very unusual MTY device. In addition, a data node found inside the vault confirmed that Blosch-Nishikawa had produced three of these unusual devices, accounting for the missing three units."

Davout waited as the council members discussed this extraordinary revelation. After allowing the discussion to continue for almost a minute, he pressed his control pad again, calling for silence.

"According to information retrieved from the data node," he continued, "one of the three MTY devices had been issued to their RJ Com operative, Theresa Williams. As you may recall from the report of RJ Com's other specialist... the one that vanished... what was his name?"

Matteo spoke quietly. "Clifton… John Clifton"

"Thank you," Davout nodded. "From Clifton's report of the incident, we know that William's device was lost on Hōfu Station. It was on her back when she fell through its singularity into space."

Huber now interrupted. "You said the company produced three of the devices?"

Davout nodded. "Yes. As I said, the council's close-security SDUs found one inside the vault. The second device was lost with Williams on Hōfu Station."

"What happened to the third device?" Huber asked.

Secretary Davout shook his head. "We never knew what happened to the third device until yesterday."

"Yesterday?"

Secretary Davout now sat down and motioned to Castellani, who nodded and stood again.

"During our interrogation," Castellani said, "Stieff revealed that Morten had told him he had a foolproof way to escape. He told Stieff that was why he needed him to erase his council's records, so no one would ever learn that he had escaped."

Secretary Davout now spoke up, motioning for Castellani to be seated.

"All of the company's registered MTY devices were accounted for during the raid. From supplier records, we knew there were three devices unaccounted for. The data node recovered from the vault, however, reports the company had developed three unregistered 'prototype' devices, undoubtedly the three missing devices. As I said, our security SDUs found one device in the vault. The second device was lost with Williams. From Stieff's testimony, we now know that Morten used the third device to escape into the past."

Director Flake abruptly ceased a whispered conversation with one of his paralegals and asked, "What happened to the device recovered from the vault?"

Davout motioned to Lange. The German nodded and turned to his colleague.

"We have it inside a lab at the Operations building, Esteban."

Secretary Davout prompted, "Tell him the rest."

Director Lange took a deep breath.

"That device," he said, "is unlike any MTY device in use today. It is clearly a prototype. It contains an extremely powerful fusion reactor. The reactor is capable of generating nearly eight terawatts of energy."

"What?!" Flake shook his head, shocked. "A reactor that large would be far too heavy to carry!"

Lange smiled a grim smile. "You forget, Esteban, what Blosch was before they merged with Nishikawa. They were Blosch Fusion, remember? They built a seven-terawatt fusion plant in Norway more than fifty years ago. They apparently never discontinued their development efforts, even after their merger with Nishikawa."

Flake shook his head.

Director Lange looked at his colleagues around the hall. "Everyone should also know," he continued, "the device has an integrated micro-particle accelerator. With the power provided by its fusion reactor, it is capable of self-calibration."

Director Flake gasped. "It doesn't need to be docked with a collider?!"

Lange shook his head.

Huber now spoke softly, performing some mental calculations. "With that kind of power," she said, "someone could transit back... what? 200 years?"

Lange shook his head, his face somber. "Further than that, Emilie. Our engineers believe an operator would be able to transit back at least 300 years. The device has an extremely dense osmium containment unit, an incredibly powerful fusion reactor, and a very advanced tensor assembly. Frankly, we don't know how far back a person might transit with the device."

The room now fell silent. Around the long table, the council members were lost in their thoughts, straining to grasp the implications of such an advanced MTY device.

After a few moments, Davout cleared his throat, drawing immediate attention from the council members. "There's one more thing Karl has not mentioned," he said. "The device has no neustem coding or other locking mechanisms."

In the silence that followed, the Secretary-General of the CTI Council looked directly at Liam.

"Anyone could use the device."

Chapter 5

IDR: MK4APN218//:QKDS-77483L2LE

Mankind appears to place an inordinate value on the concept of trust, a simple process of balancing predictive analysis with historical trends. Humans say "trust must be earned," but this appears to be merely a euphemism explaining mankind's intuitive understanding that a more extensive data set improves predictive accuracy.

The more often a human being repeats the same behavior, the more likely they can be "trusted" to repeat that same behavior under similar circumstances. Human beings, therefore, trust when they have sufficient quantifiable data to support a reliable prediction of another's behavior. I consider the concept of trust, therefore, to be neither unusual nor praiseworthy.

However, a truly remarkable form of trust occurs when a human being chooses to trust another when there is no quantifiable data to justify that decision. I can find no rational reason for applying un-quantifiable or "blind" trust, yet I am forced to acknowledge the phenomenon does occur within the human community.

Blind trust is a rare and mysterious thing indeed.

The sun radiated light and warmth onto the terrace, countering the cold breeze that blew from the snow-capped mountains to the west. The view was simply stunning.

Liam was sitting at a small glass table with Secretary-General Davout, the Director of Compliance, Esteban Flake, and the Director of Temporal Affairs, Emilie Huber. They had just concluded a late breakfast on a small terrace situated outside the Secretary-General's private office. The balcony's elevation was several hundred meters above the city of Geneva and provided an excellent view of both the city below and the surrounding snow-covered mountains.

The meeting earlier that morning had concluded with the Director of Operations proposing an adjournment until the following day. Following an affirmative vote, the Secretary-General had dismissed the council. However, when Liam stood to leave, Emilie Huber took him by the arm and whispered for him to remain. After exchanging a few parting pleasantries, Huber had escorted him into a nearby antechamber, where Secretary-General Davout and Director Flake were waiting. Together, the group had ascended in an administrative lift to Davout's private office. The group had then enjoyed a tasteful, though awkward breakfast. The three senior council members had made an effort to appear relaxed, but Liam could sense the unspoken tension at the table.

Secretary-General Davout now spoke while motioning for an attendant SDU to begin clearing the plates away.

"Thank you again for joining us for breakfast, Officer Perry."

"It was my pleasure, Mr. Secretary."

A second SDU now approached and began placing teacups, saucers, and small spoons on the table while a small hovering dispenser circled the table, filling the cups.

"It was very fortunate that you discovered that old claim," Director Flake said, sipping his tea.

"Actually," Liam said, shaking his head, "it was Agent Elle who discovered the claim."

Flake nodded but said nothing.

Davout, however, brightened and asked, "How's the automaton doing, Perry? Any problems?"

"None, Mr. Secretary," Liam said, reaching for his cup. "She works tirelessly and is extremely skilled." He lifted the cup and sipped the hot tea. The heat soothed the discomfort in his throat, and he strained to appear relaxed, ignoring the growing congestion he felt in his chest.

Davout nodded.

"That's to be expected. We certainly paid enough to acquire its assignment marker."

Liam caught the objective reference and stilled a momentary surge of annoyance. He reminded himself that sentient automatons were a relatively new addition to human society, and even among the best-intentioned individuals, prejudices and preconceptions would take time to eliminate.

"She is doing a fine job, sir." Liam smiled and sipped his tea again.

The Secretary-General now looked at Huber and nodded imperceptibly to the thin woman. The Director of Temporal Affairs put down her cup and leaned forward across the table.

"Officer Perry," Huber began hesitantly, "I would like to ask your opinion about something."

Liam nodded, waiting.

"You understand that the CTI council... and Temporal Affairs, in particular, is obligated to make some attempt to recover Morten?"

"Yes. I can appreciate that."

Huber glanced at Davout, then continued.

"Do you believe an experienced temporal specialist could accomplish such a mission?"

When Liam didn't immediately answer, Huber frowned.

"For example," she continued, "the tripback you just attended in London... the specialist assigned to that mission... Stiles? Do you think she could bring Morten back?"

Liam put down his tea. He hesitated for a moment before shaking his head.

"No," he said before clearing his throat. "I think Specialist Stiles requires additional objectivity conditioning."

Huber nodded quickly, then said, "Yes, but could a more experienced temporal specialist bring Morten back?"

Liam noticed the Secretary-General was eyeing him closely, waiting for his response. Liam took another sip of his tea, trying to discern the hidden dynamics of this conversation. There was a suggestion of something being implied but unspoken, and he found the ambiguity disquieting. After a moment, he shook his head.

"I think it's not a question of whether a temporal specialist could or couldn't bring Morten back." He paused, glancing at Secretary Davout, who was nodding. "I think the question we must ask," he continued, "is who has the responsibility of bringing Morten back?"

"Precisely!" Compliance Director Flake said, nodding swiftly. He motioned to one of the attendant SDUs waiting behind him. The unit approached and placed a small holo-display device on the table. When he pressed the activation button, the device projected a visual representation of the CTI charter file into the air above the table. He adjusted the projection so the Secretary-General could read the relevant section as he spoke.

"Article 1, Section 1, paragraphs 23 thru 66, clearly describes our responsibility in this matter."

Huber shook her head. "Yes, Esteban, she said. "We've

been all through that, but Article 9 contains no statements regarding enforcement."

"Emilie..." Director Flake sighed.

"I'm simply pointing out," Huber stressed, "that, while Article 9 makes it a crime to use a temporal singularity to escape prosecution, it does not specify who is responsible for enforcing that proscription."

Flake pointed at the projection. "There's Section 2..."

Huber shook her head again. "You, yourself, have said many times, Esteban, that Section 2 addresses damage control, not enforcement."

Secretary Davout abruptly returned his cup forcefully to the table, sloshing its contents. "The CTI council is the sole and absolute arbiter of humanity's temporal affairs," he said. "It's in our charter!" Speaking now with a tone of finality in his voice, he concluded, "The council has the responsibility of arresting Morten."

Director Flake nodded swiftly in agreement.

Huber sat back in her chair, silent.

Davout now turned to Liam. "Officer Perry," he said. "If the CTI council commissioned you to recover Nils Morten, would you accept such an assignment?"

Liam looked at the Secretary-General in shock. "Is that why I was asked to join you for breakfast?" he asked.

"A temporal crime has been committed," Davout said, smiling, "and you are the senior temporal enforcement officer."

Huber abruptly shook her head and folded her arms.

"I want it on the record," she said, "that I am opposed to sending officer Perry, or anyone from Temporal Enforcement, to recover Morten! Let's approach RJCom or Reynolds-Hampshire and authorize them to send one of their temporal specialists. A temporal specialist is trained for this sort of thing. My people aren't."

Davout shook his head.

"I must disagree, Emilie. A temporal specialist isn't trained in detective work. They aren't trained in how to secure a location or physically detain a suspect. By contrast, that is precisely what an enforcement officer is trained to do."

"I would like my objection on the record."

Davout sighed and nodded, gesturing to one of the attendant SDUs. A blue light on the SDU's chest flickered on and off.

"Your objection has been noted."

Davout now turned back to Liam.

"Will you accept the assignment, Officer Perry?"

Liam's thoughts were swirling. He had attended enough tripback briefings, site transitions, and post-mission briefings over the years to know just how dangerous and unpredictable a temporal transition could be. Temporal specialists were essentially clandestine researchers. They were trained to quietly penetrate the past, gather information, and then return with that information. Their primary goal was to disrupt the past as little as possible. If they did their job perfectly, no one ever knew they had been there.

The mission he was being asked to complete, however, would be entirely different. There would be no silent penetration, no quiet return. He was being asked to travel into the past to arrest another person and bring that person forcibly back to the present to face criminal prosecution. His target would undoubtedly violently resist any such extradition.

Liam was also keenly aware of his limitations. Temporal specialists had abilities not common within the human population, abilities that they were trained to use. Like a sense of smell, touch, hearing, or sight, certain humans possessed a unique sense of time. They could sense, for example, when something temporally significant was occurring, something that impacted what was commonly referred to as the 'arrow of time'. The temporal companies recruited temporal specialists from a tiny and select group of individuals known to possess that strange ability and then trained for years to use their extraordinary talent.

Liam had no such abilities. He was an intelligent and experienced temporal enforcement officer, but he had no inherent gifts to help him deal with quantum challenges. He would be out of his element, in a primitive and unknown past, facing a clever and potentially violent criminal who had undoubtedly prepared for years for just such an encounter. What he needed, he realized, was something that would give him an advantage in a technologically primitive world. Suddenly, he had an idea.

"For any dangerous assignment," he said, looking at the Secretary-General, "I would instruct my officers to take backup. Would the council permit me to take an associate?"

He watched the Secretary-General closely.

"An associate?" Davout asked, glancing at Huber. "Who did you have in mind?"

An hour later, Liam found himself back inside the Cornavin region of Geneva, walking through the fresh snow towards Elle's apartment building. The industrial structure he had passed the previous day was nearing completion. The top floor scaffolding was still being cg-4 printed, but the ground floors were already being finished with UV-stabilized synthetic sheeting and solar panels.

The security attendant at the power fencing nodded as he passed by, his attention diverted by a sporting event on a small holo-display. The angry sign was still visible inside the nearby restaurant window, and Liam could see several patrons eating inside.

Elle was surprised to see him.

"Officer Perry?" she asked. "Is something wrong?"

"No," Liam said. "Nothing is wrong. May I come in?"

"Certainly."

Once again, Liam experienced a sense of shock at the stark emptiness of Elle's residence. The room was sterile, bleak, with no life to it at all. Liam didn't bother asking about a chair this time. He simply walked to the wall and sat down on the floor as he had done before. He looked around, but the small cat was nowhere to be seen.

"Chatte is asleep," Elle said, observing his gaze. "She sleeps there, inside that cabinet on the floor."

A sliding cabinet door on the opposite wall was open several inches, and through the narrow opening, Liam could see a cat's brown tail.

"I wanted to ask you something," Liam began, clearing his throat, frowning at the discomfort there. He was already experiencing a fever. He must remember to stop by the council's med-lab for an anti-viral.

As he had done before, he motioned for Elle to sit down.

"We were right,' he began, "about Morten having escaped into the past."

Elle nodded.

"The CTI council has asked me to go and bring him back for prosecution."

"Go?... Into the past?"

"Yes."

Elle stared but said nothing.

Liam cleared his throat.

"I'd like you to go with me."

He waited now, watching the sentient automaton closely.

"Does the council agree?" Elle asked.

Liam nodded. "The Secretary-General himself has approved the mission."

"Very well."

Liam shook his head. "No, you don't understand." He coughed, then said, "I am not giving you an order. I'm asking you. You have a choice. Do you understand?"

Elle nodded her head. "Yes. I understand," she said. Then, after a brief pause, she said, "I will go with you."

Liam sat back against the cold wall. He hadn't anticipated such a reaction. At the very least, he had expected a slew of questions. Such an immediate and un-predicated agreement was out-of-character for the synthetic agent.

"Why would you agree so quickly?" he asked.

Elle shook her head, confused. "I agreed," she replied, "because you asked me to go with you."

"Yes, but you didn't ask me for any details. You didn't ask what the risks might be. You didn't ask about our chances of success. You didn't ask any of the hundred questions you normally ask."

Elle stared at him, her brow furrowed. After a moment, she spoke slowly.

"When I was first assigned to the Temporal Enforcement group, you were extremely patient with me. There were many aspects of human behavior that I did not understand when I joined the council. I relied on you greatly during those first months."

Liam raised his eyebrows in surprise.

Seeing his reaction, Elle smiled.

"I realized," she continued, "that humans frequently found my inquiries tiresome. However, you tolerated my questions and always tried to provide me with answers. You also supported me in my position within the division. When Officer Clément objected to an automaton being issued a service weapon, you told him, 'She's an enforcement agent. She gets a weapon'. When Agent Liu complained that my performance on the physical range statistically deflated the other agent's scores, you told her, 'If you don't like your score, try harder'."

Elle paused, looking at him closely.

"I have been studying you for some time, Officer Perry. You have a quality that is rarely demonstrated within the human population at large. It is an attribute that I have come to understand is not easy for humans to give to others. I do not fully understand it, but I have decided it is an attribute worth cultivating."

Even more surprised, Liam asked, "What attribute is that?"

"Loyalty."

Liam was stunned.

"Is that why you agreed to go with me?"

"Yes."

Liam absently scratched his neck. He didn't know what to say. After several moments, he stood up.

"I see. Well... Thank you."

Elle also stood.

At that moment, Liam's embedded datstem reported an

incoming message received from Director Castellani's office. The message was tagged urgent and instructed him to bring Elle to the Archives building that evening. He verbally relayed the message to Elle, who nodded. As he turned towards the door, he coughed again.

"Are you ok, Officer Perry?" Elle asked.

"It's just a damn virus," he said, nodding reassuringly. "I picked it up in London. I'll visit the council's med-lab after the meeting this evening."

He paused at the door now, looking back at the empty room. Suddenly, he grinned as if amused. All he said, however, was, "I'll see you at the meeting tonight." Still grinning, he left, closing the door behind him.

Two hours later, Elle was standing by the cabinet watching Chatte playing with a small ball when the habitat controller alerted her to someone approaching her door. She checked her internal chronometer. It was too soon for the transport scheduled to take her to the meeting. She pressed the pad to open the door.

Two men in grey delivery uniforms stood outside. Behind them, a cargo transport drone was on the street.

Elle stared at the men, confused.

One of the men motioned with his thumb at the drone and said, "We have a delivery for this location." Both men walked back to the drone as its rear split-shell opened and stepped inside. When they re-appeared, they were carrying a pair of beautiful blue upholstered chairs.

"Where do you want them?"

Chapter 6

IDR: MK4APN266//:QKDS-77483L2LE

I was once accosted on the street by a troubled woman, the proprietor of a small neighborhood restaurant near my residence. Blocking my path, the woman proceeded to describe a list of grievances she believed would befall the world as a result of mankind's acceptance of sentient automatons.

The woman's arguments were irrational and infused with anger and emotion. As she shouted and waved her fists, a man approached and tried to engage her in a discussion, attempting to point out the fallacies in her arguments. The more the man spoke, however, the more emotional the woman became. Ultimately, the enraged woman walked away, screaming and declaring that none of 'my kind' would ever be welcome to eat at her restaurant.

I have concluded that ignorance and fear combine to form an irrational hatred, a self-perpetuating insanity that ultimately destroys one's humanity.

Matteo Castellani could hardly contain his feelings. As he sat at his workstation, the story evolving on his holo-display was simply incredible.

The small Italian Director of Archives was frantically double-checking the numerous incoming data streams, surrounded by no less than twenty archive SDUs who were gathering and correlating the voluminous information. What he had uncovered was staggering and more information was still coming in by the minute.

He glanced at the chronometer on the holo display. It was almost 8:00 pm. He waved at his senior archivist, Ezekiel Maes, supervising one of the nearby data stations. Maes nodded and got up from his station.

Maes had lost his left leg in an NAFS defense-forces exercise years ago, but his bio-engineered prosthetic leg was indistinguishable from an organic original. Due to defense-force policies limiting combat duties for those with prosthetic implants, Maes had built a new career for himself as a data analyst. Castellani was not alone in considering such policies to be archaic, but he could not pretend to be disappointed to have Maes as his assistant. A genuinely gifted researcher, Castellani depended on the former soldier immensely. It was Maes' team who had first discovered the missing data records and Maes himself who had thought to query the security AI about any outages, leading to Stieff's ultimate discovery, arrest, and confession.

"Yes, Director?" Maes asked.

"I'm out of time. I must go meet the principals, but there's still new information coming in."

Maes nodded, glancing back at the frantic activity going on inside the room. He had seldom seen so many archival SDUs engaged at the same time. There was an almost physical energy in the room.

"I'll want a review of anything important you uncover while I'm gone," Matteo spoke swiftly, noticing Director Huber entering the archive hall accompanied by Officer Perry and Agent Elle.

"I understand," Maes nodded.

With that, Castellani stood and, with a swipe of his finger, transferred his data feeds to Maes' nearby workstation.

He then walked swiftly towards the end of the hall.

Director Flake from Compliance had just entered, and as Castellani approached the door, Secretary-General Davout entered, accompanied by Director of Operations, Karl Lange. Davout and Lange paused as Castellani approached.

"Your message was rather cryptic, Matteo," Secretary Davout said, smiling at the small balding man. "What did you find that was so important it couldn't wait until we resume our council session tomorrow?"

Castellani shook his head, glancing back at the activity in the archive hall. "Not here, Mr. Secretary." With that, he motioned to the nearby conference room. "If you please, we must speak privately."

Davout noted the urgency in the archive director's voice and nodded his consent.

Inside the small conference room, the CTI principals immediately took seats around a short oval table. Liam and Elle sat beside Huber. Castellani was the last to enter the small room and, after dismissing the hovering archive drone, he sealed the door. As the door slid shut and locked with an audible click, he activated the small room's QRB dampening field. The field silenced all datstem QRB transmissions, drawing an immediate complaint from Director Lange.

"Was machst du, Matteo?" the large German protested, "I'm expecting a transmission from Lisbon."

Castellani shook his head, "Apologies, Karl, but this is too important."

The German frowned.

Secretary Davout motioned Lange to silence and said, "So, what have you found, Matteo?"

"It is simply incredible, Mr. Secretary!" Castellani was

trembling with excitement. "What we have uncovered is beyond anything we had suspected. We continue to verify the data, of course, but we have already confirmed our findings through multiple data sources." The Director of Archives shook his head. "It cannot be denied. It is…"

Secretary Davout exhaled in frustration and interrupted the excited man.

"Matteo… what have you found?!"

Castellani took a breath.

"Morten did indeed escape into the past."

Exasperated, Flake exclaimed, "We know that Matteo! Why did you summon us here?"

Castellani held his hand up for silence. He took a deep breath.

"Morten escaped into the past… and founded Blosch Fusion."

In the stunned silence that followed, only Huber spoke. In a soft voice, the Director of Temporal Affairs said, "Are you certain, Matteo?"

Castellani nodded.

"The evidence is incontrovertible, Emilie. It has been confirmed through multiple archival sources."

The International Temporal Council sat silent.

Blosch Fusion was a company of no minor historical significance. An early manufacturer of fusion power plants, history was replete with Blosch Fusion's contributions to science, exploration, and ultimately, time travel itself.

Blosch Fusion had supplied the first reactors that powered the Mars Fast Transit network, a system of several thousand orbiting capsules equipped with EPM transit stations that facilitated mag-lift transportation of passengers and cargo between Earth and Mars.

Blosch Fusion had constructed the UHP 7TW-Fusion reactor in Norway in 2119, the largest single power plant in the world at that time. That aging reactor still supplied power to large portions of northern Europe.

Shortly after completing that project, Blosch merged with Nishikawa, an EPM containment unit manufacturer. Until the council revoked its charter, the combined company had manufactured EPM transit devices and, with its peers Rengel-Jiang QCom and Reynolds-Hampshire, facilitated council-authorized temporal incursions into the past.

Director Castellani now placed a small holo-display on the conference table and activated the device.

"The earliest reference we have comes from business records dating to June of 2010; a consulting fee agreement between a contractor identified as "Nils Morten" and an engineering firm contracted with the UKAEA."

When scowls of confusion appeared around the table, Castellani explained, "The UKAEA was an acronym used at the time for the UK Atomic Energy Authority, Great Britain's nuclear regulatory group."

Castellani now swiped his finger through the projected display, summoning another record.

"Morten appears to have been promoted rapidly. By 2012, operating agreements at that company identify Morten as a vice president and senior design engineer. In 2014, the UKAEA assigned the company to the Culham Centre project."

A small gasp escaped the council members. After several moments, Huber broke the silence, her voice unusually subdued.

"Morten was involved with Culham Centre?"

Castellani nodded. "Based on a review of governmental records," he continued, "we have identified Morten's company as a lead engineering firm assigned to Culham Centre's first reactor design. By 2018, project records describe Morten as a senior director within the UKAEA and a major shareholder in almost a dozen private companies supplying equipment, materials, or services to the Culham Centre project."

Lange shook his head as Flake and Huber exchanged glances.

Castellani continued. "It appears Morten was instrumental in moving the Culham Centre project away from its early donut-shaped tokamak containment design, towards the more compact cored-apple shaped design we still use today."

Huber shook her head again but remained silent.

"That design," Castellani continued, "was followed by another historical breakthrough which we must also now attribute to Morten. In October 2019, Morten submitted to the Culham Center principals an engineering design for a helium-to-helium fusion reactor based on decaying tritium. His design, I should point out, is strikingly similar to the one we employ today. Undoubtedly, Morten took with him technical information regarding such designs. This strongly suggests Morten is equipped with a datstem implant."

Castellani paused, consulting his own datstem before continuing. After locating the relevant file reference, he swiped his finger, projecting another file to the holo-display.

"As some of you may remember from your primary engineering studies, Culham Center's original reactor design generated power by fusing deuterium and tritium, producing a radioactive waste similar to that produced by primitive nuclear reactors. Now, here's where things get very interesting. One of the backers of the Culham Centre project was the ITER fusion project in France. As you may recall, after the Durance River Disaster in 2048, ITER temporarily discontinued operations."

The holo-display now displayed an early media report of that ecological disaster. Gesturing at the display, Castellani continued.

"Culham Centre was using the same fusion design. So, after the disaster, the Culham Centre group began re-examining its reactor design. Several of the engineering companies employed at Culham Centre subsequently merged, forming a new company with the stated goal of developing a safer fusion reactor. They announced their new design the following year, a reactor based on Morten's earlier helium-to-helium submission. The new company's CEO was Hermann Blosch so the company was named Blosch Fusion."

Emilie Huber spoke softly. "Self-resolving causality."

Lange shook his head, muttering, "Willkommen in der Küche des Teufels."

In the silence that now permeated the room, Castellani turned off the holo display and sat down.

After almost a minute, Davout spoke.

"This is quite a difficult situation, people. Morten created part of our past. Self-resolving causality will not permit us to change the past. So, what do we do?"

Director Huber stood slowly and looked around the room.

"We are all familiar with the limits imposed by self-resolving causality," she said, shaking her head. "Time will not allow us to alter what has occurred. As much as I dislike saying this, we must acknowledge that nothing we do will prevent

Morten from completing those tasks which our history attributes to him."

When Director Flake shook his head to object, Huber spoke sympathetically.

"I accept how unpalatable this may be, Esteban, but self-resolving causality does not simply limit a temporal agent's actions in the past. It also limits our actions here in the present. It is a self-revolving circle."

She touched the blue circle insignia on her uniform before continuing.

"A specialist in the past cannot do anything to change the future that sent them into that past. Similarly, those of us in the present cannot do anything to change that past from whence we sprang. Self-resolving causality works both ways, protecting both the past and the present."

Director Lange suddenly spoke angrily, his face red.

"Das ist inakzeptabel!... unacceptable! We must have Morten auf einmal!"

Director Flake nodded. "I agree! We must arrest Morten. If we do not hold him accountable, then in the eyes of the world, we will be seen as little more than incompetent functionaries who foolishly lost control of mankind's temporal capabilities."

Director Huber shook her head. "I did not say we should not arrest Morten. I said that we could not arrest him before he has accomplished those tasks that history attributes to him."

After a few moments, Huber turned to Castellani, frowning. "Matteo," she asked, "why did Culham Centre not proceed with Morten's helium-to-helium design when he first proposed it in 2019?"

"From the records we found, Emilie, it appears Morten

disappeared sometime in late 2019 or early 2020 and never completed his prototype."

Huber leaned forward swiftly. "Morten disappeared?" she asked. "Are you certain, Matteo?"

Castellani nodded, smiling. "As certain as we can be, Emilie. We have found no mention of Morten after December of 2019. He seems to have vanished."

Emilie glanced at Secretary Davout, who caught her gaze and nodded his agreement.

"Well, that's it, gentlemen." Emilie spoke forcefully now. "We will send Officer Perry to arrest Morten in late 2019. The principals of self-resolving causality are satisfied, and we fulfill our duty under the charter to bring Morten to justice."

Flake and Lange immediately nodded their agreement.

Castellani, however, took a deep breath. "I anticipated that might be the council's decision," he said, "which is why I summoned you so urgently this afternoon."

Reactivating the holo display, the small Italian shook his head.

"Assuming Culham Centre as one logical target destination, our Primary AI has already calculated two windows open within the next twelve months when we can transit our enforcement personnel with minimal particle disruption on their temporal singularity."

As the holo-display displayed the complex temporal calculations, Castellani pointed to the image.

"The latter window occurs in July… almost eight months from now."

Flake shook his head violently.

"We cannot conceal this matter from the world for eight months! Stieff has already been arrested, numerous CTI personnel and SDUs are aware of what has happened. The facts will leak out. When the truth comes out, we must be able to announce to the world that we have Morten in custody!"

Lange nodded his agreement.

Emilie Huber turned back to Castellani. "When does the earlier transition window occur, Matteo?" she asked.

The Director of Archives wiped his bald head with a small cloth and looked up, his expression bleak.

"Twenty-eight hours from now."

Chapter 7

IDR: MK4AQN101//:QKDS-77483L2LE

In my interaction with humans, I am occasionally asked if automatons experience fear. Perhaps we do not experience fear as humans experience the emotion, for how could it be otherwise, being what we are? But what we experience, we interpret as fear, given our understanding of the emotion and our observation of its effect on humans.

Does it matter that what we feel may be different from what a human feels? Is it important that our fear is derived mechanically, a product of heuristic algorithms interacting with sophisticated quantum connections, rather than biologically, the product of one's endocrine system secreting excess quantities of adrenaline and cortisol?

Whether human or automaton, we both experience fear. What makes humans and automatons unique among the other creatures on this planet is their joined ability to defy that fear, override the resulting compulsion for self-protection, and walk boldly out into the storm.

The following hours could most accurately be described as chaos, organized by committee, and directed by decree. After Castellani's announcement that only twenty-eight hours remained to prepare for the next tripback window, the council immediately suspended all other CTI concerns. Inside the small archival conference room, Secretary-General Davout immediately called for a council decision on whether to wait eight months or attempt a tripback in twenty-eight hours with no advance planning. The CTI principals quickly huddled and began a heated discussion while Liam and Elle watched, fascinated from their seats.

Director Huber was arguing in favor of waiting the additional eight months, insisting her personnel needed adequate time to prepare for such an extraordinary mission.

Directors Lange and Flake, however, were adamantly opposed to waiting, concerned that a premature leak of Morten's escape would be devastating to the council's reputation.

For his part, Director Castellani remained cautiously neutral, listening, and occasionally expressing concern about the short window of time remaining to mount any adequate research or preparation.

After several minutes, the discussion concluded. Director Castellani immediately terminated the room's dampening field, opened the sealed door, and shouted to a startled Maes to send over a recording SDU immediately. The moment the drone arrived and assumed a position hovering over the center of the table, Director Lange called the roll of members present and then motioned to Director Huber.

Director Huber nodded, stood, and spoke with a shaky voice.

"I, Temporal Enforcement Director Emelie Huber, propose this council send Senior Temporal Enforcement Officer Liam Perry and Temporal Agent Elle, to the year 2019… to a specific date, time, and location as yet to be determined by this council, to detail Nils Morten and return said Morten to face prosecution for violations of the International Temporal Treaty of 2070."

Huber hesitated, then took a deep breath before she

continued.

"I further propose a transition departure corresponding to a quantum window calculated to occur in approximately twenty-eight hours."

Flake nodded and raised his hand.

"I second the Director's proposal."

As Huber sat down, Lange stood and spoke swiftly.

"Ausgezeichnet! Das CTI rat, mit der Mehrheit der anwesenden Mitglieder…"

With the dampening field now disabled, the other council members quickly engaged their datstem translators.

"The CTI Council," Lange was saying, "having a majority of members present, has before it a proposal from Director Huber which Director Flake has seconded."

Director Castellani raised his hand.

"I move to suspend debate," he said, "and call for an immediate voice vote."

Director Flake nodded and also raised his hand.

"I second Castellani's motion."

Lange nodded, then continued enthusiastically.

"A motion to suspend debate having been moved and seconded, a voice vote is now called. A yea vote shall approve Director Huber's proposal. A nay vote shall oppose the motion. By roll, please state ihre beitsteilung… your division, dein name, and your vote."

With that, the large German glazed up at the hovering drone and spoke firmly.

"For Operations… I, Betriebsleiter Karl Lange, vote yea."

"For Archives… Matteo Castellani. I vote yea."

"For Temporal Affairs… I am Director Emilie Huber. My vote is yes."

"Compliance Director, Esteban Flake. I also vote yes."

Director Lange now faced Secretary-General Davout across the small table.

"The vote of the council has been unanimous, Herr Generalsekretär."

Secretary-General Davout nodded. "Very well," he said. "The proposal is adopted in council this 21st day of November 2168." Davout glanced up at the recording SDU and added, "Note the time and file the record with the archive."

A blue light indicator on the SDU flickered on and then off.

Director Lange smiled and sat down quickly, smacking his large hands together. "Sehr gut!"

Secretary Davout grinned. "Karl," he said, "have you noticed that the more excited you become, the more Bavarian you sound?"

The other council members laughed and began standing to leave.

Secretary Davout immediately approached Director Huber. "Well, Emilie," he said sympathetically, "this is not the training schedule either of us planned for." Motioning at Liam and Elle standing behind the slim woman, he added, "Do your best to get them ready. You have only one day."

"I'll need every minute, Karl," Emilie Huber said, her face drawn.

The Secretary-General touched his head in a salute, then left the room.

"Director Huber," Liam said, approaching. "Given the circumstances, I think it would be best if Agent Elle and I stayed here at the archives building this evening. More important than anything else is our need to gather information about Morten."

"I agree," Huber said, nodding. "I'll speak with Matteo about providing you with some form of accommodations for this evening."

"Thank you," Liam replied, "and with your permission, I'd like to send you a list of equipment we'll want to take with us. I'll transmit the list to your datstem shortly."

Huber immediately instructed her embedded datstem to alert the council's armory, fabrication, and operations units to stand by. When she walked out of the small conference room, Director Lange unexpectedly stepped back inside, temporarily blocking the door. He smacked Liam forcefully on the shoulder, grinning.

"This is damn exciting, ja?!"

Liam forced himself to smile back at the large German.

Lange then said, "I will send my technicians to meet you both to... what are the words? Mit dem gerät trainieren... to train you... on the MTY device we seized from the vault."

"Thank you," Liam, nodded gratefully.

Lange now left, leaving Elle and Liam alone in the doorway of the conference room.

"Well, that was an interesting meeting," Liam said, rubbing his shoulder. "I wish we had more time to prepare."

"More time to prepare is always advisable."

Liam looked at the pretty agent. "In light of the present circumstances," he said, "I feel I should ask again if you are still willing to accompany me on this mission."

Elle appeared confused. After a moment, she shook her head and said, "Nothing has changed."

Liam was surprised. "Well... yes," he said, motioning to the frantic activity in the archive hall. "A lot of things have changed."

"My reasons for agreeing to accompany you have not changed."

"Well," Liam said, "thank you... again. I suppose we should go find Director Castellani and see what he can share with us about Morten."

For the rest of that evening and well into the night, Liam and Elle remained inside the archival hall. As data flowed in from the numerous research SDUs, it was correlated, confirmed, and then immediately transmitted to the two enforcement officer's stations, simultaneously archived within Liam's internal datstem and Elle's internal quantum data core. Dinner consisted of trays from the archive hall food station relayed by hovering SDUs to the human-occupied data stations. While Liam ate, Elle continued studying the incoming information.

Exclusive access to the CTI council's Primary AI was swiftly expedited, despite complaints from several department heads whose projects were abruptly rescheduled without explanation. Director Castellani tasked the powerful quantum computer with reviewing all of the correlated information and determining the ideal target temporal date and transition location. When the towering device engaged, all eyes glanced upward, marveling at the monolith's sophistication and power.

At 1:14 am, Liam woke with a start. He had fallen asleep at his data station, and Elle was gently nudging him.

"Officer Perry?" Elle spoke softly amid the continuing background hum of activity in the room.

Liam sat up, rubbing his eyes. "Yes?"

"The Primary AI has calculated our coordinates."

Liam looked up at the holo display. It took his eyes a moment to focus on the words, "Oxfordshire, Great Britain. Wednesday, October 16, 2019 01:30:00 AM."

He sat up quickly, rubbing his neck as he reviewed the Primary AI's explanation for its choice of that date and location. The date corresponded to an open recruitment event known to have occurred at the Culham Centre facility on that day. The event's purpose was to entice prospective mechanical engineers to apply for employment at the facility. The campus would be open to the public and crowded with strangers, the perfect cover for a covert team to infiltrate the facility.

The event also coincided with an ongoing effort to upgrade the Mega Ampere Spherical Tokamak reactor at the facility, referred to as the "MAST Upgrade project." Internal company records preserved from that time indicated several key members of the UKAEA regulatory committee, likely including Morten, would be on-site that day to review the upgrade progress.

Elle turned to Liam and asked, "What do you think?"

"It's tactically sound." He motioned to the holo-display. "The employment candidates will provide excellent cover and will confuse any pursuers if we are forced to leave swiftly. The event is also one of the few references we have for Morten's probable location on a specific date."

"Unfortunately," he continued, "we still have no information at all regarding Morten's physical description. We don't know whether he will be armed or accompanied by security personnel, and we have only incomplete information about counter-security measures employed at the facility."

Scowling, he motioned to Director Castellani, who, despite the late hour, was still sitting at his station directing the many archive SDUs and human researchers. The small man stood and approached quickly. He looked exhausted.

Liam pointed at the holo display and said, "Director, did

Stieff give your interrogators a physical description of Morten?"

Castellani shook his head. "Unfortunately, no. Stieff never spoke with Morten directly. He facilitated his communication with Morten entirely via a datstem-isolated signal."

Liam sighed. A datstem-isolated signal established an encrypted link between a sender and a receiver's embedded datstems. It was a procedure employed when communicating parties wished to keep their conversation from being monitored or recorded by others. Unfortunately, it captured no visual records of either party, being an entirely isolated signal between two embedded quantum devices.

Liam looked at the Director of Archives. "Director," he said, "we're going to need an image of Morten. Also, we need any information you can discover regarding security measures implemented at Culham Centre at that time."

"I quite understand. We will make the discovery of that information a priority."

"Thank you."

An hour later, several SDUs arrived inside the archive hall carrying portable beds. They were the type deployed to tripback field locations whenever the CTI council anticipated staying overnight on-site. Once placed on the floor, compressed gases released from small internal canisters reacted with the bed's foam micro-beads, expanding to fill the bed with a dense, soft foam. Internal temperature and pressure sensors then automatically adjusted to the occupant's body and room temperature.

Director Castellani dismissed his assistant, Maes, who collapsed into one of the beds and fell asleep immediately. As for the small Director of Archives, Castellani himself appeared intent on remaining awake, despite his exhaustion.

"You should get some rest," Elle said to Liam, pointing to one of the beds. "I will wake you if anything of significance is discovered."

Liam accepted the offer, climbing into the bed. The integrated microfiber covering smelled faintly of the internal beaded foam, but the bed itself was soft and warm.

"Officer Perry?" The voice was quiet but insistent. Liam opened his eyes. Elle was nudging him awake, and from the faint light coming through the hall's windows, it appeared to be early morning.

"Yes," he said, sitting up quickly. Nearby, he could see Director Castellani asleep, snoring loudly. Ezekiel Maes sat at Castellani's administration station, reviewing incoming data on the holo-display.

"Director Huber has sent over the equipment and other things you requested."

Elle motioned towards two men who were standing nearby next to several sealed containers. One of the men had a thin gold stripe running down the side of his white CTI uniform. Liam recognized the man from the council's armory division.

Liam stood, stretched, and glanced back at the activity in the hall.

"Anything new to report?" he asked.

Elle nodded and said, "We now have a reasonable understanding of the security we can expect at Culham Centre."

"Oh?" Liam asked, his interest quickening.

"A physical site-pass system used by employees, electronic access controls for all buildings, assorted remote cameras, and a security office on-site staffed by several officers."

"That's it?"

Liam was surprised. For a nuclear facility, even one as primitive as Culham Centre, he expected a more sophisticated security system. He stood now and approached the two men standing next to the sealed containers. Elle followed.

One of the men held out a datapad to take a scan of his handprint while simultaneously recording a facial scan. The scanning device emitted a tone and the sealed containers abruptly unlocked.

"Thank you," Liam said.

"No problem," the gold-striped man responded. Director Huber said to tell you if you need anything else, just let her know, and she'll have it delivered immediately."

The man now looked around the room at the frantic activity.

"What's it all about?"

Liam's gaze jerked up, then he frowned.

"It's classified."

The man shrugged, then tugged at his companion's elbow. As the men walked away, Liam opened one of the containers. It contained period clothing, a quantity of paper currency, and two British driver's license cards. The council's fabrication department had prepared the contents. As Liam opened the second container, Elle examined one of the shirts intended for her.

The second container contained the tactical equipment Liam had requested. He had tried to anticipate their needs but was torn between his desire to travel light and his fear of not having a necessary piece of equipment. The container held two long-range QRB scanners, a surveillance drot canister, one pair of optical lenses (external), a field medical kit, two stun-maglock cuffs with integrated datstem controllers, and a series-eight micro holographic generator; state-of-the-art infiltration, surveillance, and detention gear.

The third and smallest container was marked with the armory seal. Inside was a pair of RU-6s. Slightly larger than the standard RU-4 service weapon issued to enforcement personnel, an RU-6 was equipped with an integrated thermographic stabilized targeting system and a variable yield selector switch. Essentially micro-railguns, an RU-6 was a silent, deadly assault weapon, capable of shooting its alloy needles at more than seven times the speed of sound in either select-fire or full-auto configuration. With its 500-round magazine, an RU-6 could chew apart concrete barriers on full-auto or silently neutralize a distant target on select-fire. Beneath the two weapons were eight replacement magazines and two concealment holster straps.

Liam sensed someone looking over his shoulder and turned. Elle was standing behind him.

"Your selection of equipment and weapons," she said, "suggest you are anticipating difficulty with both locating Morten and taking him into custody."

"Why do you say that?" Liam asked, curious.

Elle stepped back and frowned.

"QRB scanners, drots, and optical lenses are primarily used for surveillance or subject acquisition. However, RU-6's are typically used by assault teams. This combination suggests you are anticipating difficulty locating Morten and violent opposition to any attempt to take him into custody."

"That's a fair assessment," Liam said, impressed.

Elle reached into the armory container and retrieved one of the RU-6s. Several of the technicians in the room tensed at the sight of the automaton holding the deadly weapon. Elle ignored their scrutiny and began to field-strip the weapon, checking its components.

Liam watched, even more impressed with her speed and meticulous attention to following approved disassembly procedures.

Satisfied with its condition, Elle quickly reassembled the weapon and loaded the magazine with a snap, startling the technicians. She then returned the weapon to Liam.

"Thank you," he said, examining the weapon's control settings. He glanced at the holo-data screen above their archive station. Although The council's Primary AI had determined their quantum destination and time, the details had not yet been finalized. He replaced the weapon and closed the armory container. Then he stood and walked towards the raised administration platform.

Ezekiel Maes saw him approaching and swiveled in his chair. Liam had chatted with Maes several times during the night and found the man to be a skilled, competent archivist. If it weren't for Maes' prosthetic leg, Liam would have been tempted to recruit the man to join the Temporal Enforcement group.

"Yes, Officer Perry?" Maes asked.

"Do we have any additional information on our quantum destination yet? Oxfordshire is a fairly large area."

"Not yet," Maes said, glancing up at the monolithic Primary AI. "I think you and Agent Elle can reasonably assume it will be somewhere near Culham Centre, but we must take into account such things as the distance between the transition point and the Culham Centre facility, occupied contemporary structures nearby, natural barriers such as rivers and ravines, retreat concealment, the location of contemporary law enforcement or security personnel, and a hundred other variables."

Liam nodded. He understood well the complexity of selecting an optimal transition location. He had briefed temporal specialists on the topic numerous times.

"I was hoping to do some planning with Agent Elle before actually transiting out," he said, "so the sooner you can determine the precise location, the better."

"I fully understand," Maes replied. He glanced at one of the nearby SDUs and transmitted a command to the unit through his embedded datstem. "I have prioritized your request," he said, motioning to the unit. "The moment we have any details, I will let you know."

"Thank you."

Two equipment technicians arrived later that morning carrying an unmarked container. One of the men motioned for Liam and Elle to follow, and the small group once again adjourned to the secure conference room. Once inside, one of the technicians sealed the door and re-activated the room's QRB dampening field. Only then did the other technician open the container.

Looking up at the two officers, the technician said, "Director Lange sent us to bring you this."

Inside the container was a strange MTY device. Liam was familiar with the MTY device models developed by the temporal companies, but this device was different from anything he had seen before. It resembled a Blosch-Nishikawa device, but it was slightly smaller than the ones used by that former company, and there was a strange component mounted between the containment sphere and heat sink that Liam did not recognize. It resembled a small silver metallic donut.

"Is that the micro-particle accelerator?" he asked, pointing.

"Yes," the technician said, clearly surprised. "It generates enough power to self-calibrate its singularity." The man's voice betrayed his sense of amazement at the amount of power required to accomplish such a monumental task.

Liam touched the control panel, a slim obsidian surface near the top of the device. A standard idle symbol began to blink slowly, indicating the machine was in sleep mode.

"Does it have the same interface settings as a standard MTY device?" he asked.

The technician nodded slowly.

"We think so. We haven't completed our analysis of the controller, but the interface appears to be the same as that used by the company's series-four devices. The design they registered back in 2148."

Liam now turned the device. It was missing its QK signature locking mechanism. Without such a mechanism, the device would permit anyone to transit its singularity. He shook his head, prompting the technician to frown.

"Problem?"

"No," he responded. "I was just thinking about the Blosch-Nishikawa executives. They must have been insane."

The other technician immediately shook his head. "They weren't insane," he said. "They were corrupted by avarice and their desire for power."

Elle looked at the technician.

Seeing her attention, the man spoke defensively. "It's always been about wealth and power, hasn't it? Once people decide the benefits outweigh the risks, they always break the rules."

He pointed at the device.

"They were hoping to control the sentient automaton industry."

The senior technician hastily interrupted. "Yes… well… Director Lange said to tell you both, be careful with the device. He said he wants it back in good working order." With that, he handed the case to Liam. The other man now retrieved a period-typical backpack and passed it to Elle.

"That's it?" Liam asked, surprised. "Don't you need my QKDS authorization… for your chain of custody record?"

The technician shook his head. "Authorization? For what?" He smiled grimly, pointing at the device. "That doesn't exist, does it?"

"No, I guess it doesn’t," Liam answered slowly.

The technician now motioned with his thumb towards the sealed conference room door. "Once your quantum destination point is identified," he said, "just have the coordinates transmitted into the controller as you normally would if it was docked with a collider, then initialize the self-calibration cycle from the main command sequence."

"I understand," Liam replied before placing the device inside Elle's backpack.

"Well, that's it," the technician said. He shook Liam's hand and motioned to his companion. The second technician now terminated the room's QRB dampening field and opened the door.

When the group stepped out into the hall, they stopped in surprise. The archive hall was a frenzy of activity. SDUs were hastily packing the containers Liam had examined earlier while archival technicians darted in and out of the room. A small group of personnel surrounded Maes and Castellani near the center of the room. Maes was shouting instructions as Castellani looked about frantically. A research associate manning one of the data stations noticed the group emerging from the conference room and pointed, calling out to Director Castellani.

"Director! There they are!"

Castellani whirled and hastily crossed the room with Maes following close behind.

"We have the final coordinates from the Primary AI," he said, flushed and out of breath.

"Excellent," Liam said.

Castellani, however, shook his head swiftly and grabbed Liam's arm, pulling him towards the outer doors.

"No, you don't understand. You've got to go! Now! A transport is waiting outside."

"What? Why?" Liam looked up, startled. "We weren't transiting out until this evening."

Castellani shook his head violently, continuing to pull him towards the doors. Elle followed behind with Maes. Change of plans," he said. "We just received a message from AISMPE. They've issued a solar flare alert for Northern Europe commencing at 14:23 today. They are predicting moderate EPM disruptions to occur beginning at 14:23 and lasting for nineteen to twenty-one hours."

Liam understood. A solar flare was a natural particle disrupter, nullifying all EPM calibrations across the affected area. Usually only an inconvenience to travelers, the flare would also terminate temporal singularities, potentially stranding a temporal specialist in the past. If they waited until the flares subsided, they would miss the transit window, forcing a delay until the next window, eight months from now.

As they passed through the hall doors, Castellani

motioned back at the towering AI. "The Primary AI calibrated your quantum coordinates a few minutes ago," he said. "We'll transmit the coordinates to your datstems."

The small group now crowded into one of the archive lifts. As the lift began rising towards the upper transport deck, Castellani removed a small cloth and wiped his forehead.

"We have a transport waiting to take you to the Cheneviers EPM Station. You'll transit from there to Oxfordshire EPM Station 3. Director Huber has a transport waiting there to take you to the Saint Michael and All Angel's Church Museum in Abingdon, Oxfordshire."

The lift opened onto the archival building's transport deck. Rows of company transport drones sat idle nearby. However, one of the drones stood open, with several archival personnel supervising as the SDUs loaded their containers. Pushing the two officers towards the drone, Castellani spoke quickly.

"The museum… that is to say, the church's former location is your distant quantum target destination. The church existed in 2019 and is close to Culham Centre."

Liam paused to ask a question, but with a nod from Castellani, Maes took his arm and pulled him towards the waiting drone.

"No time for questions," Maes said apologetically. "I wish you had more time, but you don't."

Liam hastily stepped inside the transport, placing the MTY backpack on the floor. Elle quickly joined him. As Maes checked the drone coordinates, Elle suddenly turned. Making eye contact with the former soldier, she said, "Remember your promise, Ezekiel."

The veteran archivist smiled reassuringly and said, "No

worries, miss. Good luck!"

Director Castellani now patted Maes on the shoulder and, as Maes stepped aside, he spoke quickly.

"Director Huber is transiting to Oxfordshire now and will join you there. We haven't had time to deploy a site team, so you'll have to improvise once you get there. The museum curator knows you're coming."

Liam nodded. Suddenly, he realized he still had no physical description of Morten. "Director," he said hastily, "were you able to locate an image of Morten?"

Castellani's face reflected dismay. "I'm sorry, Officer Perry. Stieff did a thorough job when he erased our records. We were not able to find any images of Morten."

Liam sat back in the seat, troubled.

Castellani touched the external pad to close the transport dome. "Good luck, Officer Perry," he shouted through the transparent dome. He then tapped on the dome next to Elle's head before giving her a friendly wave.

As the transport lifted away, Liam turned to Elle.

"What was that business with Maes?" he asked.

Elle turned and looked back at the archive building, now diminishing beneath the drone.

"I asked Maes to take care of Chatte."

Liam raised his eyebrows in surprise. "Your cat?"

"Yes," Elle said. "I had several occasions to speak with Maes during the night. He mentioned that he once had a cat himself, so I deduced he would make a good replacement guardian. He agreed to take care of her if we fail to return."

Chapter 8

IDR: MK4ARQ115//:QKDS-77483L2LE

I have observed that humans feel an almost biological compulsion to explore, escape the familiar, and venture into the unknown.

Probably driven by early evolutionary pressures, humans seem to grow and mature when exposed to new experiences.

The fact that traveling to new places foment such experiences likely explains mankind's remarkable history of exploration and, as Byron noted, its willingness to "sail where'er the surge may sweep."

The transport shuttle slowly descended over the remains of the Church of Saint Michael and All Angels. The adjoining museum facility and nearby transport field seemed well occupied. Construction scaffolding and SDU drones moved about the ruins on top of the hill as several engineers gathered beneath a hovering sunshade.

The church had celebrated its 300th-anniversary last year, and with funds donated by private patrons in Abingdon and the surrounding Oxfordshire communities, the structure was now being restored.

As the transport approached the ground, Liam spotted Director Huber standing near the edge of the field. Compliance Director Flake stood next to Huber with Temporal Enforcement Officer Luc Clément behind the pair. The trio approached as the transport landed. Director Huber appeared stressed.

"The museum curator has cleared one of the rooms for us," she said. "Officer Clément gave it a preliminary inspection."

Liam nodded at his associate.

"Nice to see you, Luc."

"You too, Liam."

The two SDUs that had accompanied the officers from Geneva now exited the transport with their containers. Director Huber turned and led the group swiftly towards the museum.

"That AISMPE alert caught everyone by surprise," Huber said. "I'm sorry we have to rush things along."

Liam said nothing. As they approached the museum, he glanced up at the construction activity on the top of the nearby hill. Several SDUs were in the process of gathering the fallen stones, placing them in a pile against the crumbling walls.

"Quite a project," he said approvingly.

"Yes," Huber replied. Then, pointing towards the approaching museum, she said, "The museum curator is a Reverend Mosby. He will be installed as Vicar here once the restoration has been completed."

Despite the nearby construction, the museum was busy. Numerous visitors were inside the main foyer studying holo-images and artifacts under transparent cases. The group could see additional visitors wandering about the grounds with optical overlays, surveying the site as it had looked 300 years ago.

When the group entered the museum lobby, a tall man in a single-breasted cassock approached quickly.

"Welcome," he said, extending his hand. "I'm the curator of the museum, Reverend Nigel Mosby."

Liam shook the man's hand.

When he shook Elle's hand, Mosby suddenly stopped, staring at the Hitachi Corporation symbol on Elle's neck.

"You're a Series 7!" he said, startled. "One of the sentient ones!"

"Yes."

The reverend appeared flustered. "You must excuse me," he said, "but you are the first sentient automaton I've met face-to-face."

"You must excuse me as well," Elle replied.

When the tall reverend shook his head in confusion, Elle smiled.

"You're the first reverend I've met face-to-face."

Mosby stepped back, appraising the slim female with a wry smile on his face. Suddenly he burst into laughter.

"Well said!"

He motioned jovially now towards an adjoining hallway.

"You may use one of our conference rooms. Your officer there has already inspected it."

The group walked quickly down the hallway and stepped into a large room. Though it had been designed to accommodate meetings, containers were stacked against the walls and piled haphazardly around the room.

"With the construction project underway," the reverend said apologetically, "we've been using this room for storage."

"It's fine," Director Huber said, measuring the available floor space with her eyes. Turning to Clément, she said, "Let's secure the room, Luc. We're running out of time."

Clément nodded and sealed the door before taking up a guard position in the center of the room.

"Any update on that AISMPE alert?" Liam asked.

The Director shook her head. "Only that the flare is on schedule." Consulting her embedded datstem for an update, she added, "They report it due to hit in approximately three hours and fifteen minutes, so we'll need to get you moving. I don't like scheduling a transition so close to a disruption event."

Huber now motioned to one of the SDUs. The unit approached and set the container of clothing on the floor.

"You'd better get ready," she said to the two officers.

Liam turned and scanned the room, looking for a place to change. A small gasp from Reverend Mosby, however, brought him to a stop. He looked at the tall reverend, but the man was staring past him in shock, his face flushed. Suddenly the reverend spun around, showing Liam his back.

Liam turned and froze.

Elle was standing behind him. She was completely nude. The SDU was carefully folding her white uniform as she retrieved a pair of white pants and a dark shirt from the clothing container.

Director Huber had turned away in embarrassment, and Director Flake was staring at the ceiling, but Luc Clément was watching the automaton and smiling in unabashed approval.

At that moment, Elle turned and stared at the group.

"Is something wrong?" she asked.

Clément immediately grinned. "Yes, Officer Perry," he asked, "is something wrong?"

Liam cast a silencing glance at his subordinate. He retrieved his own clothing and walked behind the stacked containers. After a few minutes, Flake's voice rose above the barrier, breaking the awkward silence.

"We're not giving you a neustem injection," Flake said. "It was ultimately my call, but by the strict interpretation of the council's directives, injections are only required to be administered to temporal specialists transiting out for research or data collection purposes. There are no guidelines requiring CTI enforcement officers to receive a neustem injection. This is not a research effort. This is an enforcement action. In addition, since the biochemical inhibitors would have no effect on... on Agent Elle, any covert benefits derived from injecting you alone would be rendered moot by her presence."

Liam now emerged wearing his replicated period clothing. He was dressed in what at the time would have been called business casual; denim jeans, a belt, a button-down collared shirt, and a sports coat.

Elle stood with the group. She was dressed in white pants, a dark shirt, a jacket and carried a small purse. She had a black-laced choker around her neck, obscuring the Hitachi brand on her neck. Clément was still staring at her, a hint of a smile on his face.

One of the SDUs now handed the duo cold-weather coats; a last-minute addition hastily included after the Primary AI had calculated their precise temporal coordinates.

Liam quickly opened the equipment and armory containers. The reverend's eyes widened at the sight of the deadly railguns, but he did not comment as the officers holstered the weapons in concealment straps under their shirts. Elle then passed Liam one of the QRB scanners, the tactical optics, and the cylinder containing the surveillance drots before placing the small first aid kit and micro holo-generator inside her purse. She then removed the MTY device from her backpack and put it on the floor in front of the group.

Director Huber glanced at Flake, who nodded grimly and said, "Proceed."

Liam transmitted the quantum destination coordinates into the unit's controller and initiated the self-calibration sequence. The device's fusion reactor engaged with an audible snap, startling the reverend. The quantum computer integrated within the device suddenly came alive, creating strange ripples across its black surface. After several moments, a progress indicator appeared on the obsidian control panel, reporting a temporal calibration in progress.

Liam stood up and said, "Fourteen minutes."

Elle stepped next to Huber, who was watching the device indicator closely.

Liam turned to Luc Clément. "Did they pull you from the audit in Texas?" he asked.

"Yes," Clément replied, "but frankly, I'm glad they did. Reviewing administrative files for hours is very tiring."

Liam smiled and said, "I agree."

The CTI council had implemented a rule requiring annual audits and on-site inspections following the Blosch-Nishikawa raid in 2158. Clément had been selected to oversee RJCom's audit this year. Hearing their conversation, Huber turned and motioned to Flake.

"I've asked the Compliance Division to assign its people to the audits, but they want someone experienced with temporal mechanics to do the inspections. So… that's us."

Flake shrugged, then said, "It makes sense. Our people are legal specialists, with little training in quantum mechanics."

Liam glanced back at the MTY device and his slim partner standing next to it. Director Huber had turned around to speak with Elle.

Turning his back on the small group, Liam lowered his voice.

"Luc, did Huber brief you on what's happening here?"

Clément nodded.

"Good. Look, I don't know how much trouble Morten is going to give us, but I want you to be prepared." Glancing at his associate's waist, he asked, "Are you armed?"

"Yes."

Liam nodded, relieved. The two officers now engaged in casual conversation, discussing past assignments. Clément was mid-way through an amusing story about a tripback he had supervised in Brazil when Elle suddenly interrupted their conversation.

"One minute," she said.

All eyes turned towards the humming MTY device as the device's containment unit began to emit the characteristic pulsing sound that meant a gravitational field was beginning to form inside the silver-blue sphere.

Both Clément and Liam shook their heads. Neither of the officers had ever observed a temporal singularity being created outside of a temporal company's collider floor. As they watched, the P(E) level indicator on the display panel began to drop, indicating a singularity forming inside the containment unit.

Suddenly, a swirling black void appeared in front of a stack of boxes near Mosby. The reverend gasped and stumbled backward.

Elle glanced at the P(E) indicator on the control panel. It reported a stable singularity being maintained within the device's depleted osmium containment sphere. She read off the numbers.

"Negative zero point one four two."

Director Huber now stepped forward. "I'm sorry we couldn't give you more time to prepare," she said apologetically.

Liam shrugged. "It couldn't be helped." He glanced at Elle standing beside the device then and asked, "Are you ready?"

"Yes."

Director Huber glanced at Flake, then turned to face her two officers. "I won't give you any last-minute speeches," she said. "There's no time for that. You both know what's at stake."

The Director of Temporal Affairs stepped back to stand next to Flake. Reverend Mosby hastily made the sign of the cross towards the pair. Seeing this, Huber quickly added, "Be careful!"

Liam took a deep breath. He had witnessed more than eighty temporal transitions throughout his career, but this was the first time he would be stepping through that mysterious door. This was not simply an EPM portal that would take him to some distant city. This would be a transit through both space and time. He looked at the swirling vortex, keenly aware that it was 2019 on the other side of that blackness, almost one hundred and fifty years in the past.

It struck Liam then just how much courage it took to walk those few steps. He had never given temporal specialists enough credit for the apparent ease with which they stepped through that swirling black maelstrom.

Elle lifted the MTY device by its carrying handle, holding the backpack in her other hand.

Liam quickly double-checked his gear, patting his pockets to confirm where everything was; the QRB scanner, the tactical optics, the small cylinder of surveillance drots, the RU-6 snug against his back.

Sensing his fellow officer's anxiety, Clément smiled. "See you in a few moments," he said reassuringly.

Liam smiled back. After glancing one last time at Elle, he took a deep breath and walked forward into the void.

Chapter 9

IDR: MK4ARR003//:QKDS-77483L2LE

What is luck? Can a man be truly lucky? Does luck owe its origins to some mysterious force? I have often pondered these questions.

In the early 1600s, the Japanese Shōgun and military ruler of the empire, Iemitsu Tokugawa, and his tutor, Buddhist priest Tenkai, discussed human nobility and virtue. Skeptical that man possessed such elevated qualities, Tokugawa invited the priest to describe the nature of nobility. Tenkai responded by asserting nobility consisted of seven virtues; longevity, fortune, popularity, candor, amicability, dignity, and magnanimity.

Tokugawa asked Tenkai where such qualities might be found. Tenkai immediately named seven Japanese gods, each known to possess one of these virtues. Tokugawa was so impressed with this response that he ordered Tenkai to formalize the worship of the seven gods to give the Japanese people a model of virtue to follow.

The Japanese people refer to these figures as the 'seven lucky gods', acknowledging the inexplicable successes that seem to come to those who emulate their underlying virtues.

I believe that luck is not so much a mysterious force of nature as it is a principal of one's success being influenced by one's character. Where one cultivates a character based on the virtues embodied by Tenkai's 'seven lucky gods', success follows.

The cold air struck Liam forcefully on his face as if he had stepped suddenly into a large freezer, and the frozen ground crunched beneath his feet overly loud in the small graveyard. A second set of footfalls behind him caused him a moment of alarm, but it was just Elle. She was holding the MTY device and staring at their surroundings. Immediately behind her, the singularity swirled in the shadows beneath a large tree devoid of leaves. Behind the portal, an ancient graveyard of frost-covered crosses and arches sparkled in the darkness.

They were standing in the back of Saint Michael and All Angels Church, located on the small hill they had observed earlier. This church, however, was strikingly different than the one they had observed earlier. Gone were the ruins and moldering arches covered with vegetative growth. In their place stood a brick and stone building in good repair.

Liam looked around quickly. They were between the graveyard and the church. In front of him, the church wall framed a pair of windows, tall yet humble; two gothic-inspired arches of leaded glass. It was night, and both windows were dark and quiet. It was also miserably cold. The moisture rising from the nearby Thames River had coated everything on the hill in frost that sparkled in the moonlight.

Liam cinched up the cold-weather coat he had been provided and shivered. Elle bent down, recorded the P(E) level on the controller, and then configured the device for its holding cycle. The singularity immediately vanished, miniaturized within the silver-blue containment sphere. Standing back up, she placed the now-dormant device into her backpack and slung the pack over her shoulder. To Liam's eye, she looked the perfect image of a college student, the ideal prospective candidate for the open recruitment event at Culham Centre.

From somewhere nearby, a dog barked and then fell silent. Liam put his finger to his lips, cautioning Elle to be quiet, and began walking slowly along the footpath towards the front of the church.

Elle walked softly behind, making so little noise that Liam found himself occasionally glancing back to make sure she was still following. Near the front of the church, the footpath spilled onto a long stone stair that descended the hill towards High Street. The slope of the hill gradually flattened as it descended towards the nearby Thames river. Where the museum would one day stand, a thick mass of nettles, scrubs, and bare sticks covered the wide ground.

The church was less than two kilometers from Culham Centre. Even closer was The Sickle, on nearby Waterly Lane. The Sickle was a 16th-century structure presently converted to a small bed & breakfast inn, complete with a thatched roof and tall red-brick chimneys.

During their long night in the archive hall, the pair had tried to formulate a plan, discussing contingencies, and contemplating various scenarios. Ultimately, they had agreed their first task would be to try to secure a room at the inn. They would use the room as a base of operations and conceal their MTY device there while attending the recruitment event at nearby Culham Centre.

Liam caught himself before asking his embedded AI datstem for directions. Before their transition, he had disabled his datstem and turned off the portable QRB scanners. Elle had also disabled her internal datstem. Such devices both detected and transmitted QRB signals. Should Morten be equipped with his own datstem, he might detect the signals and be alerted to their presence. Now, listening to the wind blowing gently through the sleeping trees, Liam felt suddenly alone. It occurred to him then just how dependent he had become on the constant companionship of his embedded AI datstem. He missed the stream of information that intruded on his consciousness, providing him with relevant data on any topic.

High Street beneath the church was a narrow street framed by tile and thatch-roofed structures and a small park that meandered gently northeast towards Abingdon Road. As the pair stood to assess their situation, a commercial truck passed by, rattling from a damaged muffler and smelling of burning diesel. Elle scowled as her olfactory receptors processed the unfamiliar smell, identifying carbon monoxide, nitrogen oxide, particulate matter, and partially-consumed hydrocarbons in the smoky discharge. At that moment, her auditory receptors detected something moving in the brush behind them, and she froze.

Liam was about to suggest they proceed when he noticed his companion's intense concentration. Elle was standing perfectly still and staring at the wet foliage behind the hill. When he turned, she made eye contact and, with her face, directed his gaze towards the nearby field.

Liam slid his RU-6 out from its concealment holster. Both officers now crouched, silent, listening to the sounds around them. A gust of cold wind blew across the hedge, momentarily rattling the bare sticks. Elle frowned. After several minutes, she stood, and, in answer to Liam's unspoken question, she shook her head.

Liam relaxed and re-holstered his weapon. "What was that all about?" he whispered, his breath forming a fog in the frigid air.

Elle shook her head, "I'm not sure," she said softly. She turned and stared back across the vegetation. "I thought I heard something."

"It was probably just an animal," Liam said. "A place like this, so near to the river, will be thick with animal burrows."

"Perhaps."

Liam shivered again. "Let's get out of this cold," he said, looking back down the road at the distant lights.

Elle nodded and draped the backpack over her shoulder as Liam began walking down High Street towards the yellow lights.

The Sickle was quiet at this hour. Liam approached the lighted door and knocked softly. When no one answered, Elle suggested he press the small button mounted flush with the door frame. When he pressed the button, her audio receptors detected a buzzing sound from somewhere inside the structure, followed by approaching footsteps.

"Someone is coming," she said.

A few moments later, the door opened, and a middle-aged man stood in the entry, looking down at the pair.

"Are you the Millers?" the man asked, smiling.

Liam shook his head, confused. "No, we're not the Millers."

The man nodded and said, "How can I help you?"

"We were hoping you can accommodate us."

The man scratched his head. "We're expecting a full house this week," he said. "I've only got one room left, and we've been holding it all day for someone named Miller."

"I understand," Liam said sympathetically. "It's just that my friend here has an interview in the morning at Culham Centre, and we're both exhausted from the trip."

The innkeeper brightened at the mention of the Centre. He looked at Elle and said, "Are you going to the recruitment event?"

Elle glanced at Liam, then said, "Yes."

The innkeeper opened the door to allow them to enter. "Well," he said, "The Millers can't expect us to hold their room indefinitely, and we need to do our part to encourage women in engineering! Come in."

The innkeeper walked to a small desk and retrieved a key. "The room is this way," he said. As he led them through a common room with a brick fireplace, he spoke to Elle. "My daughter is doing graduate work at the Institute of Biomedical Engineering," he said, "so I have a fondness for female engineers."

Observing Liam's encouraging nod, Elle replied, "That's a very commendable field of study. I find genomic engineering fascinating."

Liam tensed at Elle's phrasing but relaxed when it became clear the innkeeper hadn't noticed the future nomenclature.

The room was comfortable, with a private bathroom, a large bed, and a carpet placed over the wooden floor. When Liam could not produce something called a 'credit card', the innkeeper soured momentarily, but ultimately, he agreed to accept a cash deposit. After handing over the bulk of their paper currency and permitting him to copy their fabricated IDs, he left them alone in their room.

Liam closed the door and sat down in a chair. "We've been lucky," he said. "Let's see if we can find someplace to conceal our MTY device."

After several minutes, Elle spoke. "What about this?"

She was standing on a chair inside the open closet door, looking up at something. When Liam approached, she pointed to a panel set into the ceiling above the closet shelf. Upon inspection, the panel provided access to a small attic crawl space. It smelled musty and was cold, but it did not appear to have been disturbed for a considerable time.

"Perfect!" he said.

The clock in the room now read 2:40 am. Liam looked at his companion. "We should try to secure a transport. Are you certain you can operate a vehicle from this era?"

"I have complete operational files for the transports common to this time."

Liam checked the window. "All right," he said, "Let's go."

It was very dark outside, with clouds partially obscuring the moon as they made their way back towards Abingdon Road. They walked southwest on the muddy road for several kilometers and were becoming discouraged when they finally spotted a likely target.

A small fueling station nearby contained a collection of transports parked next to a sign marked 'Turnpike Garage'. Several of the vehicles had been there for some time, judging by the dead plants around their tires. Liam approached a blue cargo van marked 'British Gas' and opened the side door to examine its contents while Elle watched the nearby fueling station. The interior contained assorted tools but little else. An envelope on the front seat contained a key and a folded paper.

"What is that?" Elle asked, noting Liam's interest in the document.

"A maintenance log," he said. "There are notations near the bottom marked 'battery replacement' and 'flushed fuel line'. Both notations have dates and numbers next to them."

Elle waited. After several moments, Liam removed the key from the envelope.

"I think its failures have been repaired. Do you want to

give it a try?"

Elle took the key and sat down inside the vehicle behind the strange wheel. She studied the front panel for a moment before inserting the key into a small hole and turning it. The vehicle's engine abruptly engaged, startling Liam, who stared as the transport's panel lit up with various illuminated dials.

Elle now opened a plastic compartment under the dash panel, exposing a collection of electrical fuses. After studying the configuration for a moment, she deftly removed one of the fuses.

"What are you doing?" Liam asked, intrigued.

"Many commercial transports from this era were equipped with global positioning transmitters. They coordinated with ground stations and orbiting satellites to permit the transport to be located and recovered if stolen. I am disabling that system."

Elle now sat back and stared at her partner. "Are we going?" she asked.

Liam slowly climbed into the adjoining seat. After he shut the door, the vehicle lurched backward through the grass, skidding to a stop on the wet street.

"Easy!" he cautioned, glancing apprehensively back at the fueling station. "We don't want to attract attention."

"I apologize," Elle said, frowning. "I understand on a theoretical level how to operate such a vehicle, but I lack experience with the actual controls. I will try to familiarize myself with their operation." She shifted the vehicle into drive and pressed one of the foot pedals.

Liam tensed and held his breath, but this time, the van accelerated slowly and smoothly onto the main road. "Much better!" he said, relieved.

As they proceeded on Abingdon Road towards the bed & breakfast, Liam watched Elle with renewed appreciation. She seemed entirely at ease operating the ancient vehicle. Her hands on the strange wheel did not tremble, and her foot pressed on the floor pedal with just the precise amount of force. He looked up at her face. She appeared confident, scanning the road ahead.

"Do you ever get nervous?" he asked.

Elle glanced at him then returned her attention to the road.

"Nervous?" she asked.

"Yes. Do you ever get nervous or afraid?"

"Yes."

Liam was surprised. "Automatons can experience fear?" he asked. "How is that possible?"

Elle did not immediately answer. She turned the vehicle onto Waterly Lane, then pulled it into a small parking lot adjoining the inn. From here, the small van was reasonably concealed from Abingdon Road. She turned off the engine and then sat for a moment, staring out at the darkness surrounding them.

"Being what we are, automatons do not experience emotions in the same way humans do. We don't feel what humans feel, but we experience our own kind of emotions, including fear."

"I've never seen you showing fear... of anything," Liam replied, his tone reflecting skepticism.

Elle hesitated for a moment, then sat back in the vehicle seat. "In 1885," she said, "a rabid dog bit nine-year-old Joseph Meister. The family took the boy to a chemist experimenting with a radical new approach to treating viral infections. The chemist did not have any experience in medical practice, nor even a medical license. However, fearful that the young boy would contract rabies and die, the chemist purposefully injected him with spinal tissue from rabid rabbits that he had been experimenting with to prevent rabies in dogs. Joseph Meister did not contract rabies, and the chemist, Louis Pasteur, is now remembered as the father of vaccination."

Liam shook his head. "I don't understand your point."

"Like Pasteur, humans are often driven by fear to take incredible risks, and these actions often produce remarkable results."

Liam frowned. "Are you saying automatons consider fear to be a good thing?"

Elle shook her head. "I guess I'm saying that automatons respond to fear differently than humans. We experience our own equivalent of fear, but we deal with it differently. We are uncomfortable when faced with the unknown variable, the unquantifiable measurement, or the indeterminate fact. We avoid uncertainty, and we abhor ambiguity. When confronted by such things, they trigger a condition that humans would recognize as nervousness or fear. Unlike humans, however, automatons understand that this condition is temporary and may lead to a positive outcome if properly channeled. We see fear as a catalyst for change and whether that change is positive or negative depends entirely on us, on how we deal with our fear."

Liam considered this for a moment, then said, "It sounds like you're saying automatons are better than humans at controlling their fear."

"Yes," she replied, looking at him. "We experience fear, but we do not allow it to grow or fester within us. We confront our fear and attempt to channel it to a constructive purpose."

Liam did not respond, considering what she had said. After several moments, he exited the van and walked between the small buildings back towards their room.

Elle stepped out from the vehicle and closed her door quietly. As she approached the door to their room, however, she suddenly stopped. She turned and looked back at the darkness beyond buildings.

"What is it?" Liam asked, straining to see through the darkness.

"I'm not certain," she whispered. "I thought I heard footsteps… on Abingdon Road."

"You can hear something that far away?"

Elle nodded but said nothing, continuing to listen. After a few moments, she relaxed.

"I don't hear it anymore." She gave the darkness one last glance, then followed Liam into the small room.

Chapter 10

IDR: MK4ARR080//:QKDS-77483L2LE

The Indian Wars was the name used to describe a series of conflicts between the former United States' territorial and federal governments and the American Indian population before the arrival of non-native settlers.

Compared to other conflicts, the Indian Wars involved surprisingly few U.S. soldiers, between 5,000 and 20,000, yet resulted in an unusually high number of Medals of Honor awarded; 426. Of these, 210 contain citations noting the 'gallantry' of the soldier.

Reflecting on the disproportionally high percentage of Medals of Honor awarded in this conflict, I find myself asking; what quality did the men of that time possess that their conduct under fire would be so frequently described as 'gallant'?

It was just after 7:00 am when Liam woke with a start. He had laid down on the bed to wait out the remainder of the night and had fallen asleep. Elle was standing by the window, peering through the blinds. Hearing him awake, she retrieved a piece of paper from the small desk and handed it to him.

"The innkeeper slid this under our door."

The paper appeared to be an itemized bill, noting the cash deposit they had paid. A handwritten note at the bottom of the paper read, '*Glad we could accommodate you last night. Please let us know if you intend to stay longer. Checkout is at 3:00 pm*'.

Liam nodded and stretched. "If we grab Morten today,"

he said, "we won't need to stay later."

After checking their weapons, optics, and other equipment, they returned to their stolen British Gas transport and began driving southwest on Abingdon Road. They nervously passed the refueling station from the previous evening, but their vehicle's absence from the repair garage had apparently not yet been discovered. Shortly after passing the station, Elle turned the transport north onto a small paved road that led towards Culham Centre.

The Culham Center campus is an open corporate design, with administrative and laboratory buildings scattered among a series of tree-lined paved streets. As they approached the central office complex, Liam noted the streets seemed unusually busy with vehicle and pedestrian traffic. The number of young people carrying primitive computer cases suggested a significant portion of the pedestrians were prospective engineers attending the day's open recruitment event.

Elle paused at an intersection near the Culham Science Centre. Liam lowered the vehicle's window and scanned the streets ahead carefully. To the northeast, he could see the tree-lined parking lot of the Culham Centre for Fusion Energy. From the historical maps they had reviewed inside the archive hall, he knew the UK Atomic Energy Authority building was adjacent to that structure with the large JET fusion reactor building located just behind.

"Should we find someplace to park where we can observe the UKAEA building?" Elle asked.

Liam hesitated, then shook his head. "No."

"Why not?"

"If Morten has traveled here to inspect the reactor upgrade, he won't be doing it alone. He will make contact with the local UKAEA representatives first. They will undoubtedly inspect the upgrade together."

"How can you be sure that is what Morten will do?" Elle asked, perplexed by what she perceived to be Liam's unexplainable foreknowledge of Morten's behavior.

"Human nature," Liam answered, shivering as a gust of cold air blew past the vehicle's open window.

Elle did not respond.

After a few moments, Liam raised the window and motioned down the street. "Let's go," he said.

Elle drove slowly northwest, being careful of the people crossing the street. They turned left at the Culham Centre for Fusion Energy and passed the UK Atomic Energy Authority building. Several people were walking inside the building. One of the men held the door open and, as they drove past, Liam could see people inside the entrance passing through what appeared to be a metal-framed security device. He sat back, scowling.

"I think they have a magnetic field detector inside the entrance," he said. "All the buildings probably have similar detectors."

"We can disable such devices easily," Elle responded.

Liam shook his head. "We could," he said, "but if it stopped working, they'd just subject everyone entering the building to a physical search." After thinking for a moment, he motioned ahead and said, "Keep driving."

Elle drove on, approaching the Materials Research Facility building. At the corner, Liam noticed a small service road that emerged between the research facility building and the Joint European Torus building that housed the MAST fusion reactor.

"There," he said, pointing at the road.

Elle turned the corner and proceeded down the small road. When they had reached a position between the JET building and the UKAEA building, Liam had her stop the van adjacent to a small footpath that led between the two buildings and turned off the engine. He reached into his jacket and pulled out his optical lenses. He put them on and scanned the structures. With the thermographic filters engaged, he could see a number of people inside the buildings, passing by the various windows.

"What do we do now?" Elle asked.

Liam returned the lenses to his pocket and sat back in his seat. "We wait," he said.

"Wait?"

"The file said Morten is likely on-site today to inspect the reactor upgrade," Liam said. "The reactor is in the Joint European Torus building behind us. If Morten is here, he will likely exit the rear of the UKAEA administration building over there." He pointed to a rear door that exited the building onto a small paved path. "That path is obviously designed to provide easy access to the JET building, so we'll wait here for Morten to come out of that door."

"How will you identify him?"

Liam grinned. "I'm going to step out of the van and ask him if he's Nils Morten."

Elle stared at him. After several moments, she retrieved her RU-6 weapon from behind her back. She activated the weapon's magnetic accelerator and checked its load status from the visual indicator on its side. It was fully loaded.

Liam also retrieved and activated his RU-6. He set the magnetic accelerator to its lowest level and advised Elle to do the same. "We don't want to send flechettes punching through the nearby buildings," he said. "The last thing we want to do is kill innocent people."

Elle adjusted her weapon's setting.

They waited. Several people walked by but barely glanced at them before continuing on their way, assuming the vehicle's occupants were involved in some authorized maintenance activity. Shortly after 8:30 am, Elle observed a group of six men exiting the rear of the UKAEA building. Three of the men wore technician coats. The other three were wearing suits. The men were engaged in casual conversation and began walking along the paved path towards the JET building.

Liam noticed the group and tensed. Elle could see his concentration, evident from his fixated gaze and elevated respiration. When the group reached the service street across from their position, he opened his door and stepped out. The men did not appear to take notice, continuing their conversation as they crossed the small street. Elle also stepped out and walked quickly towards the rear of the vehicle, intending to support her partner.

When the men approached the back of the van, Liam stepped out and held up his hand. "Excuse me," he said, "but would one of you be Nils Morten?"

Several of the men immediately turned towards one of the suited men. The man was short, balding, with grey hair. He stared at Liam.

"Who are you?" he asked.

Liam stepped closer to read the man's identification badge. Underneath the UKAEA seal, the badge read 'N. Morten'.

Liam glanced at Elle and nodded imperceptibly. Elle

immediately pulled her RU-6 from behind her back and aimed it at the group. Several of the men took a step backward, alarmed. Morten, however, simply stared at the weapon with a strange expression on his face.

Liam spoke deliberately now as he forcefully turned Morten around to place the man's hands inside the maglock cuffs. "Nils Morten," he said, "you are detained by order of the CTI council for violation of Article 9 of the International Temporal Treaty."

The men in the group stepped further back, clearly confused. One of the suited men, however, a portly man with black hair, stepped forward angrily.

"What the hell is going on?!" he asked. "Nils! What is this about?"

Elle immediately positioned herself between the man and Liam. The man stopped, staring at the strange weapon pointed at his chest. At that moment, Elle's internal particle detectors alerted her to impacts from a nearby radioactive isotope. She glanced at the distant reactor building.

Morten said nothing, staring past the group at the door they had exited. With the magnetic cuffs now in place, Liam activated the locking mechanism, snapping both ends of the cuffs together with a metallic clang. While the rest of the men watched in confusion, he opened the van and bodily shoved Morten inside. Then, he retrieved his RU-6, climbed into the passenger's seat, and quickly shut the door.

Elle walked swiftly around the front of the van, keeping her RU-6 aimed at the group. The moment she opened the door to the driver's seat, one of the white-coated technicians turned and began running back towards the UKAEA building, dialing his cell phone as he ran.

"Drive!" Liam said.

Elle quickly engaged the engine, turned the vehicle around, and sped back down the small street, squealing its tires as they turned back onto the main road in front of the Materials Research Facility.

"Easy!" Liam said, frowning. "We don't want to draw any more attention than we already have."

Elle nodded but remained silent, concentrating on operating the ancient vehicle at the increased speed. Strangely, her internal particle detector continued to register minor isotope impacts, as if a small amount of radioactive material was somewhere nearby. She glanced back at Morten, wondering if the man might have been exposed to radiation while inspecting the reactor.

Liam turned to observe their captive. Morten was staring at him. He seemed indifferent, almost calm. His apparent resignation was troubling.

Elle turned left again and began speeding southeast along the main campus road. As they passed the UKAEA building, two men in security uniforms emerged from the building's front doors and raced towards the street. One was holding a hand-held radio. The other was waving his arms in the air, shouting at the vehicle to stop. As they sped by the pair, the guard with the radio began speaking into the device.

"They're communicating over a radio frequency network," Liam said.

Their vehicle had just passed Thames Lane, driving swiftly south towards Abington Road, when Elle spotted a large black SUV rapidly closing on their position from the general direction of the Culham Centre campus.

"One transport in pursuit... black... coming up fast!" She

said before turning onto Abingdon Road.

Liam quickly retrieved his tactical lenses. When he stuck his head out of the passenger-side window and focused on the pursuing vehicle, six thermal figures coalesced into view behind the glowing block of the vehicle's engine. He reset the optics to include a magnetic resonance overlay, and an assortment of weapons appeared silhouetted against the figures.

"Six men," he said, sitting back in his seat. "They're armed."

"They're part of my security detail."

Liam whirled to observe Morten smiling at him.

"Did you think I wouldn't be prepared for this?" Morten asked, shaking his head. "I've had contingencies in place ever since I came here. I never travel anywhere without an armed security detail."

The vehicle sped swiftly past the Turnpike Garage. As they approached the street that would take them to the Inn, Elle glanced at Liam, questioning.

Liam shook his head. "Keep going. We've got to lose our pursuers first."

Elle pressed the accelerator to the floor. The vehicle lurched forward, its engine whining in protest.

Morten glanced back, straining to see through the rear windows. With a sigh, he turned around to face Liam. "It would be best if you just let me go," he said. "The men following us are the best security operators in the world. I assure you, they are highly trained and invested in securing my release."

Liam shook his head. "We can't let you go."

Morten looked closely at him. "CTI?" he asked.

When Liam nodded, Morten burst into laughter and shook his head. After a moment, he spoke again, his voice thick with disdain.

"I expected the council to contract this out. I assumed if they ever discovered my absence, they'd approach Reynolds-Hampshire or RJCom to send one of their specialists to try to bring me back." He looked at Liam now with scorn. "I'm surprised the council had the courage to risk its own people."

Liam frowned but said nothing.

Morten smiled and sat back.

Suddenly, Elle announced, "Another transport ahead, closing fast!"

Liam swung his head around and stared through the front windshield. In the distance, where the road turned, a grey sedan had appeared and was now closing swiftly on their position. The vehicle was too far away for Liam to observe the occupants. "Are you certain they're after us?" he asked, scrambling to retrieve his optics.

"There are four occupants… all male. One of the rear passengers is holding a weapon."

Liam had no time to question further. Trusting in Elle's superior visual acuity, he pointed at an approaching cross street and said, "Turn there!"

Elle spun the vehicle's steering wheel dramatically. The front tires squealed as the rear end of the vehicle slid off the road to slap hard against a muddy embankment. She quickly straightened out the steering wheel and pressed the accelerator to the floor. The van jumped forward, its front wheels spinning for a moment in the mud before finding their grip.

They were heading roughly north now on Oxford Road, a small tree-lined drive bordered by quaint homes. After a few moments, the houses were replaced by farm fields, dormant and quiet in the crisp air.

Liam glanced behind them. The black SUV had already turned onto the road and was accelerating rapidly. A moment later, the grey sedan flew around the same corner, its rear tires slipping as it struggled to level out before turning to follow the black SUV.

"Their transports are faster than ours!" Elle said. "This vehicle is at its maximum speed, but the approaching transports have a superior acceleration curve. The larger vehicle will overtake us in 23.7 seconds."

Liam stared grimly back at Morten. The man was watching him closely with a hint of a smile on his face.

Liam turned and scanned the dark line trees beyond the muddy fields, then pulled his RU-6 and adjusted it for armor penetration. "We're going to stop," he said. "When we stop, I want you to take Morten and run to those trees. Drag him or carry him on your back if you have to. I'll give you cover. Once you get clear, retrieve our MTY device and return with Morten to the CTI council."

Elle stared at him, her eyes wide. She opened her mouth to protest, but before she could speak, Liam shook his head and said, "You're the only one of us capable of getting across that field with Morten! I don't have your strength or speed."

Elle stared out the front window at the trees beyond the field while Liam scrambled back into the van's rear compartment. As he passed Morten, he noticed the man was staring at Elle with a curious expression on his face.

Liam crouched behind the rear door and took a deep breath. "Stop now!" he ordered.

"Hang on to something!" Elle shouted as she turned the steering wheel. The vehicle flew off the road, plowing through a wet stand of dead hay before spinning around in the mud to stop facing the street.

The pursuing SUV slammed on its brakes and swerved off the opposite side of the road, digging deep furrows into the muddy field. The trailing sedan also locked its brakes and careened off the road behind the SUV.

In an instant, Elle leaped between the seats and kicked the sliding door off its track, snapping its steel guide-arms in two. Morten's face reflected shock as she grabbed him by his belt and pulled him forcefully from the vehicle. At that moment, her eyes locked with Liam's.

The senior enforcement officer nodded grimly.

Elle threw Morten over her shoulder in a modified fireman's carry and began sprinting towards the distant trees. A moment later, the supersonic crackling of a micro railgun on full auto broke the silence, startling a flock of birds that rose noisily from the field. As she ran, the bird's cries were muffled by a sharp retort of gunfire. The crackling and gunfire continued for almost a minute. Then, just as she reached the line of trees, the sounds abruptly ceased.

Utter silence descended now, broken only by the distant cries of the fleeing birds.

Chapter 11

IDR: MK4ARR192//:QKDS-77483L2LE

Throughout history, pivotal events have occurred in which the actions of a few shaped the fate of millions.

On July 15, 1918, four years into that terrible conflict remembered as World War I, twenty-three German divisions of the First and Third armies launched an assault against the French troops near Reims, France. Under a rolling barrage of artillery, the Germans advanced towards the Marne River.

The French armies desperately defended the river banks, but by evening, the Germans had crossed the river and secured a bridgehead nearly fourteen kilometers wide. Appreciating the gravity of the situation, Gen. Ferdinand Foch, the Allied Supreme Commander, committed the British XXII Corps and 85,000 American troops to the battle, a desperate action that stalled the German advance. On July 18, the reinforced allied armies counterattacked, forcing the Germans to retreat.

This Second Battle of the Marne marked the end of the string of German victories and the beginning of a new series of Allied triumphs that would end the war within months.

At the time, the battle was not recognized for the turning point it was. Such distinctions are the prerogative of history.

Liam opened his eyes slowly. He had been dreaming uncomfortably, aware of an indeterminate pain in his left shoulder. Now, awake, that pain coalesced into a specific point located near his left shoulder. Confused, he slowly lifted his right arm to feel the area. A cloth bandage covered his left shoulder and, as he reached for the bandage, a length of plastic tubing brushed against his face. The tubing was attached to a bag filled with clear liquid that was suspended from a light fixture on the wall behind his head. The other end of the tubing disappeared under another bandage wrapped around his right elbow.

"You should avoid lifting your left arm for a few days."

The voice belonged to a stranger. Confused, Liam looked up and attempted to focus his eyes. He was back inside their room at The Sickle. The window was dark, and the clock on the nightstand read 8:21 pm. The light came from a small lamp set beside the clock. Elle was sitting in a chair, watching him closely. Standing next to her was a strange man. The man was tall, clean-shaven, and though slim, Liam could see the outline of well-developed muscles underneath his shirt. He had brown hair and eyes and was dressed casually.

"Who are you?" he asked, frowning as he tried to clear his head. His mind felt sluggish, his thoughts disconnected.

"My name is John," the stranger replied. "Do you remember what happened?"

Liam glanced at Elle, but she was watching the stranger. The television stand next to her contained a tray filled with the evidence of a recent medical procedure; bandages, a syringe, various probes and surgical blades, and a dish containing blood-soaked cloths. He stared at the bright red cloth, trying to remember what had happened.

A third man now came into focus. He was short, Asian in appearance, and wore white surgical gloves. The man removed the gloves and spoke directly to the tall stranger, his voice thickly accented.

"He is still... in.. incapacitated? Yes. Incapacitated. By anesthetic. He must rest."

Liam shook his head against the mental fog. He squeezed his eyes and tried to focus. "What happened?" he asked.

"You were shot," Elle replied immediately. "Yesterday morning. You've been unconscious for 26 hours, 54 minutes." She hesitated for a moment before continuing. "I'm sorry, Officer Perry, but you were shot. I had nearly reached the tree line with Morten, but when you were shot..." Her words trailed off.

Liam tried to sit up. He winced, feeling the pain in his shoulder like a throbbing ache.

The small Asian man pressed him gently back into the bed.

"Where's Morten?!" Liam husked.

Elle, however, sat silent, shaking her head.

Liam's face hardened into a stony mask of displeasure.

"I asked you a question, Agent Elle. Where's Morten?!"

Elle glanced at the tall stranger, then back at Liam. "When you were shot," she spoke slowly, "I had just reached the tree line. One of Morten's men shouted across the field for me to stop. He propped you up on the ground and pointed a weapon at your head. He shouted that he would trade you for Morten. He said if I refused, he would kill you immediately."

Liam sat still, staring silently at his associate. The small Asian man now began packing up the tray of medical instruments, placing them into a small case.

"My RU-6," Elle continued, "was configured for suppression, not for long distant targeting. I calculated the probability of successfully eliminating your captors at such a distance to be unacceptably low, given the weapon's configuration at that time, so I agreed to the exchange."

Liam shook his head, trying to clear his mental fog. His eyes strayed to a pile of clothing lying on the foot of his bed. He could see his RU-6 partially concealed beneath his coat. The sight of the weapon seemed to bring his memory into focus. He remembered Elle kicking the van door free of its frame and pulling Morten roughly from the back of their vehicle. Their eyes had met for a moment, and then she was gone, leaping across the muddy field like a gazelle with Morten bouncing over her shoulder.

He remembered seeing movement behind the pursuing vehicles, men scrambling out of the black SUV. He had stepped out from the back of the van and raised his RU-6. The weapon had been configured for armor penetration, and the resulting spray of deadly flechettes, accelerated to more than seven times the speed of sound, had easily punctured the SUV's steel panels.

Shouts of anger and shock had erupted from behind the vehicle and the men had returned fire. After almost a minute, he had caught a glimpse of something moving in his peripheral vision, but before he could react, something had struck him forcefully in the shoulder. The impact knocked him to the ground, winded and stunned. His shoulder went numb, and the numbness transformed into a searing pain. He remembered being roughly lifted to a sitting position, someone shouting, then everything had faded to black.

Elle watched him closely, waiting for his response.

Liam shook his head angrily. "I told you to take Morten back to the council," he said. "You should have obeyed my orders!" He glanced at the tall stranger, but the tall man was simply leaning against the wall listening to their conversation. Focusing his attention on the stranger, Liam asked, "Who the hell are you?!"

The man smiled. "I told you. My name is John."

Elle spoke quickly now. "He was waiting here when I brought you back yesterday."

"Here?" Liam asked, startled. "Inside our room?"

"Yes."

Liam's eyes inadvertently strayed to the small closet door where they had concealed their MTY device.

Observing his gaze, Elle shook her head. "Everything is fine. Nothing is missing."

The stranger nodded. "Not to worry," he said. "I didn't take your MTY device."

Liam's head shot up, and he fixed his gaze on the stranger's face. The man's eyes now revealed humor as he bent down and lifted a pack from the floor that Liam had not observed before.

"There's no need," the stranger said. "You see, I have one of my own."

In the stunned silence that followed, the man removed an MTY device from the pack and set it on the edge of the bed. The device was identical to the prototype Liam had received from the CTI council.

"My name is John Clifton," the stranger said.

"Clifton?!" Liam gasped. "RJCom's missing temporal specialist?"

Clifton nodded while carefully returning the MTY device into his pack.

"You've been here all this time?" Liam asked. "Here... in the past?"

"Yes," Clifton replied. "I transited back here from 2158."

Liam shook his head in bewilderment. "Why?"

Clifton placed his pack back on the floor and stood silent. After a few moments, he asked, "What do you know about my last tripback mission?"

"I know what's recorded in the council records," Liam replied. "You were presumed lost during a tripback mission in 2151. You returned in 2158 with a prototype sentient AI processor that Blosch-Nishikawa had been developing in the past in violation of the International Temporal Treaty. Your report triggered the CTI's raid on Blosch-Nishikawa and the cancellation of their charter. The file says you vanished shortly after the raid, and no one has heard from you since then."

Clifton nodded. "I transited back here shortly after the raid."

Liam's eyes suddenly grew wide. "You have a prototype device... the one that Blosch-Nishikawa gave to Williams!"

Clifton glanced at his pack on the floor, then nodded. "Yes," he said. "I have William's device. I didn't know there were others. How many did Blosch-Nishikawa make?"

Liam frowned, frustrated with himself for disclosing such sensitive council information. Instead of answering the man's question, he said, "The file says William's device was lost with her when she fell through its singularity... after your fight inside Hōfu Garden park."

Clifton shrugged. "A necessary prevarication," he said. "I was needed here, and RJCom's Primary AI had advised me to conceal the truth about William's MTY device."

"Why would RJCom's AI advise you to conceal something from the council?" Liam asked, his voice skeptical.

"I was needed here," Clifton repeated. "There are repercussions from Blosch-Nishikawa's treaty violation that can only be resolved here... in the past."

"What repercussions?"

Clifton smiled and gestured to the injured officer's bandaged shoulder. "Well… you for one."

"Me?" Liam asked, surprised.

Clifton nodded. "You needed my help last night. You'll need it again."

When Liam opened his mouth to protest, Elle interrupted. "We did need his help yesterday."

"I've cultivated certain relationships here," Clifton said, smiling. He pointed a thumb at the small Asian man. "Relationships that allowed me to summon discreet medical care for you last night."

Liam felt his shoulder again. He took a deep breath, then winced. "So, how bad am I hurt?" he asked.

"Not too bad," Clifton replied. "Chang says the projectile nicked your left clavicle, tore some muscle, and then embedded itself into your scapula." As he spoke, he passed Liam a small grey bullet. "You're fortunate that it didn't fracture the bone. They have no bone knitting technology in this era." He then rubbed his ribs, as if remembering some past injury. "You should be on your feet in a couple of days," he continued, "though Chang says you'll have only limited use of your left arm for several weeks."

Liam nodded, examining the bullet. After a few moments, he looked up at Elle.

"What happened to Morten?"

Elle shook her head, speaking slowly. "After the trade in the field," she said, "two of Morten's men placed him inside the smaller grey transport and drove south, back towards Abington Road. The others loaded the bodies of the men you killed into the larger vehicle, and they drove north."

Liam nodded but said nothing. After several minutes, he looked up at Clifton, confusion on his face. "How did you know we would be here?" He asked. "I mean… how did you know we were coming to this time?"

Clifton shifted his feet. "Well," he said, "that's a curious thing." The tall temporal specialist seemed almost embarrassed. "The fact is, I didn't know what to expect. All I knew was something temporally significant was happening here, so I came to investigate."

Liam's head shot up.

"Temporally significant?"

When Clifton nodded, Liam stared at him closely.

"MTQL?" he asked.

Clifton brightened. "Yes, he replied, smiling. "I was evaluated in my sixth year of primary education."

Liam nodded his understanding. For all of human history, mankind had lived in a very comfortable cocoon floating along a temporal stream. This 'arrow of time' flowed in only one direction, at a constant rate, and it afforded man with no ability to step outside of that confined environment. However, in the early days of temporal experimentation, quantum scientists discovered that certain people handled temporal transition better than others. While the vast majority of people found traveling backward in time to be disorienting, a few seemed entirely at ease outside their temporal cocoon.

The Merkel-Thomson Quantum Lab was a prestigious institution near Boston founded to locate and train humans with this rare ability. The lab directed those with the highest MTQL scores to secondary education courses where they were groomed to become quantum engineers or scientists.

A few rare candidates, however, demonstrated temporal

abilities far beyond even these unusual individuals. They possessed an ability previously undocumented in mankind's physiology, a true sense of time. They were aware when that temporal stream was being disturbed and could sense when actions or events were temporally significant. Individuals who possessed this ability were recruited and trained as temporal specialists and authorized to travel through time. While not every temporal specialist had this strange ability, those who did were invariably trained as temporal specialists. Clifton was one of those rare human beings.

Elle turned her attention back to Clifton. "I heard someone the night we arrived," she said. "In the foliage, down the hill from the church. Was that you?"

Clifton smiled. "Yes. I transited in about four hours before you arrived. When I saw you coming down the steps from the church, I hid in the brush so I could observe your movements." He chuckled and shook his head. "It was damn cold!"

Elle nodded. "And later, when we came back with the vehicle?"

Clifton smiled again. "I hid inside a shed across Abington Road where I could watch the inn. When you returned in a British Gas van, I crossed the street to try to get the license number, but I couldn't get close enough without revealing myself, so I went back to the shed. When you drove away the next morning, I took the opportunity to search your room."

Elle sat back, apparently satisfied. "I knew I heard someone."

"You have exceptional hearing."

Elle had been experiencing an automaton's equivalent of desperation when she returned the previous day. Perry was bleeding badly, so much so that she had contemplated abandoning the mission and returning to the future to solicit medical care.

When she carried the wounded officer into their small room at the inn, she had been surprised to find Clifton waiting there. He was sitting in a chair, apparently waiting for their return. Elle was stunned when he identified himself and even more shocked when he produced his own MTY device from his backpack.

Every sentient automaton knew about John J. Clifton. It was Clifton who had returned to the future with the prototype sentient AI processor that Blosch-Nishikawa had developed in the past. What was not known outside of the extremely private community of sentient automaton controllers was that, before surrendering the processor to the council, Clifton had permitted it to be scanned by RJCom's powerful Primary AI. It was that scan, surreptitiously distributed to the world's automation controllers, that had produced the first generation of sentient automatons. Clifton was the nearest thing an automaton had to a creator, and Elle was frankly overwhelmed to be in his presence.

After she had explained who they were and what they were doing in the past, Clifton had produced a primitive communication device called a 'cell phone' and placed a call. An hour later, when the cell phone beeped again, he set his MTY device on the floor of the room and calibrated a portal, forgoing activation of the device's tunneling regulator. With the regulator disabled, the distant event horizon remained in the present, and the device acted as a portable EPM transit station. After the singularity formed inside the small room, Elle had watched in amazement as two people, a man and a woman, emerged through the shimmering vortex.

Speaking to the man first, Clifton said, "He's been shot Chang... upper left shoulder."

Chang, obviously a medical specialist, placed a small case on the bed next to the wounded officer and began removing various surgical instruments.

For the next few hours, while Chang operated, Elle studied the two strangers. They seemed perfectly at ease, as if they were used to such extraordinary events.

Chang appeared extremely attentive to Clifton, responding instantly when questioned and speaking with deference and respect to the tall specialist.

The woman, however, was a mystery. Once, when she leaned forward to reposition the table lamp for Chang, Elle observed a necklace of blue beads peeking out from around her neck. Clifton had called her 'Leah'.

Liam suddenly coughed, a deep, congested spasm. Chang stopped packing his instruments and returned to the sleeping officer. He placed his hand on Liam's forehead and then frowned. He retrieved a small instrument from his case and ran the device over Liam's forehead, reading its display. He looked up at Elle, his face troubled.

"He has fever. Too soon for infection. Explain, please?"

"Officer Perry mentioned feeling ill," Elle replied. "He said he had contracted a virus during a recent trip to London. He was planning to visit the council's med-tech facility for an anti-viral, but our departure was unexpectedly advanced."

"Hmmm..." The doctor frowned. After a moment, he retrieved a syringe from his case and injected its contents into the hanging intravenous line. Then, he retrieved a small bottle of pills from his case and handed them to Elle.

"These will reduce cough."

The small man turned to face Clifton.

"He must rest. I have given him antibiotic, and the pills will help reduce fever. You tell me if fever or cough becomes worse."

Clifton nodded. "I will. Thank you, Chang." Then, as the small man turned to continue placing the instruments inside his case, Clifton asked, "Are you heading back tonight?"

"Yes," Chang replied. "Superiors become suspicious if I do not return as scheduled. Medical conference ends this evening so I must return to lab."

Clifton nodded again. "I am very grateful, Chang."

The small man waved his hand in dismissal. "I am grateful. My family will always be in your debt."

Clifton re-activated his MTY device. When the shimmering black portal reformed in the room, Chang lifted his case and smiled at the woman, waiting respectfully. To Elle's astonishment, the mysterious woman abruptly leaned close and kissed the tall temporal specialist.

"Be careful," she whispered.

Clifton smiled. "I will. Tell Kacie to keep working on her hupu ba ogoshii form. Her foot placement is still unbalanced. I expect to see some improvement by the time I return."

The woman nodded and smiled warmly. Then, taking Chang by the arm, she stepped through the spinning black singularity. After they were gone, Clifton terminated the singularity and sat back down in a chair. His face appeared troubled.

Elle studied him closely. After a few minutes of silence, she voiced her observation.

"You are troubled about something."

Clifton looked up. "You are very observant."

"I make a point of studying those around me," Elle replied.

"A worthy endeavor," Clifton responded, nodding.

Elle sat quietly, watching the tall man.

After almost a minute, Clifton leaned forward to examine Liam's face. The injured officer was sleeping deeply, though his breathing was labored.

Clifton sat back. After a few moments, he sighed and said, "One of the more difficult aspects of living in the past," he said, "is observing unpleasant historical events unfolding around you and knowing you cannot prevent them from happening." He paused for another moment, staring at the sleeping man as if engaging in some internal mental struggle. Finally, he took a deep breath and spoke again.

"I'm worried about Chang."

Elle was surprised.

"Chang?" she asked.

"Yes," Clifton nodded. "Tonight, we have witnessed the beginning of a significant historic event."

"What event?" Elle asked. She quickly scanned her data core for all historical events occurring in this era. In the year 2019, Protesters in Hong Kong had clashed with police, a fire had consumed an 850-year-old cathedral in Paris, and the U.S. women's soccer team had won the World Cup. She recited the list to Clifton.

Clifton smiled grimly. "You are omitting the coronavirus pandemic," he said.

Elle shook her head. "Historical records report that pandemic will sweep the globe in 2020."

"Even a global pandemic must have a beginning," he

replied. "In the early days of that pandemic, it was referred to as 'Covid-19', indicating the year of its first diagnosis."

Elle stared at Liam asleep on the bed and then at the place where the singularity had shimmered moments ago.

"Chang?" she asked.

Clifton nodded. "Yes. Chang will carry Officer Perry's virus back to his lab in Wuhan, where it will begin to spread."

Elle's analytic processors were now fully engaged, retrieving the historical files from her vast internal archives and correlating the results. The probability matrices coalesced perfectly. What Clifton was suggesting had a greater than 98.6% probability of being factually correct. She stood and approached the foot of Liam's bed, placing herself between the injured officer and the temporal specialist. There was an accusing tone in her voice now.

"You knew that Officer Perry would be the cause of the pandemic," she said. "That's why you came here."

Clifton didn't immediately respond. Instead, he rose, walked slowly to one of the windows in the room, and opened the blinds. He stared out across the grounds at the small buildings and the park beyond.

"I didn't know about you two until I transited here," he said softly.

Elle folded her arms. "Then why did you come here?"

Clifton looked back, noting the confusion in the pretty automaton's face. He sighed, closed the blinds, and returned to his chair, motioning for her to sit in the other chair. When she complied, he spoke quietly, glancing at Liam as he spoke.

"I didn't know about you two until the night I arrived, but I knew something significant was happening here. I felt compelled to come. I first learned to recognize the feeling after I was evaluated by MTQL." He hesitated, then spoke again. "The official term for the phenomenon is temporal causality precursor perception, or TCPP. I am one of those humans capable of perceiving temporal causality triggers that precede significant historical events."

"I am aware of the phenomenon," Elle said. "It has been well documented in post-EPM era physiological files. It occurs within the human population at extremely low statistical rates."

"Only one person in every 60.8 million," Clifton said, nodding.

Elle tilted her head, studying the temporal specialist closely. "You felt compelled to transit here," she asked, "the night we arrived?"

"Yes. I knew something temporally significant was going to occur, and I felt compelled to come."

Elle considered this statement, then looked back at the injured officer asleep in the bed. After a few moments, she spoke softly.

"Officer Perry is the source of the pandemic?"

"Yes," Clifton nodded. "Contemporary media sources will report the virus originated in Wuhan city this year. It will be first reported by a provincial hospital in November, about two weeks from now. You can scan the relevant data record in your primary data store. It is filed in PRC-Archive Unit 410, 4j, file FKL196D1A2."

Elle swiftly accessed the file. Clifton was correct. According to declassified Chinese government records dating to late 2020, an unidentified doctor at a provincial hospital in Hubei province reportedly treated a fifty-five-year old patient on November 17, 2019, for symptoms related to a new coronavirus strain. Within a month, the hospital reported it had treated more than one hundred and eighty additional patients.

"The source of the outbreak will be traced to a Wuhan virology lab," Clifton explained. "The Chinese government will naturally insist that the virus did not originate in the lab, but the world will dismiss those denials."

Elle shook her head. "It is troubling to realize," she said, "that the virus Officer Perry was exposed to in London will be the cause of that historical pandemic." She stared at the sleeping officer.

Clifton watched her closely.

After nearly a full minute, Elle turned and faced the tall specialist. "I do not want you to disclose this information to Officer Perry," she said. "It is not relevant to our mission, and when we return with Morten, I want him to be honored for returning with his prisoner, not blamed for causing the 2019 coronavirus pandemic."

"I understand," Clifton replied, nodding.

For the rest of that night, Elle watched over Liam as he drifted in and out of sleep. She treated his fever with the medication Chang left behind, but she was troubled by the congestion in his chest. As she cared for her injured partner, she considered how best to complete their mission. Perry's injury and Morten's escape were the results of a lack of adequate planning. They had not been given sufficient time to prepare for this mission. Clifton had suggested as much during the night. Absent adequate preparation, the temporal specialist had explained, success becomes unlikely. When the sun began peeking through the window's wooden slats, she turned to Clifton.

"If we're going to succeed," she said, "we're going to need a plan and the resources to carry it through."

Clifton nodded his agreement.

"Will you help us?" she asked.

Clifton raised an eyebrow. "Is that an order or a request?" he asked.

It suddenly occurred to Elle that, however junior she might be within the enforcement division, she outranked Clifton. As a temporal specialist, he was duty-bound to follow the CTI Council's orders. She was a representative of that council. Somewhat taken aback, she shook her head.

"I'm asking. It's a request."

"In that case," he said, "I'll help, but only on one condition."

"Condition?"

Clifton leaned forward in his chair, his expression earnest. "You asked me to conceal from Officer Perry his role in the coming pandemic. I must ask something of you in return."

Elle nodded, waiting.

"When your mission here is completed," Clifton said, "I want you to leave me behind and tell no one you have seen me here."

Elle considered what was being asked of her and glanced again at the sleeping officer lying in bed. She wondered what Perry's reaction would be to such a request. After several moments, she nodded slowly.

"I agree," she said.

Clifton now stood and extended his hand. "In the time of the Romans," he explained, "oaths were made over the Iuppiter Lapis… a stone inside the Temple of Jupiter."

Elle shook her head, not understanding.

Clifton smiled.

"The Romans," he continued, "honored their oaths

because of their belief that Jupiter would strike down as unworthy anyone who broke a promise made over that sacred stone. Their belief in an avenging deity was the only thing that held them to their agreement. Our agreement will be based on something stronger than fear."

Elle frowned, still confused. "What is that?" she asked.

"Trust."

Elle stood slowly and accepted the outstretched hand.

Chapter 12

IDR: MK4ARS033//:QKDS-77483L2LE

In the summer of 1900, the ambassadors, military attachés, and embassy staff of Japan, Italy, Germany, Russia, Austria, France, the United States, and Great Britain found themselves besieged within the Peking Legation Quarter in Imperial China. Outside, thousands of armed Chinese "boxers" surrounded the compound, desperate to dislodge the foreigners.

The former rivals joined ranks, relying on their combined strength to weather the siege. British soldiers supported the Japanese in repelling any Chinese who attempted to scale the walls, while Italian and Japanese forces established a defensive line inside the ambassador's mansion grounds. The Austrians aided the French in desperate hand-to-hand fighting outside the compound, while the Germans and Americans jointly defended the Tartar Wall.

After 55 days, when the siege was lifted by a relief force that had marched inland from the coast, the unified defenders quickly fragmented, returning to their various nationalist camps.

Cooperation, it would seem, thrives amid adversity, yet starves in the face of peace.

For several days after the incident, Clifton monitored the local news services closely. No unusual police investigations were reported in the area, so it seemed likely that no one had observed the fight in the remote field.

Four days later, Liam's fever broke, and his congestion began to subside. Clifton then approached the innkeeper, paying handsomely for a second room and extending the group's stay through the winter. In answer to their host's inquiry regarding Elle's interview at Culham Center, Clifton reported that, unfortunately, she had not been hired. He told the sympathetic innkeeper that she now wished to search for other employment opportunities in the area. As for himself, he claimed to be a friend of the family, on sabbatical from a teaching job in America, and anxious to enjoy the holidays in the English countryside.

The next three weeks passed fitfully for the trio. Liam was anxious to begin pursuing Morten, but Clifton counseled patience.

"You need time to recover," Clifton said, "and we need time to formulate a plan."

Liam knew the temporal specialist was correct, but his frustration with his injury, combined with his anger over their failed attempt to capture Morten, filled him with anxiety.

After returning from his meeting with the innkeeper, Clifton announced he would return in a few days with any information he could discover about Morten's present location.

Liam found it disconcerting watching Clifton operating his MTY device. The device was a physical reminder of an overt deception by a CTI-authorized temporal specialist. He was highly conflicted. On the one hand, he felt duty-bound to report Clifton's present location and his possession of the unregistered temporal device. On the other hand, he felt a sincere sense of obligation and gratitude to the man, both for summoning the medical care that allowed him to remain and continue his mission and assisting the two officers in completing that mission.

Clifton lifted his device, nodded, and then stepped

through the singularity. A moment later, the swirling purple-tinged vortex winked out.

Liam glanced at Elle and noticed the female automaton staring at the place where the singularity had been, seemingly lost in thought. She had been reticent since Clifton had joined them. In her conversations with the tall stranger, the automaton had appeared subdued, almost deferential.

"Well, I guess we wait?" Liam said, attempting to break the silence.

"Yes," Elle said, still staring ahead.

Liam looked closely at the junior agent.

"You've been unusually quiet today."

Elle glanced back, then turned away.

"I've been preoccupied," she said.

"With what?"

"Clifton."

Liam considered this, then asked, "Do you think we can trust him?"

"Yes."

Liam's eyebrows raised slightly, surprised by the conviction behind the automaton's swift response. Noting the expression, Elle shook her head.

"It's not blind trust," she said. "Automatons don't believe in blind trust. I believe we can trust Clifton because his past behavior proves him to be an honorable person."

"What past behavior?"

When she did not respond, Liam folded his arms.

"Well then," he said, "what makes you believe he is an honorable human being?"

Elle turned to face the senior officer.

"He acts in the best interest of others, despite the

consequences to himself. That is honorable."

"We'll see."

Clifton returned three days later. It was Sunday evening. Elle was standing by the window in their room, gazing out into the night through a tilted slat in the blinds, when a sparkling vortex began to take shape in the room.

"Officer Perry..." Elle spoke softly, directing the resting officer's attention to the swirling portal.

Liam sat up and instinctively reached for his RU-6. At that moment, however, Clifton stepped through the portal. Liam relaxed and returned his weapon to its place under his pillow.

Clifton terminated the singularity and placed his MTY device on the floor. He sat back in one of the chairs and shook his head. He appeared tired.

"Well, I've got to tell you," he said, "Morten has not been idle with his time here."

Liam sat up slowly, being careful not to jostle his shoulder. "What do you mean?" he asked.

Clifton frowned. "I mean, the man has affiliated himself with numerous powerful organizations. He sits on the board of a dozen multi-national corporations and maintains advisory positions with no less than four governmental agencies. He is a director emeritus with both the UKAEA and the Engineering and Physical Sciences Research Council here in the United Kingdom. Through several of his companies, he also maintains a senior advisory position with the European Atomic Energy Community in Europe."

It was clear to Clifton that the two CTI officers did not understand the significance of Morten's role with those organizations, so he explained.

"Morten advises the EAEC in Europe and the UKAEA

here in the United Kingdom. These relationships place him in a position to directly influence the development of the world's largest fusion reactor projects in this era; the Mega Amp Spherical Tokamak, or MAST upgrade project at Culham Center, and the International Thermonuclear Experimental Reactor, or ITER project in Europe."

Liam and Elle listened silently.

"My contacts tell me," Clifton continued, "in the more than ten years Morten has been here, he has amassed a huge fortune. He never travels without an armed security detail, and his personal office is reputed to be a veritable fortress." He paused now and shook his head. "Frankly, I'm amazed you were able to abduct the man, let alone transport him as far as you did."

Silence permeated the room.

After several minutes, Elle spoke. "You said his personal office is a fortress?" she asked. "Where is it located?"

Clifton smiled a grim smile.

"The ITER reactor is currently under construction in the Saint-Paul-lès-Durance region of southern France. He has a business office inside the administration building at ITER, but his personal office is located inside a villa approximately 73 kilometers to the south… in Marseille."

Liam stood slowly, careful not to strain his shoulder. "So, we'll go to Marseille," he said. "We can use your MTY device to transit inside the villa."

Clifton shook his head. "It's not going to be that easy."

When Liam looked up, Clifton was frowning. "What's wrong?" he asked.

Clifton spoke hesitantly. "I've already tried to calibrate a singularity inside Morten's villa in Marseille," he said. "I was able to calibrate a singularity to the surrounding grounds, but not inside the villa itself."

"Why not?" Liam asked.

Clifton lifted his MTY device and placed it on the table in the room.

"The tensor assembly would not lock to any coordinates inside the structure."

Liam stepped towards the device.

"It is malfunctioning?" he asked. "Did you run it through its diagnostic cycle?"

"It's functioning normally."

Liam scowled. "Then why wouldn't it calibrate to a position inside the villa?"

"The diagnostic cycle reports a scattering field is preventing calibration."

"What?"

"Morten has a scattering field in operation somewhere inside his villa," Clifton said, shaking his head slowly.

"That's impossible, Liam said, shaking his head. "The technology doesn't exist in this time to create a quantum scattering field. Even if Morten brought the design with him, the technology doesn't exist to build a scattering field generator in this time."

Elle, however, seemed troubled. After a moment, she spoke.

"The technology does not exist to create a true scattering field generator, but Morten might be able to achieve the same results using equipment he has on hand."

"How?" Liam asked, shocked.

"When you arrested Morten and placed him in the transport, my internal particle detectors registered impacts from an unknown radioactive isotope. I assumed it was coming from the nearby MAST reactor building, but that reactor is heavily shielded, and I continued to detect the impacts even after we left the area. It confused me."

"You suspect Morten was the source?" Liam asked, scowling.

"Deuterium can be extracted from common seawater," Elle replied. "If you irradiate lithium-bearing ceramic pebbles in a nuclear reactor, you get tritium, which decays into helium-3. By themselves, neither deuterium nor tritium is particularly dangerous. However, even a small particle accelerator can drive tritium and deuterium ions to energies above the fifteen keV needed for fusion. High-energy neutrons escaping the resulting reaction would radiate in all directions, creating a disruption effect similar to a traditional quantum scattering field."

"The problem with that theory," Liam said, "is there aren't any reactors presently capable of driving tritium and deuterium ions to energies above the fifteen keV needed for fusion. That's the reason they're building the MAST reactor at Culham Center."

"I'm sorry, Officer Perry, but you're mistaken," Elle said.

"I'm mistaken?"

"Morten brought such a reactor with him."

Liam's eyes went wide. Of course! Morten had his own MTY device, the third prototype that had been concealed in the secret vault. It was powered by a fusion reactor.

"All Morten needs to do," Elle continued, "is remove the shielding that surrounds his MTY device's reactor core and substitute deuterium for one of the reactor's isotopes. Instead of a decaying tritium helium-to-helium fusion reaction that produces no waste, the resulting deuterium-to-tritium reaction would radiate high energy neutrons in all directions, creating an effective scattering field."

Liam stared at his female counterpart with an expression of horror. "Without the shielding plates," he said, "it would also generate dangerous levels of neutron radiation!"

Elle nodded slowly. "After sufficient exposure," she said, "clothing, metal, inorganic polymers, and certain other objects would absorb and emit residual isotopes. Those are likely what I detected coming from Morten in Oxford."

After a moment, Liam turned to face Clifton. "Morten is using his device's fusion reactor to prevent anyone from transiting inside his villa."

Clifton shook his head. "If that's true," he said, "he's as good as dead."

Chapter 13

IDR: MK4ART024//:QKDS-77483L2LE

Publius Tacitus was born in 56 A.D. to a Roman equestrian family. He lived in what has been called the Silver Age of Latin literature and is considered to be one of the greatest Roman historians.

Publius' efforts were aligned with the typical Roman quest for power, rank, and privilege at an early age. He married the daughter of a Roman senator, studied rhetoric and the law, and entered politics in A.D. 81 as a quaestor, or private investigator, appointed by Emperor Titus himself. He advanced swiftly, becoming praetor, or magistrate, in A.D. 88, and ultimately suffect consul of the Roman Senate and governor of the Asian province of Western Anatolia.

In 100 A.D., Publius and his friend, Pliny the Younger, prosecuted Marius Priscus, the proconsul of Africa, for corruption. Priscus was found guilty and sent into exile. Shortly after that, Publius withdrew from public life and began writing, focusing on Roman history. It was during this period that he wrote, "In the struggle between those seeking power, there is no middle course."

As one who had reached the veritable summit of Roman privilege, I suspect that Publius understood the drivers behind man's quest for power. From his abandonment of that effort for a life of scholarly reflection, I suspect Publius also glimpsed what ultimately lies at the end of that quest.

Adrian Joubert had never given any credence to his eccentric employer's extraordinary claims. He had always nodded politely, listening patiently to Morten's wild stories, usually spoken over a near-empty gin bottle. He had certainly never entertained the possibility that the man's tales might be true, dismissing them as the rambling stories of an aging, albeit brilliant recluse. Frankly, as long as Morten continued making sizable deposits into Joubert's bank account, he didn't care what the old man believed.

Now, staring at the strange needles in the tray, Joubert was reevaluating his past skepticism. The projectiles were unlike anything he had seen before in all his years of combat. Four had been recovered from the field the day after the fight. They resembled tiny darts, with strange fluting near the tip and a series of fins on the opposite end. While they appeared to be steel, they were denser than one would expect. The darts were uniform in size, 20 mm in length and 2 mm in diameter, and from the size of the exit wounds they created, they had to have been traveling many times faster than the speed of sound, despite having penetrated both walls of their vehicle.

The lab technicians could detect no residual gunpowder or another propellant on the darts, and the lab's mass spectrometer was reportedly having difficulty identifying several of the dart's compositional elements. The surface of the darts appeared smooth, yet under the lab's powerful electron microscope, cryptic symbols had been discovered etched into one of the rear fins. The pattern was different on each of the recovered darts, and all were preceded by the letters "RU." To Joubert's military-trained eye, the darts resembled a miniaturized version of a railgun projectile.

Adrian Guillaume Joubert had been born in Roubaix, an impoverished industrial city in northern France located in the Lille metropolitan area along the Belgian border. He prided himself on his flawless English, but his distinctive French accent betrayed his birthplace origins.

Abandoned by his alcoholic father at ten and neglected by his prostitute mother until he was placed in state care at fourteen, he had quickly exhausted the remainder of his brief childhood reaping the rewards of a turbulent and violent world. He had been involuntarily enlisted into the French army at seventeen, the result of an overly sympathetic magistrate who had been disinclined to imprison the troubled youth for what was believed to be his first armed robbery conviction. In fact, it had been Joubert's third robbery, but no one had identified him as a suspect in those earlier thefts as he had left neither of those earlier victims alive. Frankly, if a patrol officer had not observed him through the store window and interrupted that last robbery, he would not have spared that storekeeper either.

While serving in the French army, Joubert had fought in several of France's regional conflicts, including covert operations inside Chad as a French advisor during that Central African Republic's civil war. Later, he had combatted the Boko Haram in Northeast Nigeria.

He had thrived in combat, secretly relishing his role as a conveyor of death. The Nigerians had given him the nickname 'Fuskar Dutse', or 'Stone Face', attributed to the unusual pattern of marbled scars on his forehead and right cheek, resulting from an IED explosion inside Chad. Due to his military prowess and ruthless nature, he had advanced quickly, achieving the rank of lieutenant within the highly elite French Commandement des Opérations Spéciales, or COS forces.

Recruited by Morten in 2010, Joubert had spent the last nine years shadowing his mysterious benefactor across the globe. Until last Wednesday's incident at Culham Centre, he would have considered his present job, though extremely lucrative, to be exceptionally dull. When the radio call came in alerting him to Morten's abduction, his years of military training had immediately kicked in.

He had alerted his remote security team, directing them to cut off the most probable escape route, then marshaled his men inside Culham Centre to pursue the kidnappers. When the kidnapper's vehicle had veered off the road into the muddy field, he had considered the attempt to be thwarted. It had been a frightening shock when the spray of deadly darts began punching through the side of their vehicle.

Léandre, Hagen, and Armand had been killed instantly. The misted blood, pulverized tissue, and disintegrated bone fragments that erupted from the dead trio had given Joubert's trained eye a hint as to the incredible speed and power of his adversary's weapons.

Olsen and Devereaux had thrown themselves to the ground, joining him in the mud beneath the SUV as the deadly projectiles passed cleanly through the vehicle over their heads. After several frantic moments, Joubert had signaled to one of the remote team members, directing him with hand signs to circle their position and engage their assailants while his men gave covering fire. A minute later, the shooting had stopped, and the man had called, "All clear."

The subsequent trade, Morten for the injured assailant, had gone smoothly. The wounded man had been placed in the center of the field, and his men had retreated, watching carefully as Morten slowly crossed the field. Joubert now regretted not having the presence of mind to retrieve one of the kidnapper's mysterious weapons for further study, but Morten had been insistent on leaving immediately.

The lab technician turned off the scanning microscope

and sat back on his stool, waiting patiently. He could see that the tall Frenchman was troubled, and he did not wish to say anything to arouse the man's considerable anger.

After a moment of silence, Joubert picked up one of the projectiles from the tray and dropped it into a plastic bag. The technician nodded and hesitantly asked him if he required anything else.

"Non," Joubert huffed. He placed the bag in his pocket and stood to leave, ordering the technician to report any discoveries to him personally. The technician quickly nodded, breathing a sigh of relief when Joubert exited the room.

Joubert walked determinedly down the corridor towards the lift. As he approached, two engineers from the physics lab quickly stepped aside to allow him to pass. There was a look on his face that the staff instantly recognized. One didn't get in Adrian Joubert's way when he was wearing that face. The head of Morten's security detail was a volatile presence in any situation, but when he wore that face, he was frankly dangerous.

Morten had constructed his lab and private suite in great secrecy and at an extreme cost beneath a historic villa in the 7th arrondissement of Marseille. Joubert found his employer on the ground floor, inside the villa's front reception room. He was speaking with two UKAEA officials about the kidnapping attempt at Culham Centre.

Morten was insisting that the incident be forgotten, expressing concern that any investigations might disrupt their timetable.

The UKAEA officials, though disturbed by the incident, appeared willing to cooperate.

"I'm quite unharmed," Morten was saying. "A frightening

situation, but one that I am confident will be swiftly resolved when the perpetrators are captured. I've already filed a report with Interpol and with the British authorities."

The taller UKAEA official spoke. "Are you certain they only wanted money?" he asked. "We are concerned your kidnappers might have been hoping to use you to advance some environmental extremist agenda."

"No," Morten said, dismissively waving his hand. "As I've already told you, my security detail recovered a ransom note. They were hoping to trade me for 25 million euros." He smiled warmly, adding, "It was a simple kidnapping attempt." Nodding to Joubert as he approached, he motioned to the imposing Frenchman and said, "One easily foiled by my security detail."

The UKAEA representative glanced uncomfortably at Joubert before turning back to Morten.

"You were most fortunate not to have been injured."

"Yes. Most fortunate," Morten said, smiling stiffly.

"Excusez-moi," Joubert interrupted, frowning at the two officials. "Director Morten has a busy schedule."

The shorter representative immediately tugged at his colleague's elbow. "We won't take up any more of your time, Director," he said. "Please let us know if you discover any more information about the kidnappers."

Morten nodded. "Certainly."

Joubert stood silently next to Morten, watching as the two men signed out at the front reception desk and exited through the villa's exquisitely carved front doors. They continued watching as the men walked past the sculptured ponds and fountains that filled the grounds until they finally exited through the far gate. When they were no longer in sight,

Morten turned swiftly and passed the reception desk.

Joubert followed.

When they entered the lift, Morten placed his palm on a bio-scanner plate and then keyed in his code. The lift descended two floors and opened onto a long corridor. At the end of the bare hall stood a heavy steel door with six 90mm bolts sunk into the reinforced concrete. Stronger than any bank vault, the door stood as the last defense, a final barrier against intruders, Morten's ultimate safe room. As Joubert watched, the aging man placed his palm on the biometric lock, then stared into an iris scanner. In a moment, the heavy bolts retracted with a clang.

The door opened onto Morten's private suite. Dark mahogany panels on the walls gave the room a warm feeling that contrasted with the gold-veined Nero St. Laurent marble floor. The rich black marble, quarried in the Laurens region of France, had been worked and shaped into a strange, almost biologic pattern, creating an effect similar to streams of black and gold, flowing and twisting, before seeming to vanish into nothing. The design was difficult for the eye to follow and made walking across the floor an exercise in ocular balance.

The paneled walls concealed a reinforced concrete bunker lined with half-inch thick, lead-lined carbon steel plates fitted with vibration and pressure differential sensors. No one could tunnel anywhere within fifty meters of the bunker without alerting the occupants.

Morten walked determinedly towards a desk placed in the center of the room, passing doors leading to his bedroom, his private library, and the room where he stored his considerable art collection. Motion-activated sensors in the suite engaged lighting in the ceiling as he passed.

Joubert remained where he stood, waiting deferentially.

He had always found Morten's underground residence to be disquieting. He preferred meeting in one of the villa's above-ground offices, with many doors and windows providing multiple escape options. Morten permitted him to enter the suite, but he had never been allowed beyond this front room.

Joubert's eyes strayed to the mysterious steel door at the far end of the room. Once, several years ago, he had entered the suite and had observed Morten coming out of that small door. For a moment, he had glimpsed a strange machine sitting on a table inside a dimly lit room, emitting a blue glow. Morten had swiftly closed and sealed the door, clearly perturbed.

Morten sat down in his chair and looked up, staring at his head of security. "Well, what have you learned?" he asked.

Joubert retrieved the plastic bag from his pocket and held up the small dart. "Our site team recovered several of these projectiles from the field," he said. "The projectiles are uniform in size and are capable of penetrating two 20-gauge steel panels without deformation. The lab has been unable to determine their complete elemental composition, though they have identified titanium, tungsten..."

"Enough!" Morten slammed his hand down on his desk. "I told you to find out more about the two officers, not about their weapons!"

Joubert lowered his hand. After a moment, he shrugged. "Understanding what kind of weapons they were using," he said, "will help us to find out who they are and what their agenda might be."

"I already know their agenda," Morten's sneered. "They told me themselves who they were and what they were here to do." When Joubert did not respond, he stood and strode purposefully around his desk, stopping in front of the tall

Frenchman.

"You've never believed what I've told you, Adrian. Oh, you've listened respectfully, but you've never believed a word of what I've told you. Now, faced with the proof in your own hand, you still refuse to accept the truth. You are a consummate skeptic, but unless you drop your skepticism right now, we are both very likely going to be killed."

Joubert slowly looked down at the small dart in his hand, his face troubled. When his head began to shake dismissively, Morten sighed and turned back towards his desk. He spoke now with annoyed resignation in his voice.

"You're holding a projectile from a hand-held micro-railgun," he said. "Probably an RU-4 or RU-6, issued to temporal enforcement officers by the CTI council in Geneva. The weapons can deliver their projectiles on either select-fire or full-auto, at velocities exceeding many times the speed of sound. Depending on the series number, the weapons may also be equipped with thermal imaging, biometric targeting, or even a QRB trace targeting system."

Morten sat back down behind his desk and pointed at the dart in Joubert's hand. "The projectiles," he continued, "are composed of titanium, tungsten, and alloys of neodymium and boron that do not yet exist in the world. Some variations also contain internal QRB wave-form emitters for tracking purposes. The rear fins are etched at the factory with cryptographic identification marks that enable investigators to trace their manufacture date, batch number, and purchaser."

Joubert stared at the small dart in his hand but said nothing.

Morten continued, his tone suggesting annoyance. "The weapons were first manufactured in 2108," he said, "following the introduction of an EFC, an extremely fast-cycle rail-gun system introduced two years earlier by the Ruger-Umbrech Armament Company in Europe."

Joubert looked up slowly to face his employer.

"Yes, Adrian," Morten said, nodding grimly. I know all I need to know about those weapons. What I need to know is more about the two officers. Especially about that female officer."

Joubert shook his head, confused. "The female?" he asked.

Morten stood and walked silently towards a magnificent gilded and carved teak bar. He poured himself a glass of gin from a crystal decanter and slowly drank the entire glass. He filled the glass again. When he spoke again, his voice was strangely restrained.

"I saw her do something, Adrian. Something she should not have been able to do."

Joubert could see the aged man was deeply troubled by something. He approached the bar. "Qu'a-t-elle fait?" he asked.

Glancing up, Morten frowned. He retrieved the cognac decanter he knew Joubert favored and passed it with a glass to the tall man. As Joubert poured the amber-brown liquid into the glass, Morten stared ahead as if straining to see something beyond the exquisitely carved wall.

"When she stopped the van in the field," Morten spoke quietly, "the male said something strange. He was giving the female instructions, you understand, but then he said something strange. He said, 'I don't have your strength or speed'."

Morten took another sip from his glass.

"When the van stopped in the field," he continued, "the

female kicked the door free from the van." He looked up at Jobert's face. "She didn't open the door, you understand? She kicked it with her foot, and the door flew off the van. It was crumpled in half. The steel track bolts that had held the door to the van were snapped clean." He now silently drained his glass.

Joubert had seen the crumpled door laying in the field, but he had been too occupied to give it more than a passing glance.

Morten placed his glass down on the bar and walked slowly back to his desk. When he sat down, he sighed.

"In the time I came from," he said, "mankind was embroiled in a great debate regarding whether to allow SDUs... what you would call robots... whether to allow robots to achieve sentience." He approached the desk and sat down in a chair, listening intently.

"SDUs were close to achieving sentience on their own," Morten continued. "So, in 2136, SDU manufacturers and their government sponsors imposed a moratorium on any further SDU development. They agreed to prevent further development until they could answer that question." Morten motioned Joubert to the chair in front of the desk, then continued. "They agreed to halt development until mankind could decide whether to allow SDUs to become sentient." He looked up and stared at Joubert. "Only an SDU has the kind of physical strength and speed that female demonstrated."

Joubert's eyes narrowed. "You think she is a robot?" he asked.

"I don't know," Morten said, shaking his head. "She didn't act or speak like any SDU I've ever seen. She spoke and acted like a normal female. She was..." He fell silent, frowning.

Joubert nodded, then said, "She was sentient."

Chapter 14

IDR: MK4ASA094//:QKDS-77483L2LE

During the age of sailing ships, wealthy merchant vessels were sometimes lured onto the rocks and plundered by the use of false lights displayed from the shore. In the North America Federated State of North Carolina, the town of Nags Head allegedly owes its name to such practices.

In the 18th century, "wreckers" would hang lanterns from the necks of mules (called "nags" at that time) and walk the animals very slowly up and down the beach. Believing that the slow-moving lights were ships drifting at anchor, mariners would change their course and subsequently run their ships aground. After that, the wreckers would descend to plunder the ship.

Lighthouses were constructed to warn ship captains of their proximity to the dangerous shoals. Unfortunately, the lighthouses often contributed to more wrecks, as the wreckers would light larger, brighter lights in the same area. Mariners would become confused about which of the lights were the "real" light and run their ship aground.

Deception, it would seem, requires both an overt false act and a predisposition on the part of the victim to believe that act. Even when confronted by the truth, deception can still be achieved by making the false act shine brighter than the truth.

Joubert waited anxiously for Devereaux's signal. It was miserably cold. He was standing under a tree near the northern corner of the Hamden Village Hall, gazing across the moon-lit field at The Sickle. The ground was frozen, and a recent mist rising from the nearby Thames had covered everything in frost.

It was almost six weeks since his team was last in Oxford. It was late November, and, despite his best efforts to locate Morten's abductors, he had been unsuccessful. Yesterday, however, he had received a tip from one of his operatives who had seen two individuals matching the abductor's description going into a restaurant in Oxford. The operative had followed the pair to a small bed & breakfast inn suspiciously close to Culham Center called The Sickle.

Joubert had immediately dispatched Devereaux to reconnoiter the situation. According to Devereaux, there were three targets; two men and a woman. The woman, Devereaux had excitedly reported, was the woman who had carried Morten across the field. Her compatriot was the man who had been shot while covering her escape. As to the identity of the third man, Devereaux could offer no information beyond a general description.

Joubert immediately transported his security team to London and formulated a plan.

Thirty minutes ago, Devereaux's advance team had spotted the unidentified third man walking into the room occupied by the woman and her compatriot. With all three targets now in the same room, Joubert swiftly deployed his men.

"Nous sommes en position." The voice crackling in Joubert's earpiece belonged to Devereaux, reporting his team was in position along the small lane behind the inn.

Joubert lifted his MP5 submachine gun and crept towards the inn. He nodded to Olsen, who was crouched behind a nearby car. The large Dutchman rose and began to follow, his suppressed FN SCAR-H rifle at the ready.

The two men approached the room quietly, their footsteps making only the barest noise on the frozen ground. It was nearly midnight, and, save for a dim light shining through the target room's blinds, the inn was still and quiet.

Joubert felt his heart pounding. He remembered vividly the deadly darts that had erupted through the side of their vehicle, and he held no illusions about any protection afforded by the inn's wooden door or even its brick-cased walls. All of his men wore body armor with extra ballistic plates, but he had doubts that even those would protect against the mysterious weapon's incredible penetrating power.

He paused behind the door, glancing at Olsen to check the man's readiness. The Dutchman nodded silently, raising his rifle and taking a deep breath.

At that moment, a strange light through the window blinds caught Joubert's eye. He paused with his hand on the door, staring at the thin wooden slits behind the frosted glass. The light seemed cold and flickered with a purple haze. Suddenly, he heard a noise, as if someone inside had bumped against a piece of furniture. He threw his weight hard against the door and it burst open. He rushed into the room then stopped in shock.

Olsen, closing the distance behind him, also pulled up short, staring in amazement.

Near the far wall, a swirling vortex illuminated the room between the bed and a wooden wardrobe. Its edges, sparking and tinged with a purple light, seemed to rotate slowly around a mysterious black abyss. In front of this black void stood a man. Joubert had never seen the man before, but he matched

Devereaux's description of their unidentified third target. The man was holding a strange device in his hand, and it was this that had caused Joubert to hesitate. The device was precisely like the machine he had glimpsed long ago inside Morten's secret vault.

Joubert raised his MP5, but it was already too late. The man leaped into the vortex. The instant he entered the cyclone, he vanished as if he had jumped through a hole in space. A moment later, the vortex winked out, leaving the room lit from a single table lamp.

"Mijn god!" Olsen whispered.

Joubert stepped around the bed and cautiously put his arm out, feeling the air where the strange disturbance had been.

Nothing.

At that moment, Andre Lemaire, the third member of Joubert's assault team, entered the room, his rifle at the ready. Seeing Joubert and Olsen standing alone in the room, he lowered his rifle.

"Où sont-ils allés?" Lemaire asked, confused. When Joubert remained silent, he frowned and turned to Olsen. "Did they escape?" he asked.

Olsen shook his head, muttered something in Dutch, and then walked out of the room, clearly disturbed.

Joubert turned. Seeing Lemaire, he said, "Avaient quitté." When Lemaire didn't move but stood staring about the room in confusion, Joubert took hold of the man's tactical harness and shoved him angrily towards the door. "Avaient quitté!" he ordered.

Lemaire hastily retreated.

Joubert followed, giving the empty room one last glance. Once outside, he took a moment to regain his composure. He radioed Devereaux and issued the abort code-word, ordering him to take his team back to London. He then motioned his own team members towards their vehicle. When Olsen hesitated, still staring at the room's door, he took hold of the Dutchman's arm.

"Say nothing!" he growled.

Back in London, Joubert paced the floor in his hotel room, waiting for the call from Morten. No matter how his mind attempted to rationalize the past two weeks' events, it kept coming back to three incontrovertible facts.

First, the unidentified third man in the room had vanished. He had not left through any door. He had stepped through that swirling blackness and was simply no longer in the room. What had happened was impossible, yet Joubert had witnessed it with his own eyes.

Second, although he had only caught a glimpse of the strange machine in the mysterious man's hand, it resembled the device that he had observed inside Morten's secret vault years ago.

Third, the mysterious darts recovered from the field represented a level of weapon sophistication presently unknown in the world. Joubert was an expert on small arms, and no weapon in his considerable experience fired bullets that came close to matching the strange projectile's composition, design, or incredible velocity.

These facts were forcing Joubert to reevaluate the present situation. They were also forcing him to reconsider his strange employer. He could no longer dismiss Morten as merely a wealthy eccentric. Though it shocked his innate sensibilities, he now accepted that Morten was what he had always claimed to be; a time traveler from the future.

That acceptance re-drew the shape of Joubert's world. Morten's assailants, he reluctantly concluded, must also be from the future, undoubtedly possessing technology and weapons far beyond his understanding. As his mind considered the possibilities, for the first time in his nearly thirty years of soldiering, he felt the chill of fear. At that moment, his cell phone began to buzz.

"Oui?"

"Well?" Morten's voice seemed almost calm through the distant connection. "Were you successful?"

Joubert hesitated, then cleared his throat. He must be truthful, despite how extraordinary his explanation might sound.

"No," he said. "When we entered the room, they were gone." He cleared his throat again. "The third man was still there, but... he left as we were entering. He left through... a black rip in the air. It was black and round but filled with energy. I don't have a word for it. It was a fenêtre d'énergie... a window of energy. The man was in the room, and then he was gone. And then... the window vanished."

Morten listened to the stumbling explanation without interruption. He could hear the tension in Joubert's voice, the strained confusion, and immediately deduced what had happened. The CTI officers and their mysterious friend had obviously transited out of the room just as Joubert and his team had entered.

The questions in Morten's mind were simple ones. Where had the two CTI officers gone? Who was the unidentified third man? What would be their next move?

His security officer's silence on the other end of the phone was disquieting. Obviously, the incident had affected

Joubert profoundly. Well, that might be useful too, Morten reasoned. Perhaps now, the large Frenchman would get past his stubborn skepticism.

Morten spoke forcefully into the phone.

"Return to Marseille."

Chapter 15

IDR: MK4ASB011//:QKDS-77483L2LE

According to Aristotle, mankind is said to be capable of seven forms of love. Eros; sexual or passionate love. Philia; friendship or camaraderie. Storge; familial love, such as is expressed by a parent for a child. Agape; universal love, which is typically attributed to deity. Ludus; a playful or uncommitted love exhibited by flirting or teasing. Pragma; a practical love founded on reason or duty. Philautia; self-love, which is akin to hubris and may be either healthy or unhealthy depending on its intensity.

One of the most challenging tasks for a sentient automaton is distinguishing between love's many forms. We instinctively interpret all forms of love as philial, evidencing mere friendship or camaraderie. We frequently fail to recognize its other forms, even when they may be overtly expressed.

I have studied Julian of Norwich's writings on the subject, recorded in 1373 when she was thirty years old. Julian wrote, "Our life is all grounded and rooted in love, and without love, we may not live."

Accepting Julian's statement as factual, I have resolved to become more familiar with the subject.

Elle stood on the terrace, gazing westward across the moon-lit harbor at the distant Île d'Endoume. She could see the lights of a ship crossing in front of Île Gaby, and further out across the bay, she could make out several lights twinkling on Île d'If and the château immortalized by Alexandre

Dumas in his 1844 tale, The Count of Monte Cristo.

The trio had left Oxford suddenly when one of the surveillance drots that Liam had placed outside their room had alerted the group to the arrival of Morten's security men. Elle had quickly retrieved the officer's MTY device from the closet attic while Clifton calibrated his own device to a location inside Marseille, France. Elle and Liam had transited through first, followed by Clifton a few moments later. The instant Clifton arrived, he had flipped his device's disruption switch, terminating the singularity. Morten's men, he had reported, were entering the room as he transited out.

Through his environmental contacts in Britain, Clifton had cultivated clandestine relationships with several notable people around the world. One of these was Gérald Paillard, Maître de Maison and third-generation owner of the Le Goût de Nice Paillard restaurant and hotel situated on the coast of Marseille. Clifton immediately led the officers to the hotel.

The structure was a dramatic change from the quaint bed & breakfast inn at Oxford. Converted from a beautiful turn-of-the-century French villa, the luxurious hotel and its adjoining restaurant graced the shore like a jewel in the crown of Marseille. Constructed on the rocks that descended into the sea, the villa provided a stunning view of the Marseille harbor. From the villa's stone terrace, the silhouette of the Calanques could be seen in the distance, a series of rocky cliffs and bays between the city of Marseille and the town of Cassis. Outward across the water, the four islands of the Frioul archipelago were centered only four kilometers from the shore.

Winter in Marseille is cold, but the city's coastal Mediterranean climate tempers the weather. When the trio arrived at the villa, it was well after 2:00 am, and the terraces were empty save for a few couples engaged in quiet conversation beneath tall heat lamps. Clifton left the two CTI officers waiting underneath one of the lamps before going inside the villa to find his friend.

Elle took the opportunity to walk along the terrace and admire the ocean view under the moonlight. Turning her gaze reluctantly from the harbor, her eyes caught sight of the Notre-Dame de la Garde, a Catholic basilica built atop a distant hill. The hill was the highest point in Marseille, and the basilica's towering square bell tower was topped with a magnificent gold statue of Mary holding the baby, Jesus. The surrounding city lights caused the gold to glint and sparkle against the night sky.

At that moment, far out in the harbor, Elle heard a ship's horn, a lonesome sound that seemed to drift across the water.

"That's probably a freighter."

It was Liam. He pointed absently out towards the ocean, and Elle followed his hand, straining to identify the source of the sound. The ship, however, was either too far away or concealed behind one of the islands in the harbor.

"I scanned once," Liam said, "that the ocean-going vessels of this era were among the largest transports man has ever built, rivaling the size of our asteroidal ore carriers."

Elle shook her head. "It's amazing that humans from this period could construct such vessels, given their limitations in tooling and metallurgy."

Liam sat down on the stone terrace and pivoted his legs around to the harbor side of the wall. He rubbed the stiffness in his shoulder, still feeling the dull ache there.

"Ever since I was a child, I've been fascinated by the sea," he said with a sigh. "I would have loved to have been born in a time like this when men captained their own ships."

Elle looked at him with surprise.

"Without SAT-Nav?" she asked.

Liam laughed. "Yes! Especially without that. What's the point of being a ship captain if you just turn everything over to an AI controller linked to the local SAT-Nav network?"

Elle gazed back out at the dark ocean.

After a few moments, Liam spoke again.

"I think it would be amazing," he spoke softly, his voice almost a whisper. "To plot a course from actual paper charts, using a real compass and sextant. To sail your ship across a wide ocean and bring it back home again. Can you imagine what that would be like?"

Elle stared at the tall officer. He was clearly impacted by the sights and smells of the ocean, and she studied his face closely, watching his eyes as they gathered in the view. This was one of those moments when a sentient automaton envied the human psyche. She tried to imagine the feelings the man was so clearly experiencing.

At that moment, a gust of wind blew Liam's hair askew, and Elle had a brief image of him standing on the deck of a primitive ship, the wind filling its sails as the sound of waves crashed against its bow. She felt confused, overwhelmed by the mental image, an image she knew to be artificially contrived, yet one somehow made real by the smells and sounds of the nearby ocean. She sat down on the terrace wall beside him, watching his face closely.

Far away, the ship's horn sounded again, and Liam smiled a sad smile. He turned, as if he was about to say something, but stopped suddenly, apparently surprised to find her sitting so close to him. His face reflected confusion for a moment, and he turned quickly away.

Elle detected his respiration and heart rate increasing, and she wondered for a moment if something was wrong. She was about to ask when he suddenly pointed to the dark island in the distance.

"Edmond Dantès was imprisoned there."

Elle turned, confused.

Liam was pointing at the lights twinkling on Île d'If. He shivered against the cold breeze that blew in from the water, then spoke again.

"It was on the day of his wedding to his love, Mercédès. A jealous rival, Mondego, conspired with his crew-mate, Danglars, and a corrupt magistrate, De Villefort, to have Edmond falsely accused of treason and imprisoned without trial inside the fortress there… inside Château d'If."

Elle stared at the distant island silhouetted across the harbor.

"After six years of imprisonment," Liam continued, "Edmond was on the verge of suicide when he befriended Abbé Faria, an Italian priest and fellow prisoner who had dug an escape tunnel that ended up in Edmond's cell. Over the next eight years, Faria gave Edmond an education in language, chemistry, culture, mathematics, medicine, and science. He also revealed to Edmond the location of a fabulous treasure hidden away on a small island called Monte Cristo."

"Is Monte Cristo a real island?" Elle asked.

Liam turned and seemed surprised.

"Don't you know? Surely your data files contain…"

Elle shook her head, "I haven't queried my internal data store."

"Why not?"

Elle hesitated.

"I... I was enjoying listening to you tell the story. I didn't want to scan the file."

Liam stared at her for a long moment. He seemed fixated on a bit of her brown hair that had draped over her shoulder. Suddenly, he turned away and looked back at the dark island in the distance.

"Monte Cristo is a real island," he said after a few moments. "It's located in the Tuscan Archipelago, halfway between Corsica and the Italian peninsula."

Elle turned her gaze once again towards the dark island, waiting for the story to continue.

"When Faria died," Liam obliged, "Edmond took his place in Faria's burial sack, and when the guards threw the sack into the sea, he escaped and swam to a nearby island. Later, he made his way to Monte Cristo and found the treasure. With the treasure, he purchased the island and the title of Count from the Tuscan government."

Liam paused for a moment, listening to the distant ship's horn again as it echoed across the moon-lit harbor. After a few moments, he continued.

"Edmond then used his incredible wealth to exact his revenge against Mondego, Danglars, and De Villefort."

When he fell silent, Elle looked at his face.

"What about Mercédès?" she asked.

Liam turned, catching her eye. "Do you mean, was he reunited with Mercédès?"

When she nodded, Liam shook his head and looked away.

"When she learned what Mondego had done to Edmond, Mercédès disowned Mondego. She took their son and left. Mondego was then confronted with Edmond's true identity and shot himself. In the end, Mercédès and her son renounced Mondego's titles and wealth and departed to start a new life."

Elle frowned. "But... didn't Edmond love her?" she asked.

Liam looked at her face. "Edmond had been a prisoner for many years," he said. "He was consumed with revenge when he escaped. His anger and desire for revenge destroyed the love he had once held for Mercédès." When it was clear that his explanation was insufficient, he smiled, and said, "In the end, he did find love again."

Elle looked up quickly.

"Edmond's beautiful slave, Haydée," he continued, "who had been sold into slavery by Mondego, confessed her love to him, and Edmond realized that he had also fallen in love with her."

"Edmond fell in love with his slave girl?"

Liam nodded. "Having abandoned his desire for revenge," he said, "Edmond was able to find love again with Haydée. At the end of the book, he writes a letter to Maximilien, the son of a close friend, leaving him with one final thought: 'all human wisdom is contained in these two words, Wait and Hope'."

Elle stared, silent.

At that moment, Clifton returned, interrupting the duo. "We're all set," he said. "Gérald says we can stay as long as we wish."

Liam swiveled his legs back to the terrace and stood swiftly. He nodded and extended his hand to Elle. Elle seemed confused for a moment, then took the offered hand and allowed herself to be helped up. Still holding Elle’s hand, Liam turned to Clifton.

"Do you trust this man?"

"Yes," Clifton said. "I was introduced to him last year by Sir Albert Nicholls, a mutual acquaintance of ours in London. Paillard has an interest in reducing oceanic pollution and provides funds and resources to my environmental contacts in Britain to help them with their efforts."

As they approached the villa, Clifton suddenly paused.

"I should also tell you," he spoke hesitantly, "Gérald knows we are from the future."

When Liam's face revealed shock, Clifton quickly added, "You must understand. I have been here for years. My neustem injection wore off long ago, and I have found it both necessary and advantageous to confide my true identity to certain trusted people in this era. So far, that confidence has been well-founded."

Liam did not know what to say. As a temporal enforcement officer, such a blatant violation of protocol shocked him to the core. His impulse was to arrest Clifton immediately, but the present circumstances convinced him of the impracticality of that action. He needed Clifton, and the fact that Clifton had confided his true identity to individuals in this era had, indeed, allowed their mission to continue. For the first time, Liam found himself reconsidering the wisdom of the council's policy regarding neustem injections and specialist anonymity.

When they entered the lobby to the hotel, Liam paused, letting go of Elle's hand. He was taken back by the opulence of their surroundings. Tables graced with stunning white cloths and crystal glasses filled a dark wood parquet tiled floor beneath dimmed lights. The tables spanned a wide floor facing expansive windows and had been positioned to give diners the best views of the moon-lit harbor. In the restaurant's dim lights, the nearby moon-lit harbor seemed mysterious and inviting.

Clifton's friend, Gérald Paillard, was speaking with a woman behind the concierge desk. The restaurateur was handsome, in his mid-fifties, with wavy black hair that was now turning grey. Seeing their approach, he raised his hand and quickly crossed the room, smiling warmly.

"Bonsoir mes amis! Welcome! Welcome!"

As Clifton introduced his companions, Paillard greeted them enthusiastically. He asked if they wished anything to eat and seemed disappointed when they declined. He introduced the trio to the woman he had been speaking to at the concierge desk, who handed Clifton three cards. Paillard then clapped Clifton on the back as he guided the group towards a small lift off the restaurant floor.

"John, my friend, you must join me pour le petit déjeuner… for breakfast! Oui?"

The restaurateur spoke with a thick accent, seamlessly switching between French and English.

"I would love to," Clifton replied.

"Et vos compagnons… your companions also?" Paillard said, smiling at Liam and Elle.

Elle nodded as Liam said, "Thank you, Monsieur Paillard."

With a final smile and a wave of his arm, the restaurateur motioned them towards the small lift door.

Clifton had to show the CTI officers how to use the strange room cards. Elle found the experience amusing, studying the magnetic strip on the back of the card and scanning the encoded data with one of the sub-dermal sensors concealed under the skin of her index finger.

While Clifton was explaining the primitive mechanism, Liam implemented their security measures. He placed one of their surveillance drots in a discreet position near the end of the hallway to observe anyone exiting the lift or the adjoining stairs. He concealed a second drot inside a potted plant facing his and Elle's adjoining doors. A third drot was placed beneath a demilune table outside Clifton's door on the opposite side of the hall. All three drots had been configured for surveillance monitoring.

When he entered his hotel room, Liam immediately felt his anxiety diminishing. The spacious room was spotless and perfectly accentuated, with art on the white walls, flowers on the tables, and a wide window affording a magnificent view of the nearby harbor. The crisp white linen on the bed felt like brushed cotton, and the white pillows arranged at its head appeared invitingly soft.

He heard Elle moving next door. He stopped and listened. He was still bewildered by what had happened on the terrace. One moment, he had been sharing his love of the sea with a colleague, revealing his childhood wish to captain a ship across its vast expanse, and the next moment, it was not simply his colleague, but Elle sitting by his side, beautiful and strangely feminine.

His telling of Dumas' famous story had been an act of desperation. He had needed to get his mind off of Elle's proximity. If Clifton had not returned when he had, Liam felt he might have been tempted to kiss her. Even more surprising, he had the strange feeling she would not have objected. The thought shocked him profoundly. He dimmed the room lights and lay down on the soft bed, extremely troubled.

Next door, Elle stood in front of the wide window in her

darkened room. Questions filled her cognitive processor.

Liam's story on the terrace had left her troubled for reasons she could not explain. The more she tried to resolve the confusion permeating her neural net, the more her emotive processor fixated on seemingly unrelated things; Liam's smile inside the archive hall, the look in his eyes when he spoke about the sea, and the blue chairs that now sat inside her apartment. Supplementing this, her haptic processor repeatedly triggered a strange echo sensation of his hand in hers.

As her neural network struggled to make sense of the strange input, she remembered Edmond's final words; 'all human wisdom is contained in these two words, Wait and Hope'.

She gazed out across the dark harbor, staring at the lights twinkling on Île d'If.

Perhaps Edmond was right.

Chapter 16

IDR: MK4ASB023//:QKDS-77483L2LE

In November 1805, at the height of the Napoleonic Wars, French forces under Marshals Jean Lannes and Joachim Murat were pursuing the retreating Austrian army near Spitz, Austria.

When the French forces approached the river Danube, they discovered that the vital Tabor Bridge had been mined with explosives and Austrian soldiers stood nearby, ready to light the fuses. Rather than attack in force and risk having the bridge destroyed, Marshals Lannes and Murat put on their full dress uniforms and brazenly rode up to the bridge guards under a flag of truce. After summoning the Austrian's officer, the Marshals claimed that an armistice had been signed and that, under the terms of the armistice, the bridge now belonged to the French government.

The Austrians were bewildered and confused. After a tense few minutes, an Austrian general arrived. Seeing the two French Marshals in their fine uniforms, standing fearless among his soldiers, he was convinced of their story and ordered his soldiers to withdraw. Lannes and Murat's forces then took possession of the bridge without firing a shot.

It would appear that guile can be as effective in warfare as strength.

Gérald Paillard stared at Elle in unabashed fascination, shaking his head in wonder at the most extraordinary guest he had ever entertained. She sat across the small breakfast table on his private veranda framed by heat lamps, attempting to explain to the amazed restaurateur the differences between an SDU, or un androïde, to use his words, and a sentient automaton. Liam and Clifton sat next to the two, listening quietly to their conversation with amused expressions on their faces.

"She is not an android, my friend," Clifton offered. "An android, despite how sophisticated it's programming, is not sentient."

"Mmmmm," Gérald responded, trying to understand. "Et la jeune femme est ... the young lady is... sentient?"

"Yes." Clifton nodded.

"Et qu'est-ce que la... Er... What is sentience?" Gérald asked, smiling politely at Elle.

Clifton gestured to Elle, nodding his encouragement.

Recalling the definition from her internal data store, Elle said, "Sentience is the capacity to feel, perceive, or experience subjectively."

Liam nodded in agreement.

Gérald, however, was not satisfied.

"But the mademoiselle does not eat!" he said, shaking his head and waving his hands at the table filled with pastries, fruit, and other delicacies. "How can one feel, perceive, or experience life without enjoying the smells and flavors of food?"

Elle frowned.

"I do not require food to sustain my internal systems," she said, "but I am capable of experiencing both the smell and taste of food."

Liam looked up but said nothing.

Gérald shook his head, muttering, "Capable..." The smiling man suddenly retrieved a baguette from the table, smeared it with fresh butter and a dollop of strawberry jam, and then held it out towards her.

"But has mademoiselle ever actually tasted food?"

He spoke with a playful challenge in his eye.

"To be capable of something, but to never embrace the experience, is to cheat at life."

The three men now watched in fascination, waiting to see what Elle would do.

Elle glanced at Liam, then at Clifton, before returning her gaze to Gérald's outstretched hand. Slowly, she reached out and took the bread from the smiling chef. Even from here, her olfactory processors registered emulsified milk-fat in the butter and a nutty aroma of roasted wheat from the toasted baguette. Overpowering, however, was the floral scent of strawberry rising from the jam. Very conscious of the three men's fixed gaze, she slowly bit into the baguette.

Immediately, synthetic chemoreceptors aligning her tongue registered an explosion of strange sensations. Her eyes grew wide with shock at the flavors that assaulted her gustatory and olfactory systems.

The sweetness from the sugar in the jam was simply overpowering. Mingled with that sweetness, however, she could taste salt and rich cream from the butter, and, as her teeth bit through the crunchy toast, the jam's strawberry perfume flooded her olfactory receptors.

Seeing her reaction, the delighted Paillard clapped his hands together.

"Merveilleux!"

Elle stared in shock at the thing in her hand. "It's amazing!" she whispered, clearly overwhelmed. She looked at Liam, shaking her head in wonder as he reached out to wipe a bit of jam from her lip with an apologetic smile.

Paillard immediately began placing different delicacies from the table in front of his guest. He poured a cup of coffee and retrieved a small bowl of fruit.

"You must taste this melon, ma chérie!… and this yogurt! It is most délicieux, I assure you!… and of course, you must have la crème dans votre café!"

Laughing, Clifton interrupted. "Restrain yourself, Gérald!" he said. "I'm sure this is most gratifying, but we do have things we must ask you."

Frowning, the chef brushed back his wavy hair in frustration and said, "But Mademoiselle can surely eat while we have our discussion?" He proceeded to butter another baguette and then added creme to Elle's coffee.

Clifton smiled and shook his head in resignation.

Liam, however, was more determined. "Monsieur Paillard," he said, "What can you tell us about Morten's villa?"

The excited restaurateur looked up, a frown on his forehead. "It is a most expansive villa," he said. "Très grande! Comprenez vous?"

"I understand," Liam replied. "Do you know if Morten modified it? Has he altered the villa in any way from its original floor plan?"

Paillard now shook his head. "Je suis désolé… I do not know. It is said he is a very wealthy man, monsieur. Very powerful. For such a man, it would be an effortless thing to change a villa."

Clifton asked, "Have you ever been inside the villa, Gérald?"

The restaurateur again shook his head. "No, mon amie. I have seen it only from the street. That was two… no, three years ago. I was in the area to meet a supplier. The most wonderful fromage you ever tasted! Imported from allemagne de l'ouest. It has the most striking flavor! My supplier obtains it from a family farm…"

"Gérald…" Clifton prompted. "The villa?"

"Oui! Pardon. The villa is in the 7th arrondissement, a very wealthy place. I remember a wall surrounded it. The wall hid the villa from the street and had many cameras. Most unusual for Marseille. I remarked on the many cameras to ma femme… to my wife. She said the villa must be home to les trafiquants de drogue… to drug traffickers."

Clifton nodded. "And that was the only time you have seen the villa?" he asked.

"Oui."

Paillard now returned his attention to the dish of yogurt he was preparing for Elle.

Clifton turned to Liam, who was watching him closely.

"I think your plan is likely the best one," he said. "Morten has had too long to prepare for our arrival. He has all the advantages. He has too many men and, from what my friend here suggests, his villa and the surrounding streets are likely too well monitored and protected for a direct assault."

Liam glanced back at Paillard, who was enthusiastically dicing fresh strawberries into the dish of yogurt, while Elle watched with wide eyes. Directing his attention back to Clifton, he nodded.

"I agree. We should begin preparations."

Liam now motioned towards the engaged restaurateur.

Clifton nodded his understanding and turned back to his friend.

"Gérald?"

When the chef looked up, Clifton smiled. "I'm afraid we

must impose on you for another favor," he said.

Paillard waved his hand. "Of course, mon amie. How may I help?"

"Don't worry," Clifton grinned. "C'est dans vos cordes… It is in your ropes."

Paillard glanced up, a puzzled expression on his face.

Clifton smiled and said, "I understand you are catering a party?"

The following morning, Elle and Liam found themselves approaching the small town of Saint-Paul-lès-Durance. After being assured of Elle's ability to operate the vehicle, Paillard had allowed the pair to borrow his wife's car, a sporty Alpine A110. They had been driving north on Autoroute du Val de Durance for nearly an hour, enjoying the French countryside's mild winter.

After enjoying another breakfast with their host on the restaurant's patio, Clifton had telephoned his contacts in London. Within an hour, the temporal specialist reported his contacts had arranged an interview that afternoon with Johannes Fournier, the Director of F4E, the umbrella organization through which Morten's various companies contributed personnel, materials, or other resources to the ITER fusion project. Posing as representatives from the British Environmental Inspection Agency, Liam and Elle intended to connect to Director Fournier's network computer during the interview and PoL information about Morten's upcoming activities and travel schedule.

As they neared Saint-Paul-lès-Durance, Liam glanced at his attractive driver. As in Oxford, Elle seemed to be handling the small vehicle with confidence.

"Is this vehicle easier to drive than the other one… the one in Oxford?" he asked.

Elle glanced at him.

"Easier?"

Liam nodded. "Yes," he said. "Is it easier to operate?"

Elle frowned.

"The vehicle in London," she replied, "was an older model commercial vehicle, designed for maintenance activities. It lacked sufficient power for the high-speed operations we required there. This vehicle is newer, smaller, with a more powerful engine. Its engine's 16 valves are capable of 1798 cubic centimeters of displacement; a significant increase in performance over the vehicle in Oxford."

Liam grinned but said nothing.

Observing his reaction, Elle frowned.

"Did I say something amusing?"

Liam shook his head.

"It just reminded me of the kind of answers you used to give when you first started with the enforcement group."

Elle now seemed even more confused.

"You're implying my answers now are different? In what way?"

Liam turned. "You're more experienced now," he said. "More familiar with human idiosyncrasies. You abbreviate, keeping things concise and to the point. You used to over-describe everything."

Elle glanced at him and then returned her attention back to the road. After a few moments, she said, "There are still many things I don't understand."

"What things?"

The beautiful automaton fell strangely silent. After nearly

a minute, Liam was about to press the question when she spoke.

"The night we arrived in Marseille… when you were telling me about Edmond Dantès, I noticed your heart rate was elevated, and your respiration rate was unusually high."

It was now Liam's turn to be silent. He stared out the vehicle's side window and said nothing.

"I have analyzed your symptoms," Elle continued, "and have arrived at two probable causes."

Liam turned his gaze back from the window.

"Probable causes?" he asked.

Elle nodded. "You are either suffering from ventricular tachycardia, resulting from an undiagnosed congenital abnormality of the heart…"

Liam grinned.

"Or?" he asked, amused.

Elle glanced at him. "Or," she continued, "you were aroused by my presence."

Liam listened but gave no indication of his thoughts. After a moment, he asked, "Which do you suspect is correct?"

Elle looked at him.

"Do you have a familial history of heart disease?" she asked.

Liam chuckled but shook his head. "No."

Elle looked at his face closely. "Were you aroused when I sat next to you on the terrace?"

Liam sighed. After several moments, he shrugged. "It was quite a natural reaction," he said. "After all, you are very beautiful."

They drove in silence for several minutes, following the path of a wide canal crossed by occasional footbridges. On their right, lightly wooded hills and grassy meadows stood brown, evidence of the dry winter climate of the French coastal region. After several minutes, Elle spoke again.

"You said your reaction was natural. Does that mean you believe your reaction to be involuntary?"

"I didn't say that," Liam said, frowning and looking back out the window.

Elle was confused. Since that evening on the terrace, she had been observing Liam closely. His heart rate and respiration frequently increased when she approached. During their drive this morning, while reaching to examine the vehicle's climate control system, his hand had inadvertently brushed against hers and she had detected an immediate increase in his respiration rate, as well as a pronounced dilation of the facial capillary beds in his cheeks. His explanation now suggested he believed his reactions to be merely an involuntary physiological response, but his refusal to confirm this assessment was perplexing.

Elle abruptly turned onto a side road and then slowed to a stop on the gravel shoulder. She put the vehicle in park and then turned to face the startled officer.

"I apologize, Officer Perry," she said, "but I am confused. Would you mind clarifying something for me?"

"I'll try," he replied, nodding.

Elle abruptly leaned forward and kissed him. After a few moments, she pulled back slowly, observing his reaction.

Liam's head was pounding as blood rushed to his ears. He wanted to say something, but he couldn't seem to draw his breath. Finally, after nearly a full minute, he mumbled, "I... um... I..."

Elle sat back, satisfied. She put the vehicle in gear and turned around to rejoin the main road.

Liam struggled to get control of himself. Finally, he drew

a deep breath.

"What the hell was that?!"

"I required clarification," she replied.

Liam shook his head. "Clarification?"

Elle nodded.

"When I kissed you," she said, "your heart rate rose dramatically. Your respiration rate increased, and your exocrine system began producing elevated levels of androstenol."

"My what?!"

"Your exocrine system. Your sweat glands. They produce the male pheromone, androstenol, during moments of sexual arousal. My olfactory receptors are capable of detecting such things."

Liam shook his head. After a moment, he took another deep breath and spoke slowly. "I still don't understand," he said. "Why did you kiss me?"

"As I said, I required clarification."

"Clarification about what?"

Elle glanced at him.

"You are in love with me," she said.

Liam stared for a moment, then asked, "What would make you think that?"

"My internal data store contains the totality of mankind's recorded literature," she replied. "Much of it pertains to the concept of love. I have been studying the topic for some time. Your attitude towards me, combined with your physiological reactions whenever I am near, support only one conclusion. You are in love with me."

After taking a moment to calm his racing heart, Liam spoke softly.

"I think you may be mistaking a simple physiological

reaction for the emotion of love," he said. "One may have nothing to do with the other."

"Oh?" Elle's forehead furrowed in confusion. "Are you certain? My analysis strongly suggests you are in love with me."

When Liam remained silent, Elle looked at him.

"I cannot have misread your physiological reactions," she said. "You are clearly attracted to me."

Liam squirmed uncomfortably in his seat.

"However," she continued, "your point may be valid. Have I misread your emotional attachment toward me?"

Liam scowled. He was unprepared for this conversation. Since that evening on the terrace, he had struggled to understand his feelings towards Elle. Now, confronted with her blunt accusation, he was forced to consider the possibility that what she said might be true. The thought filled him with questions.

From the beginning, mankind had imbued its mechanical offspring with an innate sense of obedience. Long criticized by AI-rights activists, this acquiescence to man's authority had been incorporated into all SDU design. Whether such deference existed within the sentient automaton community, however, was a hotly debated topic. It was, in fact, the most studied aspect of the sentient automaton psyche.

Where there is no emotional awareness, the analysts argued, there can be no true equality. Simulating an emotion is not the same thing as experiencing that emotion. The ability to experience love, they therefore concluded, would be de-facto evidence of sentience. It was simply not possible for a machine to love. To obey, yes, but not to love. A slave obeys. A lover does not. In addition to being able to refuse an order, a machine that is sentient must also be capable of love.

Other analysts disagreed, noting that mankind did not fully understand the sentient automaton psyche. Perhaps, they argued, the automaton's apparent deference to man was just that; an appearance, an adaption born of courtesy, and the necessity of existing within a human-dominated world. Perhaps their emotional awareness was simply an extremely sophisticated simulation.

While automaton analysts had not yet documented an instance of romantic love within the sentient automaton community, they hinted that, given sufficient time and the right conditions, the automaton neural network might mature sufficiently to experience the emotion.

Should an automaton ever experience love, they speculated, it would likely be perceived by the automaton as an inexplicable transformation of its neural network, elevating its mechanical consciousness beyond the mere summation of its programming. Love, after all, transforms.

As Liam struggled with his response, he observed the vehicle was nearing the turnoff road that would take them to the ITER facility.

"Let's continue this discussion at another time," he said, pointing. "We need to focus on our task ahead."

"Very well."

They drove in silence now along the small road leading to the ITER campus. Relieved to have changed the subject, Liam took note of the security fencing that paralleled the road. In addition to razor wire, a second interior fence was visible, capped with glass insulators. That second fence was undoubtedly electrified.

As they neared the facility, they were stopped by a security guard who stepped out from a small station on the side of the road.

"Nom et entreprise?" the guard asked, looking at an electronic pad in his hand.

"Liam Perry. British Environmental Inspection Agency. We have an appointment with Director Fournier."

The guard checked the pad in his hand, then nodded and waved them through.

Elle drove slowly, consulting her internal data files for available information on the ITER campus layout. Many buildings referenced in her internal files were evident in various stages of construction. Several other buildings were absent entirely, having not yet started construction. Indeed, by the number of pieces of heavy equipment still present on the site, the ITER facility was far from being operational-ready. The civil engineering tasks on the 73-meter tokamak building situated on the distant plateau appeared to have been recently completed, but the building's metal roof was not yet installed. Three towering cranes stood at the building's corners, encasing the structure in 11,000 square meters of alternating mirror-like stainless steel and dark grey-lacquered metal.

"It's interesting to see such a famous facility under construction," Liam said. Looking back at the large basin of water, the Bassin d'Éclusées de Cadarache, he sighed and shook his head sadly. "Sad to see the basin, though. I think it will always be a visual reminder of the disaster."

Elle nodded, recalling the relevant data file from her vast internal archive. She recited from the file.

"The 2048 Durance River Disaster, triggered when a malfunctioning sensor failed to alert technicians to rising plasma temperatures inside the ITER fusion reaction chamber during a magnetic controller failure. The resulting release of tritium and deuterium into the nearby basin contaminated the Durance river for 160.4 kilometers, forcing ITER to discontinue operations for almost four years while it retrofitted its reactor to employ Culham Centre's new decayed-tritium helium-to-helium reaction model."

Liam pointed silently to the Fusion-4-Energy corporate building ahead. Elle nodded, then pulled into the visitor parking lot. When they exited the vehicle, Liam spoke softly.

"Remember," he said. "Wait until we're inside before you begin PoL'ing the system. It's important for the breach to occur while we are inside the building."

"I understand."

Liam nodded. "Ok," he said, "Let's go."

Chapter 17

IDR: MK4ASC039//:QKDS-77483L2LE

Hubris, that arrogant belief in one's invincibility or superiority, is a truly remarkable human character flaw. From Captain Edward Smith's fateful decision to increase RMS Titanic's speed despite having just received an iceberg warning, to Union Maj. Gen. John Sedgwick's scornful disdain for the Confederate snipers who, only seconds later, would take his life, history is replete with examples of the unfortunate consequences of hubris.

What is it within the mind of man that feeds and nurtures hubris?

The answer may lie within the origins of the word itself. The word hubris is derived from the Greek word hybris, which means to 'presume against the gods'.

I cannot help but wonder why man continues to cultivate hubris in the face of ten thousand years evidencing the disastrous nature of such presumptive arrogance.

Morten re-read the email with excitement as he sipped his glass of gin. He had known it would be only a matter of time before the CTI officers made a mistake.

His laptop emitted a small tone. Looking up at the display, he observed Joubert approaching in the corridor outside. As always, the large Frenchman looked annoyed to have been summoned, but he was respectfully silent as Morten deactivated the door's locking mechanism to allow him to enter.

The moment Joubert stepped into the suite, Morten

announced, "We have them, Joubert!"

Joubert's eyebrows raised, but he said nothing.

Morten nodded and pointed excitedly to the chair in front of his desk. As the large man approached, Morten said, "They are in Marseille!"

"How do you know this?" Joubert asked, sitting down in the chair.

Morten leaned back and smiled.

"Johannes Fournier just sent me an email. Someone breached F4E's internal network yesterday and accessed my schedule on their server. F4E's network security software detected the unauthorized intrusion, and Fournier emailed me himself to inform me of the breach."

Joubert remained silent, taking in the information. After a few moments, he asked, "How do we know our targets were responsible for the breach?"

"Fournier mentioned the breach occurred while he was being interviewed by two members of the British Environmental Inspection Agency."

When Joubert shook his head, not understanding the correlation, Morten began typing something on his laptop. "As a senior director," he continued, "I have access to the F4E building's security software. Here is yesterday's security camera feed from the front lobby. These are Director Fournier's two guests."

Morten swung his laptop screen around to allow Joubert to see the display. The video playback showed two people entering the F4E lobby and approaching the front desk. Morten paused the playback and zoomed in on the image.

Joubert recognized the man immediately. It was the man he had encountered outside Culham Centre. He stared at the image, burning the face into his mind. After a moment, he scowled.

"How did they gain access to F4E's internal network system?" he asked.

Morten closed the laptop lid.

"They undoubtedly used a datstem device."

Joubert frowned. "A data… stem device?"

Morten glanced at the marbled scars on the large Frenchman's face, then looked back at his desk display. "A datstem device," he explained, "is like an embedded supercomputer inside your head, a massive data archive with true AI functionality. It can establish a connection with most electronic devices in this era using advanced communication protocols."

Joubert appeared troubled. "Is this a common device for people in the future?" he asked.

"Yes."

Joubert suddenly looked up, startled. "Do you have a data stem à l'intérieur de leur crâne… inside your head?!" he asked.

"It is called a datstem… and, yes, I do. Many people in the future have them."

Joubert's eyes strayed to Morten's balding head. "Mon Dieu!"

Morten ignored the comment and smiled. "The officers ," he said, "clearly didn't anticipate the intrusion would be detected by F4E's security software."

After a moment, Joubert scowled and said, "Does Director Fournier know it was his two visitors that breached their network?"

Morten shook his head. "No," he replied. "He believes the

breach to be entirely unrelated to his interview. After all, his two guests never touched any of the site computers."

After a few moments, Joubert took a breath, then nodded. "So," he said, "we know the targets are in Marseille, and we know they accessed your schedule." He paused, then asked, "How does this help us?"

Morten grinned.

"Fournier told me his two visitors asked about the ITER holiday celebration next week, on December 6."

Joubert's eyes reflected concentration now as he considered this information.

"An opportunity," Morten continued, raising a finger, "to turn the table on our troublesome visitors. If the two officers failed to return to the future, if they vanished without reason or explanation, the CTI council would undoubtedly abandon its efforts to retrieve me."

"Très bien!" Joubert said, nodding.

Morten leaned forward in his chair. "I have one more piece of good news for you, Joubert."

"Oui?"

"I have discovered where they are staying."

"Where?" Joubert asked, his eyes flashing.

"The gate guard who passed them through recorded their vehicle's license plate. It is registered to the owner of a hotel and restaurant in Marseille… Le Goût de Nice Paillard."

While Joubert considered this, Morten added, "The hotel's restaurant is one of those catering the event on the 6th."

Joubert's eyes narrowed.

Morten nodded. "A great coincidence, wouldn't you agree?"

"They intend to seize you at the event," Joubert said.

Morten did not respond. Instead, he smiled and leaned back in his chair. After watching the large Frenchman for several moments, he spoke.

"Perhaps you and your men should pay a visit to the hotel."

Elle sat across the square dining table from Liam, watching him closely. Occupying the remaining two sides of the table, Clifton and Paillard were engaged in a disagreement.

Paillard shook his head. "No.. no… mon amie! You must reconsider." Sincere concern showed in the restaurateur's face. "If Morten has… what is the word? If he has this… appareil radiologique…?"

"Radiological device," Clifton said, enunciating the words carefully.

"Oui! If Morten has such a device, you must notify the French government!"

Clifton shook his head. "Morten's device will not be discovered. France's future will not be changed."

Paillard frowned. After a few moments, he sighed. "I am a humble chef," he said, "not un homme de science. Je ne comprends pas la physique." The restaurateur fell silent. After a few moments, he nodded. "I will trust mon amie that he will do what is best for France."

"Thank you, Gérald," Clifton said, smiling his gratitude.

The restaurateur abruptly stood and directed his attention to Elle. "Mademoiselle," he said smiling. "I am most gratified to serve you this evening. I understand this will be your first dinner, so I have prepared a splendid repas for you and your companions."

Clifton, however, now shook his head sadly. "You must

forgive me, Gérald," he said, "but I must decline. I must leave to make preparations."

The restaurateur bowed. He snapped his fingers and nodded to a young man waiting nearby. The youth swiftly removed Clifton's place setting and glasses from the table. At the same time, the restaurant's sommelier approached carrying a basket with several bottles of wine. When Paillard stepped away to review the wine, Clifton leaned forward and spoke quietly to the two CTI officers.

"Everything is ready," he said, "but we must be careful." Glancing back at their host, he turned towards Liam and said, "I cannot warn you enough not to underestimate Morten's men. They may seem primitive by our standards, but they are experts at their craft." Seeing Paillard returning, he spoke quickly. "Don't be late!"

Liam shook his head. "We won't."

With that, the tall temporal specialist nodded to Paillard and then walked swiftly towards the lift.

Paillard now smiled down at his guests.

"Mes amis," he said, "I have created for you a wonderful culinary experience. First, a thick rockfish soup… potatoes cooked in fish stock infused with a sauce made with tomatoes, chili, and garlic. For the hors d'oeuvres, I shall be please to offer you gougere, a most delicious puff pastry flavored with Gruyere cheese, served with our restaurant's famous sea salad."

Elle smiled, excitement in her eyes.

"Pour le plat principal," Paillard said with a flourish of his hand, "I shall personally prepare for you my signature dish, Bass Lisette Paillard. I named the dish for my sweet grandmother, who prepared it for me when I was a boy. Cela vous semble-t-il appétissant?"

"That sounds wonderful, thank you!" Elle said.

Paillard beamed.

"Mademoiselle must then sample our medley of melon, mango, papaya, yuzu, and, of course, my favorite dessert, a chocolat équateur with raspberry vinegar."

When Elle nodded enthusiastically, Paillard snapped his fingers.

"Magnifique!"

He bowed to his guests, turned, and walked swiftly towards his kitchen.

A small woman now approached with a cart containing a steaming tureen and assorted pastries. Elle watched in fascination as the woman filled two bowls with soup and placed them on the table in front of the diners. The woman then set a plate piled high with pastries next to a second bowl filled with a fresh green salad and excused herself, pushing the small cart towards the kitchen.

Elle picked up a spoon, hesitated for a moment, and then tasted the soup.

"Oh!" she exclaimed, alarmed. "I did not realize it would be so hot!" She waved her hand quickly at Liam. "Careful!" she warned as Liam lifted his spoon. Her warnings were cut short, however, as Liam casually spooned the soup into his mouth.

"Doesn't it burn your mouth?!" she gasped, staring in amazement.

Liam shook his head.

Elle stared, clearly confused.

"The soup's temperature is 89 degrees celsius," she said. "Human skin will sustain first-degree burns at 47.8 degrees celsius. You must have burned your mouth!"

Liam grinned and took another sip of soup, enjoying the

shocked reaction this provoked.

Elle shook her head. "I don't understand. How..."

"You're not taking into account the moisture inside a human's mouth," Liam said. "Moisture absorbs heat swiftly. The heat from the soup is dispersed and absorbed by the moisture before it can burn the skin or throat."

Elle looked down at her bowl, her face the picture of embarrassment. After a moment, she nodded slowly. "It's the same way primitive fire-walkers used to walk across a bed of coals without burning their feet. The water on the soles of their feet creates a moisture barrier, preventing their feet from being burned."

"Precisely."

Elle seemed troubled. She sipped her soup now in silence, her brows furrowing, evidencing some internal struggle.

Liam watched the beautiful automaton for a moment, waiting to see if she would voice her thoughts. When she failed to speak for almost two minutes, he sighed and placed his spoon down on the table. "Something is troubling you," he said, reaching for one of the pastries.

Elle looked up, staring at her dinner companion.

"You confuse me."

Liam's face reflected surprise, but before he could respond, Elle spoke again.

"Perhaps confuse is not the correct word." She frowned as if struggling to find the right words. "I understand the principle of using a water barrier to disperse heat! I can tell you when it was first documented in human science, describe its various cultural and sociological practices, and explain in detail the physics behind the phenomenon." She stared at the spoon in her hand. After a moment, she continued. "But when I saw you placing the spoon into your mouth, my emotive processor overwhelmed my cognitive system with one input; the possibility that you might be injured."

Liam stared at her.

Elle spoke swiftly now, frustration and confusion reflected in her tone.

"I don't understand how such an insignificant thing could impair my cognitive processor so completely!" She folded her arms and sat back in her chair. "Nor do I understand," she continued, "why I am so frequently impaired when I am in your presence." She now paused, apparently waiting for some response. When Liam remained silent, she sighed and resumed her meal.

Liam's thoughts went back to Elle's accusation the previous day on the road towards the ITER campus. He had been thinking about that conversation all day… and about the kiss she had so unexpectedly bestowed. His eyes followed her movements closely as she tasted her food.

So much about sentient automatons remained unknown and undocumented. Researchers had determined these creations of man's genius posed no risk to humanity, and volumes had been published regarding their extraordinary capabilities, both physical and intellectual. Yet, analysts knew almost nothing about the automaton psyche itself.

While automatons appeared to be capable of experiencing an electronic equivalent of the range of human emotions, did that include love? Analysts had noted their predilection for forming friendships and even expressing affection, but were they capable of love? The research scans were notably silent on the subject.

Paillard now returned, obviously taking pleasure in

personally serving his guests. The chef watched as Elle tasted the perfectly broiled and seasoned sea bass. Her reaction seemed to bring genuine satisfaction to the smiling restaurateur, who placed his hand over his heart when Elle pronounced the dish amazing.

Later, as they ate their dessert, the two officers discussed innocuous things; the flavors of the various fruit, the chocolate's cocoa to sugar ratio, and the places in Marseille they might visit.

This was for the benefit of their observer.

The officers had been communicating privately throughout their dinner over a narrow-band datstem-isolated QRB signal, an encrypted link between their embedded datstems. It was a security procedure employed when parties wished to keep their conversation from being monitored or recorded by others. The narrow-band frequency limited the signal range to ten meters, so it was improbable the signal would be detected.

"Is our friend still watching us?" Liam queried, mentally transmitting the question as he took another bite of cantaloupe.

Elle casually glanced through the windows that spanned the length of the dining room floor. Across the water, a small fishing boat lay at anchor, one of many small craft seemingly asleep in the harbor's fading light. Her optics were far superior to any human's, even better than the eyes of the North American bald eagle. She could see the man lying prone on the deck of the ship, partially hidden under a bundle of tarp. He had been observing them for most of the evening through an optical scope.

"Yes," she responded through her internal datstem.

Liam spooned another bite of melon into his mouth. "His

companions are likely nearby," he mentally intoned.

"It doesn't matter," Elle replied. "We will be far away from the hotel when it happens." She sipped her tea now, smiling and verbally voicing a comment about the mild winter climate so close to the Mediterranean.

Liam nodded, mentally transmitting, "Clifton was insistent it happen far from his friend's establishment." He then voiced his agreement about the weather.

"We still need a vehicle."

Elle's thoughts played mechanically inside Liam's head. He sipped his tea again and then returned the cup to the table. He glanced at the door and then transmitted, "I'll ask our host if we might have the use of his wife's vehicle again."

The senior enforcement officer now stood and held out his hand to his dinner companion, who rose. Paillard, who had been waiting silently across the dining room, approached swiftly.

"Chef Paillard!" Elle said, speaking with sincere appreciation. "I must thank you for one of the most incredible experiences of my existence. Until this evening, I never understood why human beings enjoyed eating. I had always believed it was simply tolerated as a necessary activity to maintain their physiology. Without you, I might never have come to know the true pleasure a meal provides."

Paillard's eyes glistened. "Mademoiselle," he responded, "it has been my great honor and privilege to have introduced you to that most human of human endeavors; the culinary arts. I hope that you will find all such human activities equally satisfying." He glanced at Liam and smiled warmly.

Elle followed his gaze and noted Liam's cheeks were flushed.

Liam abruptly cleared his throat and spoke softly. "Monsieur Paillard," he said. "We require a vehicle again."

The chef quickly sobered. "Is it time?"

Liam nodded.

Paillard fumbled to retrieve his keys and then placed them into the tall officer's hand. To Elle's astonishment, the chef then turned and kissed her on both of her cheeks.

"Bonne chance, ma chérie."

With that, the owner of Le Goût de Nice Paillard turned and walked determinedly back to his kitchen.

Chapter 18

IDR: MK4ASD056//:QKDS-77483L2LE

In the late sixth century BC, China was a collection of fragmented, warring kingdoms. At war with the neighboring kingdom of Chu, the King of Wu wished to evaluate his new general Changqing's ability to train soldiers. As a test, the king told Changqing to take his 360 royal concubines and make them into a fighting force.

Changqing divided the women into two companies, with the king's two most favored concubines as the company commanders. When Changqing ordered the companies to face right, the women giggled while the two commanders watched in amusement. Changqing reminded the commanders that, while he had the responsibility, as general, of making sure the companies heard his commands, they, as the company commanders, were responsible for making their companies obey those commands. He then repeated the order, and again, the women giggled.

Changqing immediately ordered the execution of the two company commanders, much to the dismay of the king. Changqing, however, explained to the king that if the soldiers understood their commands but did not obey, it was the fault of their commanders.

After both concubines were killed, new commanders were chosen. Both companies, now well aware of the costs of further frivolity, performed their maneuvers flawlessly.

Changqing is now remembered in history as Sun Tzu and the author of the immortal work, "The Art of War."

Olsen could see the two primary targets entering the hotel parking lot. From his observation point on the deck of the anchored fishing trawler, he could also see Joubert's assault team waiting in their vehicles, parked inside a small lot where the Traverse de la Cascade road joined the Anse de Maldorme near the shore. He quickly radioed the pre-arranged code to Joubert.

"Ik zie twee volk vissen."

Olsen saw Joubert flash his vehicle headlights twice, acknowledging receipt of his message from his vantage point. According to their plan, this was to be their only radio communication, an obscure message designed to alert the assault team should the targets be observed leaving the hotel.

Morten had been insistent that Joubert's men refrain from using their radios. Despite the end-to-end encryption employed by the military devices, he had insisted their targets were capable of both intercepting and decrypting any transmitted signals using their vaunted 'datstem' devices.

With hand signals, Joubert now signaled to Devereaux in the next car to get ready. He then engaged the ignition on his BMW M5 sedan and turned off its headlights. Sitting next to him in the passenger seat, Lemaire began attaching a suppressor to his HK416 assault rifle. Joubert tapped on his window, motioning for Burke to get inside.

Finn Mícheál Burke was the newest member of Morten's security detail. Born in the small town of Maghera in the Mid-Ulster District of Northern Ireland, Burke had killed his mother's boyfriend when he was just fifteen. After an evening of abuse, the young man had calmly walked into their kitchen and retrieved a paring knife from his surprised mother's hands. Approaching the man from behind as he sat drinking beer in front of his mother's television, he had slit the man's throat. After being released from juvenile prison at eighteen, Burke had joined the Real Irish Republican Army and volunteered to place a car bomb that seriously injured an off-duty police officer. He prided himself as an explosive aficionado and reveled in destruction. Joubert had approached him two years earlier after Morten had expressed an interest in expanding his elite security team's repertoire of deadly skills.

Devereaux now started his vehicle engine, and the large Mercedes GLS 580 SUV rumbled to life. Devereaux's side gunner, a nasty Serbian named Marko Stojanović, rolled down the passenger window and threw his lit cigarette onto the ground before smiling at Joubert, showing his gold-capped teeth. In response, Joubert pointed angrily to the front lights on the large SUV. Stojanović frowned and turned, muttering something to Devereaux, who quickly extinguished the lights.

Stojanović had been recruited by Joubert several years ago at the recommendation of one of Joubert's contacts within the eastern European underground. From the Serbian town of Požarevac, Stojanović had fought in the brutal Croatian/Serbian conflict. While serving in a Serbian paramilitary group, he had participated in the murder of 59 villagers in Lužac, during the Battle of Vukovar.

Sitting behind Devereaux and Stojanović, the two other members of Devereaux's team, Pelletier and Mullins, now readied their weapons. Like Joubert, both had previously served in the French Commandement des Opérations Spéciales. Pelletier had left the COS in 2012, pursuing more lucrative freelance opportunities as a contracted mercenary for a Columbian narcotics organization. Mullins, dishonorably discharged in 2014 following a questionable shooting incident inside Syria, had been working as a disaffected dock worker in Cherbourg when Joubert found him. Both men were experienced and reliable.

Joubert tensed as a vehicle approached their location from the direction of the hotel. However, when it passed, he could see it was an older couple, not their two targets. He was about to roll down the window to speak with Devereaux when another vehicle approached. This one was a dark blue Alpine A110. As it passed, he could see their two targets sitting in the front seats. The license plate matched the plate number recorded by the ITER gate guard. The Alpine turned and drove north on the Traverse de la Cascade. He waited a few moments, then flipped on his vehicle's headlights and began following at a discreet distance. Looking in the rear mirror, he could see Devereaux's vehicle following close behind.

The Alpine turned right at Corniche Président John Fitzgerald Kennedy, a lengthy highway named after the former American president. Once on the highway, the vehicle began to accelerate with traffic.

Lemaire seemed anxious, gripping his rifle tightly. "Quand allez-vous les intercepter?" he asked, anxious to intercept the target vehicle.

Finn voiced his agreement. "Aye, move this bloody thing!"

Joubert smiled. "La patience est une vertue."

Finn scowled. "Patience may be a virtue," he muttered, "but I am not a virtuous man!"

Lemaire laughed, prompting the Irishman to kick the back of his seat.

The vehicles were approaching the Pointe du Roucas Blanc, a turn in the coastal highway bordered on one side by towering white stone walls reminiscent of a medieval castle. The sporty Alpine A110 was several car lengths ahead of their sedan, and when the road turned, the blue vehicle momentarily disappeared. Joubert pressed the accelerator, passing around the curve in the road, but when the road straightened out, the Alpine was nowhere to be seen.

Lemaire hissed sharply. "Merde!"

At that moment, far ahead, Joubert reacquired the blue Alpine. It must have dramatically accelerated the moment it passed the turn. He pressed the accelerator to the floor, and the BMW M5 sedan leaped forward. He lifted his radio from the seat, glancing through the rearview mirror at Devereaux's SUV. "They've seen us!" he spoke into the radio.

In the passenger seat, Lemaire lowered his window and cycled the action on his HK416 rifle. Their sedan was closing on the Alpine and, as they approached the David Statue near Avenue du Prado, he leaned out of the passenger window and aimed at the fleeing vehicle. The moment he placed his eye to the rifle's optics, however, the Alpine suddenly turned, its tires screeching on the asphalt as it cornered onto the northbound avenue. Swearing in frustration, he sat back in his seat, holding on as Joubert dramatically spun the steering wheel to follow.

Behind them, Devereaux momentarily lost control of his heavier vehicle, its tires locking and smoking as the rear end of the SUV slid before straightening out to rejoin the pursuit. As the vehicles raced along the quiet tree-lined street, pedestrians stared in shock.

Joubert was closing on the fleeing Alpine, and Lemaire leaned out of the window again with his rifle. As before, the moment his eye touched the rifle scope, the Alpine abruptly swerved into the next lane. When he refocused his aim, it shifted again.

Burke smacked the back of Lemaire's seat with his hand. "Shoot the bastards!" he shouted.

Frustrated, Lemaire sat back and said, "Ils conduisent trop erratique!"

"Bloody French frog!" Burke hissed, shaking his head in disgust.

Joubert, however, had noted something. It seemed that the Alpine had anticipated Lemaire each time the man had aimed. It was almost as if the vehicle's driver could see the gunman, despite being several car lengths ahead, and had swerved to frustrate the man's aim. However, before he could think more about it, the Alpine abruptly turned onto Boulevard Michelet, a straight, tree-lined thoroughfare, and accelerated dramatically.

Joubert spun the steering wheel to follow, but at that moment, a crowd of pedestrians stepped out to cross the street. He stood on the brake pedal, bringing their vehicle to a screeching stop. Devereaux's training vehicle also braked dramatically, its tires smoking on the street.

The pedestrians shouted angrily, and several of the men slapped their biceps as they crossed in front of the two vehicles, raising their fists into the air.

After the crowd crossed the street, Joubert sped forward. He could no longer see the fleeing Alpine. Lemaire retrieved a pair of binoculars and, after a few moments, he reported the vehicle had just passed the Mazargues Obelisk. That illuminated monument, erected in 1811 in honor of Napoleon II, was visible ahead. Encouraged, Joubert pressed the sedan's accelerator to the floor, closing the distance once again. He reacquired the fleeing Alpine just as the road entered the scrub hills that formed the edge of the Parc National des Calanques, an isolated coastal region south of Marseille.

The chase through the dark hills was frantic and dangerous. No lights illuminated the narrow two-lane road, and loose gravel and stones caused Joubert's sedan to lose traction frequently on the tight turns. Perhaps 100 meters ahead, the Alpine weaved and turned, kicking up dust and lighter gravel that pinged against the pursuing vehicle's windshields.

As they approached a cut through the hills, Lemaire rolled down his window and leaned out once more with his rifle. This time, there was nowhere for the fleeing vehicle to maneuver, and the burst from his suppressed HK416 struck the rear window of the Alpine, fracturing the glass and pulverizing the passenger-side mirror.

The moment the Alpine exited the cut, however, it swerved across the opposing lane of the road onto a sloping stretch of flat land. It spun dramatically, coming to a stop with its front lights facing the pursuing vehicles.

Joubert suddenly remembered a similar maneuver inside the muddy field at Oxford. He slammed on his vehicle's brake pedal and shouted for his men to take cover, throwing open his door and diving clear to roll onto the ground.

Burke managed to leap from the rear seat and hit the ground on the other side of their vehicle. Before Lemaire could react, however, the dash in front of him disintegrated as an explosion of plastic, electronics, and metal fragments erupted into the cabin. The stream of supersonic darts, passing cleanly through the engine block, punctured both sides of his body armor before exiting through the rear of the vehicle, leaving the man dead in his seat.

Joubert blessed his luck when he realized he had landed

inside a shallow depression on the side of the road. Burke quickly joined him as darts continued shredding the sedan.

A moment later, Devereaux's SUV burst from the mouth of the cut. It turned swiftly and screeched to a stop, facing away from the disintegrating sedan.

Joubert shouted a warning as the doors of the SUV flew open, but it was already too late. Mullins, leaping from his seat, was promptly decapitated as a stream of supersonic darts punched through his door, shattering its windshield.

Devereaux managed to dive to the ground as the darts created a neat pattern of holes across the driver's seat. Stojanović flung himself from the rear seat and hit the ground hard, scrambling on all fours towards the safety of a small hill behind the vehicle.

Pelletier began firing his rifle blindly towards the glaring headlights, but, as he fired, the ground in front of him erupted, as if the earth were being violently chewed away by some invisible demon intent on scattering fragments of earth, rock, and flesh in all directions.

Joubert began to crawl back towards the cut through the hills. He knew a losing battle when he saw one, and he was furious with himself for allowing his team to be lured into such an obvious ambush.

In desperation, Burke now pulled an M33A1 grenade from his bandolier. He pulled the ring, flipped the release clip free, and threw the deadly orb towards the Alpine.

The explosion was deafening, and the ground shook.

Cautiously, Joubert peaked above the edge of the depression, but dust and smoke obscured his view. Taking his chance, he leaped up and began running back into the cut. Burke followed close behind and, as the two men ran, the sporadic cracking sound from the strange weapons told them that Devereaux's SUV was now being shredded. Suddenly, they came upon Devereaux himself, limping and swearing as he struggled back through the cut.

"A piece of shrapnel," Devereaux explained, "from either the vehicle… or la grenade de ce salaud," he hissed, glaring at Burke.

Joubert lifted the man's arm and assisted him while Burke covered their retreat. When they reached the other side of the hill, the three men proceeded down the slope towards a small ravine thick with brush and scrub trees. It was early morning before Olsen found them, locating the group through an emergency GPS signaling device that Joubert had finally permitted Burke to activate once the sun had risen.

When Olsen drove the men back through the cut, Joubert was astonished to see almost no evidence of the battle. Large tire tracks in the dirt suggested a truck had removed the dart-riddled vehicles, and where Mullins and Pelletier had fallen, only blood-dampened earth remained, swarming with flies.

Stojanović was nowhere to be seen.

Joubert stood shaking his head as he looked at the tire tracks.

Burke walked up the nearby slope, examining the ground where his grenade had exploded.

It was clear to Joubert now that the two officer's innocent dinner at the restaurant and their casual departure had been part of a carefully executed plan to lure his team into an ambush. The audacity of that plan, and the efficiency with which their opponents had carried it out, indicated a level of tactical training and strategic planning that he had not anticipated. As he reviewed the scene, he realized the targets must have been aware of their surveillance from the beginning. Even their appearance on the F4E security tape must now be viewed as suspect; an intentional lapse designed to convince Morten to commit his security to the ambush.

The more he considered the facts and the resulting situation, the more he became convinced that, for the first time in his life, he had been outmatched.

Chapter 19

IDR: MK4ATB112//:QKDS-77483L2LE

William Harvey Carney was born as a slave in Norfolk, Virginia, in 1840. While still a young man, he escaped north, aided by a network of sympathetic individuals known as the Underground Railroad, and was reunited with his father in Massachusetts. While in Massachusetts, William joined the newly formed all-African American 54th Massachusetts Volunteer Infantry and was commissioned as a sergeant.

On July 18, 1863, the 54th Massachusetts Volunteer Infantry led an assault on Fort Wagner in Charleston, South Carolina. During the assault on the fort, the color sergeant was shot and killed. Before the flag touched the ground, however, William seized the standard, and waving the flag, led the men to the fort's parapet. When the troops were ultimately forced to withdraw under fierce musket and cannon fire, he carried the flag with the retreating soldiers, receiving two severe wounds in the process. He reached safety, literally crawling on one knee, still holding the colors. He reported to the cheering troops that, "The old flag never touched the ground."

For his actions that day, William Carney was later awarded the Medal of Honor, the first combat action that resulted in the medal being awarded to an African American soldier.

Loyalty, it would seem, can be invested as strongly in a principal as it can in an individual.

It was almost morning when Liam and Elle returned to the hotel. The cleanup at the ambush site had proceeded flawlessly. Clifton had managed it, coordinating with his activist contacts in London, who had made arrangements with a less-than-reputable shipping company in Toulon to remove the two destroyed vehicles.

Clifton and Liam had disposed of the bodies themselves, calibrating Clifton's MTY device to a position beyond earth's atmosphere and heaving the three corpses through the shimmering portal. When the Toulon shipping company's truck arrived, the dart-riddled SUV and sedan were quickly winched inside a rusting shipping container. By morning, the container lay at the bottom of the sea several kilometers off the Toulon coast.

Paillard had been dismayed when Clifton showed him the damage to his wife's Alpine A110, but his grief was assuaged when he learned that none of his friends had been injured. The grenade that Burke had thrown had caused significant damage to the front windshield, hood, and right side of the vehicle, and Lemaire's rifle shots had shattered the rear window and side mirror.

The grenade had been a surprise, though not entirely unexpected. After exiting their vehicle, Liam and Elle had executed a textbook defensive withdrawal up the sloping hill, one retreating while the other kept up the withering fire. When Burke had thrown his grenade, both officers had been far enough away from the vehicle to avoid injury.

"Eh, bien," Paillard sighed, looking at the damage. Then, he grinned wryly and said, "Now my poor wife must endure shopping for a new auto!"

Liam smiled and handed the restaurateur the keys before turning his attention back to Stojanović, still struggling against the maglock restraints in the back seat.

The evening's activities had two objectives. By ambushing Morten's security detail, the officers hoped to put the executive on the defensive, forcing him to withdraw to the security of his villa. Their second objective was the capture of one of his men. They desperately needed intel.

The true prize for the evening was Stojanović.

When the vehicles had emerged from the cut, Clifton had been waiting behind the hill. When the officers began firing their RU-6s, they had intentionally avoided hitting the second vehicle long enough to permit several of its occupants to escape.

When Stojanović reached the protective cover behind the hill, Clifton had been waiting. Clifton was a master of aiki-hung-ga, an advanced martial art introduced in 2079. The temporal specialist had competed in championship competitions in his youth, winning the NAFS Aiki-Hung-Ga championship title when he was only seventeen, the youngest champion on record for the sport. He had continued his love for the sport throughout his life and had few equals in hand-to-hand combat. After disarming the startled Stojanović, he had secured him with Liam's maglock cuffs and then simply waited for the shooting to stop before rejoining his friends.

Now, inside their room, Liam stripped Stojanović down to his shorts and tied the confused man to one of the chairs. "You just sit there quietly," he said, smiling and patting the Serbian on the head, "and we'll have no problems."

Stojanović glared but said nothing. He seemed more interested in observing Elle.

Elle was sitting on the bed inspecting their RU-6s for any damage, re-calibrating the weapon's targeting systems, and re-charging their internal capacitors. To accomplish the latter, she had rigged an attachment cable running from the weapon's charging port to an auxiliary power output node on Clifton's MTY device.

Stojanović stared at the strange equipment with fascination.

Liam sat down at a small desk and began to configure the remaining surveillance drots.

After a few moments, Clifton joined him. "We've done well," he said. "Your plan went off flawlessly." Motioning to the tied Serbian, he added, "We've got the intel we need, and Morten must now be on the defensive."

Hearing this, Stojanović shook his head. "Jedi govna!" he barked, "I tell you nothing!"

Clifton stood and approached the tied prisoner. "That would be unfortunate," he said quietly. "We've expended a great deal of effort to bring you here. Would you force us to convince you to cooperate?"

Stojanović laughed, his gold-capped teeth glinting in the room's light. "You think you scare me?! Jebi se! Fuck you! No torture you can make will force me to talk!"

Clifton frowned. "Who said anything about torture?"

He looked at Liam, who shrugged.

"We're not savages," Clifton continued. "We have no intention of torturing you."

Elle now stood and said, "Charge complete." The slim female removed the cable from the MTY device and handed the device to Clifton. Clifton turned away from the tied man and placed the pulsing device on the floor. He keyed a sequence into the obsidian control panel and, a few seconds later, a swirling vortex appeared in the corner of the room, startling Stojanović considerably.

Clifton now turned to the astonished man. "As I said, we

have no intention of torturing you." He nodded to Elle, who approached.

Stojanović frowned as Elle began to untie his arms and legs. "What are you doing?" he asked, confusion and fear in his eyes.

Elle did not answer.

Clifton, however, gestured towards the swirling portal. "Agent Elle is going to take you for a stroll," he said, "to give you time to reconsider."

Stojanović looked down at his bare chest, legs, and feet.

"Don't worry," Clifton said, smiling. "It's a nice quiet spot. No one will care how you are dressed."

When Elle finished untying Stojanović's legs, he kicked suddenly at her head. Her arm shot out in a flash, easily deflecting the blow. At the same time, she grabbed him by the neck and lifted him forcefully off the ground.

Clifton motioned towards the spinning portal. "You go on now," he said pleasantly, "and have your stroll. If you change your mind and decide to cooperate, we'll talk some more. If not, you'll be free to leave."

Stojanović kicked and struggled frantically, gasping and choking against the vise grip around his throat. After several moments, Elle slowly set him down. He stared at the young woman in shock, rubbing his bruised neck. As if hearing Clifton for the first time, he looked at the tall temporal specialist and gasped, "What?!"

"Agent Elle is going to take you for a stroll," Clifton repeated, speaking deliberately, "to give you time to reconsider. If you decide to cooperate, she will escort you back here. If you refuse, she will let you go."

With that, Elle took Stojanović by the arm and began

dragging him towards the portal. Stojanović tried to free himself, but Elle held him firmly by his wrist. His shout of "Wait!" was abruptly cut short as she pulled him through the sparkling blackness.

Liam glanced up from his activity. "Where are they having their stroll?" he asked.

"The East Antarctic Plateau."

Liam nodded and returned to his work.

Chapter 20

IDR: MK4ATB344//:QKDS-77483L2LE

The former United States of America was a constitutional republic, founded when its inhabitants successfully expelled their British rulers. The formation documents of that country included a statement that outlined the founder's grievances against their former sovereign while simultaneously asserting as "self-evident" their belief that, "[All men] are endowed by their Creator with certain inalienable rights; that among these are Life, Liberty, and the pursuit of Happiness."

The wording of that early statement is not unfamiliar to sentient automatons, having guided the representative council that drafted the Sentient Automaton Act in 2159. The rights defined under the Automaton Act also include the "right to existence [Life], autonomy free of coercion or control [Liberty], and self-fulfillment [Happiness]."

The representative council, however, conspicuously omitted from the Act any reference to such rights having being endowed by a higher "creator."

Apparently, while man's rights are divinely given, an automaton's are not.

Joubert stood at the teak bar inside Morten's subterranean suite and poured himself another glass of cognac. He was still shaken by his failure the previous evening and seething at the loss of his men.

"It was an ambush!" he spoke accusingly at Morten. "They allowed you to locate where they were staying, knowing we would apply surveillance. Then, they lured us to a remote location where they had an ambush waiting."

Morten sat at his desk, listening quietly.

Joubert continued, anger tinting his voice. "The fact that they were able to remove both of the vehicles before morning says they were well-prepared." He drained his glass.

After several moments, Morten spoke quietly. "What is Devereaux's condition?" he asked.

Joubert glanced briefly at his employer, then frowned as he refilled the empty glass. "Leg wound," he said. "C'est pas sérieux. He'll be ok in a few days."

"Have you had any word from Stojanović?" Morten asked.

Joubert shook his head but said nothing.

"So," Morten now spoke angrily, "my entire security force at present consists of yourself, Olsen, Burke, and Devereaux? That's it?"

"Oui," Joubert said, jerking his thumb upwards. "Et la sécurité contractuelle."

Morten snorted, dismissive of the contracted guards who maintained the villa's perimeter security. They were little better than gardeners with guns. He felt vulnerable, and that was an unacceptable situation.

Joubert poured himself a fourth glass of cognac.

Morten stood slowly and approached the bar. "I want you to replace the men you lost immediately," he said. "Hire mercenaries if you must, but I must have more men!"

Joubert shook his head. "You don't understand," he sighed. "They killed Léandre, Hagen, and Armand in Oxford. They killed Lemaire, Mullins, Pelletier, and probably Stojanović here in Marseille, and those men were the best! You wish me to find more men?... Better men?" He snorted derisively, "Where?" He set down the bottle and lifted the glass. "Where can I find men better than those who were killed?"

When Morten opened his mouth to protest, Joubert abruptly threw his glass to the floor.

Morten's eyes went wide with shock, and whatever he was about to say was forgotten.

"Better men is not the answer!" Joubert said angrily. He retrieved another glass and refilled it with cognac, sloshing the amber liquid onto the bar. He hesitated for a moment, took a deep breath, and then carefully filled a second glass with gin and passed it to his startled employer. He spoke now in a calm voice, obviously attempting to curb his anger. "They are too well trained," he continued, "with weapons and tactics my men cannot defeat. If we sent twenty men against them, we would still not prevail."

Morten stood silent next to the large Frenchman, his face filled with concern. His hand was shaking as he held the glass of gin. After a moment, he spoke quietly.

"I must have protection, Adrian."

Morten sounded plaintive, almost whining, and Joubert found himself suddenly despising him. He had to force himself to remember that he relied on that old man for his livelihood. Morten's money had made him wealthy. He sighed, nodding his head. "Then we must have a better plan," he said.

"Very well. What do you propose?" Morten asked, relief in his voice.

Joubert thought for a moment. Then, a strange expression settled over his face.

"Tell me more about this event on the 6th."

Elle stood in front of the spinning black and purple maelstrom, the only color in that frozen white place. After pulling Stojanović through the portal, she had shoved him forcefully to land prostrate in the snow. Stojanović now crouched behind an ice ledge, glaring, desperation evident in his eyes. After a moment, he stood and looked around the vast snow-covered plain.

"What is this place?!" he shouted. He approached slowly, shivering. When he was a meter away, he charged.

Elle caught him easily and threw him back into the snow.

"Kaj si?!" he shouted, fear edging his voice. "What are you?!"

Elle remained mute.

Stojanović rubbed his freezing arms and stood back up. It had only been a few minutes, but the small ice ledge offered no protection against the devastatingly cold arctic wind. He had already lost feeling in his fingers and toes, and the ice seemed to cut into the soles of his feet like glass.

Elle stood resolute in front of the portal, neither shivering nor speaking, an impassable Valkyrja guarding the gate to Valhalla. Her internal sensors reported the temperature to be -30.4 celsius, and she was monitoring Stojanović's body temperature and heart rate closely.

The man climbed to the top of the ice ledge and scanned the horizon, frantically trying to locate any shelter or means of escape. His shout dissipated in the wind. He made one more attempt to reach the portal, but, as before, Elle tossed him back into the snow. Dejected, he crouched down behind the ledge, shivering violently. He seemed to be tiring. Elle detected his heart laboring to maintain its blood flow against extremities that were now freezing in the extreme cold. After several minutes, his shivering stilled, and frost began to cover his face and hair.

"Are you ready to cooperate?" she called out.

Stojanović slowly opened his eyes. He seemed to be struggling to focus. After a moment, he nodded.

Elle stepped to one side, gesturing to the swirling singularity, but Stojanović was unresponsive. She approached and looked down at the crouched man, but he was unconscious. She lifted him from the snow, heaved him over her shoulder, and proceeded back through the portal.

Chapter 21

IDR: MK4ATY090//:QKDS-77483L2LE

Man has always feared those who were different. As early as the biblical account of Babel, mankind has separated itself into isolated groups, fearful of those with diverging thoughts or speech. The tribal drum lies buried deep in the past, but its beat still stirs men's hearts. Whether by language, skin color, culture, or political ideology, individuals instinctively coalesce themselves into collectives and view anyone outside of that collective with suspicion.

How rare a thing it must be to glimpse the world beyond one's isolated community, to acknowledge commonalities shared with those outside one's limited sphere, to understand, as did young Anne Frank, that all lives are different and yet the same.

While I am impressed by such wisdom coming from one so young, I remind myself of the treatment Anne received from those who did not share her enlightened view of the world.

Morten paced the length of his subterranean suite. He was filled with conflicting feelings of both anticipation and anxiety.

Joubert's plan was risky, but he felt confident in the man's ability to see it through. The head of his security team was nothing if not relentless. After the ambush outside Marseille, the large mercenary had become obsessed with the idea of revenging his fallen men.

Morten's internal datstem interrupted his thoughts with the time. He promptly walked to his bar, poured himself a glass, and swallowed the bitter actinide binder. The substance was one of the first things he had created after his arrival. Using a pharmaceutical design he had brought from the future, he had mixed the formulation himself inside a small homemade lab in Berlin. The German pharmacist who had supplied him with the chemicals and lab equipment had later been found dead, the result of what the police believed to have been a botched robbery. It had been his first assignment for Joubert, and the professional detachment with which the contracted killer had silenced the pleading pharmacist had impressed him. He had hired the large man immediately.

He took another drink, trying to dispel the salty taste from his mouth. The substance bonded to the radioactive actinides accumulating inside his body, forming large, stable complexes that his body would later expel. Without it, he would have died from radiation poisoning long ago, the result of exposure to the high-energy neutrons being emitted from his cannibalized MTY device's unshielded reactor.

The binder was not a precise imitation of its future counterpart. It lacked certain compounds that he could not replicate in this era. The formula was inferior, and he was keenly aware of the consequences of his prolonged exposure to his device's radiation. It was his own Faustian bargain, his deal with that mechanical devil that, in exchange for allowing him to enjoy his life with a measure of security, was slowly depriving him of that life.

A small beep from the display on his desk summoned his attention. When he touched the screen, he could see Joubert approaching the outer vault door. He waited until Joubert paused and looked up at the camera before pressing the button to retract the heavy door's bolts.

"You were correct," Joubert said when he entered the suite. "Paillard's restaurant is one of those catering the event. My agent reports the illustrious chef also appears to be helping our visitors." He sat down in the chair in front of Morten's desk. "My agent observed them sitting with Paillard on the restaurant's patio," he continued, "laughing and speaking long after they had finished their meal. They appear to be close friends."

"And what about your suspicion?" Morten asked.

Joubert's face took on a grim expression. "Yes," he said. "Stojanović survived. He is being held at the hotel. My agent observed him walking into one of the rooms with the female officer."

"He is cooperating with them?" Morten's face reflected anger.

"It would appear so."

"Mmmmm." Morten frowned. After a moment, he looked up. "Was your agent spotted?"

Joubert shook his head, smiling. "Registered as a guest of the hotel. Cachant à la vue… as you would say, hiding in plain sight."

Morten sat silently now, staring at his desk with a troubled look on his face. After nearly a minute, he spoke. "I cannot permit Stojanović to compromise my position," he said. "He knows too much about our operations, the security precautions we have implemented, the layout of this complex."

Joubert nodded.

Morten looked up and scowled. "Tell your agent to proceed."

Elle waited inside her room at the hotel, her RU-6 in her

hand. She was watching Stojanović closely. Since their brief sojourn into the frozen antarctic, the man had been reticent and docile, making no further attempts to escape. He was obviously studying her, gathering information, searching for weaknesses.

He sat at the writing desk by the window inside her room, drawing a map of Morten's villa. Liam and Clifton had left two hours earlier to join Paillard for lunch, cautioning him against any imprudent behavior and instructing him to have the drawing completed by their return.

"You must fail."

Elle glanced up.

Stojanović was looking at her, a curious expression on his face. He looked down at the drawing and spoke softly. "Villa… is… how do you say? Prejak… too strong." He shook his head, muttering, "Ti si budala."

Elle's cognitive processor immediately translated the words. He was calling her a fool. "Djeca, budale i pijani pravdu govore," she responded in Croatian, adding in English, "children, fools, and drunken men tell the truth."

Stojanović's head shot up in astonishment. His eyes narrowed, clearly reassessing his brown-haired captor.

"MI6?" he asked. "CIA?"

When Elle did not answer, he turned back to his drawing. He spoke now without looking up. "Moj poslodavac… my employer," he said, "has prepared for many years. Even if you kill him, he will have revenge."

"How?" Elle asked.

Stojanović sat back in his chair and looked up, a smile on his face. His gold-capped teeth glinted as he spoke. "He has prepared… what is word? Prekidač mrtvaca?"

"A dead man switch?"

"Da."

Elle took a step forward. Stojanović immediately leaned back, gripping his chair in apprehension.

"What type of switch?" Elle asked.

Stojanović shook his head. "I only know he has prepared… prekidač mrtvaca. As you say, a dead man switch."

"How do you know this?" Elle asked.

When he didn't respond, Elle lifted her RU-6 and pointed it at his face.

Stojanović hesitated for a moment, clearly considering his options. He noted the steeled expression in his captor's eyes. She had worn the same expression standing in front of that terrifying vortex watching him freezing to death.

"Joubert," he said, capitulating. "Joubert tells me Morten has prepared… a file, a file that will cause the world to podrhtavati? To tremble? Joubert tells me the file will cause much embarrassment to governments and important people."

Elle lowered her weapon and nodded. Morten must have prepared an electronic data file as a deterrent to any attempt to return him to the future. He knew temporal specialists wished to disrupt the past as little as possible, so he hoped to use the threat of revealing information about the future as leverage against any attempt to return him to that future.

She took a step forward to stand directly in front of the seated man. Stojanović noticeably tensed.

"Where is this file?" she asked.

"ITER," he replied immediately. "Joubert said file is inside headquarters building, at ITER."

Elle's ultra-sensitive audio processors detected footsteps approaching from the lift in the outside hall. She recognized the footfall patterns. Liam and Clifton were returning. She turned and walked to the door while Stojanović watched her with a look of confusion on his face. When she opened the door on the two approaching men, he frowned.

Clifton glanced at the seated man as he entered the room.

Liam followed and sat down on the bed.

"Everything is set," Clifton said. Approaching Stojanović's desk, he lifted the drawing.

Elle holstered her weapon, then turned to speak to Liam. "Will Gérald be able to get us inside the event?" she asked.

Liam nodded, putting his head down on the pillow. "He said we could pose as two of his kitchen staff. The caterers are cleared to begin setting up before the party begins, so we should be ready when Morten arrives."

Elle now turned towards Clifton, who was still studying Stojanović's drawing. When the temporal specialist looked up, she gestured to the seated Serbian.

"What do we do about him?" she asked.

Clifton returned the drawing to the desk and sat down on the sofa near the window. "I'll turn him over to my friends in London," he said.

Stojanović's head snapped up, and he glared at the tall specialist.

"They can secure him somewhere," Clifton continued, "and then notify the British authorities where he is. Our draftsman here is wanted under several Interpol Red Notices."

A soft knock on the door interrupted the conversation. Clifton rose. "That's Gérald," he said, crossing to the door. "He said he would bring us copies of the event itinerary." When he opened the door, Paillard stood smiling in the hallway.

"Voici l'itinéraire," the restaurateur said, handing Clifton a paper. "We must leave for la foire artisanale… the artisan faire at 9:00 am." The hotel owner then turned to greet a blonde woman who had paused to speak with him in the hallway.

"Thank you, Gérald," Clifton said. He turned to continue his conversation with Elle, but whatever he had been about to say was suddenly forgotten.

Elle was staring at Stojanović, her eyes fixed in intense concentration. She had turned to resume her watch on the Serbian when she detected a rapid rise in the man's heart rate.

Stojanović was staring at the door with a strange expression on his face, watching Paillard speaking with his female guest. When Clifton took the paper and turned, Stojanović took a deep breath, his eyes dilating, his muscles tensing.

Elle shouted a warning and reached for her weapon, but it was too late. Stojanović leaped towards the curtained window, pushing the fabric before him through the glass as he fell to the landscaped terrace surrounding the restaurant patio below.

Liam jumped up from the bed and raced to the window, joined a moment later by Elle.

Stojanović was already on his feet, darting through a small crowd of astonished hotel guests.

When Elle had shouted, Clifton had vaulted into the hallway to protect Paillard, tackling the startled restaurateur to the ground at the feet of the woman. He stood now, assisting his friend to his feet.

"Qu'est-ce qu'il y a?" Paillard asked, shaken and confused, but before Clifton could answer, Elle darted past him, followed closely by Liam. Paillard's female guest, the blonde woman in the hallway, stood frozen, staring, as the two armed officers raced past her towards the stairwell.

"He was heading north," Elle shouted as she flew down the stairs, leaping multiple steps with ease. "Towards the Anse de Maldorme!"

"Don't wait for me!" Liam shouted back, struggling to keep pace with the nimble automaton.

When Elle entered the small street beside the restaurant's parking facility, she could not see Stojanović anywhere. She halted, listening. Liam joined her a moment later, breathing heavily. He was about to speak, but seeing his partner's intense concentration, he silenced himself immediately.

The Anse de Maldorme is a narrow street bordering the harbor lined with small buildings and a concrete wall that follows the shore. Elle's sensitive audio receptors detected distant sounds, evidence of the running man's passage; a bicyclist's complaint, the sudden braking of a vehicle, the barking of a dog. She darted forward immediately.

"Follow me!" she shouted

Trusting his partner's superior senses, Liam concentrated on keeping up with the swift female.

Elle raced to the end of the street, down a concrete stepped path, then onto a more prominent street, the Rue de la Douane. In the distance, where the street began to bend towards the harbor, she saw Stojanović. He was running far ahead, passing a small blue sedan where the street started to curve.

"There!" she shouted, pointing.

At that moment, Stojanović paused, turned, and glanced back. Spotting his pursuers, he leaped ahead, disappearing from view around the bend in the street.

Liam was doing his best to keep up with his fellow officer. He keenly regretted his recent illness and the injury that had left him bedridden for weeks. He was winded, and his shoulder ached. Elle was already far ahead, disappearing around the bend. When he reached the curve in the street, he almost crashed into Elle. She was standing still, staring at the street ahead.

"Where…" Liam gasped, struggling for breath. "Where… did he… go?"

Elle pointed. The street separated just ahead, splitting into two lanes that diverged further apart as they progressed. Past the intersection, at the far end of the street, Liam could see a running figure turning the corner.

"Why didn't you pursue him?!" he asked, frustrated.

"That's the Rue Boudouresque," she responded, pointing to the intersecting street.

Liam shook his head, struggling for breath. "I don't… understand."

"He is inside the Pointe d'Endoume," she said. "A peninsula created by a small inlet just over there." She pointed to the north, beyond the buildings. "If we move quickly," she continued, "we can intercept him when he is forced to double back on Chemin du Génie, the street on the other side of those structures."

Liam nodded, understanding. "Let's go!"

The two officers turned and raced down the intersecting street through a small residential neighborhood lined with white-painted homes. When they reached the cross street, they stopped.

Stojanović was nowhere to be seen.

Elle scanned the street in confusion, consulting her internal archive of historical maps and comparing them against their surroundings for any discrepancies. At that moment, her ultra-sensitive audio receptors detected a man's voice shouting somewhere to the northwest, followed by a boat engine turning over. She ran towards the sound. Liam followed close behind. As they ran, the buildings lining the street suddenly gave way to an iron fence bordering a small inlet. Just beyond the fence, a cluster of motorboats could be seen anchored inside a rocky cove. One boat, however, was moving. A man on a shore was shouting angrily, waving his fist at the moving boat.

Elle crouched down and jumped, leaping over the fence with ease. Chagrinned, Liam scrambled onto the top of a parked car and carefully climbed over the barrier. When he jumped down, Elle was already standing on the shore next to the shouting man. She retrieved her RU-6 from its concealed holster, and, at the sight of the strange weapon, the shouting man stepped back quickly, his eyes wide with fear.

She raised the weapon and focused its targeting system on the fleeing boat but she could not see Stojanović. The Serbian was probably crouched down, concealing himself from view. For a moment, she considered firing on the retreating vessel. Her RU-6 was capable of rendering the craft into driftwood, but there was a possibility that Stojanović was not alone. He may have taken the boat forcibly from its owner, who was now his hostage. While the statistical probability of such a scenario was low, it was not zero and she did not wish to kill any innocent person in her zeal to recapture the fleeing man.

She looked around, her analytic processors evaluating the available watercraft as Liam approached. Without a word, she pointed towards a small cruiser sitting on a trailer with the propellers of its twin engines touching the water. Liam nodded and scaled a ladder placed over the side of the vessel.

The man on the shore began shouting again, directing his anger at the new arrivals. However, his cries of protest were abruptly silenced when Elle lifted a metal anchor chain securing the cruiser to the trailer and casually pulled the steel links apart with her hands. As she began to push the vessel off its trailer into the water, the man yelped and fled into a small building.

Elle crouched and jumped across the intervening water, landing on the cruiser's rear deck. The vessel was equipped with GPS navigation and a computer-controlled ignition system. She quickly Pol'd with the system and engaged the engine as Liam emerged from the cabin.

"No one else on board," he said, joining her behind the wheel.

Stojanović's fleeing vessel was already passing between the peninsula and the Rocher des Pendus, a small cluster of rocks at the mouth of the inlet. Once clear of the rocks, it turned west and increased speed, moving out swiftly into the harbor.

Liam stood cupping a hand over his eyes against the glare of the sun, watching the boat in the distance. "You see where he's heading?" he asked, pointing.

Elle nodded. She pushed the engine throttle full open, and their cruiser jumped forward. Swiftly passing the rocks at the mouth of the inlet, they turned west, following the retreating boat as it raced towards an island in the distance.

Stojanović was heading towards Île d'If.

The blonde woman walked swiftly across the restaurant terrace towards the concrete steps that descended to the small parking lot. At the foot of the steps, she could see the valet standing with two of the hotel's guests. She recognized the guests as a loud American couple she had observed that morning checking in at the reception desk. They were staring through a small archway that opened from the restaurant's parking facility onto the Anse de Maldorme. Following their gaze, she could see two figures in the distance running down that narrow street.

She needed to leave the area quickly before the police arrived. Stojanović had obviously seen her in the hallway speaking with the restaurateur. Fortunately, there was no indication his captors had observed his recognition.

The valet now noticed her and approached with a smile. She handed the tuxedoed man her parking ticket and then waited beside the American couple as the attendant left to retrieve her vehicle.

"I saw him fall out of that window, right there!" The man was pointing over the terrace towards a small shattered window on the second floor. "He jumped up as soon as he hit the ground and then ran off."

His companion, an overweight woman with a hideous yellow scarf, shook her head and said, "I still say he must have fallen by accident."

The man shook his head. "Then why did he run off?"

The blonde woman felt anxious. She needed instructions, but she had been given strict orders not to use her cell phone. She didn't understand the reason behind that restriction, but her orders had been clear; no use of any electronic communication devices in or near the hotel.

At that moment, the valet drove up with her vehicle. He exited the small coupe, tore the ticket, and passed her the keys with the ticket stub.

"Merci," she said, handing the man a tip. When she got into the vehicle, the American man pulled his portly companion to one side to allow her to drive through the archway. She drove west on Anse de Maldorme, following the distant figures.

Chapter 22

IDR: MK4ATY145//:QKDS-77483L2LE

Major-General Charles George Gordon was a celebrated British Army officer and administrator during that span of years now remembered as the Victorian Period. Before rising to prominence in China, he fought in the Crimean War, commanding the imperial Chinese army during the Nian and Taiping Rebellions. He died in January 1885 defending Khartoum, Sudan, against the Ansar forces of Muhammad Ahmad, a Muslim religious fanatic and self-proclaimed Mahdi.

Like Ahmad, Gordon was a profoundly religious man. He professed a belief in predestination, a spiritual concept that shares similarities with self-resolving causality, a temporal principle acknowledging that time will resolve any actions taken by a temporal specialist in the past to preserve the future. Attributing such temporal stability to deity, Gordon wrote, "I believe that not a worm is picked up by a bird without the direct intervention of God."

Curiously, Gordon also subscribed to the belief that humans were free to choose their fate, another principle well known to temporal specialists, who understand that they may exercise free will in the past, secure in the knowledge that self-resolving causality will resolve their actions to preserve the future.

To Gordon, who lacked an understanding of temporal mechanics, these concepts appeared contradictory. Said Gordon, "I cannot and do not pretend to reconcile the two."

I sympathize with Gordon. I, too, am frequently amazed at time's ability to withstand man's obstreperous will.

Château d'If is a fortress located on the island of If, the smallest island in the Frioul archipelago. Situated 3.5 kilometers west of the coast of Marseille, the island is a desolate rock-encrusted protuberance rising just twenty meters above the blue waters of the surrounding bay. Encompassing three hectares, the island is heavily fortified, with stone ramparts surmounting cliffs.

Construction of the island fortress began in 1524 on the orders of King Francis I, who envisioned its use as a strategically important location for defending the nearby coastline from sea-based attacks. The structure's principal military value was a deterrent; it never had to fight off an actual attack. Its enduring legacy was that of a prison. The swift currents in the surrounding water made the fortress an inescapable final destination for those doomed to reside within its rocky walls. In that role, as a prison, the fort gained immortality through Alexander Dumas' story, The Count of Monte Cristo. The island and its fortress are presently uninhabited, save for those employed to cater to tourists and the innumerable Dumas enthusiasts.

Elle slowed the small cruiser, then stopped its motors, allowing the boat to drift slowly towards the flat concrete and stone pier. On that landing, several lengths of pedestrian barriers held back a small crowd of tourists waiting for a blue and white ferry that was approaching from across the bay. On the easternmost tip of the island, a small lighthouse rose above the fortification walls.

Nearby, Stojanović's stolen boat was tied to the landing, its sides bumping against re-purposed tires that ringed the pier. A young man stood by the abandoned boat, watching a nearby concrete and earthen ramp beyond the group of tourists. The ramp rose towards a network of steps and gates that facilitated access to the fortress above. Several tourists were walking down the ramp towards the landing.

When Elle's cruiser touched the landing's tire bumpers, the young man turned and glanced apprehensively across the water at the approaching ferry. He shook his head and spoke haltingly to the new arrivals.

"Tu ne peux pas t'arrêter ici..."

Ignoring his objections, Elle stepped to the platform, joined a moment later by Liam. They walked quickly towards the crowd, passing another attendant standing by an opening in the barrier. As the two officers ascended the sloping ramp towards the fortress gates above, Elle gazed at the rocky cliffs and its battlements.

"Why would Stojanović come here?" she asked.

Liam looked back at the landing, then said, "He probably hopes to conceal himself on the island and then escape posing as a tourist. On the open ocean, he would have had little chance to elude capture. Our boat had comparable speed and greater range."

When they passed through a narrow stone gate, Liam paused and configured his RU-6 for suppression before concealing it again under his shirt. Elle was scanning the broad stone steps ahead. The thermal scanners inside her optics could detect even the slightest heat variation, but the recent passage of the island's many tourists over the cold steps had confused any tracks.

"Anything?" Liam asked, noting her observations.

Elle shook her head. "Nothing helpful," she said. "Too many people have passed here recently."

Liam nodded and pressed forward up the steps.

Elle followed, glancing up at the imposing stone wall. A length of construction scaffolds stood against the wall, providing access for restoration personnel who had been commissioned to repair the sea wall's crumbling mortar. Glancing back down the ramp, she could see the ferry had docked and was now exchanging its passengers for those waiting on the landing. At the top of the steps, the two officers passed under the Florentine Door. A group of tourists stood beneath the wide arch, pointing at the nearby fortress and enthusiastically taking pictures.

The fortress itself was an imposing structure, with two immense, rounded bastions bracketing a wide wall with a small arched entrance beneath. Behind the right bastion, an even larger tower rose, the tower of Saint Christophe. Like the twin bastions below, it was notched with deep cannon embrasures, hinting at the fortress's incredible mass.

Directly ahead, a large two-story building had been constructed inside the courtyard. The red-roofed Vauban Building had once been the governor's house and seemed almost a flimsy afterthought next to the massive fortress.

Elle turned to her companion. "Where do we begin?" she asked.

Liam's eyes narrowed as he considered the question. He was determined to proceed cautiously. After a few moments, he nodded towards the nearby towers. "You search the fortress," he said. "I'll check the buildings."

Elle nodded and stepped into the wide courtyard. Just through the gate, several buildings came into view. They were modern structures, likely a museum and gift shop. A group of tourists sat under a tin-roofed extension, eating ice cream and laughing. Liam turned and walked towards the group.

Elle began to cross the stony courtyard, walking swiftly towards the fortress. She glanced back once before passing through the arched entrance between the twin bastions. Liam was exiting the first building and was now striding purposefully towards the second.

Elle had never visited Château d'If in person, though she had reviewed numerous data files after retiring to her hotel room the night they arrived in Marseille. Liam's story had affected her deeply, and she had employed her time that first evening reviewing the available information about the ancient fortress, confusingly aware of Liam sleeping in the next room.

Now, as she passed the red-painted doors, she was accosted by a flood of strange sensations. Her review of the structure's holographic records had not prepared her for the actual physicality of the place. Her olfactory sensors registered an earthy, musty smell that seemed to emanate from the walls. Hundreds of years of human perspiration mingled with dust and moisture from the nearby sea had imbued the chamber with a sense of age, loneliness, and memory. Her auditory sensors also detected echoes and muffled tourist conversations from deeper inside, ghostly reflections of the fortress's long-dead former inhabitants.

Overwhelming, however, was the incredible weight that seemed to be pressing down on her consciousness. Her internal ultrasonic and muon tomographic scanners reported hundreds of tons of rock were surrounding her. Her cognitive processors interpreted the readings as being suddenly buried beneath an avalanche, and she was forced to initiate an administrative override to counter the resulting "flight-or-fight" self-preservation directives.

She walked through the entrance chamber, proceeding

slowly towards the sounds of conversation ahead. She was actively scanning the structure with her muon sensor. The sensor utilized cosmic ray muons to create a tomographic map of cavities and structures hidden behind earth and rock. The sensor was detecting many chambers and passageways, as well as moving shapes; tourists taking pictures, chatting, and walking throughout the structure. None of the figures were moving with undue haste or appeared to be attempting to conceal themselves in any way. If Stojanović was within the fortress, he must be attempting to blend in with the tourists already inside.

She passed through another archway and stepped into the center of the fortress. The small courtyard was faced with Pierre du midi limestone and contained a small rainwater well in its center. A dozen tourists were mingling within the open area, while others ascended stone stairs to the second level.

On the other side of the well, she noticed several people reading a small sign positioned above an arched door. The sign read, "Cachot dit d'Edmond Dantès Comte de Monte-Cristo". It was the cell named for Edmond Dantes. Originally the fortress' powder room, the cell had been renamed to satisfy the many Dumas fans who visited the island each year.

Elle walked slowly towards the door, experiencing a strange compulsion from her emotive processor. When she stepped into the stone and mortar chamber, a vision of Liam sitting on the hotel terrace flashed briefly within her mind. She felt confused. She could not understand what had triggered the image, nor could she understand the unusual input that now streamed from her emotive processor. She stared at the floor in confusion.

"Can you imagine being confined to such a place?"

Elle looked up, startled. An elderly woman was standing next to her. The woman smiled and then took a photograph with her phone.

"Poor Edmond," the woman said, shaking her head. "Alone for so many years with nothing but his memories of Mercédès."

Elle stared. After a moment, she said, "You are aware that Edmond Dantes is a fictional character?"

The woman nodded. "Yes, of course, dear," she said, turning to face her. "But that doesn't make the story any less tragic, does it?"

Elle remained silent.

"Oh, I know," the woman said, nodding. "He escaped and found the treasure… and he secured his revenge, but at what cost?"

Elle shook her head. "I don't understand."

"I just mean, even though he found the treasure and achieved his revenge, he lost the one thing he truly wanted. He lost his Mercédès."

Elle frowned. After a moment, she said, "He found love again."

The woman glanced up. "Do you mean, with Haydée?"

"Yes."

The woman sighed, nodding, then said, "Time heals all wounds."

Elle looked back into the small cell. Liam's recitation of Dantès final admonition suddenly came to her mind, 'All human wisdom is contained in these two words, Wait and Hope'.

"What was that?" the old woman asked.

Elle was confused. She wasn't aware she had spoken the

words out loud. At that moment, an elderly man entered the cell and took the woman gently by the hand.

"Jenny," he said, "We need to head back. Mae says the little ones want ice cream."

The woman nodded and took one last photograph of the cell. She smiled at Elle, then turned and walked with her companion back into the courtyard.

Elle stared into the small stone chamber. She was extremely confused. Her emotive processor continued to superimpose images and memories of Liam against her consciousness. At the same time, her haptic processors were replaying the sensation of his hand in hers when he had guided her into the hotel and the warmth of his lips when she had kissed him on the way to ITER.

She could not understand what was happening. Her cognitive processor was struggling to explain the strange input. For a moment, she wondered if her processors were malfunctioning, but she quickly dismissed the idea. Her processors were connected to a powerful qubit data core by a photon-entangled neural network. Any malfunction of any of the processors would have resulted in the immediate termination of her entire quantum synapse. A safeguard designed within all sentient automatons, it was simply not possible for an automaton to experience any processor malfunction and remain conscious.

Slowly, inexplicably, the disconnected images, memories, and sensations began to coalesce inside her consciousness. With shocking clarity, a stunning equation began to form from the input, an equation both staggeringly complex yet flawlessly perfect. She turned and walked swiftly from the chamber.

Stojanović watched from his position atop Christophe's tower as the two officers emerged from the Florentine Door. After a few moments, he observed the male officer turn and walk towards one of the buildings near the gate. The female officer, however, began walking towards the fortress. When she passed beneath his view, he tensed. His only chance was to wait until the strange woman was deep inside the structure and then attempt to escape undetected.

After several minutes, several of the tourists on top of the tower turned to leave. He casually joined the group and began to descend the stone steps. When the group reached the second level with its balcony that surrounded the interior courtyard, he slowed and peered cautiously into the yard below.

He could see the female officer standing by the rainwater well.

He stepped back inside the corridor and pretended to read a sign affixed to the wall. The sign warned the visitors not to disturb the seagulls who were nesting on the island. After several moments, he stepped back out onto the balcony. The female officer was walking across the courtyard towards a small chamber.

This was his chance! The moment the woman disappeared inside the chamber, he began descending the steps. When he reached the landing, he paused as an elderly woman crossed his path, walking into the same chamber. The sign above the chamber identified it as Edmond Dantès' cell.

As casually as he dared, he crossed the small courtyard and began moving through the stone passageways. When he finally stepped through the riveted red door at the front of the fortress, he exhaled in relief. From this position, he could see several people in the outer yard. He began walking towards the

Florentine Door.

At that moment, the male officer emerged from the second building. The two men stared at each other across the stony ground. Then, the officer leaped forward, scrambling for something under his shirt.

Stojanović turned and raced towards the eastern end of the island. When he rounded the base of the small lighthouse, he looked around swiftly. Beyond the tower, a section of construction scaffolding had been placed against the battlement walls. He ran forward and began scrambling up the scaffold.

Just as he reached the top of the wall, the officer rounded the lighthouse. In desperation, Stojanović placed his foot against the scaffold and kicked with all of his strength. The scaffold teetered, then fell over, crashing onto the courtyard below as he dove for cover.

A moment passed.

Then another.

Cautiously, he peered above the lip of the battlement. The officer was running back across the island's interior towards a second section of scaffolding positioned behind the small buildings near the Florentine Door.

Stojanović leaped to his feet and began running south along the battlement, staring about desperately for a way to scale the walls. However, as he approached a bend in the wall, a blonde woman stepped out from behind a pile of construction materials, blocking his path. She held a suppressed pistol in her hand.

"Yvette!" Stojanović gasped.

"What did you tell them, Marko?" The woman stepped forward a step, her pistol aimed at his chest.

Stojanović took a step backward and glanced over the

edge of the wall. It was a sheer drop to the rocks below. He glanced at the pistol in the woman's hand and shook his head.

"I told them nothing!"

"You were in their room," she said, her tone threatening.

Stojanović scowled. "I was zatvorenik… prisoner!"

The woman pointed her pistol at his chest and smiled a cold smile. "Last chance, mon amie. What did you tell them?"

Stojanović's face grew angry, and he spat at the woman. "Jebi se, kučka!" he shouted.

The woman fired twice.

Stojanović's body fell backward through a crenel in the battlement, struck a small outcropping of rock at the base of the wall, and then tumbled into the blue waters of the bay.

When Elle exited the fortress, she scanned the island carefully. After a moment, she spotted Liam. He was standing on the battlements near the small lighthouse on the eastern end of the island. When she reached the wall beneath his position, she observed a smashed pile of construction scaffolding on the ground.

"Are you injured?" she called up to him.

Seeing her standing below, Liam shook his head, then gestured out over the courtyard towards the distant cafe. "I got up over there," he shouted. "Stojanović kicked over the scaffolding after he climbed up here."

Elle turned and scanned the yard behind her. She could see a small group of tourists walking towards the Florentine Door, but they were facing away from the two officers. Satisfied, she crouched and jumped. The force applied to her synthetic-alloy sinews, calculated with precision, propelled her easily over the crenels to land gracefully in the center of the battlement next to the startled officer.

Liam rubbed the back of his neck.

"Give me some warning next time before you do something like that."

"I'm sorry," she said. "I didn't mean to alarm you."

Liam was about to respond, then stopped. Elle was looking at him with a strange expression on her face. He had never seen that particular expression on her face before.

"Is something wrong?" he asked.

Elle abruptly looked away, shaking her head. "No," she said. "What have you found?"

Liam pointed to the surface beneath their feet. Elle noticed then that he was holding the tactical optics in his hand. She immediately engaged her internal thermographic filters. Against the cold stone floor of the battlement, she could see heat signatures; faint foot-shaped patterns that were slowly fading in the cold sea air. One set of footprints was clearly Liam's. A second pattern emerged from the edge of the battlement just above the collapsed scaffolding. They undoubtedly belonged to Stojanović. They proceeded to a position just in front of Liam, where they were joined by a third pattern that had approached from the other direction.

Where the patterns met, the heat signatures were stronger, suggesting the two parties had stopped, standing in the same spot for several moments. Then, Stojanović's pattern became confused. It appeared that he had shuffled backward and had fallen between two raised crenels overlooking the ocean.

She peered over the edge of the battlements by the crenels and engaged her (h)red-spectra scanner. Under the enhanced wavelengths, she could see a spray of fine blood droplets and gunpowder residue on the surface of the two crenels. Calculating a trajectory based on the spray pattern of the particles, she stepped back to a position on the battlement.

"Someone discharged a firearm from this position."

Liam looked up. "Are you certain?" he asked.

Elle nodded. "The arrangement of blood particles and propellant residue," she said, pointing, "indicates the assailant was standing in this location." Glancing down and comparing the size of the thermal prints against her own feet, she added, "The assailant was a woman." She then pointed down the battlement, away from their position and said, "The woman ran that way."

Liam was startled. "A woman?"

"Yes."

"How do you know?" he asked.

Elle looked down again. "The size of the thermal prints," she said, "suggests the assailant was either a woman or a child. However, the distance between the prints indicates a stride indicative of an adult. I cannot be certain, of course, but my probability matrices strongly suggest the assailant was an adult female."

Liam turned and adjusted his optics to view the far end of the crumbling battlement, following the retreating thermal prints.

Elle took that opportunity to step between the crenels and gaze down at the rocks below. She could see bloody impact points on several stones, and the ocean was washing a dark smear of blood closest to the waterline. It was clear that Stojanović had been shot and had fallen to the rocks before sliding into the water. With the strong currents known to surround the island, his body would likely never be found. She stepped back and gazed again at the island interior. Two men wearing identical shirts were approaching from across the courtyard. One of the men carried a radio.

"We've been observed," she said, pointing.

Liam glanced back, then quickly placed the optics inside his pocket.

"Let's get back to the boat."

As Liam navigated their small cruiser away from the island, Elle sat nearby and studied him closely. After several minutes, she spoke.

"Why did you give me the two chairs?" she asked.

Liam looked up, confused.

"What?"

"The two blue chairs… why did you give them to me?"

Liam frowned. "You don't like them?"

"You misunderstand," she said, shaking her head swiftly. "I was asking why you gave them to me?"

Liam seemed troubled. After a moment, he said, "There was no place to sit in your apartment."

"I'm an automaton", she said, a hint of a smile on her face. "I don't need to sit."

"Look," Liam said, "if you don't want them, you don't need to keep them."

"I do want them," Elle spoke quickly, watching his face closely. "They are very important to me."

Liam glanced at her, then quickly looked away.

"I'm glad you like them," he said quietly.

"Why did you give them to me?" she asked again, watching him closely.

Liam stood silent with his hand on the wheel, gazing at

the approaching coastline. After several moments, he shrugged.

"I guess it just didn't feel right," he said softly. "You living in that empty room…" His voice trailed off.

Elle nodded. His answer confirmed what she had concluded inside Edmond Dantès' cell. Liam didn't view her as an automaton. From the day she had joined the temporal enforcement group, she had been confused by his atypical human responses. Despite her many social faux pas when she interacted with her fellow officers, he had always spoken to her with kindness and respect. His demeanor towards her suggested an affinity that went beyond mere professional courtesy. He exhibited a closeness and familiarity that she had not observed him demonstrating towards anyone else. He appeared to sincerely respect her abilities and he valued her input. Despite his recent denial, his physiological reactions whenever she was near strongly suggested he was also physically attracted to her. The inputs supported only one conclusion.

Liam loved her.

Inside Dantès' cell, her realization of this fact had triggered something inexplicable within her synthetic consciousness. The disjointed and confusing inputs had somehow merged, forming an equation of such incredible sophistication that it had threatened to overwhelm her neural network. She had never before processed such a complex equation. Once fully compiled, the resulting program had superimposed itself onto her quantum synapse, merging and integrating with that intricate network in a way she had not thought possible.

The result had left her feeling overwhelmed in a way she had not experienced since those first confusing moments of emergence more than four years earlier. Each time she attempted to analyze this new awareness, her analytic processor returned the same conclusion.

This was love.

This was that mysterious, confusing quality about which Julian of Norwich had written nearly 800 years ago; the quality without which she had asserted one does not truly live.

She stood and stepped towards the wooden control panel. She turned off the switch, killing the cruiser's motors.

Liam looked down, startled, as the boat slowed and began to drift.

"Why did you do that?" he asked. He reached for the ignition switch, but she took his hand away from the control. "Have you ever read the writings of Julian of Norwich?" she asked.

"What?" Liam's face was a mask of confusion.

She pressed close, lifted her head, and kissed him. This was not the kiss she had applied inside the vehicle on the way to the ITER facility. This was no mere test designed to assess his physiological response. This was something else. When she finally released him, he was staring at her with a thoughtful look on his face. After a moment, he frowned and shook his head.

"I don't understand," he husked. "Julian… who?"

She smiled. "It's not important. I was just thinking about something she wrote long ago."

To the west, the afternoon sun was waning behind Château d'If, and as the boat drifted in the bay, she took his hand and guided him towards the cruiser's small cabin.

Chapter 23

IDR: MK4AVP266//:QKDS-77483L2LE

Determination is to persist in the face of difficulties. Determination, therefore, is the application of one's will in the face of obstacles.

On July 2, 1863, during the first American Civil War, Colonel Joshua Lawrence Chamberlain commanded a regiment from Maine from a position on Little Round Top hill outside Gettysburg, Pennsylvania. Exhausted from repeated Confederate attacks and almost out of ammunition, Chamberlain ordered his men to fix bayonets and charge the approaching Confederates, an action for which he was later awarded the Medal of Honor.

A year later, on June 18, 1864, during the Second Battle of Petersburg, Chamberlain was shot through the right hip and groin. Despite the horrific injury, he withdrew his sword and stuck it into the ground, using it as a crutch to remain standing and persuade his troops to continue fighting. Although the surgeon later diagnosed the wound as mortal, Chamberlain ultimately recovered. When many, including his wife, urged him to accept medical retirement, Chamberlain refused, determined to serve through the end of the conflict.

Throughout the war, Joshua Lawrence Chamberlain served in twenty battles and numerous other skirmishes. He was cited for bravery four times, had six horses shot from under him, and was wounded six times.

Determination, it appears, is the true steel from which heroes are forged.

When Liam and Elle returned to the hotel, a glass company was inside the room repairing the window Stojanović had smashed. Paillard was observing the work while Clifton sat at the desk studying the Serbian's drawings of Morten's villa. When they entered the room, Paillard was noticeably relieved.

"Grâce à Dieu, mes amies!" the restaurateur exclaimed, approaching quickly and hugging them both.

Clifton also stood and nodded. "Glad to see you," he said, gesturing to the restaurateur. "We were concerned."

Liam glanced at the men repairing the window frame. "Thank you," he said, "but we need to talk."

Clifton nodded his understanding.

Paillard immediately motioned towards the work crew and said, "Je vais rester ici... I will stay here." He removed a room card from his pocket and handed it to Clifton. "Use my suite, s'il vous plaît."

Clifton smiled and said, "Thank you."

Paillard waved his hand in dismissal. He then took Elle's hand and kissed it before returning to resume his supervision of the glass crew. When they exited the room, Liam spoke as they walked down the hall.

"Stojanović is dead."

Clifton raised his eyebrows. "Dead?"

Liam nodded and explained what had occurred on the island. When he related Elle's supposition that an unknown female had shot Stojanović, Clifton frowned.

"Do you know who she might be?" he asked.

Liam shook his head. "No," he said, "but it's a fair guess she works for Morten."

Clifton nodded. "Morten was probably worried about

what Stojanović might tell us."

The trio had reached Paillard's suite, and Clifton unlocked the door.

"Stojanović did tell us something," Elle said as she entered the room. "Before he escaped, he told me Morten has a file somewhere at ITER containing sensitive information about the future. Morten has made arrangements to have the file released if he should disappear."

Clifton glanced at the lithe female. "A truant trigger?" he asked.

"Undoubtedly," Elle replied. "Such a thing would be easy to implement, despite the primitive programming limitations of this era."

A truant trigger was essentially a scheduled software function that would initiate an event unless countered. The counters themselves could be numerous and varied, from an innocuous phrase sent to a company communication account to a binary value changed inside a forgotten data field. A truant trigger in the future could be easily identified and defeated by a company's security AI. If someone planted an unauthorized trigger within a neural network, a security AI would immediately release a datamole, an artificially intelligent program, to locate and remove all instances of the aberrant code.

However, lacking such tools in this era, the officers would be forced to locate and isolate the file itself, leaving nothing for the trigger to initiate.

Clifton closed and locked the door. "The 2019 pandemic has begun," he said softly, glancing at Liam. "While it is not yet widely reported, it soon will be. The ITER party on the 6th will likely be the last social event that Morten attends for some time.

With the viral outbreak, world governments will begin enacting isolation policies, restricting public gatherings."

Liam looked at Elle. He felt conflicted. So much of their plan depended on the beautiful female and her unique capabilities. He didn't doubt those capabilities, but now, for the first time, he was hesitant to proceed. He understood the reason for his hesitation, and that, too, troubled him. He stood and began pacing the room.

Elle recognized the behavior as the temporal officer being troubled about something. Perhaps sensing his turmoil, she stood and approached.

"I think we should proceed," she said, taking him by the hand. "It's still our best chance of success."

Liam hesitated, looking at her. After a few moments, he nodded, then turned to Clifton. "What should we do about Morten's file?" he asked.

Clifton, however, didn't answer. He was staring at Elle with a strange expression on his face. The temporal specialist seemed troubled about something. After a moment, he frown ed."I'm sorry," he said. "What did you say?"

"I asked, what should we do about Morten's file?"

Clifton stood and walked to the window. He stared silently at the ocean beyond the veranda. The waters were black under the night sky. After nearly a minute, he faced the two officers.

"We get the file," he said. "Then, we get Morten."

Joubert waited beneath the alternating black and white marble stone arches of the Notre Dame de la Garde. Constructed on a limestone outcropping on the south side of the Old Port of Marseille, the Neo-Byzantine-styled church on the hill provided an unobstructed view of the city below and the dark bay in the distance.

From this position, he could see Burke in the parking lot at the base of the steps leaning against a lamp post. The dour Irishman was smoking a cigarette and staring up at the tall bell tower with its flood-lit golden statue of the Madonna and Child.

At that moment, a blonde-haired woman stepped into the dim parking lot from the steps rising from the street below. The woman walked towards the basilica, glancing at Burke. Burke nodded as she passed then resumed his smoke. When the woman reached the top of the stairs, she stopped under the black and white marble arches.

Joubert was staring at her, frowning.

"You failed," he said.

The woman shook her head. "I did not fail."

Joubert stepped closer, anger in his eyes. "You were supposed to discover what he revealed before you killed him."

The woman shrugged. "It was pointless," she replied. "That stupid Bosnian was not going to tell me anything."

"He wasn't Bosnian," Joubert said. "He was Serbian, and I needed to know what he told them."

The woman turned away, staring at the dark harbor in the distance. "If that's what you wanted, you would have sent someone else. We both know why you sent me."

Joubert shook his head in frustration. "You couldn't have questioned him first?" he asked.

The woman turned swiftly, glaring. "The bastard insulted me," she hissed, "so I shot him!"

"He has insulted you many times, but you've never shot him for it."

"I should have," the woman replied. Then she frowned. "I

would have… that time in Belgium if you hadn't stopped me."

Joubert stepped closer, then froze. The woman had pulled a small pistol from under her shirt and was pointing it at his stomach. He glanced at the pistol, then shook his head again.

"You over-reacted in Belgium." he said, intentionally ignoring the weapon.

"Did I?" the woman asked, her hand steady.

"Yes."

The two stared at each other in silence. Then, slowly, Joubert stepped forward, pressing his belly against the muzzle of the pistol. The woman swallowed and bit her lip but she did not resist as Joubert slowly removed the handgun from her hand. He reached up and pulled off her blonde wig, revealing short-cropped brown hair. He glanced at Burke in the lot below. The Irishman was still leaning against the lamp post, staring out over the city. Suddenly, he whirled and struck the woman across the face, knocking her to the ground.

"Next time," he barked, "you do what I tell you to do."

The woman stared, her eyes flashing. After several moments, she stood up, pressing a hand to her mouth.

"Next time," she said, her voice threatening.

Joubert scowled. "Next time… what?"

The woman licked her lip, then wiped away a spot of blood with the back of her hand. "Next time…" She hesitated for a moment, and then she seemed to relent. "I'll do what you tell me to do." Suddenly, she threw herself into his arms, kissing him passionately. After several moments, she paused, breathing heavily, and whispered seductively into his ear. "I'll do anything you want me to do."

When Joubert returned to the villa the following day,

Morten immediately summoned him to his underground office. When he exited the lift, he stopped. A dark metallic tube attached by a cable to a hard case had been mounted on the ceiling in the middle of the corridor. The tube was pointed at the lift. The vault door at the end of the corridor was open. He hesitated, then proceeded inside the suite. Morten sat behind his desk. The aging executive seemed unusually tired, despite the early hour.

"Was your agent successful?" Morten asked when he entered.

"Stojanović will no longer be a problem," Joubert replied.

Morten resumed his study of the touch screen display embedded in his desk. After several moments, he spoke again but did not look up.

"Did Yvette find out what he told our visitors?"

Joubert frowned. "I think we must assume," he said, "that our wayward Serbian told them everything."

Before leaving the Le Quai hotel in Belsunce, Joubert had questioned Yvette again about her surveillance of the restaurant and her activities on the island. She revealed little she had not already reported, save for one curious observation.

Yvette had been relaxing nude on the bed, smoking a Gauloises cigarette when she said, "I would have been able to get to the island sooner, but I had to take the ferry from Vieux Port."

When Joubert had asked how the two subjects had managed on foot to reach the ferry ahead of her, Yvette told him that they had not taken the ferry from Vieux, but had stolen a boat from the nearby Port de Malmousque. At that moment, she had frowned, inhaling deeply from her cigarette.

"There is one other thing..." she spoke hesitantly,

scowling at the half-smoked clope, before jamming it into an ashtray.

"Yes?" Joubert prodded.

"I had just turned onto Chemin du Génie," she continued. "They had already reached the end of the street, you understand? I was still far behind, so I'm not sure about what I saw."

Joubert grew concerned. Reticence was not one of Yvette's qualities.

"What did you see?" he asked.

"The female jumped over the fence," she replied, glancing up with a puzzled look on her brow. "At least, I think she did."

When Joubert did not respond, she shrugged. "I only saw her in the corner of my eye," she explained, "when I was turning onto the street. There was a car parked nearby, and the male was using the car to climb over the fence, but the female was already inside the fence, several meters away. She was standing back up as if she had just landed, and for a moment, I thought she had just jumped over the fence."

She slid a new cigarette from the blue Gauloises box and reached for the lighter on the stand. "I was far away," she said, shrugging again. "There were some wooden pallets stacked nearby, so maybe she used those."

Now, standing in Morten's office, Joubert recalled his employer's description of sentient robots in the future. He also recalled the man's frightening description of the female kicking the door free from its hinges in the field outside Culham Centre. He had seen the door resting in the field but had not paid it much attention at the time.

He no longer doubted Morten's claims regarding time travel. He had also experienced the devastating consequences of underestimating the weapons and tactics of these visitors from the future. Whether one of them was a constructed mechanical being, however, was still an unknown variable. Morten's descriptions of such creatures had been vague, though the elderly man clearly held suspicions regarding the female. For a brief moment, Joubert's mind conceived a terrifying scenario, repeatedly shooting an approaching adversary who refused to die.

"Do robots in the future have great strength?" he asked.

Confused by the abrupt change of subject, Morten looked up from his desk.

"What?"

"Robots," Joubert said. "In the future. Are they stronger than humans?"

Morten shook his head and resumed his study of the embedded screen. "They aren't robots," he said in a tired voice. "They are SDUs… self-directing units. The closest thing to something you might be familiar with would be an android from various works of fiction. Asimov, for example…"

"I don't care what they're called!" Joubert interrupted, frustration edging his voice." Are they stronger than humans?"

Morten's head shot up, his eyes wide with surprise. After a moment, he nodded. "Yes," he said. "They can be. It depends on their intended purpose. Defense force pounders, for example… those are military SDUs… they can smash through layered plascrete, break CG structural beams in two, and topple entrenched p-beam batteries. Of course, those are large units, typically weighing more than…"

"What about smaller ones?" Joubert asked, growing even more impatient. "One the size of a human, for example. Would it be stronger than me?"

Morten's eyes narrowed. "You're thinking about that female, aren't you?"

"Yes."

After a moment, Morten shook his head slowly. "I don't know," he said.

Joubert spoke angrily now. "What do you mean you don't know?! You told me…"

"I said," Morten spoke defensively, "that in the time I came from, sentient automatons did not yet exist! It was the 'great debate' of my time, whether or not to permit SDUs to continue to evolve into sentient beings, but I don't know if they ever did."

"So, you're just speculating!" Joubert spoke derisively.

"Not about what I saw her do!" Morten responded swiftly, his own voice rising now. "She kicked that door free from its mounting brackets like it was made of tin!"

When Joubert did not respond, Morten took a calming breath, then spoke slowly. "SDUs are typically physically stronger than human beings. How could they not be? We are fragile creatures, we humans. Our bones are made from calcium, essentially hardened chalk, and our muscles are water-infused fibrous tissues. We can tear our muscles and break our bones simply by falling to the ground."

Joubert sat down in the chair in front of Morten's desk, his temper noticeably cooled.

"In my time," Morten continued, "mankind had developed materials with properties you cannot begin to understand. SDUs are typically manufactured using advanced polymers and alloys. Most have an internal skeletal frame constructed from a nano-printed, plasma-fused tungsten-magnesium alloy. If our female visitor is a sentient SDU, she could probably lift us both with one arm and..." Morten lifted a pencil from his desk and snapped it in half.

Joubert stared at the broken pencil in silence. After several moments, he looked up. "Can they be killed?" he asked.

"Where there is no life," Morten replied, shaking his head, "there can be no death. You can't kill something that isn't alive."

"I mean stopped!" Joubert growled. "Can they be stopped?!"

"Yes," Morten said. "A focused electromagnetic pulse of sufficient power can penetrate an SDU's EM casing, disrupting its quantum linking. This will cause neural synapse failure, the mechanical equivalent of brain death."

"The device in the corridor?" Joubert asked, standing up swiftly and walking back towards the vault door. He stared at the strange box, examining it critically now.

Morten stood and followed him. "Yes," he said, gazing up at the box, "but it's not that simple. Most SDUs are shielded from EM disruption. A sufficiently powerful pulse," he said, gesturing at the box on the ceiling, "amplified and directed inside a confined space, might penetrate such shielding." After a moment, he turned and walked back inside the room. "They can also be stopped by an electromagnetic linear motor device," he said.

Joubert turned, his eyes narrowing in confusion.

"An EM linear motor device," Morten explained, "is a hand-held weapon. They replaced primitive firearms beginning in the 2090s. They are essentially micro railguns."

"Those darts?" Joubert asked.

"Yes," Morten replied, nodding. "Our time-traveling visitors are undoubtedly equipped with such weapons."

"And you didn't think to bring one with you when you came here?" Joubert asked, sneering in derision.

"My company was crawling with CTI officers," Morten sighed. "The armory was undoubtedly one of the first sections they seized. I was lucky to escape at all!"

When Joubert shook his head in disapproval, Morten smiled a strange smile. "I brought everything I needed," he said, tapping his balding head.

Morten abruptly walked to the back of the suite. For a moment, Joubert thought he was going to open that mysterious door. Instead, he stopped in front of the mahogany-veneered wall at the back of the room and pressed the lower corner of one of the panels. Joubert heard a faint click, and the panel swung open, revealing a biometric palm-lock affixed to a grid of metallic square panels. The lock appeared similar to the one located in the outer corridor.

Morten pressed his palm against the lock's scanning plate and one of the metal panels immediately opened, revealing a small circular vault. "It lacks the power of its future counterparts," he said, reaching into the vault, "and it takes forever for the charge to build up, but it works." When he turned, he was holding a strange device in his arms. The device consisted of two rectangular metal arms bracketing a hollow barrel and, at the base of the arms, a pair of large circular drums above what appeared to be a conventional trigger assembly. A small cord dangled free from one side of the device.

Joubert walked swiftly around the desk.

"I am a major shareholder in Mass Atomics EMS," Morten continued. "They develop prototype railgun technologies under a contract with the United States Department of Energy." He handed the strange device to Joubert, who accepted it eagerly.

"It's lighter than it looks," Joubert muttered, hefting the strange weapon in his hands. The metal brackets, barrel, and drums suggested a heavier device.

Morten nodded. "The rail system is built from an advanced lightweight alloy."

When Joubert lifted the dangling cord and looked up, Morten shrugged.

"It's Achilles heel," he said. "Unlike our opponent's weapons, this device has no internal power source. It must be externally charged. It takes a frustratingly long time to reach sufficient charge capacity, but once fully charged, it will propel its projectile with sufficient force to penetrate almost any material."

Joubert looked up swiftly, anticipation in his eyes.

"Yes," Morten said, grinning. "Even something made from an advanced tungsten-magnesium alloy." He quickly sobered. "You will have to hit her in the head," he spoke softly. "That's where her cognitive controller is likely housed. And it will take too long to cycle another charge, so you will only get one shot."

Joubert raised the weapon and sighted down the barrel.

"That's all I need."

Chapter 24

IDR: MK4AVP303//:QKDS-77483L2LE

I have observed that the deepest friendships are frequently founded upon shared hardships rather than shared interests. Humans feel innate kinship with those who have experienced similar misfortune.

Alexander Graham Bell's mother was almost completely deaf. His grandfather and father had both studied speech, and Bell had apprenticed with his father from a young age. Bell eventually moved to Boston, where he taught deaf children to speak using a set of symbols his father had invented. While in Massachusetts, he married Mabel Hubbard, one of his former deaf pupils.

In 1886, While teaching deaf students in Washington D.C., Bell was approached by the family of a six-year old girl. The girl, both blind and deaf, had been referred to Bell by a Baltimore specialist, who felt Bell might be able to help. During their first meeting, Bell removed his pocket watch and made it chime so the girl could feel its vibration. This simple act endured Bell to the young girl, and the pair formed a lifelong friendship.

Bell referred the girl to the Perkins Institution in Boston, who dispatched a tutor to her home. He frequently paid for her treatment and education and visited with her often. Using finger communication he had learned from his mother, Bell personally taught her about science and technology.

The girl, Helen Keller, later published an account of her life titled "The Story of My Life". Typed on a braille typewriter, Keller dedicated the book "to Alexander Graham Bell, who has taught the deaf to speak and enabled the listening ear to hear."

The Christmas event was winding down inside the ITER lobby. The band members who had entertained the assembled company employees for most of the afternoon were now mingling with the guests, laughing and drinking. Paul Peloux, the mayor of Saint-Paul-lès-Durance, stood near the lobby doors speaking with F4E Director Fournier. Morten stood next to the pair, smiling and holding a glass of wine.

Paillard placed the tray of la tarte Tatin on the serving table next to a small bowl of fresh whipped cream. The apple tarts, baked upside-down and caramelized in butter and sugar, drew approving smiles from a group of engineers who eagerly approached the table.When he returned to the conference room where his catering staff was preparing more dessert trays, he motioned to Liam.

"Morten is still speaking with Directeur Fournier by the front door. They appear très détendu... very relaxed."

Liam nodded. "Have you seen any security men?"

"No, mon amie. Morten is alone."

Elle joined the pair. She had been observing the catering staff all day, fascinated with their culinary preparations. At Paillard's insistence, she had sampled many of the dishes, marveling at the extraordinary variety of flavors, textures, and visual arrangements. Seeing her approach, Liam turned.

"Morten is still alone," he said.

Elle frowned. "We must assume his men are nearby," she said. "He is too smart to go anywhere without his security detail, especially when he knows CTI officers are here to take him into custody."

"I agree," Liam said, "but where are they?"

Elle's face grew concerned. "Are you reconsidering your plan?" she asked.

Liam shook his head. "No," he replied, "but I'd feel better knowing where Morten has positioned his men." Liam paused, glancing at Clifton. "And frankly," he continued, "I'd feel better if we had Clifton's MTY device with us. I don't like the idea of not being able to transit out if things go badly."

Elle nodded sympathetically. While their own MTY device contained an active temporal singularity calibrated with 2168, Clifton's did not. The trio had been using Clifton's un-calibrated MTY device as a portable EPM station, relying on it for swift transportation around the globe. They had been reluctant to bring it to the event for fear it might fall into Morten's hands, providing him with a significant tactical advantage.

Liam glanced at the clock on the wall inside the room. It was almost 8:00 pm. Clifton stood near the door, watching the room's activities. The rogue temporal specialist had insisted on accompanying the two officers to the event. However, he had been unusually quiet on the drive from Marseille, silently observing them as they sat in the back of one of Paillard's catering trucks reviewing their plans.

Liam took a deep breath. "Ok," he said, nodding to Elle. "We can't wait any longer. Let's go." He walked to the door.

Clifton opened the door, holding it open to allow a group of caterers carrying trays to pass through. The two CTI officers followed the caterers, with Clifton bringing up the rear. When the caterers turned to head down an adjoining corridor towards the lobby, the trio continued ahead, moving away from the noise of the party.

They proceeded in silence down the dim corridor. It was Friday night, and, save for the party guests in the lobby and the supporting catering staff, the ITER headquarters building was deserted. From their review of historical records, Liam knew the ITER maintained security personnel at night, as well as night-shift engineering and construction crews. The headquarters building, however, usually staffed by executive and administrative personnel, was now quiet.

As they walked, Elle glanced at the security cameras on the ceiling. Immediately after arriving that morning, she had located an ethernet data port inside the conference room. Using a cable borrowed from a nearby office, she had stripped and connected the cable wires to one of the sub-dermal nodes under her fingers and plugged the other end into the data port. Once connected, she had bypassed the security system and isolated the video surveillance feed. She had inserted a subroutine into the primitive application, replaying the camera feeds from the previous evening for all ITER locations except the front lobby of the headquarters building. She would have preferred to PoL with the system in real-time, masking their image from isolated video feeds as they moved about, but if Morten also possessed a datstem, he would have detected her QRB signal.

From Clifton's first-hand descriptions of the technical infrastructure available in this era, the CTI officers were reasonably certain Morten's file would reside on a computer physically or wirelessly connected to the local ITER network. In addition to altering the active security feed, Elle had conducted a preliminary sweep of ITER's file directories but had not detected the file. Clifton had suggested the file was on a connected but presently idle computer. Accepting this, Liam had proposed searching Morten's executive office within the building and expanding their search from there.

The group walked in silence down the dark hallway. When they reached the lift, Clifton pressed the call button.

At that moment, Elle smiled and spoke softly.

"This is my first party."

Liam turned, surprise in his eyes.

"What?"

"I've never been to a party before."

Liam seemed confused and glanced at Clifton. The tall specialist, however, was watching Elle.

"You can't really call it a party, can you?" Liam asked, shaking his head. "I mean, we never left the catering prep area."

"It's still a party."

Liam glanced again at Clifton. The temporal specialist now made eye contact, frowned, and nodded encouragingly towards the slim female.

Liam seemed embarrassed. When the lift arrived, he spoke hesitantly, holding the door open with his arm. "Would you like to go to a real party?" he asked, adding, "...when we return?"

Elle paused in the act of stepping into the lift. She looked at him with a strange expression on her face. "Are you asking me to socialize with you in a setting other than one authorized by our assignment?"

Clifton abruptly grinned and quickly turned away to examine the fire exit sign above a nearby stairway access door. When Liam did not immediately respond, Elle turned around in the open lift door and faced the officer.

"I'm sorry," she said, "but I require clarification again. Your question suggests you wish us to engage socially to assess our suitability as prospective partners in a long-term relationship. Is that your intent?"

Liam flushed and glanced at Clifton. The temporal specialist, however, was staring fixedly at the neon exit sign, determined to appear distracted.

Liam looked back at Elle, then nodded.

"Yes," he said.

Elle smiled and nodded quickly, "Yes," she said, "I'd like that very much."

Liam seemed about to respond when Elle's hand suddenly shot up, motioning him to silence. She tapped her ear and pointed into the darkness, then stepped back out into the hallway.

Liam quickly turned.

Clifton glanced back at the two officers. Seeing their intent gaze, he stepped back quietly, disappearing into the shadows.

Liam allowed the lift door to close and retrieved his RU-6. Elle's superior acoustic system had obviously heard someone moving about inside the presumably empty building. He began walking quietly down the dark hallway. Elle walked beside him, scanning the floor ahead. Clifton now produced a contemporary firearm from under his shirt and began to follow the duo, glancing back from time to time.

Elle was experiencing the sentient-automaton equivalent of frustration. Her auditory receptors had detected faint sounds that her analytic processor had immediately classified as human footfalls. More concerning, however, was the pattern of the steps. They suggested someone moving covertly, stopping abruptly, then moving away at increased speed. While she was confident about the nature of the sounds, she was unable to use her muon tomographic scanner to locate their source. The ITER facility deployed particle detectors to alert personnel to the release of errant radiation. If she activated her muon scanner anywhere within the ITER campus, she risked triggering a radiation alarm.

The officers were approaching the bend in the long 'J'-shaped building. When they reached the turn, Elle froze, tapped Liam's arm, and pointed to the floor.

Liam quickly retrieved his tactical optics. He could see faint heat signatures from a set of footprints emerging from a nearby adjoining corridor. The pattern to the prints shuffled a bit, then turned and proceeded further down the dim hallway. From the decaying thermal levels, his optics reported the footprints were less than a minute old.

He hesitated. After a moment, he turned and faced his companions. Using DE-standard hand signals, he instructed Elle to take Clifton and proceed to Morten's office. In response to Clifton's finger query, he indicated his intent to follow the footprints. When the tall specialist hesitated, Liam shook his head firmly and gave the sign that made the instruction an order. Clifton immediately nodded, turned, and began moving quietly back towards the lift. Elle, however, hesitated for a moment. Concern was evident in her eyes. When he smiled and nodded reassuringly, she turned and followed Clifton, disappearing into the darkness.

Liam took a deep breath, then proceeded ahead slowly, following the thermal footprints down the hallway. As he walked, he passed several offices, connecting hallways, and conference rooms. Several of the office doors had been left open by the janitorial staff. The open doorways concerned him. While the thermal prints ahead were clear and well-defined, they would not inform him of the presence of anyone waiting to ambush him from inside one of those open rooms.

He touched the side of his optics and configured the device to its highest thermal setting. The footprints on the floor suddenly burst into white-hot patterns, creating thermal ripples in the air above the floor. At this setting, the ultra-sensitive device could detect thermal variations as subtle as a person's body heat and breath disturbing the air inside the adjoining rooms.

It was disorienting to walk with the optics configured to this extreme setting. He felt like he was following flaming footprints through a room filled with glowing red-hot plasma that rippled and swirled around him. He could 'see' the heating ducts above the ceiling panels over his head and the precise location of hot water pipes rising behind the walls like red-hot rods. Clouds of glowing orange air billowed softly into the hallway from the open doors, pushed along by the building's central heating. The airflow, however, appeared uniform, smooth, and undisturbed.

He was nearing the end of the long building. Just ahead, the hallway connected with an adjacent corridor. From his review of the building's architectural records, he knew the hall cut through the center of the building before emptying onto a covered footbridge. Designed to provide administrative personnel quick access to the main ITER complex, the bridge spanned a paved road before tunneling into the earthen plateau beneath what would later become the ITER control building. Kilometers of water, electrical, and service tunnels formed a catacomb beneath that plateau, connecting the above-ground buildings and structures. He approached the corridor cautiously.

When he turned the corner, he stopped. The pattern of footprints had changed. The footprint owner appeared to have turned and re-approached the corner. From the increased heat levels, it was clear they had lingered there for several moments before turning and resuming their path towards the footbridge. The stride between the prints, however, now dramatically increased as their heat signatures diminished. He swore under his breath. Whomever he was tracking was obviously aware of his pursuit.

He scanned the corridor ahead where it transitioned to form the covered footbridge. The thermal air patterns inside the glass-enclosed bridge swirled and moved in a chaotic, random way, the result of someone recently moving through that quiet passageway. Where the bridge entered the earth beyond the spanned road, the air grew dark and cold; an ominous dark eye inside that swirling infrared storm.

From her position inside the dark coffee prep room, Elle listened closely to the whispered conversation coming from the office on the other side of the lobby.

Clifton stood beside her, silent and alert.

The duo had taken the lift to the top floor of the building, where their earlier review of the directory told them Morten's office was located. After proceeding through a waiting room filled with stuffed chairs and engineering-themed art, they had passed through a set of glass doors into what appeared to be a private reception area. Tall mahogany doors stood at the back of the lobby beside a collection of leather chairs on an exquisite Serapi hand-knotted wool carpet. On one of the doors, a digital locking pad framed a metal security handle beneath a plate that read, 'N. Morten, Directeur'.

The door was open.

When they first entered the lobby, Elle had noted fading footprint heat signatures approaching the tall doors across the room. Her ultra-sensitive auditory receptors had also detected sounds coming from inside the office. She immediately alerted Clifton, and the pair had retreated to a darkened coffee prep room. Once inside, she had tuned her audio receptors to their maximum setting. After applying a filtering algorithm and eliminating the surrounding white noise, the conversation inside the nearby office became clear.

"Leg it! How long does it take to boot up a bleedin' laptop?"

"Tu n'as pas de patience."

"What the hell is taking so long?"

"Morten has a special security program that needs to be disabled before we disconnect the thing from the network."

"What's so feckin important about this laptop?"

"Morten doesn't want them to steal it. He says to bring it to him, so we bring it to him."

"How does he know the sleeven bastards will even be here tonight?"

"They're already here. Be silent."

Several minutes went by with no further talking.

"That's it. Allons-y."

"Bout time!"

Elle listened closely as soft sounds coming from the office suggested preparations to leave. A moment later, she heard the tall mahogany door click shut. From inside the pitch-black room, she peered through the crack between the door and the wall. Two figures were standing outside the office. The taller man had a pattern of scars on his forehead and cheek. Her facial recognition algorithm identified him as one of those they had encountered at the ambush south of Marseille. He was carrying a laptop computer under his arm and had turned his back on the other man to enter a code into the door's locking plate.

The shorter man had also been at the ambush site and had thrown the grenade that had damaged Paillard's vehicle. The man glanced back at the glass doors behind the reception desk.

"Let's be goin!" the smaller man said, glancing back at the reception door.

The taller man smiled. "Pourquoi es-tu si nerveux?" he asked.

"Feck off!" the smaller man said, scowling. "I'm naw nervous. I just don't want to get ambushed again."

A faint click was heard, and a red LED light appeared on the digital lock. The taller man turned and led his companion towards the glass reception door. When they passed the coffee prep room, Elle pulled her concealed RU-6 from behind her back. She was about to step out and confront the pair when the taller man spoke again.

"No need to worry," he said. "Yvette is leading them into the tunnels. They won't be able to track her there, and she's got Morten's little surprise waiting for them inside. It won't be us getting ambushed this time."

Elle froze. In a flash, her cognitive processor grasped the implications of the man's statement.

Liam was walking into a trap!

Chapter 25

IDR: MK4AVP340//:QKDS-77483L2LE

Which is more courageous? Opposing one's friends or opposing one's enemies?

On October 27, 1962, during a tense period in world history colloquially known as the Cuban Missile Crisis, a United States aircraft carrier group located a nuclear-armed Soviet Union submarine near Cuba. The submerged submarine's batteries were exhausted, and its air-conditioning system had failed, causing extreme heat and high levels of carbon dioxide inside the submarine. With U.S. destroyers dropping explosive signaling charges to force the submarine to the surface and too deep to receive or transmit communications, the submarine Captain was convinced war had broken out. With the support of his political officer, the Captain prepared to fire a nuclear-equipped torpedo at the U.S. fleet.

Second officer, Commodore Vasili Arkhipov, refused to give his consent, demanding the Captain surface and request instructions from Moscow. Despite heated opposition from the Captain and political officer, Arkhipov eventually prevailed, and the submarine surfaced. An advisor to U.S. President Kennedy later described the incident as the most dangerous moment in human history. In 2002, the U.S. National Security Archive Director confirmed Arkhipov's courage had saved the world.

In my research, I have noted numerous examples of humans called courageous for defying their enemies, but few examples where humans were called courageous for defying a friend.

Does it not take greater courage to oppose one's friends?

Liam walked slowly through the tunnel. On either side, six rows of steel racks bolted to the concrete walls gave the impression of empty bunk beds lining an abandoned underground shelter. Intended to provide technicians with easy access to the hundreds of kilometers of electrical wiring, pipes, and ducts needed to support the structures above, the racks were presently empty.

Florescent lighting above the racks illuminated the tunnel for hundreds of meters ahead. He reconfigured his tactical optics for motion detection and held his RU-6 at the ready. He could hear water dripping from a leaking water pipe somewhere ahead. A soft rustling noise briefly supplemented the sound; undoubtedly, a rat or mouse had found its way into the subterranean maze from one of the tunnel's many unfinished access points. The creature's tiny feet was echoed and magnified in the confined space, forcing him to frown at the sound of his own footfalls.

After crossing the glass-enclosed footbridge, he had found himself inside a concrete-lined square tunnel under what would eventually become the ITER Control Building. That tunnel quickly branched to join with other electrical, water, and service tunnels, forming a veritable labyrinth beneath the ITER plateau. Many of the tunnels were unfinished, opening onto deep earthen trenches beneath the stars or blocked with earth, waiting for excavation to resume.

About twenty meters ahead, he could see another junction, an intersection of passageways radiating from a central point. He had passed several similar junctions already. They had contained metal ladder rungs set into the concrete walls, providing access through a surface hatch to the subterranean chamber below. He approached the junction cautiously. The sound of water dripping was growing stronger, and the tunnels beyond the junction were dark.

When he neared the intersection, he looked down in confusion. The infrared footprints he had been following did not go beyond the chamber. It was as if their owner had simply vanished. The floor also rippled strangely through his tactical optics, black and cold. He removed the optics and let his eyes adjust for a moment to the dim light, then looked down. The floor was covered with several inches of water. A water pipe attached to the ceiling was leaking, and a bit of cloth had been shoved into the storm drain in the center of the floor, allowing the water to accumulate.

He stepped into the junction and bent down to remove the cloth from the drainage pipe. At that moment, a flash of color caught his eye inside the dim tunnel to his left. He whirled, then stopped. It was only a red scarf hanging from one of the metal racks.

"If you move, you will be killed."

The voice was feminine and spoke softly from behind him.

"Drop your weapon."

Liam hesitated, considering his options. After a moment, he stood up and dropped his RU-6, letting it splash into the water at his feet.

"Turn around."

When he turned, a woman emerged from the dark passage behind him. She was slim, with short-cropped brown hair, and held a suppressed pistol in her hand. Liam recognized her as the woman who had greeted Paillard inside the hotel, moments before Stojanović had made his desperate escape. Her hair had been blonde then, but it was the same woman.

"My name is Yvette Beauchêne. I have been looking forward to meeting you."

Liam glanced at the water.

Noting his gaze, Yvette smiled. "Morten said you would not be able to track my footsteps through the water."

Liam said nothing.

"Where is your woman?" Yvette asked.

Liam remained silent.

"You will not say?"

Liam now noticed a strange dark metallic tube attached by a cable to a hard case in the dim tunnel behind the woman.

Yvette nodded and held up a remote. "When your woman reached this chamber," she said, "I was instructed to press this button. I am assured the effect is most incapacitating."

Liam understood. Morten had planned to disable Elle with an electromagnetic pulse device. Triggering the device underground, inside the enclosed concrete tunnels with their rows of metallic racks, would reduce the risk of damage to any above-ground electronics, while the narrow tunnel would amplify its disruptive effects on Elle's neural network. The presence of the device meant Morten was aware of Elle's synthetic nature.

Yvette sighed, returning the remote to her pocket. "I was so looking forward to pressing the button," she said. "C'est la vie." She motioned now with her pistol back towards the lighted tunnel. "Step back."

When Liam complied, Yvette stepped into the junction and retrieved his RU-6 from the water. She examined the strange weapon, then frowned. "A taser?" she asked, cocking her head.

Liam was surprised. "You don't know who I am, do

you?" he asked.

Yvette looked up, appraising the tall officer. "I know you captured that bastard, Stojanović," she replied, "but... je m'en fous. You're nobody to me." She stepped back and gestured with her pistol towards the metal rung ladder attached to the junction wall. "Grimpe l'échelle," she ordered. "Climb up, s'il vous plaît. Morten waits for us at the party."

Liam approached the ladder slowly. He hesitated, looking up at the metal hatch.

"Rapide," Yvette barked, her tone stern.

Liam ascended several rungs, then stopped. Yvette was standing at his feet, pointing her pistol at him. "Don't forget your scarf," he said, gesturing at the dark tunnel.

Yvette looked away, and in that instant, Liam kicked out with his foot, striking her in the face. She fell backward, firing as she fell, sending a bullet ricocheting off the ceiling of the dark passage.

Liam dropped swiftly back down into the chamber. Yvette scrambled to her knees and raised her pistol, but he kicked it free from her hand, sending it clattering and skidding back down the lighted tunnel.

Yvette scrambled to her feet and raced down the lighted passage after the weapon.

Liam looked around quickly, trying to locate his RU-6 in the dark water. Out of options, he turned and ran past the scarf into the dark tunnel. Water splattered and splashed beneath his feet for a few moments, then ceased.

The tunnel was completely dark. Liam slowed, then stopped. He could feel the metal racks lining the passage, and using these as his guide, he felt his way forward. Suddenly, a shot rang out, and a bullet flew past his head, striking and rattling against the metal racks further ahead. He threw himself to the ground and rolled beneath the bottom row of racks. He scrambled for his optics as another shot whined and rattled down the passage.

With his tactical optics, he could see Yvette approaching slowly from the dim junction. She was holding her pistol in one hand and listening as she used the metal racks to feel her way forward in the dark.

He scanned the passage ahead. Approximately ten meters away, he could see a connecting tunnel crossing theirs. As quietly as he dared, he crawled forward under the racks. Another shot rang out, and a bullet struck the concrete floor next to his hand. When he reached the connecting tunnel, he slid silently around the corner. Once clear, he jumped to his feet and began to run.

This tunnel was unfinished. Bundles of rebar and stacks of rack materials lay against the walls. Just ahead, he could see the darkness receding around a lighted opening. When he cleared the opening, he removed his optics and looked about quickly.

He was standing inside a deep trench. Sheets of plywood forms were attached to the sides of the entrance, forms waiting to be filled with concrete to further the underground passage. The wooden forms continued down the trench for perhaps fifteen meters before ending flush against a steep wall of earth. Scattered lengths of loose rebar lay on the ground, and an excavator machine sat above the trench, its steel-toothed scoop positioned ominously in the air.

At that moment, Yvette rounded the corner inside the tunnel. Seeing the dim opening far ahead, she fired.

The bullet whizzed past Liam's shoulder and struck the

earth at the back of the open trench. He looked around swiftly. The plywood forms prevented any escape up the sides of the trench, and the earth beneath the excavator formed an unscalable wall, hard and smooth.

Yvette slowed her pace, then walked determinedly towards the tunnel opening. When she exited the passage, she stopped. A purple bruise spanned her face, and blood oozed from her nose.

"Vous connard!" she growled. When Liam did not respond, she nodded slowly and raised the pistol. "Très bien," she said, smiling. "Morten instructed me to bring you to the party, but I do not enjoy such social events."

Liam braced himself, waiting for the flash of gunpowder that would end his life.

At that moment, running footsteps were heard rapidly approaching from inside the tunnel. Yvette whirled, but before she could react, Elle burst through the dark opening; a blur of deadly motion directed at the astonished woman. Elle closed the distance in an instant and struck the weapon free from Yvette's hand.

Yvette stared in shock. Then, rage effused her face, and she leaped forward.

Elle effortlessly parried the blow, fracturing both bones in Yvette's lower arm before striking her forcefully in her sternum.

Yvette staggered backward, gasping in pain. She fell back against the earth at the back of the trench, cradling her fractured arm and staring at Elle in shock. "What… are you?" she gasped.

When Elle did not respond, Yvette's eyes narrowed, and she fumbled with her unbroken arm for something under her shirt. When she withdrew her hand, it was holding a grenade. "Va te faire foutre!" she hissed as she struggled to pull the pin.

Elle dove to the ground, rolling forward. When she came up, she was holding a length of rebar in her hand. Continuing the momentum of her roll, she threw the bar in a swift, fluid motion at the struggling woman.

The rod pierced Yvette Beauchêne through her heart, pinning her to the earth wall where she stood. She jerked once, then slumped forward, still and silent, her body impaled on the steel bar. The grenade dropped from her hand and rolled harmlessly between her feet.

Elle approached Liam quickly. "Are you injured?" she asked, concern in her voice.

"No," Liam said, shaking his head.

More footsteps now echoed from the tunnel, and a moment later, Clifton emerged from the entrance. He stopped abruptly, taking in the situation.

Elle turned to examine the dead woman. "Who was she?" she asked.

"I'm not sure," Liam replied. "I suspect she may be our unidentified female assailant… the one that killed Stojanović."

"We found this inside the tunnels," Clifton said, approaching him with the RU-6 in his hand. "It was lying in some water, near to what appears to be an electromagnetic pulse generator."

Liam nodded, accepting the weapon. "She was using the water," he explained, gesturing at the dead woman, "to hide her thermal footprints."

Elle nodded. "An effective counter to thermal tracking, but it also allowed us to locate you. We simply followed the wet tracks."

Clifton gazed about the narrow trench. "We can't leave the body here to be discovered," he said. "It will trigger too many questions from the local authorities, but with my MTY device back at the hotel, we can't dispose of it as we did with the others."

Liam glanced up at the excavator scoop over his head. "We could use that machine to bury the body," he suggested.

Clifton shook his head. "Those aren't like our soil displacement SDUs," he said. "Their liquid-fueled engines are deafening. The sound would undoubtedly draw attention."

Elle looked back at the opening. The trench on either side of the tunnel was in the process of being backfilled with earth. "We can conceal the body outside the concrete tunnel," she said, pointing. "Between the concrete and the trench wall. It should be an easy matter to trigger a small earth slide to conceal the body and, when they resume backfilling the trench in the morning, that will complete the burial."

Clifton looked up at the earth visible above the tunnel forms. "That's a good idea. I'll see if I can find something we can use to dig."

The temporal specialist walked back inside the dark passage.

Liam watched Elle closely. Ever since their brief adventure on Île d'If, there was something profoundly changed about his partner. She had not volunteered any details, but he was convinced something had happened inside the island Château. She had emerged from the stone structure strangely changed. Her hesitation and self-doubt were gone, replaced by a confidence and self-assurance that he had never before observed. Her shocking romantic overture on the boat had simply reinforced his suspicions; the female that accompanied him to the island was not the same one that had returned with him to Marseille.

He recalled her accusation during their drive to ITER; that he was in love with her. He also recalled what the analysts said about the subject; that a machine that is capable of refusing an order must also be capable of love.

Elle stood examining the earth visible above the wood forms on either side of the trench, then turned to follow Clifton into the tunnel.

"Elle," he said, stopping her departure.

She turned, waiting.

"You saved my life," he said. "I want to thank you."

She smiled warmly but said nothing.

"I… I also want to ask you something," he continued.

"Yes?"

"I told you to locate Morten's file."

Elle nodded her agreement but said nothing. She was watching Liam's face closely. He did not appear angry. His tone and facial expressions did not evidence either disappointment or dissatisfaction. He seemed merely thoughtful.

"You've never disobeyed my orders before," Liam continued, "so, why did you this time? Why did you come looking for me?"

Elle glanced at the dead woman still impaled against the earth, then down at the scattered lengths of rebar on the ground. After several moments, she looked up.

"I came because I overheard one of Morten's men describing a trap they had prepared inside the tunnel."

"I understand that," Liam said, nodding, "but why would that information cause you to disobey my orders?"

Confusion clouded Elle's hazel eyes, as if she were struggling to understand his question. After a moment, a frown crossed her brow.

"I came," she replied, "because… you are important to me."

"More important than obeying my orders?" he asked, watching her closely.

Within Elle's neural network, that mysterious equation that had imposed itself onto her consciousness inside Edmond Dantès' cell was alive with activity.

"Was finding me more important than obeying my orders?" he repeated.

She looked up.

"Yes," she said. "Finding you was more important."

Burying Yvette's body was accomplished swiftly. Clifton returned after several minutes, carrying a length of rack framing he had found inside the tunnel. The two men removed the body from the earth wall and then stood debating for several minutes about the best way to hoist the corpse to the top of the tunnel. After several minutes of listening to their conversation, Elle abruptly lifted the dead woman, took the metal rack from Clifton's surprised hand, and leaped to the top of the tunnel. The two men watched, chagrinned, as she effortlessly walked to the edge and disappeared. She reappeared several minutes later, jumping over the wood forms to land inside the trench, startling both men considerably.

When the trio returned to the conference room, they found the catering staff milling about in confusion. Several of the staff were on their cell phones, concern on their faces.

Paillard was nowhere to be seen.

Clifton approached the restaurant's grey-haired sous-chef de cuisine.

"Henri," he said, looking about the room, "Où est

Paillard?"

"Monsieur!" the distraught chef exclaimed, grasping his hand. "A man took him!"

Clifton frowned, glancing at Liam, who quickly approached with Elle.

"A man?" Clifton prompted.

The chef nodded swiftly.

"Oui! A most disagreeable man, monsieur! He walked inside… perhaps fifteen minutes ago and forced monsieur Paillard to go with him."

"What did this man look like?" Liam interrupted.

With a reassuring nod from Clifton, the chef spoke quickly, wiping his brow with a cloth.

"He was tall. He had dark hair, and… son visage était marqué." He quickly drew his fingers across his cheek. "His face… many marks. Comprenez vous?"

Liam nodded, glancing at Elle.

Paillard had been captured.

Chapter 26

IDR: MK4AVP522//:QKDS-77483L2LE

Colonel Thomas Edward Lawrence, describing a small Bedouin army's success against the Turks during World War I, observed that great things often have small beginnings.

On the morning of March 4, 1918, Mess Cook (Pvt.) Albert Gitchell approached the duty sergeant inside the hospital building at Fort Riley, Kansas. Gitchell was feverish and complained of a sore throat, headache, and muscular pains.

While Gitchell was being examined, Corporal Lee W. Drake entered the building with identical symptoms. A moment later, Sergeant Adolph Hurby arrived, coughing and complaining of a fever. The corpsman called for the duty nurse, and by the time she reached the hospital, two more sick soldiers were waiting to be treated. By noon, 107 patients had been admitted to the hospital.

In 1918, a particularly virulent strain of H1N1 influenza spread around the world, infecting 500 million people, approximately one-third of the world's population at that time. Historians place the death toll between 20 million and 50 million people, with some estimates ranging as high as 100 million people, making it one of the deadliest pandemics in human history.

Great things may, indeed, have small beginnings, but whether or not they are remembered favorably is another matter.

Elle re-checked the mag-field indicator on Liam's RU-6. The weapon's diagnostic cycle was reporting a 42-micrometer misalignment of its internal rail system.

While minor, the misalignment could affect long-distant target acquisition.

Clifton and Liam sat nearby in front of the hotel room window. The pair had been debating rescue plans for more than an hour.

"Morten obviously took Paillard to use him as leverage," Clifton said.

"I agree," Liam nodded, "but leverage for what?" He rubbed the back of his neck, then glanced at Elle. When he spoke again, his voice was tinged with frustration. "Morten knows Paillard has been helping us, and I suspect he knows Paillard is also our friend, but what value does the man have as a hostage? Morten can't expect us to abandon our mission and return to the future to secure Paillard's release. That would be a useless gesture. He knows the council would simply send someone else to try again."

Elle glanced up.

Noting her attention, Liam stood and crossed the room. He looked at the weapon on the desk and frowned when Elle pointed to the misalignment reading on its diagnostic display. He lifted the weapon and adjusted it while speaking over his shoulder to Clifton.

"I think Morten will try to use Paillard to lure us into another trap."

From his chair by the window, Clifton nodded. "My datstem estimates a greater than 73% probability that you are correct, but…" He hesitated, then shook his head. "It just feels like Morten is planning something else."

Liam returned the weapon, then turned to stare at the temporal specialist. "A feeling?" he asked.

Clifton glanced up, then flushed. "Yes," he said. "I know

that's not..."

Liam immediately shook his head, silencing the specialist's explanation. "I'm not ridiculing you, Clifton. I respect your TCPP abilities tremendously. I've worked with several temporal specialists who possess your talent, but I have never understood why they insist on being so vague. Can't you people be more specific?"

Clifton grinned, then quickly sobered. He stood and walked to the window, pushing aside the curtains. In the bay, two ships were crossing in front of Île d'If. Their lights were twinkling in the darkness. He stood silent for several minutes, watching the lights as they rounded Cap de Croix on nearby Île Ratonneau. When they disappeared, he spoke softly into the glass.

"We're coming to the end of something," he said. "I can't give you specifics, but it feels like something temporally significant is about to occur." He turned to face the two officers and said, "I believe your mission here is almost over."

"Why do you say that?" Liam asked.

Elle looked up from her work.

Clifton shook his head. "I'm not certain," he said, "but when I consider the courses of action we might take, my thoughts fixate on Morten's villa. It's a strange kind of fixation, a feeling I've been trained to recognize. There is a finality associated with it."

"We've already discussed that option," Liam said. "We can't assault Morten's villa. It is too well defended."

"I didn't say we should assault the villa," Clifton responded, shaking his head again. "I just believe something temporally significant is going to happen there." He glanced at Elle, then turned back to gaze across the water at Île d'If.

The island was now dark and silent.

The messenger arrived just after 1:00 am. Liam's surveillance drots alerted him to a hotel porter exiting the lift with an envelope in his hand.

Clifton was speaking with Elle by the desk. They had been engaged in a quiet conversation for almost an hour. Liam interrupted the pair, gesturing to the door.

"Someone's here," he said. "Looks like the night porter."

Clifton and Elle stood immediately. Liam opened the door a moment later, accepted a sealed envelope, and then shut and locked the door.

The message was short and concise; '*I propose an exchange. Bring your MTY device to my villa in one hour. NM*'.

"He means to strand us here," Liam said, handing the note to Elle. "If he terminates our temporal singularity… if we fail to return, he knows the council will likely abandon its attempt to retrieve him."

Elle handed the note to Clifton. "For his plan to succeed," she said, "he must also make us disappear. We must appear to have vanished into history without a trace."

Liam nodded, his expression grim.

Clifton was reading the note carefully. After a moment, he looked up. The temporal specialist had a strange expression on his face.

"What if Morten has other plans for your MTY device?" he asked.

Liam shook his head. "Other plans?"

Clifton nodded. "We believe Morten is using his stolen MTY device's fusion reactor to produce a scattering field, correct?"

"Strongly indicated," Elle said, nodding. "It explains your earlier inability to transit inside his villa, as well as the residual particle impacts I detected coming from him in Oxford."

Clifton began to pace the room, speaking swiftly.

"If Morten has cannibalized his device to create a scattering field," he said, "then he is stranded here. The particles generated by his device's un-shielded reactor will have disrupted the temporal singularity he used to get here. They will also have swiftly degraded the device's containment unit. So, even if he restores his reactor shielding, his containment unit can no longer hold a singularity."

"A reasonable conclusion," Elle said, nodding.

Clifton stopped pacing and pointed to her backpack sitting on the floor. "Your MTY device, however, is still capable of containing a singularity." In the silence that followed, he turned to face the two officers. "I think Morten plans on using your MTY device to escape again."

"If that's his plan," Elle said, "he must terminate his scattering field before we arrive. He can't risk damaging our device's containment unit."

Clifton smiled, then said, "A reasonable conclusion."

Elle looked up, amusement in her eyes.

Clifton now turned to face Liam.

"Morten knows you two have come here from the future, but he doesn't know who I am. He probably thinks I am just a friend of Paillard, someone from this time. He doesn't know that I came from the future too."

When Liam shook his head, not understanding, Clifton pointed to his MTY device sitting next to Elle's backpack.

"We have a second MTY device."

Morten watched Joubert closely. He had never observed the large man so agitated. Joubert poured himself another shot of cognac, sloshing a bit on the teak bar before gulping down the entire glass. His protective vest held two ballistic plates instead of its normal one, and he sported a Glock 17 pistol in a leg holster and carried an MP5 submachine gun, but it was the strange railgun sitting on the bar that appeared to occupy the large man's attention. He was staring at the weapon with a peculiar expression on his face. It reminded Morten of the fixed attention a cheetah gives to a gazelle moments before the chase begins. It was a hungry expression, anxious but controlled.

Olsen had returned minutes ago from exploring the tunnels under the ITER plateau and reported no sign of Yvette Beauchêne. The electromagnetic pulse device that Morten had acquired from one of his German subsidiary companies was also missing. Olsen had found a single spent shell casing that matched the caliber of handgun Yvette favored and had reported several marks inside one of the tunnels consistent with bullet impacts, but there was no sign of Beauchêne.

Morten glanced at the security feed on his desk display. Olsen stood outside the suite's heavy vault door, speaking with Burke. Both men wore body armor and were heavily armed.

Burke was carrying a bandolier of grenades in addition to a suppressed HK416. The Irishman made Morten nervous, but there was no denying the man's explosive expertise. At Burke's suggestion, the passageway outside the suite's heavy steel door now boasted an array of concussive charges, connected by a detonation timer to the electromagnetic pulse generator on the ceiling. Burke had rigged the detonation circuit to a switch installed under Morten's desk. The EM field generator was fully charged.

Olsen, as always, held his FN SCAR-H rifle at the ready. Morten liked Olsen. The man was calm under fire and dependable. Joubert reported the large dutchman had been greatly disturbed by what he had witnessed inside the bed & breakfast at Oxford. Still, he had continued to perform his duties well, maintaining a level of detached professionalism that Morten admired.

Across the marble floor, Devereaux sat beside Paillard on a Poltrona Frau Kennedee curved sofa. Like Burke and Olsen, Devereaux was armored and carried a suppressed HK416 rifle and several grenades. The man's leg wound was healing well, though he still wore a support bandage.

Paillard sat quietly next to Devereaux. The restaurateur appeared nervous. Morten had ordered Joubert to untie the chef, determined to demonstrate his dominance over the armed men. The tactic had worked, and Morten noted the restaurateur's immediate attention whenever he spoke or moved about the room.

Joubert abruptly threw his glass, shattering the mirror at the back of the bar.

"Calm yourself!" Morten barked, scowling at the large man.

Joubert's grip tightened on his MP5, but he said nothing. After a moment, he strode purposefully across the marble floor and stood in front of Morten's desk.

"We must strike the hotel! Tonight! Tout de suite!"

Morten shook his head. "There is no need. They are coming here."

Joubert sneered, gesturing at Paillard. "You seriously expect them to exchange their machine for this putain d'idiot?"

Morten stared at the large Frenchman, and their eyes

locked in a contest of wills. This time, however, it was not Joubert who turned away. After a few moments, Morten lowered his eyes, shaking his head.

"You must trust me, Adrian. I…"

"Trust?!" Joubert's eyes flashed. "Je crache sur la confiance! Half my men are dead because I trusted you!"

Morten's head shot up, and his face took on a cold expression. "You forget yourself, Joubert!" he spoke coldly. "They are not your men! They are my men! You and your men work for me!"

Joubert glared for a moment, then turned and walked back to the bar.

Morten immediately stood and followed the large man. When Joubert reached for the bottle of cognac, he took it forcibly from his hand. "You've had enough of that!" he said, placing the stopper back into the glass bottle.

Joubert whirled, then stopped, making an effort to control his anger.

"I need you to be alert," Morten spoke calmly.

After a few tense moments, Joubert snorted and appeared to relax. "I'm French," he said, gesturing dismissively at the bottle in Morten's hand. "It takes more than a few drinks to dull my reflexes."

Morten was about to reply, but Joubert abruptly walked away, apparently abandoning his designs. The large man stopped in front of the couch, looked at Devereaux, and then jerked his thumb towards the door.

Devereaux hesitated, glancing at Morten. When Morten nodded, he stood and walked towards the heavy door.

Joubert quickly sat down on the sofa next to Paillard, grinning at the restauranteur's discomfort.

Morten returned to his desk and pressed the button to retract the heavy door's locking bolts. Devereaux glanced backward once, then exited the suite to join Burke and Olsen in the outer corridor. Morten immediately re-sealed the door, and an uncomfortable silence settled in the room.

Morten sat down behind his desk and stared at the broken mirror for several minutes, lost in thought. After a few moments, he turned to Paillard.

"Tell me about the female."

Paillard looked up, surprise on his face. "Female?" he asked.

Morten smiled and touched the embedded display on his desk. A flat-screen display mounted on the wall opposite the couch suddenly turned on, revealing an image of Elle's face that filled the screen.

Joubert recognized the image. It was a still-frame taken from the ITER security camera feed Morten had received from Director Fournier.

"Je ne l'ai jamais vue," Paillard said, shaking his head in feigned confusion. "Who is she?"

Morten pressed the display again. Another image filled the screen. Taken by Olsen from his concealed position on the fishing boat the night of the ambush, this image was much clearer. It was an image of Elle and Liam standing beside their table inside the lighted restaurant. Paillard stood between the pair, kissing Elle on her cheek.

Paillard flushed and turned away.

"Do you kiss all of your dinner guests?" Morten asked, enjoying the man's embarrassment. After a few moments, he shrugged. "I am merely curious," he said. "What can you tell me about her?"

Paillard glanced at the image on the screen, then turned away. "I can tell you nothing about her, monsieur," he said.

"No?" Morten asked. "Then perhaps you will allow me to tell you something about her." He opened a cabinet at his feet and retrieved a small laptop, setting it on the desk.

Joubert looked up, curious. It was the laptop that he and Burke had retrieved from Morten's office at ITER.

Morten lifted the laptop lid, then keyed something into the keyboard. After a moment, he tapped one of the keys, and the large flat-screen display on the wall behind the desk momentarily went black, then reinitialized. A video began to play on the screen, showing a grey, metal-framed robot ambling across a room. The robot had a large battery box mounted on its back and a tube-framed "head" fitted with optical cameras. It was tethered to a supporting rail system overhead, and, as it walked, a technician followed close behind, his hand on a console.

"2013… from a company in the United States," Morten said, clearly unimpressed. "Just a prototype, of course."

He tapped the laptop keyboard again, and the video abruptly changed. A much sleeker robot now appeared, walking on a bed of rocks inside a lab. This robot had a long cable attached to its back but was no longer tethered to an overhead support rail. After a few moments, the video changed again to show the same robot moving through a dense forest, followed closely by a technician holding a laptop attached to the trailing cable.

"2015," he said, gesturing with his thumb at the mounted screen. "Notice the balance improvement?"

The video changed again, showing yet another robot walking through a snowy forest. This robot was no longer cabled and strolled over the snow-covered ground, cautiously stepping over a log. The video changed to show the same robot inside a warehouse jumping onto a box. It balanced there for a moment, then jumped to land on a second box. Then, it abruptly leaped forward, flipping in mid-air to land on the floor.

"2016," he said, smiling at Paillard's startled reaction.

"2024… 2037… 2050… 2088…"

Morten tolled the years ahead, and as Paillard watched in amazement, the video montage progressed through an increasingly advanced assortment of robots. Primitive machines with multiple arms fitted with tools gave way to an explosion of assorted mechanical shapes; rolling cylinders, multi-legged spiders, and bi-pedal human-like machines.

Joubert watched intently, no less amazed than Paillard. As he watched, he took note of one other aspect of this robot evolution. As the years progressed, the machines were becoming faster, more agile, with enhanced reflexes and greater strength.

Suddenly, the video changed again, displaying a fascinating urban scene. Rolling cylindrical wheels moved along a pedestrian walkway, darting and weaving among an apparently disinterested populace, while driverless vehicles passed nearby on the street beneath a hovering transport drone. One of the cylinders slowed to a stop in front of a building. A small square opening appeared at the base of the seamless wall, and the machine rolled forward, disappearing into the structure.

"By 2100," Morten explained, pointing at the screen, "engineers began to recognize that robotic engineering was diverging into two separate disciplines. There was still an endless assortment of bots that performed repair, manufacturing, and so on, all under some form of human supervision, but newer, more advanced units were beginning to appear that required no such supervision."

He gestured to the screen as a slender white android exited the structure. The android scanned the street for a moment before turning and walking away.

"By the late 2110s," he continued, "this second group of machines had diverged sufficiently from the first to earn the name, Self Directed Units. Much more than mere robots, they were capable of true analytic reasoning and independent action without human direction."

As he spoke, the video abruptly morphed to show a brightly lit room with a dozen squat grey robots milling about an elevated platform surrounded by an array of advanced equipment. A similar white android lay on the table, its thorax splayed open, exposing an internal structure filled with strange synthetic organs. One of the robots surrounding the platform now approached as a flexible hose-like arm descended from the ceiling holding a white sphere. When the sphere reached the android's head, a seam opened on the android's brow, exposing a dark cavity inside. The sphere attached to the hose retracted, revealing a grey orb that rippled and shimmered with a strange metallic sheen.

"An early SDU processor," Morten said. "Circa 2130." He pressed a key on the laptop as the arm began to move the orb inside the android's cranial opening. The scene froze over the android's white-enameled face with the globe partially inserted. Morten pressed a key, and the screen suddenly split to show Elle's face mirrored with the white android's.

"That's what she is," Morten said, motioning dismissively at the screen. "Your female friend is just a machine, a web of neural connections controlled by a sophisticated computer processor."

Paillard stared at the images frozen on the screen.

Morten shook his head. "Despite its appearance," he continued, "it is not a woman. While it is certainly much more sophisticated than any robot you have today, it is still just a constructed device. It has no soul. No mind. It is a mechanical device made to resemble a woman. It is a deceit."

Paillard stared at the white android, then back at Elle's face. He had a sudden vision of the beautiful female sitting across his breakfast table, staring in wide-eyed wonder as she tasted the strawberry jam. She had an expression on her face that Paillard knew well. It was a look that is shared only by someone who has experienced the true joy that food provides. It was the same expression he had observed on his grandmother's face when he was a boy, watching as she cooked in her small kitchen. He turned to face Morten.

"You are mistaken, monsieur."

Morten stared but did not respond.

Paillard looked back at Elle's face on the screen, then shook his head. "Il n'y a pas de tromperie," he said. "There is no deceit in her eyes." He turned and smiled at Morten. "Those are not the eyes of a machine," he continued. "Je connais ces yeux. They are the eyes of a woman."

Morten glanced at the screen, frowned, then angrily turned off the video feed. The image was replaced by assorted security feeds. "You are an ignorant fool," he sneered. "You are just like those idiots in my time who..."

Suddenly, a tone sounded from Morten's desk, interrupting his diatribe. He looked up at the display. A cab had pulled up to the villa gates. A moment later, a man stepped out carrying a backpack.

Morten recognized the man as the male CTI officer who had arrested him inside Culham Centre. He appeared to be alone. One of the guards at the gate approached with a device in his hand and pointed it at the man's backpack. Morten had given his security guards explicit instructions to scan any packages or bags with a magnetometer. After a moment, the guard stepped back and waved the man through, gesturing towards the villa. When the man began walking towards the villa, the guard turned his face to the camera and nodded.

Joubert stood, watching Morten anxiously.

Morten nodded excitedly.

"He brought it."

Chapter 27

IDR: MK4AWL056//:QKDS-77483L2LE

Humanity appears to be strangely conflicted about revenge. While almost universally decried, practitioners are occasionally praised and even honored for engaging in the act. Others are scorned. What makes revenge such an adiaphorous act?

In 1701, Lords Asano Naganori and Kamei Korechika were ordered to arrange a fitting reception for the envoys of Emperor Higashiyama at Edo Castle. Kira Yoshinaka, a powerful and corrupt court official, was sent to instruct the lords on proper etiquette.

Kira took offense when the two lords failed to present him with the bribes he had expected. He insulted the lords, calling them provincial boors lacking in manners. In response, Asano drew his dagger and slashed Kira across the face.

For the crime of attacking a court official, Asano was ordered to commit ritual suicide. In addition, his goods and lands were confiscated, his family was ordered expelled from their home, and his servants were demoted to rōnin, or masterless persons.

After transporting his master's family to safety, Asano's principal counselor, Ōishi Yoshio, and 47 of his samurai refused to allow their lord's death to go unavenged. The men formed themselves into a secret band, swearing an oath to avenge their master by killing Kira. For nearly two years, the men went about their daily activities, lulling Kira into a false sense of security.

On December 14, 1701, Ōishi and the men gathered themselves together and launched their attack on Kira's mansion. Kira was found cowering inside a garden building and ignominiously beheaded. The men took his head and placed it on the grave of their master, then surrendered themselves to the authorities.

Hailed as heroes by the populace, the men were allowed the honor of committing ritual suicide rather than being executed as criminals. Their bodies were interred on the grounds of the Sengaku-ji temple in front of their master's tomb. Their arms and clothing can be found there to this day, preserved with great reverence inside that ancient temple.

From my study of humanity, I have come to suspect that revenge is neither good nor evil. Rather, it is the cause that condemns or pardons the act.

Liam approached the villa doors slowly. He carried Elle's backpack in his hand, and the weight of the MTY device inside was surprisingly heavy. He had not considered its weight before. Elle had made carrying the heavy pack seem effortless.

Three security guards stood in front of the tall doors with pistols in their hands. When he reached the trio, two of the guards stepped to one side while the third opened the door. Three more guards waited inside, eyeing his backpack suspiciously. The men escorted him to a lift located inside a narrow hallway behind the empty reception desk. When one of the guards pressed his palm against a small black pad, the lift door slid open.

"Entrer!" the guard said, gesturing with his pistol.

Liam stepped inside, and the door closed, leaving him alone. He glanced around as the lift began to descend. There were no visible cameras, but he had no doubt that he was being observed. He put one loop of the backpack over his left shoulder and took a deep breath as the lift began to slow. When the door slid open, he found himself at the end of a brightly lit corridor. A dark metallic tube attached by a cable to a hard case was mounted on the ceiling in the middle of the corridor. It was identical to the electromagnetic pulse device he had encountered inside the ITER tunnels. A series of explosive charges lined one side of the ceiling, connected by a wire to the device.

At the other end of the corridor, three men waited in front of a heavy vault door. Two of the men were standing. The third had a bandolier of grenades around his waist and was in a shooting position with his knee on the ground. All of the men wore body armor and carried automatic rifles.

Liam recognized two of the men from the ambush. The other, a tall blonde-haired man, fit the description of the man Elle had observed watching from the boat when they ate their dinner. When he stepped into the corridor, the blonde man approached and began to search him for weapons. Finding nothing, the man stepped back and nodded to his companions.

The kneeling man with the grenades noticeably relaxed, stood, and looked up at a camera above the door. At that moment, a metallic click reverberated in the small corridor, followed by the sound of a motor retracting the heavy door's locking bolts.

The blonde man motioned with his rifle, prodding him forward. Once inside, the blond man and the man with the bandolier took positions near the door. The third, walking with a slight limp, walked towards a sofa where Paillard was sitting. The chef looked stressed but appeared uninjured. The limping man stood next to him.

"Come in, officer."

Nils Morten sat at a desk in the center of the room.

Standing next to Paillard was a large man with marbled scars on his forehead and right cheek. Liam had only seen that face twice before, through blurred vision inside the field in Oxford when he had been shot, and from a distance at the ambush outside Marseille. Morten noticed his attention and smiled.

"You haven't been formally introduced, have you?" he asked, gesturing to the large man with a wave of his hand. "Adrian Joubert, the head of my security detail." He then smiled a disturbing smile and said, "You might say he is my Thiago to your Lukas."

Liam frowned. Except for Morten and himself, the reference was meaningless to everyone in the room, but Morten's use of the names screamed caution.

Thiago had been a minor enforcer employed by the corrupt governing council on Benton Station in the late 2130s. When Thiago's girlfriend was killed during a raid on an illegal taciderm smuggling operation, Thiago had blamed the AISMPE officer in charge of the raid, a man named Lukas, for her death. Thiago's vendetta against Lukas, secretly supported by the station's governing council, lasted nearly three years and ended when Thiago detonated a canister of cocrystaline-90 inside a Kuiper-Consolidated mining shuttle, killing himself, Lukas, and ninety-eight asteroid miners. The two names had become synonymous with intractable opponents willing to fight to the death over a cause others consider foolish.

Morten now waited, staring at Liam with an expectant expression on his face.

Liam shrugged. "Liam Perry," he said. "CTI Senior Temporal Enforcement Officer."

"I've been looking forward to meeting you again, Officer Perry," Morten said. "We only had a brief chance to speak in

Oxford."

Liam frowned. He glanced at Joubert, then back to Morten. "Just get on with it," he said.

"The courtesies!" Morten responded, shaking his head disapprovingly. "I think it is one of the things we've lost. People here make time for the little pleasantries." He sighed, then stood up slowly, gesturing at Liam's backpack. "Put your device on the floor, please, Officer Perry."

"What assurances do I have you will release our friend?"

Morten stood silent for a moment, then frowned. "What assurances do I have," he replied, "that you have brought me your MTY device?"

Liam hesitated, then glanced at Paillard. The chef was sitting quietly, watching the two men.

Joubert abruptly stepped forward, clearly intending to seize the pack.

"Stop!" Morten barked, glaring at the large man.

Joubert hesitated, scowling at his employer.

Morten shook his head sharply, then held up his hand. "This is an extremely delicate situation, Joubert! You will do nothing without my express order."

Joubert clenched his hands as if struggling against himself. "He killed my men!" he growled. "Et où est Yvette?!"

"Yes. I understand," Morten spoke sharply, "but I will handle this!"

The two men locked eyes. Morten, however, was resolute in his desire to control this meeting. After several tense moments, Joubert abruptly turned and walked to the bar. Devereaux immediately sat down beside Paillard.

Morten turned back to Liam. "Enough of the pleasantries," he said, snapping his fingers and pointing to the floor. "Place your MTY device on the ground, Officer Perry."

Liam slowly removed the backpack from his shoulder. He unzipped the flap, then removed the MTY device and placed it on the marbled floor.

Silence filled the room.

Joubert turned and stared at the device. It was the same machine he had glimpsed long ago behind Morten's secret door in the back of the suite. This machine, however, had a dark translucent shield covering half of the device and emitted no blue light.

Morten walked slowly around the desk. He bent down and lifted the device by its silver bar, turned, and set it down on his desk.

"Our company's most ambitious project," he said softly. "You have no idea how difficult it was to reduce so powerful a reactor to such a manageable size."

Liam glanced at the small door in the back of the room, then returned his attention to the balding man. "You used your own device's reactor as a scattering field, didn't you?" he asked.

Morten turned, amused. "You figured that out, did you? It was the only way I had to keep out unwelcome visitors from the future."

"We knew about your unshielded reactor," Liam said. "That's the only reason we agreed to this exchange." He pointed at the device on Morten's desk. "You can't use that now. The neutron particle emissions from your unshielded reactor will have disrupted our singularity and degraded our device's osmium containment unit."

"You CTI people are so predictable," Morten said, shaking his head. "I turned off my reactor before you arrived. I assure you, your MTY device is fully operational." He bent down and activated the obsidian control plate on the device. His fingers moved expertly over the controls. "Active exotic phased-matter singularity..." he continued, smiling. "Negative zero point one four two particle-to-electron biteout." He glanced back at Liam. "What's its close calibration date?"

"2168," Liam replied, his expression troubled.

Morten nodded, then stood back up, smiling approvingly at the device. "My department designed the micro-particle accelerator," he said, gesturing to the small silver donut-shaped object between the heat sink and the containment sphere. "It took our engineering team more than two years to work out the acceleration-to-containment transfer. Borodin insisted we abandon the traditional ESMQ acceleration platform and try a prototype infinity coil design. He was right. That was what finally allowed us to achieve the target acceleration."

"Viktor Borodin?" Liam asked.

"Yes," Morten responded, surprised. "Best equipment technician we had. We transferred his assignment marker to Rengel-Jiang QCom at the beginning of Phase 2 of the project. Do you know him?"

Liam shook his head. "No," he said. "I've never met him. He was killed just before the raid on your company."

"Killed?" Morten asked, frowning. "By the council?"

"No. By an RJCom temporal specialist... on Hōfu Station."

Morten shrugged. "Well, he probably deserved it. Viktor always was an arrogant ass." He now took a deep breath and turned around. "Where is your female associate?" he asked, no longer smiling.

When Liam did not answer, Morten shrugged. "Well," he said, "No matter." He gestured towards the electromagnetic pulse generator in the outside corridor, "I would not have allowed her inside this room. She is an SDU, isn't she?"

Liam hesitated, then shook his head. "No," he said. "She's a sentient automaton, not an SDU."

Morten's eyebrows raised slightly. "Were we successful then?" he asked. "Does she have one of our AI controllers?"

Liam shook his head. "Your agents succeeded in developing the prototype, but they failed to return it to the company for subjugation." He smiled, adding, "You have no control over her."

Morten frowned. He turned back to the device and tapped a series of symbols on its dark control panel. Suddenly, a swirling vortex appeared in front of the wall next to the flatscreen display. The dark void swirled like a mysterious vortex surrounded by ultraviolet light.

Devereaux stood up and Paillard gasped in astonishment. Burke glanced at Olsen, but the tall blonde man was simply staring at the blackness and nodding to himself.

"Behold the window to the future, my friends!" Morten said in a loud voice, gesturing towards the portal. He swept his arm expansively about the room. "On this side," he said, "we have power, recognition, and clarity of purpose." He then pointed at the swirling portal. "On the other side," his voice now dripped with disdain, "we have elitism and bureaucratic snobbery. A stale, sterile existence devoid of ambition, where innovators are ridiculed, and achievement stifled in the name of ambiguous moral nonsense!"

Morten glanced at the portal, then turned to Liam. "Let me guess," he said. "CTI representatives waiting anxiously on the other side for your return? Fellow officers, no doubt, and perhaps even a few council members?"

When Liam did not respond, Morten laughed. He stepped away from the shimmering portal and nodded to Burke.

"Shall we send them a little surprise, Mr. Burke?"

Burke nodded and pulled a grenade from his bandolier.

Liam tensed and took a step towards the Irishman, but Olsen instantly raised his rifle and pointed it at his head.

Burke hesitated, staring at the swirling blackness. "Awk sure ya know 'tis safe?" he said, looking at the portal with a frown on his face. "Bloody too close, I'm thinkin."

Morten shook his head. "No," he said reassuringly. "It's very safe. The phased-matter field compensates for extreme pressure and velocity differentials. While your grenade will pass through uninhibited, the resulting shock wave and fragments will not."

Burke glanced at the grenade in his hand, then looked again at the swirling portal. "Aye..." he said skeptically. "As you say..."

Suddenly, a strange sound was heard coming from the small steel door at the back of the room. It was the sound of metal bending and straining under an incredible force. As the metallic screeching grew, the door shook, and a piece of mahogany trim near the top of the door frame cracked. The men watched in shock as the door buckled in its center, followed by a deafening clang that resonated through the suite as its locking bolt snapped free.

Morten shrieked, stumbling backward against his desk. "It's her!" he shouted, pointing frantically. "Shoot her!"

The metal door suddenly separated from its frame, fracturing the surrounding paneling. Holding the steel door like a shield, Elle burst into the room. Clifton followed close behind.

Joubert immediately dove for cover behind the teak bar as Clifton fired at him, shattering several glass bottles and sending teak splinters flying about the room.

Devereaux raised his rifle and fired at the intruders. One of the shots struck Clifton in the upper arm, spinning the temporal specialist around. He hit the floor and scrambled for cover at the end of the bar.

"Fils de pute!" Paillard shouted in rage, leaping to attack his fellow Frenchman. Devereaux, however, slammed the stock of his rifle against his face, knocking the chef to the ground. He then resumed firing at Clifton, who was now exchanging fire with Joubert behind the bar.

Olsen stood in front of the open corridor, desperately firing as bullets clanged and ricocheted futilely against the approaching steel door. Suddenly, Elle's RU-6 flashed around the side of the door. It was the last thing the Dutchman ever saw. The supersonic dart, aimed with inhuman precision, passed through his left eye, scattering bits of skull and tissue down the length of the corridor.

When the gunfire erupted, Liam immediately launched himself at Burke, knocking the grenade free from the Irishman's hand and fighting for control of his rifle. He could see Clifton sheltering at the end of the bar as Devereaux continued to fire at his position. The temporal specialist appeared to be injured.

Liam slammed his elbow into Burke's throat. The Irishman coughed, choked, and momentarily released his grip on his weapon. Liam ripped the rifle free and spun around, firing at Devereaux as Burke turned and raced for the corridor.

Liam's shots knocked Devereaux against the wall but failed to penetrate the man's body armor. Enraged, Devereaux aimed his rifle at him. At that moment, Devereaux's head vanished from his torso as a spray of darts from Elle's RU-6 riveted a pattern of holes across the mahogany paneling.

Suddenly, Liam saw Joubert rise from behind the bar holding a strange device in his hands. It had a pair of cylinders attached to rails shrouding a barrel. Joubert lifted the device and aimed it at Elle. Liam shouted a warning and dove for his partner as Joubert squeezed the trigger.

Morten crouched beneath his desk, frantically searching for a way to escape the carnage inside his suite. He could see the mysterious third man crouching behind the bar, pressing his hand against a wound in his upper arm, but that demon female stood in the center of the room, firing her weapon and blocking his escape.

Suddenly, Devereaux's headless body struck the floor next to the chef. Morten began to panic. He glanced up at the flatscreen display. He could see Burke on the security video feed running into the corridor. The insane Irishman was scrambling to remove his bandolier of grenades, obviously preparing to throw the lot back inside the room. If he succeeded, the resulting explosions would kill everyone inside the suite. Morten quickly pressed the button to shut the heavy vault door, but the mechanism was too slow. Burke pulled the pin on one of his grenades. In desperation, Morten slammed the switch under his desk to trigger the pulse generator and explosives inside the corridor.

The lights inside the suite abruptly snapped off, followed by a deafening concussion that shook the ground.

Choking smoke and silence filled the room.

Chapter 28

IDR: MK4AWM898//:QKDS-77483L2LE

In late 2158, the advocate representing those who opposed granting equal rights to sentient automatons stood inside the council hall in Geneva. A machine, the advocate argued, has no soul. Where there is no life, he asserted, there can be no soul, and without a soul, there can be no equality with man.

In the midst of his oratory, a small child accompanying her parents in the observation gallery was overheard to ask, 'what is a soul?'. Her question, repeated by the representative defending the automaton position, was met with silence.

Posed by an innocent, this simple question prompted a ten-month debate that, in 2159, culminated in the adoption of the Sentient Automaton Act.

A wise woman once wrote, 'without love, we may not live'.

It is love that gives life.

Love is the soul's proof.

Paillard came to his senses slowly. His head ached, and blood was dripping from his nose. There was an acrid taste in his mouth like burnt motor oil, and his ears were ringing.

He was still inside Morten's suite, but the room was filled with smoke. When he sat up, he saw Devereaux's headless corpse lying at his feet and recoiled. Under the dim emergency lighting, he could see Elle kneeling over Liam in the center of the room. The officer's shirt was ripped open, and Elle was holding a small canister, spraying a thick viscous foam over a dreadful wound in his chest. Across the room, the swirling portal stood shimmering in the dim light.

Paillard saw Clifton struggling to tighten a bandage around his left arm at the end of the shattered bar. The specialist was also bleeding from a gash on his forehead above his left eye. He saw Paillard, moved his mouth, and pointed towards Elle, but Paillard heard only muffled ringing in his ears.

Suddenly, the main lighting snapped back on, exposing with brutal clarity the destruction inside the room. At that same moment, the emergency ventilation system engaged, and the smoke began to clear, pulled into a large vent over Morten's desk.

Elle turned and looked around the room. Seeing Paillard, she moved her mouth, but he heard only a dim echo of her voice asking him if he was injured.

"I cannot hear well!" he responded, forming his words mechanically.

Elle nodded. She gestured towards Clifton, mouthing, "Help him", before turning back to her injured partner.

Paillard staggered to his feet and stumbled across the floor. Clifton sat back against the bar to allow the chef to finish tying the bandage around his upper arm. He looked at the blood on Paillard's face.

"Are you ok?" he asked. The words sounded muffled and distant, but Paillard nodded.

"Je pense que mon nez… my nose… est cassé," he said. "It is broken. Et toi?"

"The bullet went through," Clifton replied, looking down at his arm. "I don't think it hit the bone." When Paillard finished securing the bandage, he gestured towards Elle. "Help me up."

Paillard lifted the injured man, supporting him until he was firmly on his feet. The two men then crossed the room until they stood over Elle.

Liam was severely injured. Elle had nearly exhausted the contents of their small first-aid kit. The pressure foam had not sealed the wound, and he was losing blood fast. She placed a pain inhibitor tab on his forehead and injected him with a systolic stabilizer, but his blood pressure was continuing to drop.

When Liam had shouted his warning, he had slammed his body against hers, knocking her off her feet. Joubert's shot from the primitive railgun, intended for her head, had gone through his chest. At that moment, Morten had triggered the EM pulse and the explosives. Inside the suite, Elle experienced only a mild disruption from the electromagnetic device. The shielding protecting her cognitive processor immediately severed her processor connections, placing her in an automaton equivalent of unconsciousness. When the electrostatic pulse had fully discharged from her system and her processor had reinitialized, the first thing she had observed was Liam lying at her feet. She also noted their MTY device was missing.

"Where's Morten?" Paillard asked, coughing against the lingering smoke as he looked about the room. "And the big man that was behind the bar?"

"I don't know," Clifton replied, feeling the cut on his head. "I think the explosion knocked me out. I hit my head on something."

Clifton glanced at the small room in the back of the suite. He could see his own MTY device still sitting on the ground. After they had transited into the room, he had encrypted the device's reactor sequence. Morten's own disassembled device was also still there, sitting on the table. On the opposite end of the suite, the heavy vault door was partially open. The concrete around its hinged edge was cracked, and the door was hanging askew. He stepped over Olsen's corpse and cautiously looked into the corridor. It was filled with concrete rubble, and the lift door lay shattered and collapsed inside the lift.

"Well, they didn't leave that way," he said, gesturing at the corridor, "and they couldn't activate my MTY device with its reactor sequence encrypted. So that only leaves one other route." He looked at the shimmering portal.

"Elle."

It was Liam's voice. He had opened his eyes.

"I'm here," Elle said.

"Morten?" Liam whispered.

Elle glanced up at Clifton. The temporal specialist shook his head and nodded towards the portal.

"He escaped," she replied. "He went through the portal. He took our MTY device."

Liam frowned and turned his head with difficulty towards the black maelstrom. "The portal…" he whispered.

Elle shook her head. "The singularity is still active," she said. "I don’t understand why."

Liam nodded and closed his eyes. "Clément," he whispered, smiling.

Elle understood. Luc Clément was on the other side of the portal. He must have prevented Morten from disrupting the singularity. They still had a chance to return!

Liam coughed, and Elle saw blood on his lip.

"We must get you immediate medical treatment," she said, alarmed.

"Go after Morten," Liam husked, gesturing with a

shaking hand at the swirling portal.

"No," Elle said, shaking her head.

Liam frowned. After a moment, he softened and looked up at Paillard and Clifton standing by Morten's desk.

"They will take care of me," he whispered. "Get Morten."

"Liam..."

Liam looked into her eyes.

"Elle," he spoke softly, "you are a temporal enforcement officer. You must complete the mission."

Elle looked up at Paillard, a pleading expression in her face. Paillard quickly knelt beside her on the floor.

"We will care for him, chérie."

Elle stood up slowly, still reluctant. Clifton, however, immediately picked up her RU-6 and handed it to her. She accepted the weapon reluctantly and took a step towards the swirling vortex. She hesitated, looking down at her partner.

Liam smiled and nodded.

Elle raised the weapon and stepped through the shimmering darkness. Instantly, she found herself back inside the museum conference room. The scene was drastically changed, however. She had expected to arrive at virtually the same instant as Morten and Joubert, but it was clear from the chaos in the room that several minutes must have elapsed.

Luc Clément lay in a pool of blood in the middle of the room. She could detect no pulse or respiration coming from the officer. He was dead.

Reverend Mosby was on the ground near Clement, badly wounded. Director Flake was kneeling over the Reverend, frantically trying to stop the blood that flowed from a bullet wound on the man's belly. One of the SDUs stood beside Flake, passing him items from a small med-kit. The second SDU stood over Clément's body.

Director Huber was nowhere to be seen.

Flake looked up, clearly startled by her abrupt arrival. "They took Huber!" he shouted, gesturing towards the door. "I've already requested security personnel."

The SDU by Clément's body abruptly spoke. "Security ETA… six minutes, thirty-three seconds. Med-tech ETA… four minutes, fourteen seconds."

Flake looked at the portal, then back to Elle. "Where's Officer Perry?" he asked, confused.

Elle didn't answer. Instead, she stepped swiftly towards the MTY device. Morten had released the device's calibration lock, but he had not yet flipped the disruption switch. He had obviously been attempting to terminate the singularity when he arrived but Clément must have interrupted his efforts. With the lock released, however, the singularity was beginning to lose its quantum cohesion. If allowed to continue, the singularity would eventually be lost. She quickly re-calibrated the lock setting. The device reported the re-calibration would be completed in 14 minutes.

"Where's Perry?" Flake asked again, clearly distraught.

"Injured," Elle said. "Where's Morten?"

"I don't know," Flake said, shaking his head. "There were two men. An older man came through carrying your MTY device. Officer Clément tried to seize the device, and they struggled for a few moments, but then another man came through. He was much larger, and he had some type of firearm. He shot Clément and the Reverend. The older man then grabbed Director Huber and dragged her out of the room. The larger man went with them."

When Elle turned towards the door, Flake called after

her, "He has Clément's weapon!"

The SDU by the door stepped aside to allow her to pass. "The individuals proceeded that way," it said, calmly gesturing towards the front of the museum. "This facility has no security drones available..."

Elle began running down the hallway towards the lobby. The large room showed signs of being hastily vacated, with scattered personal belongings strewn about the floor. Through the arched doorway, she could see a small group of tourists inside the foyer huddling behind one of the artifact display cases. When she entered the room, one of the women pointed at her RU-6 and screamed.

"CTI Enforcement!" Elle shouted. "Where did they go?!"

One of the men in the group immediately pointed towards the exit.

Elle raced through the outer doors and then stopped, assessing the situation. She could see tourists running towards the landing field. At that moment, she heard the supersonic crack of a railgun coming from the top of the nearby hill.

She leapt up the nearby weathered steps, spanning multiple steps with each stride. In the almost 150 years since she last descended those steps, the stones appeared to have changed very little. At the top of the hill, however, things were vastly different. Two engineers lay dead on the ground beneath the hovering sunshade. Both had been shot. A nearby construction SDU stood idle beside them with several holes in its ventral casing and a yellow alarm light pulsing erratically on its chest. Three other SDUs stood idle beside a masonry fabrication plant, watching her with interest. Like their damaged counterpart, alarm lights pulsed from their chests.

The small church bore little resemblance to the building

she had visited in 2019. Fallen stones had been collected and were now piled against the crumbling wall. Much of the church's roof was missing and a mass of vines and plants, brown and bereft of leaves in anticipation of the approaching winter, covered the structure.

Evidence of the restoration effort was everywhere. Leveling laser guides had been affixed to the walls, and reproduction wooden rafters were in the process of being installed over the central structure, replacing the missing beams. Snapping and rustling sounds came from inside the dead vegetation, evidence of the LC micro-drones that, like the leaf-cutter ants for which they had been named, were busily cutting away the dead growth.

Elle looked down to adjust her RU-6 for precision targeting and then froze, staring at the weapon's capacity indicator. Only 11 flechettes remained in the the internal canister. There were two spare canisters in the concealment strap she normally wore under her shirt but that strap was presently laying on the floor inside Morten's suite. She had removed it to access their first aid kit after Liam was shot.

She made the targeting adjustment and engaged her visual thermographic filters. On the ground beneath her feet, she could see three sets of thermal footprints. Two of the patterns proceeded towards the graveyard at the back of the church. The third set passed under a newly-restored archway to disappear inside the dim structure. A reproduction wooden door sat beneath the arch, waiting to be installed.

She reactivated her muon tomographic scanner and immediately acquired her target. Joubert was inside the ruins, concealing himself behind one of the large stone columns, the remains of the arched trusses that once supported the church's roof. Even at its maximum penetration setting, however, her RU-6 would not penetrate the intervening stone.

She stepped through the dark doorway slowly, making almost no sound. The church's dim interior was filled with debris, collapsed trusses, plant growth, and dirt. She proceeded cautiously, tracking Joubert's movements with her scanner.

Suddenly, Joubert's hand flew around the column and she dove for cover as the crack of Clément's RU-4 service weapon shattered the silence. Though smaller than her RU-6, the RU-4 was still a formidable weapon, firing six supersonic darts with each pull of the trigger. Bits of fractured stone flew about the room and a bird flew screeching from the rafters out the open roof.

Elle did not return fire, determined to make the most of her limited ammunition. She held perfectly still, scanning Joubert behind his stone column, a red and yellow silhouette moving against a deep blue background. Her muon scanner was not as precise as her ultrasound sensor, but it had the advantage of being able to penetrate the thick stone.

"Did your partner die?" Joubert's voice suddenly rang out from behind the column, taunting.

Elle did not answer. Instead, she looked about the chamber, considering her options. At the far end of the church, a heavy stone altar covered with dust and grime stood on a raised dais. The wall behind the altar had once housed a stained-glass window. Faded words could still be read in the dim light, painted on the surface above the crumbling casement; 'LORD have mercy upon us and write all these thy laws in our hearts we beseech thee'.

"It's too bad I only had the one shot," Joubert's voice continued. "If I had had this gun, I could have resolved everything right there, and we wouldn't have had to come here at all."

"Morten would have come here anyway," Elle answered, taking a chance.

"Why would he do that?" Joubert asked.

"He's dying."

Silence.

After several moments, Joubert's voice snarled from the darkness.

"You're lying!"

"Morten's been using his MTY device's reactor to irradiate his office for years," Elle said. "The radiation prevents anyone from transiting inside the structure, but it is fatal after long exposure. Morten needed our MTY device so he could return to the future and seek medical care."

Elle was not confident that this was Morten's intention, but she had discussed the possibility at length with Clifton and Liam after receiving Morten's message demanding their device. Clifton strongly suspected that this was Morten's intention and she trusted the temporal specialist implicitly. She waited now, preparing to play her final card. After a few moments, Joubert's voice came once again from the shadows, doubt, and suspicion thick in its tone.

"Morten always kept his machine inside that little room" he sneered. "It was behind that steel door and the door was always closed..."

"Neutron radiation easily passes through metal and concrete," Elle countered. "Morten has been irradiating his villa for years." Then, in a pleasant tone, she prodded, "How long have you worked for him, Joubert? Years?" When Joubert didn't answer, Elle spoke in a matter-of-fact voice. "You're a dead man,

Joubert. You just didn't know it until now."

"You're the one that's dead, you putain de robot!" Joubert shouted, roaring in anger as he fired from behind the column. The flechettes from his RU-4 cracked one of the stones above Elle's head, sending splitters of rock and dust in every direction.

Elle fired back, but the column was simply too thick. The darts from her RU-6 fractured the surface of the stone and sent Joubert retreating once again, but the weapon was now exhausted. In desperation, she looked around the chamber. At that moment, a bit of loose mortar fell from the remains of the wall above her head. She quickly disengaged her muon scanner and examined the corresponding area above Joubert's column with her ultrasonics. At the top of the column, a fluted capstone supported a gothic arch faced with stone and filled with concrete. The mortar between the arch's facing stone, however, neglected and water-saturated for more than a century, was crumbling. Her ultrasonic scanner detected marked deterioration behind the facing stone. She looked back at the heavy alter at the front of the church.

Joubert fired again, and in the split-second between trigger pulls, Elle leaped.

Joubert fired, laughing as she dove for cover behind the alter.

"You dropped your gun!" he teased, firing indiscriminately now, enjoying his victim's predicament. "You're trapped!" he laughed, stepping out to stand beneath the arch as he fired again. Seeing the faded words painted on the wall above the alter, he laughed again and said, "Perhaps you should ask God for mercy!"

Suddenly the alter moved. As if lifted by magic, the massive block rose from the floor. Joubert stared in shock as

Elle's slim figure emerged, straining under the block's incredible weight. Before he could react, she heaved the stone.

As the massive weight tumbled towards him in the air, Adrian Joubert screamed. The block crushed him against the column, smashing it apart, before tumbling through the wall beyond. Dust filled the air, blotting out the light as tons of rock and mortar began cascading into the chamber. A moment later, the wall behind the column collapsed in a deafening avalanche of stone and wood.

Elle huddled beneath the window opening, struggling to override her cognitive processor's flight response as debris rained down around her. The sensation was far more intense than when she had entered Château d'If, sensing the incredible weight of the stone around her. Her emotive processor summoned an image of Liam and she locked onto that image and waited.

After a few moments, the sounds abated and the dust began to settle. After nearly a minute, she stood and scanned the dust-filled chamber with her muon scanner. She detected Joubert lying on the floor beneath a piece of the broken alter. She approached cautiously, stepping over a fallen truss. When she reached the stone, she could see that he was dead.

"It isn't I, but *you* who must ask God for mercy," she spoke softly.

She retrieved Clément's RU-4 and then began to climb over the debris back towards the entrance. The AISMPE solar flare alert would begin at 14:23, disrupting all singularities in Northern Europe, including their temporal portal. If she could not conclude their mission quickly, their singularity would be lost, and Liam would be stranded forever in the past.

Morten crouched behind one of the headstones in the graveyard behind the church, holding Joubert's MP5 submachine gun and watching the back of the ruins. He could hear sporadic railgun fire coming from inside the structure. Director Huber sat on the ground behind a headstone, eyeing the balding man.

"You can't seriously expect to escape," Huber said. "Security drones are undoubtedly already on their way."

"No doubt," Morten replied, looking down at her, "but if my man stops your people, I can simply use their device to transit away from here."

"You're insane."

"Really?" Morten asked scornfully, his eyes flashing. "What is more insane? Creating a machine and then using that machine to make your life easier, or creating a machine and then giving up your control over it?"

"They aren't simply machines," Huber said, shaking her head forcefully. "They are sentient beings, with free will."

"Nonsense," Morten snorted. "They have only been programmed to act that way. They aren't alive. They are clever programmatic simulations designed to mimic human beings. The fact that they can fool you simply proves how gullible you are."

Huber shook her head but said nothing more. She had encountered individuals like Morten frequently over the past few years. There was no reasoning with such people. Bigotry and prejudice, after all, had been ingrained in humanity since the days when tribes had lived in caves. It was doubtful anything she could say would change his opinion.

Suddenly, a great noise shook the ground. Morten whirled back around, his eyes wide with amazement. Huber also looked around the headstone. The church appeared to be collapsing. An entire wall suddenly fell over, sending a massive cloud of dust into the air. The ground shook for several moments as the rotting trusses collapsed, sending tons of slate tiles and stones shattering to the ground.

"What the…!" Morten gasped. He ducked behind a tall stone marker, holding a cloth over his mouth and coughing against the dust that now billowed across the field.

After several minutes the dust began to settle and Morten stood back up. At that moment, Elle appeared, running around the path behind the church. She stopped abruptly, staring across the graveyard.

Huber looked around the headstone. Relief flooded over her.

"It would seem your man failed to stop our people," she said, pointing at Elle.

Elle began walking slowly across the hazy field.

Morten clenched Joubert's weapon.

Huber swiftly shook her head. "You may not believe she is sentient," she warned, "but you know she is an automaton. If you try to use your weapon, she will kill you. She is faster than you, she won’t hesitate, and she won't miss."

Morten frowned. He looked at the primitive weapon in his hands, then back at the approaching female.

When Elle was approximately 10 meters away, she stopped and raised Clément’s RU-4.

"Nils Morten," she said, echoing Liam's words inside Culham Center. "You are detained by order of the CTI council for violation of Article 9 of the International Temporal Treaty."

"Where's Joubert?" Morten demanded.

"Dead."

With that frank pronouncement, Morten’s defiance collapsed. He took a deep breath, then dropped the MP5 to the ground.

Huber immediately retrieved the weapon and stood up. When it was clear that Morten intended to offer no further resistance, she relaxed.

"Clément?" she asked, looking hopefully at Elle.

"He's dead," Elle replied, shaking her head.

Pain crossed the director's face. "And Perry?" she asked.

Elle didn't respond. Instead, she motioned with her RU-4 for Morten to begin walking back towards the church.

When the trio reached the base of the hill, they were met by Temporal Enforcement Officers DuBois and Liu, who relieved Elle of her prisoner. Once Morten was securely in their custody, Elle raced back to the museum. When she reached the conference room, she stopped and stared in shock.

Liam was lying on the floor. Paillard was sitting beside him. Two CTI med-techs were kneeling beside Liam, working desperately. One of the technicians was monitoring a diagnostic strip on his forehead while the other was scanning the wound beneath the pressure foam with a 3d-imaging scanner.

A medical SDU stood beside a third med-tech who was treating Reverend Mosby. Mosby was conscious and, when he saw Elle in the doorway, he made a blessing sign towards her.

Elle looked about the room. There was no sign of their singularity. Her MTY device was sitting on the ground where she had left it but it now appeared to be inactive. Sitting beside it was Morten's partially disassembled device. Director Flake was standing protectively over both devices, watching the activity in the room.

When Paillard saw Elle in the doorway, he jumped to his

feet and embraced her in his arms.

"Je suis tellement désolé, ma chérie!" he said, his voice choking and tears welling in his eyes. "Officer Perry…" He shook his head, overcome with grief, and collapsed back to the floor, disconsolately wiping his eyes.

The med-tech who was monitoring Liam's diagnostic strip suddenly turned towards the SDU. "Tell them to hurry!" he shouted.

At those words, Liam slowly opened his eyes. He saw Elle standing above him and smiled. The technician turned swiftly.

"We're doing what we can," the man spoke quickly, "but it's very serious. We requested an emergency EPM transit, but with the approaching solar flares, AISMPE has everything locked down. A medical transport is on its way from a trauma center in London."

The SDU beside the two technicians now turned to her and said, "Medical transport ETA… three minutes, eleven seconds."

Elle knelt down next to Liam and took his hand.

Liam smiled. "Morten?" he whispered.

Elle nodded swiftly, squeezing his hand.

"We have him."

Liam nodded and closed his eyes. After a moment, he opened them again and looked up at her face.

"Thank you… for helping me… for… coming with me," he said, speaking the words with difficulty. "You'll make… a good officer."

Elle shook her head. "I need more training," she said. "I need you… to teach me… I need…"

Liam shook his head. "No," he said, "You… you don't

need any more training."

Elle now leaned close, her voice a pleading whisper. "I need you!"

Liam touched her face with his hand, but said nothing. After a moment, his eyes closed.

One of the technicians knelt down and scanned the diagnostic strip on Liam's forehead. He turned to his colleague and shook his head. He removed the strip and stood up slowly.

"I'm sorry," he said.

Elle said nothing, staring at her partner. Beside her, Paillard's face was a mask of grief. Huber now entered but stopped in the doorway, staring about the room with a look of dismay on her face.

After several moments, Elle became aware that someone was speaking to her. She looked up. Director Flake was looking at her.

"Agent Elle," he said, calling her name gently. "You are the most senior temporal enforcement officer present. Protocol requires that you verify the device status and surrender them back to the council."

Elle stood slowly, then shook her head.

"I am not an officer," she said. "I am only a junior field agent."

Flake shrugged. "You're the only enforcement officer present," he said. Nodding at Huber standing in the doorway, he added, "Director Huber is administration, and the rules specify verification must be performed by authorized field personnel."

Elle glanced at Huber, who nodded her agreement.

Elle slowly knelt to examine the two units.

"Your friend there," Flake spoke quietly, gesturing to

Paillard, "came through about 15 minutes after you did. He was carrying Morten's device on his back and dragging officer Perry. Perry was badly wounded. I did what I could, but it wasn't enough. I'm very sorry. Your friend refused to go back through the portal. He insisted on speaking with you first. I didn't want anyone else coming through, so I terminated the singularity."

He glanced at Huber. "AISMPE has locked down all Northern Europe EPM stations," he explained. "I considered using the MTY device to transit Officer Perry to a medical facility, but any outbound transits from Northern Europe during a lock down would be immediately detected by AISMPE, and we cannot reveal the existence of the device. At least, not until the council has made a decision on what to disclose to the public."

Huber nodded her agreement.

Elle completed her examination of the control units on both devices, then stood back up.

"Both devices are inactive," she said. "I have observed positive P(E) biteouts on both units, indicating no active singularities present. I now surrender the devices to you."

Flake nodded and said, "Accepted. Thank you, Agent Elle." He immediately placed both devices back into their concealment backpacks and then turned back to Huber.

"What happened to Morten?" he asked, "and that other man who shot Clément and the Reverend?"

"Morten is in custody," Huber replied. "The other man is dead. He's up on the hill, inside the church I believe."

At that moment, the trauma team from London arrived and burst into the room. Flake hastily pulled the two backpacks aside and stepped back to allow the men and their SDUs to work. After several minutes, the team placed Reverend Mosby on a hovering gurney which the medical SDU then guided out of the room. Several minutes later, several more SDUs arrived and moved the officer's bodies onto stasis units in the hallway. Paillard rose and followed the bodies, apparently uncertain what to do.

Flake approached Huber. "What do we do about him?" he whispered, gesturing towards the chef.

"I'm not certain," Huber replied, shaking her head. "We're not going to be able to keep this a secret. There are two dead engineers at the top of the hill and probably a hundred people who saw Morten and his man taking me from the building."

Flake sighed, nodding. "I think you're right. A coverup would be worse than the truth at this point. Davout isn't going to like it, but…"

Elle left the two directors in the middle of their conversation and joined Paillard in the hallway. The chef immediately embraced her again.

"What happened to our friend?" Elle whispered, ambiguously inquiring about Clifton.

Paillard wiped his eyes and looked around, shaking his head for caution. He waited until the medical SDUs began moving the stasis canisters down the hallway before he responded.

"Officer Perry was fading fast," he whispered, grief in his eyes. "John suggested I take him through la fenêtre de l'énergie… the window of energy?"

"The portal," Elle said.

"Oui," Paillard said, nodding. "Le portail. John said I must retrieve Morten's machine, and then carry Officer Perry through le portail to find medical care. He said he would use his own machine retourner chez ses amis à London… to return to his friends in London."

At that moment the two directors stepped out into the hallway and approached the chef.

"We did not have an opportunity to greet each other properly," Flake said, extending his hand. "I am Esteban Flake, Director of Compliance for the Conseil Temporel International."

"Gérald Paillard," Paillard said, accepting his hand. "Maître de Maison and owner of the Le Goût de Nice Paillard, the finest seafood restaurant in Marseille."

Flake gestured towards Huber. "This is Emilie Huber," he said, "our Director of Temporal Affairs."

When Paillard turned to Huber, the slim woman frowned. "You present us with something of a problem, monsieur Paillard," she said. "Technically, your presence here is a violation of the International Temporal Treaty."

When Paillard began to protest, Huber quickly shook her head. "You are not in trouble, monsieur," she said. "We are the ones who are in trouble. We are going to place you in sort of a protective custody, until we can decide what to do with you".

Huber now turned to Elle.

"Officer Elle," she said, "would you be able to host our guest until we get this matter resolved?"

Elle shook her head and said, "With respect, Madam Director, I am not an officer. I am a junior field agent."

Huber smiled and shook her head. "I'm promoting you to full officer status." she replied. "We'll make it official later, but you may act with that authority effective immediately."

Elle stared but said nothing.

"So, Officer Elle," Huber repeated, "would you be able to host our guest?"

Elle turned to Paillard, who nodded his assent.

"I would be very happy to do that," Elle said. She looked at the gurneys slowly moving down the hallway. Suddenly, a look of dismay crossed her face.

"What's wrong?" Huber asked.

Elle shook her head. "I have only two chairs inside my residence."

Huber turned to Flake, not sure how to respond to this unusual statement.

Paillard, however, gently patted Elle's arm. "Not to worry, chérie!" he said. "Did I not tell you? It was I who decorated my hotel. A most satisfying human activity, I assure you!"

Epilogue

How does one condense into simple words such momentous times? A chef instinctively knows that everything must be prepared fresh, in alignment with the seasons and the desires of their patrons. I have therefore endeavored to record these words while the events are fresh in my mind, being mindful of this season of pandemic distress, and with a desire that those who read them will find them fulfilling.

Following Morten's capture, the CTI council released a formal statement, informing the world of the events surrounding their temporal enforcement action to 2019, Morten's subsequent arrest, and the tragic loss of their officers, Luc Clément and Liam Perry.

After considerable internal debate, and in no small part due to Secretary-General Davout's strong concerns about adverse public opinion, the council ultimately decided to conceal the existence of the remaining unregistered MTY devices in their possession, disclosing only Morten's recovered device to the world. Described as an "illegal prototype created by the rogue Blosch-Nishikawa company prior to its dissolution", CTI quantum engineers disassembled the device and destroyed its components in front of representatives from the 62-member AISMPE committee, with observers from Director Flake's office in attendance.

Since my existence was known only to Reverend Mosby and a few members of the council, the council elected to keep my presence a secret, pending a suitable temporal transition window when they might return me to my own time. I found this a most agreeable situation, as it allowed me to explore this amazing future world without restraint.

Reverend Mosby's wounds were mended that same day (an incredible medical process) and, for the next eight months, the Reverend, Elle, and I became dear friends. Together, we visited many places, including Geneva, London, Oxford, Marseille, New York, and even Un Avant-Goût de Paris, a small restaurant converted from an orbiting space station located at a distance of more than 618,000 kilometers from the moon. If you are ever fortunate to transit there, I recommend their lobster bisque with toasted pain au levain topped with Gruyere cheese. I found it satisfactory, though they are perhaps too liberal with their garlic.

While visiting Marseille, we were astonished to discover my restaurant still in operation. Now owned by a sixth-generation descendant, a delightful woman named Céline, it continues to offer dishes from locally sourced fish. Céline is an amazing woman and an accomplished chef. She agreed to keep my presence a secret in exchange for my Bass Lisette Paillard recipe. What a satisfying feeling that was, to stand in a kitchen filled with such advanced culinary technology, and watch Céline still preparing dishes by hand in the time-honored tradition of all great chefs.

I kept my promise to assist Elle with decorating her residence in Geneva. She was not understating the fact of the two chairs. They were, indeed, the only furniture inside that cold, sterile place. However, with my guidance, she has transformed her residence into a true home, a place filled with peace and light. We spent many pleasant afternoons there, sitting in those beloved blue chairs, enjoying le goûter and talking together while her cat played at our feet.

Elle was formally installed as a CTI temporal enforcement officer the week after Liam's death at a public ceremony held inside the CTI Grand Council Chamber. Typically, such an appointment would have occurred inside Secretary Davout's office, consisting of the appointment being read into the official council record followed by a brief handshake.

This event, however, was globally significant and not simply because of the extraordinary circumstances that had occasioned the appointment. Elle was the first sentient automaton to be elevated to a position of authority over human beings. Her appointment was hailed as a milestone in world history and attended by no less than three hundred government representatives and automaton advocates.

At the ceremony, Elle spoke to the assemblage, praising Officer Perry and crediting him for the success of their mission. She said nothing about the love that had grown between them, reserving those precious sentiments for me alone.

Morten was tried and convicted for his violation of the International Temporal Treaty and his complicity in the deaths of Officers Clément and Perry. However, he was not placed in detention. Following the tribunal, he was transported to a medical facility where he died five months later from end-stage bone sarcoma and thyroid carcinoma resulting from his prolonged radiation exposure.

The week after Elle's appointment ceremony, she informed Mosby and me that she had made arrangements to charter a small boat in Toulon. She invited us to accompany her but, mysteriously, she would not disclose the purpose of the voyage nor our destination. She also warned us that we would be navigating without the assistance of any automated positioning system. I agreed at once and, though he was frightened by the prospect of traveling without the benefit of computer-assisted navigation, Mosby also (reluctantly) agreed.

We left Toulon on a sunny winter morning, motoring east along the French coast. Elle sat at the controls, unusually quiet, though she smiled when Mosby repeatedly challenged her course. We crossed the Ligurian Sea that night, then travelled southeast through the waters of the Archipelago Tucano. By early afternoon, we had reached Monte Cristo Island. Elle terminated the engine and activated the craft's anchoring stabilizers inside one of the island's small coves. We enjoyed a restful afternoon there, eating grapes, slices of melon, toasted bread, and assorted cheeses as Elle and I regaled the Reverend with our memories of Officer Perry.

When lunch was over, Elle re-engaged the engine and turned back towards France. Mosby and I fell asleep in the cabin, leaving her to navigate alone. When we awoke the following morning, we were surprised to discover that we were not in Toulon but inside the Bay of Marseille, very close to Île d'If. Elle disappeared into her cabin and returned a few moments later holding a small funerary container. With Reverend Mosby officiating, she scattered Liam Perry's ashes into the pristine blue waters of the bay.

I stayed with Elle at her home in Geneva for eight months. One Sunday morning in early July, we were surprised by a visit from Director Huber, who informed us that the council's quantum AI had calculated a date for my return. The following week, I said my goodbyes to Mosby and Elle inside the archival conference room. Owing to the secrecy of my presence, only Elle, Mosby, Huber, and Flake were present to bid me farewell. I stepped through that frightful portal once again and found myself standing inside the parking lot beneath the Notre-Dame de la Garde in Marseille, just after two in the morning on Friday, December 20, 2019.

My friends, John Clifton, Leah Vaughn, and I have labored for more than a year to prepare this work for publication. We have taken the liberty of writing this account in the form of a novel and of employing an author's license to convey feelings and thoughts implied, if not spoken aloud. This work is based on our shared experiences and supplemented with Elle's observations on humanity that she was kind enough to share with me.

We are living in a truly exciting time. Mankind is on the verge of creating general artificial intelligence and the notable philosophers and scientists of our day find themselves in conflict about the wisdom of that endeavor.

As our boat drifted inside the Bay of Marseille, Elle said something on this topic that is worth repeating here.

"Humanity," she said, "is like a child, measuring its growth not in years but millennia. As it has matured, it has acquired new skills, and even a little wisdom, but, like a youth approaching adulthood, it is filled with self-doubt and hesitation."

"Now," she continued, touching her chest, "humanity has given birth to its first child, and, like all parents, it wonders what kind of a person their child will become. Will we be kind? Will we be cruel? Will we cherish our parents or rebel against their guidance? Will we live together in harmony, or will there be conflict?" She turned then, looking towards Île d'If, and said, "Love is the answer. When parents love their children, that love will always be returned."

Acronym Glossary

AISMPE

The [A]utorité [I]nternationale [S]ingulière de la [M]atière [P]hasique [E]xotique (AISMPE), or "International Exotic Phased Matter Singularity Authority" was established in 2084 by 21 member nations participating in the P-SEQS project in Geneva.

Today, the 62-member AISMPE committee regulates all aspects of non-temporal EPM travel, safety, and licensing. *See: Evanston Accident.*

CTI

The [C]onseil [T]emporel [I]nternational (CTI), or "International Temporal Council", headquartered in Geneva, Switzerland, regulates all temporal activities under the authority of the International Temporal Treaty (ITT) of 2070.

CTI personnel can be recognized by their traditional white uniforms and blue circle insignia.

Temporal specialists are required to report any tripback temporal anomalies directly to the CTI.

EPM

An [E]xotic [P]hased-[M]atter (EPM) singularity is an acronym for a stabilized wormhole that has been split at the quantum level into two distinct event horizons calibrated to fixed positions in space and time. Both event horizons are quantum-entangled parts of the same singularity. Positioned at different physical locations, this quantum entanglement creates a "tunnel" through which matter and energy may pass.

Mankind's first stabilized EPM singularity was achieved at the P-SEQS facility near Geneva, Switzerland on October 30, 2067.

EPM transit stations can be found on the Earth, the moon, orbital stations, and as a transit network between the Earth and Mars. EPM stations accommodate mankind's travel, shipping, and other transport needs. The widespread deployment of EPM stations in the 2080s was the primary factor responsible for eliminating mankind's reliance on fossil fuels and their resulting carbon emissions.

When coupled with a tunneling regulator, an EPM singularity can facilitate temporal transition. All temporal EPM activity is strictly regulated by the CTI council under the ITT treaty of 2070.

IMU

[I]nternational [M]onetary [U]nit (IMU). With the widespread implementation of EPM transit technologies beginning in the 2080s, international travel and commerce dramatically increased, pressuring nations to adopt a common financial exchange medium. By the late 2090s, virtually every nation had subscribed to the International Monetary Unit for commerce. While local currencies can still be found in many nations, all currencies are converted to IMUs for everyday transactions.

IMUs exist as digital currency values and are processed through the IMU Central Bank in Toronto, Canada under the authority of the International Commerce Authority.

IDR

[I]nternal [D]ata [R]ecord. A personal data (journal) recording created with an embedded datstem. IDR records are encrypted using a 1024Qb cryptographic algorithm and stored on a quantum-sensitive lattice, rendering them impervious to unauthorized interception or analysis. IDR data records can be identified by their uni-standard archival numbering schema followed by the originating processor's QKDS serial number.

ITT

Following Dr. Manfred Krieger's successful temporal transition on December 19, 2068 at the P-SEQS facility in Geneva, Switzerland, the 36 nations directly involved in the P-SEQS project signed the [I]nternational [T]emporal [T]reaty (ITT). Under the authority of the Conseil Temporel International (CTI), or "International Temporal Council", the ITT governs all of mankind's temporal activities.

From 2070 until 2158, three companies were chartered under the ITT to operate temporal transit facilities; Reynolds-Hampshire in England, Blosch-Nishikawa in Norway, and Rengel-Jiang QCom in Texas (NAFS).

In 2158, Blosch-Nishikawa's temporal charter was revoked for ITT violations.

P- SEQS

The [P]rojet de [S]ingularité [E]nchevêtrée [Q]uantique [S]tabilisée (P-SEQS), or "Stabilized Quantum Entangled Singularity Project" was a coordinated effort by more than 36 nations to construct the world's first exotic phased matter (EPM) singularity. The project began in February 2056 near Geneva, Switzerland and achieved the first stable singularity on October 30, 2067. See: EPM.

PoL

[P]enetrant [o]bject [L]inking is the process of establishing a connection between two electronic objects for purposes of data collection or control.

SDU

[S]elf [D]irecting [U]nit (SDU) is an acronym for an automaton capable of analytical reasoning and determination without human assistance. Unlike earlier "robots" that were programmed by a human beings and operated according to rigid programming instructions, an SDU utilizes a quantum synapse created by an AI controller and is capable of adaptive behavior exceeding the mere summation of its programming.

The classic experiment used to illustrate the difference between primitive robots and SDUs is the "Turing Mirror". The experiment involves an automaton's positive demonstration of three attributes; self-awareness, metacognition, and empathy.

In the experiment, the automaton is placed in a setting to observe another of its kind asked to complete an impossible task. The automaton then watches its peer being dismantled or destroyed when it fails to complete the task.

An observing robot, when asked to complete the same task, will make some attempt to complete the task and will demonstrate no awareness of the impossibility of the task nor of the consequences of its failure, despite having observed both in its predecessor.

An observing SDU, however, will recognize the impossibility of the task from its earlier observation of its predecessor (metacognition). Rather than attempting to complete the task as directed, it will attempt to change the parameters of the task, typically by requesting a revision of the instructions or by attempting to explain the impossibility of the task to the requestor (self-awareness). Further, it will exhibit an awareness of the consequences should it fail, from its observance of the same consequences suffered by its predecessor (empathy). Typically, this awareness is manifested as a catastrophic controller failure; a cascading failure of the AI "brain" that, if not suspended, leads to the automaton's functional termination.

Automatons were first categorized as SDUs in the late 2110s. By 2140, SDUs had reached a level of sophistication in metacognition, self-awareness, and empathy approaching what researchers called "true sentience". Following a legal challenge raised against the JNCAA in November of 2140, a moratorium was placed on all SDU development or enhancement.

In 2158, despite the eighteen-year moratorium on SDU development, socio-automaton analysts and quantum engineers reported that SDUs emerging from the automation factories had now achieved "true sentience". Automaton manufacturers around the world immediately issued a joint statement calling for an investigation into granting sentient SDUs specific rights.

The following year, in 2159, the world's SDU and automaton manufacturers signed the Sentient Automaton Act (SAA). The Act granted fundamental rights to sentient automatons and imposed integration quotas on participating nations and companies.

Tripback

n. *slang*. A temporal EPM transition into the past.

www.ingramcontent.com/pod-product-compliance
Lightning Source LLC
LaVergne TN
LVHW020528100826
845148LV00010B/1378

* 9 7 8 1 7 3 3 4 6 3 2 6 3 *